DETECTIVE BARNES

TWO FICTIONAL CASES FROM THE 1890S

DETECTIVE BARNES

TWO FICTIONAL CASES FROM THE 1890s

by RODRIGUES OTTOLENGUI

Edited with an Introduction by
SAMANTHA SMITH

WHITLOCK PUBLISHING
ALFRED, NY

A Modern Wizard by Rodrigues Ottolengui first published 1894.
A Conflict of Evidence by Rodrigues Ottolengui first published 1893.

First Whitlock Publishing edition 2015

Whitlock Publishing
P.O. Box 472
Alfred, NY 14802

ISBN 13: 978-1-943115-06-8

This book was set in Adobe Garamond Pro on 55# acid-free paper that meets ANSI standards for archival quality.

Printed in the United States of America.

TABLE OF CONTENTS

ACKNOWLEDGEMENTS

A huge thank you to Dr. Allen Grove, without whom, this edition of Ottolengui's novels would have never been a possibility.

Also, a huge thank you to Brooke Tillotson for all her help with the book cover's wonderful design.

In addition, a huge thank you goes to Louis N. Sorkin who helped me find information on Rodrigues Ottolengui and his involvement with the New York Entomological Society.

NOTES ON THE TEXT

The text for *A Modern Wizard* is based off of the 1894 edition of the same novel.

The text for *A Conflict of Evidence* is based off of the 1893 edition of the same novel.

A Modern Wizard and *A Conflict of Evidence* were printed in reverse order of their original publish date because the age of the main character is younger in *A Modern Wizard* than he is in *A Conflict of Evidence*.

Obvious typographical errors and misinformation have been corrected as follows:
On page 276, "s tove" has been changed to "stove."
On page 303, "page 41" has been changed to "page 297."
On page 457, "Anoble" has been changed to "A noble."

INTRODUCTION

"I am not reading detective stories to improve my knowledge of literature, but because these stories help to increase the analytical quality of the mind."

Benjamin Adolph Rodrigues "Rod" Ottolengui was born on March 15, 1861 in Charleston, South Carolina. In his 16th year, he moved to New York City to become apprenticed to a dentist. Although dentistry seems to have been his first academic love, Ottolengui had many other hobbies and interests including taxidermy, autopsy, entomology, photography, and detective novel writing.

Ottolengui was accustomed to holding important positions in the fields he studied. He was among the first to use x-rays in dentistry, and he was one of the first fiction writers to present dental patterns as a method for identifying a corpse. His non-fiction work, *Methods of Filling Teeth*, was used as a standard textbook to teach dentistry for decades. He also served as Vice President of the New York Entomological Society, and focused his time on researching a species of moths. Ottolengui wrote extensively during his life: four detective novels, eighteen detective short stories, two non-fictional books on dentistry, a fictional serialization in a Charleston newspaper, as well as many different scientific articles on photography, dentistry, and entomology.

The majority of his fictional work deals with two men: Detective Barnes and Detective Mitchel (both first seen in his 1892 novel, *An Artist in Crime*). Detective Barns is a seasoned detective, while Mitchel is an amateur. Sometimes they work together and sometimes they work against each other while attempting to solve the crime. *Before the Fact* (2012) is a recently collected selection of detective short stories about Mitchel that were published in several magazines from the early 1900s. The stories *Before the Fact* focus on Mitchel's claim that he can figure out and stop a crime before it even happens.

DETECTIVE FICTION

Most critics view detective fiction as a relatively new genre, starting in 1841 with "The Murder in the Rue Morgue" by Edgar Allan Poe. Some of the basic elements of detective fiction, however, can be seen in works written well before 1841. In *Arden of Faversham* (1592), one can see some of these early elements. The play is centered on the characters attempting to figure out who murdered Arden, a wealthy land owner with a cheating wife. However, many critics do not consider this play to be detective fiction because solving the murder is not the main point of the play itself. Even fiction as old as the Ancient Greek tragedies contains hints of detection. In *The Libation Bearers* from *The Oresteia* by Aeschylus, Electra uses a crude form of deduction (with clues so full of holes that Sophocles later makes fun of Aeschylus' work) to determine that it is her brother who has been at her father's grave.

The Oresteia and *Arden of Faversham* would both be better classed as crime fiction instead of detective fiction. Although all detective fiction can be classed as crime fiction, not all crime fiction can be considered detective fiction. Any work that includes a crime can be labeled "Crime Fiction," while a label of "Detective Fiction" requires the main character to be a detective who is actively trying to solve a crime using deduction, the logical gathering of facts and clues by either an amateur or professional detective to identify the perpetrator of the crime. Detective Fiction contains miraculous deductions based on the smallest clues, involves crimes that can be explained through reason, and can employ the "locked room" concept, created by Edgar Allan Poe, in which the detective tries to figure out how a murderer killed a man and then left the room without being noticed, in the process leaving the door locked from the inside.

After Poe, many authors such as Emile Gaboriau and Sir Arthur Conan Doyle expanded and contributed to the detective fiction genre. Gaboriau's detective was the first to make a plaster cast of foot prints, and Doyle is responsible for the most famous detective of all time: Sherlock Holmes. These three authors, and many others, incorporated the newest crime fighting techniques in their stories, reflecting the advances of the science at the time. This style of detective fiction, created by Poe, Gaboriau, and Doyle, was popular until the late 1920s, when another type of detective fiction became popular, the hardboiled detective fiction (see "Contemporary Detective Fiction," page xviii).

We can see the Poe/Gaboriau/Doyle style reflected in Ottolengui's works. Not only is Ottolengui's detective Barnes, like Sherlock, able to make large deductions from seemingly small clues, but he is also not afraid to do the foot work and get his hands dirty while going after evidence and clues. Barnes takes the cases slowly, attempting to make absolutely no assumptions until everything has been eliminated and nothing is left but the truth. Preferring to let the evidence speak for itself, he listens to every possible side of the case. Detective Burrows at one point discovers a large amount of incriminating evidence that would put the wrong man behind bars, and despite Burn's arguments that not all the facts fit the case, Burrows is determined to go through with his assumptions. It is Barnes who tirelessly exhausts every possibility that the evidence shows him until he has the true story that fits all of the evidence. To do this, he goes against his partner, and even leaves his job, intent on seeing the proper justice done. For him, a wrong must be righted, no matter what.

In a detective story, the crimes cause a disruption in society to the point where order needs to be restored. A detective appears to fill the vacuum left by the lack of order, solve the crime, and restore order to the community. Because the detective does this using logical reasoning and deduction, the reader often follows along, attempting to interpret the clues at the same time as the detective. The case becomes a race between the reader and the characters to be the first to determine the perpetrator of, and the motives behind, the crime.

This is where Ottolengui's defensive quote comes in: "I am not reading detective stories to improve my knowledge of literature, but because these stories help to increase the analytical quality of the mind." Detective fiction represents a lower form of literature because it is a type of genre fiction defined by specific conventions and restrictions. There are at least five concrete events that must happen in detective fiction: a crime must take place, a detective or detectives get involved somehow, they follow the clues to find the perpetrator, they follow the wrong clue once or twice, and then they find the criminal and end the story with the case being solved. Readers can rely on finding these traits which makes the books predictable. Many people scoff at genre fiction because they believe that the authors don't have to be very creative to write a story with such a prescribed storyline. In the case of detective fiction, many critics question a story that can only be read once because the first reading takes out all the mystery, and knowing the answer of "whodunnit" undermines everything written in the novel before the big reveal. As Priestman says in "The Detective Whodunnit from Poe to World War I":

> "A form which is often meticulously clever on many narrative and stylistic levels encounters a kind of glass ceiling when it attempts to claim serious literary status: how can a text be held up as a shining example of plot, or indeed of anything related to the final outcome [. . .] when it is a kind of cardinal sin against the form to reveal to others—or even to recall for oneself—what that plot or that outcome actually is?"

Ottolengui argues that this does not matter. It doesn't matter that we can only read the story once because then if reread it, we remember who did it the first time. The point of detective fiction is not for the story arc to be overly fresh or exotic. The point is that detective fiction sharpens our minds by pushing us to draw our own conclusions before the detective beats us to it.

Sometimes though, Ottolengui has the detective tell us things instead of taking us along as he discovers the clues. There are many details that a typical reader might overlook that the detective does not because he knows that even seemingly trivial clues might be vital. One notable instance is in *A Conflict of Evidence* when Detective Barnes and Detective Burrows draw a map of footprints in the snow surrounding the scene of the crime and then explain the significance of each set in great detail. This happens early on in the story, however, and would have been fairly tedious to read had the detectives not explained how important those tracks were. The significance of the knowledge given doesn't become apparent to us until much later in the story, and if we had not had the detectives to point it out to us, we would likely have completely missed it. By having his detectives split up to follow the footprints and then regroup to tell each other what they have discovered, Ottolengui quickly and easily delivers important information to the reader.

CONTEXTUAL HISTORY

During the nineteenth century, criminals shifted from being thought of as ordinary people who made mistakes to persons with a deviant characteristic that made the committing of a crime no longer easily explained by motives. Because of that, a new school of thought came into being: crimes could be almost completely motiveless, committed simply because the criminal wanted to do so; certainly traditional motives need not apply. The criminal was seen as an artist, creating a destruction of life for whatever reason the perpetrator was happy with, or simply for the effect of not following social norms or standards. Poe's writing reflects these changing thoughts on the criminal's lack of motive and gives it a name, perverseness:

> "PERVERSENESS. Of this spirit philosophy takes no account. Yet I am not more sure than my soul lives, than I am that perverseness is one of the primitive impulses of the human heart [. . .] Who has not, a hundred times, found himself committing a vile or a silly action, for no other reason than because he knows he should not? Have we not a perpetual inclination [. . .] to violate that which is Law, merely because we understand it to be such? [. . .] It was this unfathomable longing of the soul to vex itself—to offer violence to its own nature—to

do wrong for the wrong's sake only—that urged me to continue and finally to consummate the injury that I had inflicted upon the unoffending brute [. . .] in cool blood" ("The Black Cat").

These shifting modes of thought were not reflected in detective fiction; the crime always has an explanation that the detective discovers fully. The reason behind the crime is always along the lines of what was considered a traditional motive, "money, power, sex, and revenge" (Harpham "Detective Fiction and the Aesthetic of Crime"). The criminal was not an artist, performing the crime just because he could; the criminal was simply an ordinary Joe or Jane who would eventually be caught, despite his or her attempts to get away with the crime.

Most often, it is the detective in the story who is seen as the artist. His job is to reverse-construct the crime as he works backwards from the effect (the crime being committed) to determine the cause (means and motive that lead to committing the crime). Detection is the medium he uses to solve the case in an artistic and flawless manner, if done correctly. The objective is to discover the correct perpetrator of the crime, the motive behind it, and restore the world as close to its original pre-crime state as possible. This is seen in *A Conflict of Evidence* when Detective Barnes does everything in his ability to right the wrong conclusion that Detective Burrows comes to, almost costing an innocent suspect his freedom.

In order to achieve these goals, the detective has to have an appreciation for the crime committed and an ability to look at any crime scene without missing details or being disturbed by any potential gory surroundings. Most often the motivation for a detective was to serve, protect, and restore order for the masses. One anomaly however is Sherlock Holmes.

SHERLOCK HOLMES

Sherlock Holmes was created in the 1890s and reportedly based off of a teacher of Doyle's: Joseph Bell. Doyle wanted to "try [his] hand at writing a story where the hero would treat crime as Dr. Bell treated disease." It is well reported that Dr. Bell could look at a patient and tell what disease he had often before even exchanging words with the patient. It is highly ironic that one of our great televisions minds, Dr. Gregory House, a diagnostician from the TV show *House, M.D.*, was based upon Sherlock Holmes, a character based upon a real life doctor who did the same things as Dr. House.

As a detective, however, Sherlock is confusing in that he doesn't have a discernible, or maybe just not a traditional, motive. He is fascinated by the crimes, and it is evident he enjoys himself while chasing down a clue. His motives to solve the crime do not include payment, power, sex, nor a moral compass that states he must help the masses. He is not afraid to get his hands dirty or to act in a seemingly immoral fashion to solve the case.

Instead, Sherlock has a flair for the aesthetic of the crime. He appreciates the mystery laid out before him, taking only the crimes that interest him most, and citing the criminal Moriarty as his intellectual equal. The political, psychological, and social trappings under Sherlock's decisions are what has us reading and rereading his adventures.

In Doyle's autobiography *Memories and Adventures* (1924), Doyle claimed, "It had struck me that a single character running through a series, if it only engaged the attention of the reader, would bind that reader to that particular magazine." Doyle's idea was spot on. Sherlock is one of the best known detectives. A great many writers have followed in Doyle's footsteps by writing entire series about one or the same detectives. Hundreds of books were published under the name Carolyn Keen (actually there were a bunch of ghost writers that contributed to the novels) all with the same detective, Nancy Drew. The same could be said for the Hardy Boys. Most of Ottolengui's works also involved either Detective Barnes or Detective Mitchel. Ottolengui was possibly influenced by the sensation that was Sherlock Holmes, which came out mere years before Ottolengui tried his hand at writing detective fiction.

CONTEMPORARY DETECTIVE FICTION

In the 1920s, a new form of the genre appeared: hard-boiled detective fiction. Instead of focusing on the intellectual side of the detectives, the focus was more on the experiences of that detective. The emphasis shifted from the solution of the crime, to the steps it took to solve the crime. The hard-boiled detective showed a man (or, by the 1980s, a woman) who was ordinary, someone with whom the reader could identify, who made mistakes but still restored the order by the end of the novel. The excitement of these stories comes not from the deduction but from the action and violence that takes place in order to get the clues. The crimes no longer happen in mansions or little hamlets that are cut off from the outside world; they take place in locations that readers can recognize and happen to people to whom readers can relate.

The hard-boiled detective also has the hardest moral decisions to make and sometimes has to take the law into his own hands, often by killing the perpetrator somehow. Ottolengui foreshadowed this in 1893 with *A Conflict of Evidence*. Near the end of the story, Detective Barnes has a decision to make on how to deal with the truth now that he has solved the crime. He needs to decide how much he should tear apart the world of the victim's family in order to let an innocent man go free. He may take the law into his own hands, but it's not to the extreme that the hard-boiled detectives had to decades later.

As the century progressed, detective writers started using their work to explore issues other than the crime. Issues such as gender, environmental concerns, race, equality, and the masculine environment were open to examination through the lens of the detective story. The 1970s showed a shift from independent detectives to police-procedurals in which the detective has a slew of people working with him to help solve the crime. *The New Centurions* (1970) by Joseph Wambaugh, the *Inspector Maigret* novels by Georges Simenon, and the *87th Precinct* series (starting in 1956) by Ed McBain are just a few examples. The police-procedural as a form of detective fiction came about as a response to surfacing doubts that one detective could do it all. Just like criminals don't need any more of a motive than "because I wanted to," sometimes the detective just cannot find all the evidence or interpret it all by himself. In a world where there are now fingerprint and DNA databases, gunshot ballistics, and ever-evolving computer technology, no detective could be experts in it all. Detectives today need the help of teams and the ability to outsource evidence if they want to figure out everything. Dr. House has his team of doctors and the lab, Scooby Doo is the gang of five teens and a dog, and the television series NCIS is about one group with the backing of an entire government agency, the technical expertise of a state-of-the-art forensics lab, and the collaboration of other agencies and local police. No one detective has to do all the work anymore; it has become a group effort.

~ Samantha Smith

BIBLIOGRAPHY

Doyle, Sir Arthur C. "Memories and Adventures." *Memories and Adventures.*

Greene, Douglas G. *Classic Mystery Stories.* Mineola, NY: Dover Publications, 1999.

Harpham, John S. "Detective Fiction and the Aesthetic of Crime." *Raritan* 34.1 (2014): 121-41.

Leddy, Chuck. "Loot vs. Literature: Genre and Literary Fiction." *The Writer* 121.1 (2008): 8-9.

Ottolengui, Rodrigues. *Before the Fact.* Ed. Douglas Greene. Eugenia, Ont.: Battered Silicon Dispatch Box, 2012.

Poe, Edgar A. "The Black Cat." *The Complete Tales and Poems of Edgar Allan Poe.* Ed. Dawn B. Sova. New York: Barnes & Noble, 2006. 531-38. Print.

Priestman, Martin. "The Detective Whodunnit from Poe to World War I." *Crime Fiction: From Poe to the Present.* Plymouth: Northcote House, 1998. 5-18. Rpt. in *Short Story Criticism.* Ed. Janet Witalec. Vol. 59. Detroit: Gale, 2003.

Routledge, Chris. "Detective Fiction." *St. James Encyclopedia of Popular Culture* (2000): 693-95.

Snyder, Laura J. "Sherlock Holmes: Scientific Detective." *Endeavour* 28.3 (2004): 104104-108.

Weiss, Harry B. "Rodrigues Ottolengui, 1861-1937." *Journal of the New York Entomological Society* 59.2 (1951): 93-98.

Xu, Wenru. "Edgar Allan Poe and His Detective Fictions." *Studies in Literature and Language* 7.2 (2013): 59-62.

TIMELINE – B. A. RODRIGUES "ROD" OTTOLENGUI

1861   Born on March 15 in Charleston, South Carolina

1877   Travels to New York City to become apprenticed to a dentist

1885   Becomes Master of Dental Surgery

1890   Serializes *Conya: A Romance of the Buddhas* in a Charleston newspaper

1892   Nonfictional book *Methods of Filling Teeth* is published

        First detective novel, *An Artist in Crime*, is published

1893   *A Conflict of Evidence* is published

        Vice President of the New York Entomological Society

1894   *A Modern Wizard* is published

1895   Starts writing short stories with detectives Barnes and Mitchel (characters from *An Artist in Crime*)

1896   *The Crime of the Century* is published

        Becomes editor of *Items of Interest* later titled *Dental Items of Interest*

1898   Collects the Barnes and Mitchel short stories into a volume called *Final Proof, or the Value of Evidence*

1900   *An Artist in Crime* is translated into Icelandic by Sigtryggur Jonasson; published in Winnipeg under the title *Leikinn Glaepamaour*

1901   *The Crime of the Century* translated into Icelandic "Höfuo-Glaepurinn, Saga"

        Ainslee's Magazine publishes six stories under the general title "Before the Fact"

1928   *Table Talks on Dentistry* is published

1933   (Circa.) Retires from practicing dentistry

1937   Dies from heart ailment and stroke Sunday, June 11th

Rodrigues Ottolengui

A Modern Wizard

BOOK 1

CHAPTER I
LAWYER AND CLIENT

Early one morning, in the spring of eighteen hundred and seventy-three, two young lawyers were seated in their private office. The firm name, painted in gilt letters upon the glass of the door, was DUDLEY & BLISS. Mortimer Dudley was the senior member, though not over thirty years old. Robert Bliss was two years younger.

Mr. Dudley was sorting some papers and deftly tying them into bundles with red tape. Why lawyers will persist in using tape of a sanguine color is an unsolvable mystery to me, unless it may be that they are loath to disturb the many old adages in which the significant couplet of words appears. However that may be, Mr. Dudley paused in his occupation, attracted by an exclamation from his partner, who had been reading a morning paper.

"What is it, Robert?" asked Mr. Dudley.

"Oh! Only another sensational murder case, destined, I imagine, to add more lustre to the name of some lawyer who doesn't need it. Mortimer, I wonder when our turn will come. Here we have been in these rooms for three months, and not a criminal case has come to us yet."

"Don't be impatient, Robert. We must not give up hope. Look at Munson. He was in the same class with us at college, and we all considered him a dunce. By accident he was engaged to defend that fellow who was accused of poisoning his landlady. Munson actually studied chemistry in order to defend the case. His cross-examination of the prosecution's experts made him famous. Who knows! We may get an opportunity like that some day."

"Some day! Yes, some day! I believe there is a song that begins that way. I always detested it. I do not like that word 'some day.' It's so beastly indefinite. I prefer 'to-day' or even 'to-morrow.' But let me read to you the account of this case. It is about that young woman who died so mysteriously, up in the boarding-house on West Twenty-sixth Street."

"I don't know anything about it, Robert. I haven't read the papers for three days. Tell me the main facts."

"Well, it is really a very curious story. It seems there was a young girl, twenty or thereabouts, living in town temporarily, whilst she studied music. Her name was Mabel Sloane. She is described as pretty, though that is a detail that the reporters always add. But, pretty or ugly, she died last Sunday morning, under rather peculiar circumstances. The doctors differed as to the cause of death."

"Why, there is nothing odd about that, is there?" Mr. Dudley smiled at his own wit. "Doctors disagree and the patient dies. That is the old adage. You have only reversed it. Your patient died, and the doctors then disagreed. Where's the odds?"

"The odds amount to this, Mortimer. One doctor signed a certificate of death, naming diphtheria as the cause. The other physician reported to the Board of Health that there were suspicious circumstances which led him to think that the woman might have died from poison."

"Poison? This is interesting."

"The more you hear, the more you will think so. In yesterday's papers it was announced that the Coroner had taken up the case, and that an autopsy would be held."

"Does this morning's paper give the result of the post-mortem?"

"Yes. Listen! 'The autopsy upon the body of Mabel Sloane, the beautiful young musician'—you see they still harp on the beautiful—'young musician, whose mysterious death was reported yesterday, shows conclusively that the girl was poisoned. The doctors claim to have found morphine enough to kill three men. Thus the caution of Dr. Meredith, in notifying the Health Board of his suspicions, is to be commended. It is but just to say, however, that the doctors who made the post-mortem, entirely exonerate Dr. Fisher, the physician who certified that the death was caused by diphtheria, for they claim, curiously enough, that the woman would undoubtedly have died of that disease even if the morphine had not been administered. This opens up a most interesting set of complications. Why should any one poison a person who is about to die a natural death? It might be claimed that the murderer did not know that a fatal termination of the disease would ensue. This brings us to the most interesting fact, that the one who is suspected by the police is no other than the girl's sweetheart, who is himself a physician. Thus it is plain that he should have known that the disease would probably prove fatal, and under these circumstances it is almost inconceivable that he should have resorted to poison. Nevertheless, the detectives claim that they have incontestible evidence of his guilt, although they refuse to reveal what their proofs are. However, some facts leaked out yesterday which certainly tend to incriminate Dr. Emanuel Medjora, the suspected man. In the first place, Dr. Medjora has suddenly and completely disappeared. Inquiry at his office elicited the statement that he has not been there since the day before yesterday, which it will be remembered was the time when the Coroner first came into the case. Dr. Medjora has not been at his residence, and none of his friends has seen him. In short, if he had been swallowed by an earthquake he could not have vanished more swiftly. He was supposed to have been engaged to marry Miss Sloane, and as she was a beautiful girl, accomplished, and altogether charming, it has puzzled all who knew her, to understand why he should wish to destroy her. Some light may be thrown upon this, however, by the discovery at the autopsy, that she has been a mother. What has become of the child, or where it was born, is still a part of the mystery. Miss Sloane has lived at the Twenty-sixth Street house about three months, and as she has always been cheerful and happy, the boarders cannot reconcile this report of the doctors with what they knew of the woman. They claim, with much reason, that if her baby had died she should have had moments of despondency when her grief would have been noticeable. Or if the child were alive, then why did she never allude to it? Another significant fact is, that Dr. Medjora has been seen driving in the Park, recently, with a handsome woman, stylishly dressed, and evidently wealthy, as the coachman and footman wore expensive livery. Did the Doctor tire of his pretty little musician, and wish to marry his rich friend who owns the carriage and horses? His disappearance lends color to the theory.' There, what do you think of that?" said Mr. Bliss, throwing aside the newspaper.

"What do I think?" answered his partner. "I think that this will be a great case. A chance for young men like us to make fame and fortune. If we could only be retained by that man—"

The door from the outer office opened and young Jack Barnes, the assistant, entered and handed Mr. Dudley a visiting card. The lawyer looked at it, seemed astonished, said "Show the gentleman in," and when Barnes had left the office, turned to his partner, handing him the card, and, slightly excited, exclaimed:

"In heaven's name, Robert, look at that!"

Mr. Bliss took the card and read the name:

EMANUEL MEDJORA, M.D.

The two young men looked at each other in silence, startled by the coincidence, and wondering whether at last Dame Fortune was about to smile upon them. A moment later Dr. Medjora entered.

Dr. Emanuel Medjora was no ordinary personage. His commanding stature would attract attention anywhere, and the more he was observed the more he incited curiosity. First as to his nationality. To what clime did he owe allegiance by birth? One could scarcely decide. His name might lead to the conclusion that he was Spanish, but save that his skin was swarthy there was little to identify him with that type. Perhaps, more than anything, he looked like the ideals which have been given to us of Othello, though again his color was at fault, not being so deep as the Moor's. He wore a black beard, close trimmed, and pointed beneath the chin. His hair, also jetty, was longer than is usually seen in New York, and quite straight, combed back from the forehead without a part. The skull was large, the brain cavity being remarkably well developed. Any phrenologist would have revelled in the task of fingering his bumps. The physiognomist, also, would have delighted to read the character of the man from the expressiveness of his features, every one of which evidenced refined and cultured intellectuality. The two, summing up their findings, would probably have accredited the Doctor with all the virtues and half of the vices that go to make up the modern man, not to mention many of the talents commonly allotted to the rare geniuses of the world.

But according these scientists the freest scope in their examinations, and giving them besides the assistance of the palmist, clairvoyant, astrologist, chirographist, and all the other modern savants who advertise to read our inmost thoughts, for sums varying in proportion to the credulity of the applicant, and when all was told, it could not be truthfully said that either, or all, had discovered about Dr. Medjora aught save that which he may have permitted them to learn. Probably no one thoroughly understood Dr. Medjora, except Dr. Medjora himself. That he did comprehend himself, appreciating exactly his abilities and his limitations, there cannot be a shadow of a doubt. And it was this that made him such a master of men, being as he was so completely the master of himself. Those who felt bound to admit that in his presence they dwindled even in their own estimation, attributed it to various causes, all erroneous, the true secret being what I have stated. Some said that it was a certain magnetic power which he exerted through his eyes. The Doctor's eyes certainly were remarkable. Deep set in the head, and thus hidden by the beautifully arched brows, they seemed to lurk in the shadow, and from their point of vantage to look out at, and I may say into, the individual confronting him. I remember the almost weird attraction of those eyes when I first met him. Being at the time interested in an investigation of the phenomena which have been attributed to mesmerism, hypnotism, and other "isms" which are but different terms for the same thing, I could not resist the impulse to ask him whether he had ever attempted any such experiments. Evading my question, without apparently meaning to shirk a reply, he merely smiled and said, "Do you believe in that sort of thing?" Then he passed on and spoke to some one else. I relate the incident merely to show the manner of the man. But on the point, raised by some, that he controlled men by supernatural means, I think that we must dismiss that hypothesis as untenable in the main. Of course those who believed that he possessed some uncanny or mysterious power of the eyes, might be influenced by his keen scrutiny, and would probably reveal whatever he were endeavoring to extort from them. But a true analysis would show that this was but an exhibition of their weakness, rather than of his strength. Yet, after all, the man was excessively intellectual, and as the eyes have been aptly called the "windows of the soul," what more natural than that so self-centred and wilful a man should find his lustrous orbs a great advantage to him through life?

At the moment of his entrance into the private office of Messrs. Dudley Bliss, those two young men had partly decided that he was a murderer. At sight of him, they both abandoned the conclusion. Thus it will be seen that, if brought to the bar of justice, his presence might equally affect the jury in his behalf. He held his polished silk hat in his gloved hand, and looked keenly at each of the lawyers in turn. Then turning towards Mr. Dudley he said:

"You are Mr. Dudley, I believe? The senior member of your firm?"

Mr. Bliss was insensibly annoyed, although very fond of his partner. Being only two years his junior, he did not relish being so easily relegated to the secondary status.

"My name is Dudley," replied the elder lawyer, "but unless you have met me before, I cannot understand how you guessed my identity, as my partner is scarcely at all younger than I am." Mr. Dudley understood his partner's character very well, and wished to soothe any irritation that may have been aroused. Dr. Medjora grasped the situation instantly. Turning to Mr. Bliss he said with his most fascinating manner:

"I am sure you are not offended at my ready discrimination as to your respective ages. It is a habit of mine to observe closely. But youth is nothing to be ashamed of surely, or if so, then I am the lesser light here, for I am perhaps even younger than yourself, Mr. Bliss, being but twenty-seven."

"Oh, not at all!" exclaimed Mr. Bliss, much mollified, and telling the conventional lie with the easy grace which we all have acquired in this nineteenth century. "You were quite right to choose between us. Mr. Dudley is my superior—"

"In the firm name only, I am sure," interjected the Doctor. "Will you shake hands, as a sign that you forgive my unintentional rudeness? But stop. I am forgetting. I see that you have just been reading the announcement"–he pointed to the newspaper lying where Mr. Bliss had dropped it on a chair, folded so that the glaring head-lines were easily read–"that I am a murderer!" He paused a moment and both lawyers colored deeply. Before they could speak, the Doctor again addressed them. "You have read the particulars, and you have decided that I am guilty. Am I not right?"

"Really, Dr. Medjora, I should hardly say that. You see—" Mr. Dudley hesitated, and Dr. Medjora interrupted him, speaking sharply:

"Come! Tell me the truth! I want no polite lying. Stop!" Mr. Dudley had started up, angry at the word "lying." "I do not intend any insult; but understand me thoroughly. I have come here to consult you in your professional capacity. I am prepared to pay you a handsome retainer. But before I do so, I must be satisfied that you are the sort of men in whose hands I may place my life. It is no light thing for a man in my position to intrust such an important case to young men who have their reputations to earn."

"If you do not think we are capable, why have you come to us?" asked Mr. Bliss, hotly.

"You are mistaken. I do think you capable. But think is a very indefinite word. I must know before I go further. That is why I asked, and why I ask again, have you decided, from what you have read of my case, that I am guilty? Upon your answer I will begin to estimate your capability to manage my case."

The two young lawyers looked at each other a moment, embarrassed, and remained silent. Dr. Medjora scrutinized them keenly. Finally, Mr. Dudley decided upon his course, and spoke.

"Dr. Medjora, I will confess to you that before you came in, and, as you have guessed, from reading what the newspaper says, I had decided that you are guilty. But that was not a juridical deduction. That is, it was not an opinion adopted after careful weighing of the evidence, for, as it is here, it is all on one side. I regret now that I should have formed an opinion so rashly, even though you were one in whom, at the time, I supposed I would have no interest."

"Very good, Mr. Dudley," said the Doctor. "I like your candor. Of course, it was not the decision of the lawyer, but simply that of the citizen affected by his morning newspaper. As such, I do not object to your having entertained it. But now, speaking as a lawyer, and without hearing anything of my defence, tell me what value is to be put upon the evidence against me, always supposing that the prosecution can bring good evidence to sustain their position."

"Well," replied Mr. Dudley, "the evidence is purely circumstantial, though circumstantial evidence often convinces a jury, and convicts a man. It is claimed against you that you have disappeared. From this it is argued that you are hiding from the police. The next deduction is, that if you fear the police, you are guilty. Per contra, whilst these deductions may be true and logical, they are not necessarily so; consequently, they are good only until refuted. For example, were you to go now to the District Attorney and surrender yourself, making the claim that you have been avoiding the police only to prevent arrest, preferring to present yourself to the law officers voluntarily, the whole theory of the police, from this one standpoint, falls to the ground utterly worthless."

"Very well argued. Do you then advise me to surrender myself? But wait! We will take that up later. Let me hear your views on the next fact against me. I refer to the statement that poison was found in the body."

"Several interesting points occur to me," replied Mr. Dudley, speaking slowly. "Let me read the newspaper account again." He took up the paper, and after a minute read aloud: "'The result of the autopsy, etc., etc., shows conclusively that the girl was poisoned. The doctors claim to have discovered morphine enough to kill three men.' That is upon the face of it a premature statement. The woman died on Sunday morning. The autopsy was held yesterday. I believe it will require a chemical analysis before it can be asserted that morphine is present. Am I not correct?" The Doctor made one of his non-committal replies.

"Let us suppose that at the trial, expert chemists swear that they found morphine in poisonous quantities."

"Even then, the burden of proof would be upon the prosecution. They must prove not merely that morphine was present in quantities sufficient to cause death, but that in this case it did actually kill. That is, they must show that Mabel Sloane died from poison, and not from diphtheria. That will be their great difficulty. We can have celebrated experts, as many as you can afford, and even though poison did produce the death, we can create such a doubt from the contradictions of the experts, that the jury would give you the verdict."

"Very satisfactorily reasoned. I am encouraged. Now then, the next point. The drives with the rich unknown."

"Oh! That is a newspaper's argument, and would have no place in a court of law, unless—"

"Yes! Unless—?"

"Unless the prosecution tried to prove that the motive for the crime was to rid yourself of your *fiancée* in order to marry a richer woman. Of course we should fight against the admission of any such evidence as tending to prejudice the jury against you, and untenable because the proof would only be presumptive."

"Presumptive. That is as to my desire to marry the woman with whom I am said to have been out driving. Now then, suppose that it could be shown that, since the death of Mabel Sloane, and prior to the trial, I had actually married this rich woman?"

"I should say that such an act would damage your case very materially."

"I only wished to have your opinion upon the point. Nothing of the sort has occurred. Well, gentlemen, I have decided to place my case in your hands. Will five hundred dollars satisfy you as a retaining fee?"

"Certainly." Mr. Dudley tried hard not to let it appear that he had never received so large a fee before. Dr. Medjora took a wallet from his pocket and counted out the amount. Mr. Bliss arose from his chair and started to leave the room, but as he touched the door knob the Doctor turned sharply and said:

"Will you oblige me by not leaving the room?"

"Oh! Certainly!" replied Mr. Bliss, mystified, and returning to his seat.

"Here, gentlemen, is the sum. I will take your receipt, if you please. Now then, as to your advice. Shall I surrender myself to the District Attorney, and so destroy argument number one, as you suggested?"

"But, Doctor," said Mr. Dudley, "you have not told us your defence."

"I am satisfied with the one which you have outlined. Should future developments require it, I will tell you whatever you need to know, in order to perfect your case. For the present I prefer to keep silent."

"Well, but really, unless you confide in your lawyers you materially weaken your case."

"I have more at stake than you have, gentlemen! You will gain in reputation, whatever may be the result. I risk my life. You must permit me therefore to conduct myself as I think best."

"Oh! Certainly, if that is your wish. As to your surrendering yourself, I strongly advise it, as you probably could not escape from the city, and even if you did, you would undoubtedly be recaptured."

"There you are entirely wrong. Not only can I escape, as you term it, but I would never be retaken."

"Then why take the risk of a trial? Innocent men have been convicted, even when ably defended!"

"Yes, and guilty ones have escaped. But you ask why I do not leave New York. I answer, because I wish to remain here. Were I to run away from these charges, of course I should never be able to return."

"Then, Doctor, I advise you to surrender."

"I will adopt your advice. But not until the day after to-morrow. I have some affairs to settle first."

"But you risk being captured by the detectives."

"I think not," said the Doctor, with a smile.

"Should we wish to communicate with you, where may we be able to find you, Doctor?"

Doctor Medjora appeared not to have heard the question. He said:

"Oh! By the way, gentlemen, you need not either of you study up chemistry, as did Mr. Munson. You remember the case? I know enough chemistry for any experts that they may introduce, and will formulate the main lines of their cross-examination myself. Let me refer to a point that you made. Did I understand you that if we can show that Mabel died of diphtheria, our case is won?"

"Why, certainly, Doctor. If we can prove that, we show that she died a natural death."

"Of course, I understood that. I merely wished to show you what a simple thing our defence is. We will convince the jury of that. I will meet you at the office of the District Attorney at eleven o'clock on the day after to-morrow. Good-morning, gentlemen."

The Doctor bowed and left the room. The two lawyers looked at one another a moment, and then Mr. Dudley spoke:

"What a singular man!"

"The most extraordinary man I ever met!"

"Robert, why did you start to leave the room?"

"Mortimer, that is a very curious thing. I had a sort of premonition that he would go away without leaving his address. I meant to instruct Barnes to shadow him, when he should leave. I wonder if he read my thoughts?"

"Rubbish! But why not send Jack after him now? He will catch up with him easily enough."

Acting upon the suggestion, Mr. Bliss went into the outer office, and was annoyed to be told by the office boy that Jack Barnes had gone out half an hour before.

CHAPTER II
JACK BARNES INVESTIGATES

Jack Barnes, at this time, had just attained his majority. He was studying law with Messrs. Dudley Bliss, and acting as their office assistant. But it was by no means his intention ever to practise the profession, which he was acquiring with much assiduity. His one ambition was to be a detective. Gifted with a keen, logical mind, a strong disposition to study and solve problems, and possessing the rare faculty of never forgetting a face, or a voice, he thought himself endowed by nature with exactly the faculties necessary to make a successful detective. His study of law was but a preliminary, which, he rightly deemed, would be of value to him.

Anxious, as he was, to try his wits against some noted criminal, the chance had never been his to make the effort. He had indeed ferreted out one or two so-called "mysterious cases," but these had been in a small country village, where a victory over the dull-witted constabulary had counted for little in his own estimation.

Naturally he had read with avidity all the various newspaper accounts of the supposed murder of Mabel Sloane, and it was with considerable satisfaction that he had read the name upon the card intrusted to him to be taken to his employers. It seemed to him that at last fortune had placed an opportunity within his grasp. Here was a man, suspected of a great crime, whom the great Metropolitan detective force had entirely failed to locate. From what he had read of Dr. Medjora, he quickly decided that, though he might consult Messrs. Dudley Bliss, he would not intrust them with his address. Jack Barnes determined to follow the Doctor when he should leave the office. Thus it was, that he was absent when Mr. Bliss inquired for him.

Descending by the elevator–a contrivance oddly named, since it takes one down as well as up,–he stationed himself in a secluded corner, whence he could keep watch upon the several exits from the building. Presently, he saw Dr. Medjora step from the elevator, and leave the building, after casting his eyes keenly about him, from which circumstance Barnes thought it best not to follow his man too closely. When, therefore, he saw the Doctor jump upon a Third Avenue horse-car, he contented himself with taking the next one following, and riding upon the front platform.

He saw nothing of Dr. Medjora until the Harlem terminus was reached. Here his man alighted and walked rapidly across the bridge over the river, Barnes following by the footpath on the opposite side, keeping the heavy timbers of the span between them as a screen. But, however careful Dr. Medjora had been to look behind him when leaving the lawyers' offices, he evidently felt secure now, for he cast no anxious glances backward. Thus Barnes shadowed him with comparative ease, several blocks uptown, and then down a cross street, until at last he disappeared in a house surrounded by many large trees.

Barnes stopped at the tumbled-down gate, which, swinging on one hinge, offered little hindrance to one who wished to enter. He looked at the house with curiosity. Old Colonial in architecture, it had evidently once been the summer home of wealthy folks. Now the sashless windows and rotting eaves marked it scarcely more than a habitat for crows or night owls. Wondering why Dr. Medjora should visit such a place, he was suddenly astonished to hear the sound of wheels rapidly approaching. Peeping back, he saw a stylish turn-out coming towards him, and it flashed across his mind that this might be the equipage in which the Doctor had been said to drive in the Park. Not wishing to be seen, he entered the grounds, ran quickly to the house, and admitted himself through a broken-down doorway that led to what had been the kitchen. He had scarcely concealed himself when the carriage stopped, a woman alighted, and walking up to the house, entered by the same door through which the Doctor had passed. Barnes was satisfied now that this meeting was pre-arranged, and that it would interest him greatly to overhear the conversation which would occur.

Seeking a means of reaching the upper floor, he soon found a stairway from which several steps were absent, but he readily ascended. At the top, he stopped to listen, and soon heard low voices still farther up. The staircase in the main hall was in a fair state of preservation, and there was even the remains of an old carpet. Carefully stepping, so as to avoid creaking boards, he soon reached a level from which he could peep into the room at the head of the stairs, and there he saw the two whom he was following. But though he could hear their voices, he could not distinguish their words. To do so he concluded that he must get into the adjoining room, but he could not go farther upstairs without being detected, as the door was open affording the Doctor a clear view of the top of the stairway.

Barnes formed his plan quickly. Reaching up with his hands, he took hold of the balustrade which ran along the hallway, and then, dangling in the air, he worked his way slowly from baluster to baluster, until he had passed the open doorway, and finally hung opposite the room which he wished to enter. Then he drew himself up, until he could rest a foot upon the floor of the hall, after which he quickly and noiselessly swung himself over and passed into the front room. That he succeeded, astonished him, after it had been done, for he could not but recognize that a single rotten baluster would either have precipitated him to the floor below, or at least by the noise of its breaking have attracted the attention of Dr. Medjora, who, be it remembered, was suspected of no less a crime than murder.

Looking about the room in which he then stood, he took little note of the decaying furniture, but went at once to a door which he thought must communicate with the adjoining room. Opening this very gently, he disclosed a narrow passageway, from which another door evidently opened into the room beyond. Stealthily he passed on, and pressing his ear against a wide crack, was pleased to find that he could easily hear what was said by the two in the next room. The conversation seemed to have reached the very point of greatest interest to him. The woman said:

"I wish to know exactly your connection with this Mabel Sloane."

"So do the police," replied the Doctor, succinctly.

"But I am not the police," came next in petulant tones.

"Exactly! And not being the police you are out of your province, when investigating a matter supposed to be criminal." Barnes learned two things: first that the Doctor would not lose his temper, and therefore would not be likely to betray himself by revealing anything beyond what his companion might already know; and second, that she knew little as to his relation with Mabel Sloane. This was not very promising, yet he still hoped that something might transpire, which would repay all the trouble that he had taken. The woman spoke again quickly.

"Then you are not going to explain this thing to me?"

"Certainly not, since you have not the right to question me."

"I have not the right? I, whom you expect to marry? I have not the right to investigate your relations with other women?"

"Not with one who is dead!"

"Dead or alive, I must know what this Mabel Sloane was to you, or else—" She hesitated.

"Or else?" queried the Doctor, without altering his tone.

"Or else I will not marry you."

"Oh! Yes, you will!" replied the Doctor, with such a tone of certainty that his companion became exasperated and stamped her feet as she replied in anger:

"I will not! I will not! I will not!" Then, as though her asseveration had slightly mollified her, she added: "Or if I do—" and, then paused.

"Continue!" exclaimed the Doctor, still calm. "You pause at a most interesting period. Or if you do—"

"Or if I do," wrathfully rejoined the woman–"I'll make your whole life a burden to you!"

"No, my wife that is to be, you will not even do that. Perhaps you might try, but I should not permit you to succeed in any such an undertaking. No, my dear friend, you and I are going to be a model couple, provided—"

"Provided what?"

"That you curb your curiosity as to things that do not concern you."

"But this does concern me."

"As I have intimated already, Mabel Sloane being dead, you can have no interest whatever in knowing what relations existed between us."

"Not even if, as the newspapers claim, she had a child?"

"Not even in that case."

"Well, is there a child?"

"I have told you that it does not concern you."

"Do you deny it?"

"I neither deny it, nor affirm it. You have read the evidence, and may believe it or not as you please."

"Oh! I hate you! I hate you!" She was again enraged. "I wonder why I am such a fool as to marry you?"

"Ah! This time you show curiosity upon a subject which does concern you. Therefore I will enlighten you. You intend to marry me, first, because, in spite of the assertion just made, you love me. That is to say, you love me as much as you can love any one other than yourself. Second, you are ambitious to be the wife of a celebrated man. You have been keen enough to recognize that I have genius, and that I will be a great man. Do you follow me?"

"You are the most supreme egotist that I have ever met." The words, meant as a sort of reproach, yet were spoken in tones which betokened admiration.

"Thank you. I see you appreciate me for what I am. All egotists are but men who have more than the average ego, more than ordinary individuality. The supreme egotist, therefore, has most of all. Now, to continue the reasons for our marriage, perhaps you would like to know why I intend to marry you?"

"If your august majesty would condescend so far." The Doctor took no notice of the sneer, but said simply:

"I too have my ambitions, but I need money with which to achieve success. You have money!"

"You dare to tell me that! You are going to marry me for my money! Never, you demon! Never!"

"I thought you had concluded to be sensible and leave off theatricals. You look very charming when you are angry, but it prolongs this conversation to dangerous lengths. We may be interrupted at any moment by the police."

"By the police! In heaven's name how?" In a moment she showed a transition from that emotion which spurned him, to that love for him which trembled for his safety. Thus wisely could this crafty physician play upon the feelings of those whom he wished to influence.

"It is very simple. As much as you love me, you love your own comfort more. I asked you to come up here quietly. You came in your carriage, with driver and footman in full livery. Is that your idea of a quiet trip?"

"But I thought—"

"No! You did not think." The Doctor spoke sternly, and the woman was silent, completely awed. "If you had thought for one moment, you would have readily seen that the police are probably watching you, hoping that, through you, they might find me. Fortunately, however, I have thought of the contingency, and am prepared for it. But let us waste no more time. No! Do not speak. Listen, and heed what I have to say. I have decided not to follow your suggestion. You wrote to me advising flight. That was another indiscretion, since your messenger might have been followed. However, I forgave you, for you not only offered to accompany me, but you expressed a willingness to furnish the funds, as an earnest of which I found a thousand dollars in your envelope. A token, you see, of a love more intense than that jealousy which a moment ago whispered to you to abandon me. From this, and other similar circumstances, I readily deduce that after all you will marry me. But to come to the point. I have consulted a firm of lawyers, and by their advice I shall surrender myself on the day after to-morrow."

"You will surrender to the police?" The woman was thoroughly alarmed. "They will convict you. They will—ugh!" She shuddered.

"No," said the Doctor more kindly than he had as yet spoken. "Do not be afraid. They will neither convict me, nor hang me. I will stand my trial, and come out of it a freed man."

"But if not? Even innocent men have been convicted."

"Even innocent men! Why do you say even? Do you doubt that I am innocent?"

"No! No! But this is what I mean. Although innocent you might be brought in guilty."

"Well, even so, I must take the chance. All my hopes, all my ambitions, all that I care for in life depend upon my being a free man. I cannot ostracize myself, and reach my goal. So the die is cast. But there is another thing that I must tell you. We cannot be married at present."

"Not married? Why not? Why delay? I wish to marry you now, when you are accused, to prove to you how much I love you!" Thus she showed the vacillation of her impulsive, passionate nature.

"I appreciate your love, and your generosity. But it cannot be. My lawyers advise against it, and I agree with them that it would be hazardous. Next, I must have money with which to carry on my defence. When can you give it to me? You must procure cash. It would not be well for me to present your check at my bankers. The circumstances forbid it, lest the prosecution twist it into evidence against me."

"When I received your note bidding me to meet you here, I thought that you contemplated flight. I have brought some money with me. Here are five thousand dollars. If you need more I will get it."

"This will suffice for the present. I thank you. Will you kiss me?" A sound followed which showed that this woman, eager for affection, gladly embraced the opportunity accorded to her. At the same moment there was a loud noise heard in the hall below, from which it was plain that several persons had entered.

"The police!" exclaimed the Doctor. Then there was a pause as though he might be listening, and then he continued, speaking rapidly: "As I warned you, they have followed you. Hush! Have no fear. I shall not be taken. I am prepared. But you! You must wait up here undisturbed. When they find you, you must explain that you came here to look at the property, which you contemplate buying. And now, whatever may happen, have no fear for my safety. Keep cool and play your part like the brave little woman that I know you to be."

There was the sound of a hurried kiss, and then Barnes was horrified to see the door at which he was listening, open, and to find himself confronted by Dr. Medjora. But if Barnes was taken by surprise, the Doctor was even more astonished. His perturbation however passed in a moment, for he recognized Barnes quickly, and thus knew that at least he was not one of the police. Stepping through the door, he pulled it shut after him, and turned a key which was in the lock, and, placing the key in his pocket, thus closed one exit. Barnes retreated into the next room and would have darted out into the hall, had not the strong arm of the Doctor clutched him, and detained him. The Doctor then locked that door also, after which he dragged Barnes back into the passage between the two rooms. Here he shook him until his teeth chattered, and though Barnes was not lacking in courage, he felt himself so completely mastered, that he was thoroughly frightened.

"You young viper," hissed the Doctor through his teeth. "You will play the spy upon me, will you? How long have you been listening here? But wait. There will be time enough later for your explanations. You remain in here, or I will take your life as mercilessly as I would grind a rat with my heel." As though to prove that he was not trifling, he pressed the cold barrel of a revolver against Barnes's temple, until the young man began to realize that tracking murderers was not the safest employment in the world.

Leaving Barnes in the passageway the Doctor went into the front room, and Barnes was horrified by what he saw next. Taking some matches from his pocket he deliberately set fire to the old hangings at the windows, and then lighted the half rotten mattress which rested upon a bedstead, doubly inflammable from age. Despite his fear Barnes darted out, only to be stopped by Dr. Medjora, who forcibly dragged him back into the passageway, and then stood in the doorway watching the flames as they swiftly fed upon the dry material.

"Dr. Medjora," cried Barnes, "you are committing a crime in setting this house afire!"

"You are mistaken. This house is mine, and not insured."

"But there are people in it!"

"They will have ample time to escape!"

"But I? How shall I escape?"

"I do not intend that you shall escape."

"Do you mean to murder me?"

"Have patience and you will see. There, I guess that fire will not be easily extinguished." Then to the amazement of young Barnes the Doctor stepped back into the passageway, and closed and locked the door. Thus they were in total darkness, in a small passageway having no exit save the doors at each end, both of which were locked. Already the fire could be heard roaring, and bright gleams of light appeared through the chinks in the oak door. At this moment voices were heard in the next room. The Doctor brushed Barnes to one side and took the place near the crevice to hear what passed.

"Madam," said the voice of a man evidently a policeman, "where is Dr. Medjora?"

"Dr. Medjora?" replied the woman. "Why, how should I know?"

"You came here to meet him. It is useless to try to deceive me. We tracked you to this house, and, what is more, the man himself was seen to enter just before you did. We only waited long enough to surround the grounds so that there would be no chance to escape. Now that you see how useless it is for him to hide, you may as well tell us where he is, and save time!"

"I know nothing of the man for whom you are seeking. I came here merely to look over the property, with a view to buying it."

"What, buy this old rookery! That's a likely yarn."

"I should not buy it for the house, but for the beautiful grounds."

"Well, I can't stop to argue with you. If you won't help us, we'll get along without you. He is in the house. I know that much."

"Sarjent! Sarjent! Git outer this! The house is on fire!" This announcement, made in breathless tones by another man who had run in, caused a commotion, and, coming so unexpectedly, entirely unnerved the woman, who hysterically cried out:

"He is in there! Open that door! Save him! Save him!"

Dr. Medjora smothered an ejaculation of anger, as in response to the information thus received, the police began hammering upon the door. Old as it was, it was of heavy oak and quite thick. The lock, too, was a good one and gave no signs of yielding.

"Where is the fire?" exclaimed the sergeant.

"In the front room," answered the other man.

"Get the men up here. Bring axes, or anything that can be found to break in with." The man hurried off, in obedience to this order, and the policeman said to the woman:

"Madam, you'd better get out of this. It is going to be hot work!"

"No! No! I'll stay here."

Barnes wondered what was to be the outcome of the situation, and was surprised to hear the sound of bolts being pushed through rusty bearings. Dr. Medjora was further fortifying the door against the coming attack. Barnes would have assailed the other door, but from the roar of the flames he knew that no safety lay in that direction. Presently heavy blows were rained upon the door, showing that an axe had been found. In a few moments the panel splintered, and through a gap thus made could be seen the figure of the man wielding the axe. It seemed as though he would soon batter down the barrier which separated Barnes from safety, when at the next blow the handle of the axe broke in twain. A moment more, and a deafening crash and a rush of smoke into the passageway indicated that a part of the roof had fallen in. The sergeant grasped the woman by the shoulders, and dragged her shrieking, from the doomed house, which was now a mass of flames. The little knot of policemen stood apart and watched the destruction, waiting to see some sign of Dr. Medjora. But they saw nothing of the Doctor, nor of Barnes, of whom, indeed, they did not know.

CHAPTER III
A WIZARD'S TRICK

All New York, that afternoon, was treated to a sensational account in the afternoon "Extra" newspapers, of the supposed holocaust of the suspected murderer of Mabel Sloane. Yet in truth not only was Dr. Medjora safe and well, but he had never been in any serious danger.

As soon as the police had abandoned the effort to batter in the door, Dr. Medjora turned and said to young Barnes:

"It would serve you right were I to leave you in here to be burned, in punishment for your audacity in spying upon me. Instead of that, I shall take you out with me, if only to convince you that I am not a murderer. Give me your hand!"

Barnes obeyed, satisfied that even though treachery were intended, his predicament could not be made worse than it already was. By the dim light which occasionally illuminated the passageway, as the flames flared up, momentarily freed from the smoke, and shone through the crack in the door, already burned considerably, Barnes now saw the Doctor stoop and feel along the wainscoting, finally lifting up a sliding panel, which disclosed a dark opening beyond.

"Fear nothing, but follow me," said the Doctor. "Step lightly though, as these stairs are old and rickety." Much astonished, Barnes followed the Doctor into the opening, and cautiously descended the narrow winding stairs, still holding one hand of the man who preceded him. He counted the steps, and calculated that he must be nearing the basement, when a terrible crash overhead made him look up. For one moment he caught a glimpse of blue sky, which in a second was hidden by lurid flames, and then darkness ensued, whilst a shower of debris falling about him plainly indicated that the burning building was tumbling in. The hand which held his, gripped it more tightly and their descent became more rapid, but beyond that, there was no sign from the Doctor that he was disturbed by the destroying element above them. In a few more moments they stood upon a flat cemented floor.

"It seems odd," said the Doctor, with a laugh that sounded ghoulish, considering their position, "that I should need to ask you for a match when there is so much fire about us. But I used my last one upstairs." Barnes fumbled in his pocket, and finding one, drew it along his trouser leg until it ignited. As the flame flared up, a dull red glare illuminated the face of Dr. Medjora, making him seem in his companion's fancy the prototype of Mephistopheles himself. Again the Doctor laughed.

"Afraid to trust me with fire, eh? Is that why you lighted it yourself? Never mind. I only wished to get my bearings. It is long since I have been in this place. See, here is a door to the right." He grasped the iron handle, and after some exertion the bolt shot back, but when he pushed against it the door did not yield. At the same moment the match spluttered and the flame died.

"Help me push this door," said the Doctor. Barnes obeyed most willingly, but their combined efforts still failed to move it.

"Well," said the Doctor, "my young friend, it looks as though we were doomed, after all. In case we should fail to escape, when we are thus unexpectedly hurried into the presence of the secretary of the other world, in making your statement, I trust you will not forget that you cannot blame me for the accident which curtails your earthly existence. It was no fault of mine that you were in the passageway above, nor could I foresee that we could not open this door."

This sacrilegious speech, made in a tone of voice which showed in what contempt the speaker held the great mystery of life and death, chilled young Barnes so that he shivered. It made him more than convinced that this man was fully capable of committing the murder which had been attributed to him. At the same time, as the Doctor appeared to have abandoned the effort to escape, despair rendered Barnes more courageous and sharpened his senses so that he could think for himself. Freeing his hand from the other's grasp, he felt about until he found the edge of the door, and rapidly searched for the hinges. In a few moments a cry of gladness escaped from him.

"It is all right, Doctor. The hinges are on our side. We must pull the door to open it, and not push it as we have been doing."

"Good!" said the Doctor. "I knew that. I was only trying you. You are clever. And courageous. Too much so for me to run any risks." The last words were spoken as though to himself. He continued: "Come. We must get out of this before it is too late!" He opened the door, which moved so easily that Barnes readily comprehended that the Doctor must have held it firmly shut whilst the two had been trying to open it, else his own shaking would have disclosed the fact that it opened inward. Thus he saw that Dr. Medjora spoke truly, and had only been submitting him to a test. He followed through the door, glad once more to have hope before him, for had the Doctor intended to destroy him, it would have been easy enough to shut the door, leaving him behind, fastening it, as he did now, with a heavy bolt.

"There is little chance of our being followed," said the Doctor, as he thus barred the way behind them, "but it is as well to be careful. And now that we are safe, for this vault is fire-proof, I will let you see where you are." In a moment the Doctor had found a match and lighted a lamp, and Barnes gazed about him bewildered.

At most he had expected to find himself in some forgotten vault or old wine-cellar. What he saw was quite different.

The apartment, if such a term may be employed was spacious, and formed in a perfect circle, with a hemispherical roof. This dome was covered with what, in the dim light, appeared to be hieroglyphical sculpture. What puzzled Barnes most was that no seams appeared, from which he concluded that the entire cavern must have been hewn out of the solid rock. The floor also was of stone, elaborately carved, and, appearing continuous with the ceiling, at once presented an impossible problem in engineering. For the door through which they had entered evidently had no connection with the original design of the structure, since it was of modern style, and, moreover, the doorway, cut for its insertion, had destroyed the continuity of the carvings on the wall, which, to the height of this doorway, represented a seemingly endless procession, interrupted only by the cutting of the opening, which thus showed curiously divided bodies of men and women along its two edges. In the centre of the place was a singular stone, elaborately carved, with a polished upper surface. Upon this Dr. Medjora seated himself, after having lighted the lamp which hung like a censer from the centre of the roof. Barnes looked at him, awed into silence. Allowing him a few minutes to contemplate his surroundings, the Doctor said:

"You are Jack Barnes, the assistant of Dudley Bliss. You are ambitious to become a detective. Therefore, when you read my name on my card this morning, you thought it a good opportunity to track a murderer, did you not? Answer me, and tell me no lies!"

"Yes," said Barnes, surprised to find that a curious sensation in his throat, as though he were parching, precluded his saying more.

"Well, you have tracked the murderer to his den. What do you think of the place. Safe enough from the police, eh!" The Doctor laughed in a soft congratulatory way, which grated upon his hearer's ear. He continued, as though to himself: "And Dudley Bliss warned me that I could not escape from the police. I, Emanuel Medjora! I could not escape!" Then he burst out into a prolonged ringing peal of laughter which made Barnes tremble affrighted, as a hundred echoes for the moment made his imagination picture myriads of demons chiming in with the merriment of their master.

"Come here," cried the Doctor, checking his laugh. Barnes hesitated and then retreated. "Come here, you coward!" said the Doctor, in a sterner voice. The taunt made the blood course more swiftly through the young man's veins, and the laugh of the demon echo having died away, he threw his head up and approached the stone, stopping within a few feet of Dr. Medjora, and looking him in the eye.

"Ah! As I thought. A strong will, for a youngster. I must use strategy." This so softly that Barnes did not comprehend the sense of the words. Then the Doctor spoke in his most alluring manner:

"You are plucky, Mr. Barnes. This is a gruesome place, and I have brought you here under such peculiar circumstances that you might well be alarmed. But I see that you are not, and I admire you for your courage. It is his courage that has made man the master of all the animal world. By that he controls beasts, who could rend him to a thousand bits, with ease: only they dare not. So, for your courage, I forgive your impudence, and I might say imprudence, in following me this morning."

Barnes was mystified by this alteration of manner, and was not such a fool that he did not suspect that it boded him no special favor. He did not reply, not knowing what to say. The Doctor jumped up from his seat, saying pleasantly:

"I am forgetting my politeness. You are my guest, and I am occupying the only available seat. Pardon me, and be seated." Barnes hesitated, and the Doctor said, "Oblige me!" in a tone which made Barnes think it wise to comply. He therefore seated himself on the stone, and the Doctor muttered low to himself:

"How innocently he goes to the sacrifice," words which Barnes did not hear and would not have understood had he done so. Then the Doctor laughed with a muffled, gurgling sound, which, answered by the echoes, again made Barnes feel uncomfortable.

"Now then, Mr. Barnes," began Dr. Medjora, "I have no doubt that your curiosity has been aroused, and that you would like to know what sort of place this is, and how it came here. It is a very curious story altogether, and as we shall find time hang heavily on our hands whilst the fire is burning upstairs, I cannot entertain you better, perhaps, than with the tale. You know, of course, or you have heard, that I am a physician. But no one knows how thoroughly entitled I am to the name. I am a lineal descendant of the great Æsculapius himself." Barnes stared, wondering whether the man were mad. Having begun his recital, Dr. Medjora apparently took no more notice of Barnes than though he had not been present. But whilst he spoke, with his hands clasped behind his back, he began to pace around the room, thus walking in a circle about Barnes, as he sat upon the stone in the centre.

"The ancient Mexicans worshipped a god to whom they built pyramids. This was no other than my great ancestor Æsculapius. He was also known to many of the races that inhabited the great North country. Here in this place, a powerful tribe built a great pyramid, the top of which was this dome, hewn from a single rock, and carved, as you see, with characters which, translated would tell secrets which would astound the world. The man who acquires all the knowledge here inscribed, may well call himself the master of this century. I will be that man!"

He had increased his pace as he walked around, so that during this speech he had made three circles about Barnes, who, astonished as much by his actions as by his words, had followed him with his eyes, turning his head as far as possible in one direction to accomplish this, and then rapidly turning it to the opposite side so that he might not lose sight of the Doctor. As the last words were uttered, the Doctor stopped suddenly before him, and hurled the words at him as though they contained a menace. But Barnes flinched only slightly, and the Doctor continued his walk and his narrative.

"Yes, for here on these rocks are graven the sum of all the knowledge of the past, which the great cataclysm lost to us for so many centuries. This dome was the summit of the great temple. This floor was a hundred feet below it, and was the floor of the edifice. Then came the flood. The earth quaked, the waters rose, the earth parted, the temple was riven, and the dome fell, here upon this floor, and the record of the greatest wisdom in the world was buried beneath the earth. Lost! Lost! Lost!!"

His gyrations had increased in rapidity, so that he had run around Barnes six times during the above speech, and, as before, he stopped to confront him, fairly screaming the last words. Barnes began to feel odd in his head from turning it to watch this man who, he had now decided, was surely a madman, and as the Doctor screamed out "Lost! Lost! Lost!" almost in his face, he started to his feet, standing upon the stone and prepared to defend himself if necessary. As though much amused at this action, Dr. Medjora threw back his head and laughed. Laughed long and loud! Laughed until the answering echoes reverberated through the place as though a million tongues had been hidden in the recesses. Stopping suddenly, he began racing around again, and resumed his story:

"And so came that great cataclysm which all corners of the world record as the flood. So the great Atlantis, the centre of the civilization of the world, was lost for centuries, until at last re-discovered and re-christened America. Æsculapius perished, and his wisdom died. His records were hidden. But he left a son, and that son another, and from him sprung another, and another, and another, and so on, and on, as time sped, until to-day I am the last of the great line. Ha! You doubt it. You think that I am lying. Then how comes it that I am here? Here in the treasure house of my great ancestor? Because among my people there are traditions, and one told of this temple. I studied it, and worked it out, until I located it. Then I came here and found this old house built over it. And I knew that it covered the greatest secret in all the world. But it contained another secret too. A simple, easy secret for a man like me to solve. A secret staircase, built by some stupid old colonist, to lead him down to a secret wine-cellar, which is on the other side of that stairway. But Providence would not permit the old drunkard to turn to the right, in digging for his vault, or he would have entered this chamber, as I have done. I found this staircase, and cut my way into this place, which I closed with that iron door. And you, you fool, thought that I did not know how to open a door that I had built myself." His laugh rang out again, and the piercing shrieks, coming back from the echoes, darted through Barnes's brain, confused by his pivotal turning on the stone as he tried to follow the Doctor racing around the chamber, and as the man now rushed at him screaming:

"Now! Now! You fool, you are mine! Mine! All mine!" Barnes felt as though something in his brain had snapped, and, tottering, he threw up his arms, and then sank down, to be caught by Dr. Medjora, who lifted him as though he had been a child, and laid him upon the floor. Placing his ear to his heart a moment, the Doctor arose to his feet with a satisfied expression and speaking low, said:

"He is now thoroughly frightened, but the shock will not kill him. When he wakes he will be mine indeed! I will play the little trick, and I can be safe without fear from this." He kicked the prostrate form lightly with his foot, and then lifted Barnes up and sat him upon the stone as he slowly revived, supporting him until he had sufficiently recovered not to need assistance. Then he placed himself in front of Barnes, and as soon as the young man seemed to have regained his senses he folded his arms and said sternly:

"Look at me!" Barnes obeyed for a moment and then turned away and would have risen, but the doctor called out authoritatively:

"You cannot get up! You have no legs!" Barnes reached down with his hands towards his legs, only to be stopped by the words:

"You cannot feel! You have no hands! Now look at me! Look! I command you!" Barnes gazed helplessly into the Doctor's eyes, and the latter continued, in a voice of peremptory sternness:

"Now answer me when I speak to you. Do you understand?"

"Yes, I understand. I will answer!" The voice did not seem to be the normal tones of the young man, and a smile passed over the Doctor's face as he went on.

"Do you know who you are? If so, tell me!"

"I am Jack Barnes!"

"And who am I?"

"Doctor Medjora!"

"Do you know where you are?"

"Yes! In the chamber of Æsculapius!"

"If I let you go from here, what will you do?"

"I would tell the police what I know!"

"Good! Now listen to me!"

"I am listening!"

"You wish to escape?"

"Yes!"

"I am your master?"

"You are my master!"

"You must obey my commands! You understand that?"

"I must obey your commands. I understand that!"

"You are asleep now?"

"Yes, I am asleep!"

"But if I give you a command now when you are asleep, you will obey it when I allow you to awaken?"

"What you command when I am asleep, I will do when you let me be awake!"

"You followed me to-day?"

"I followed you."

"You will forget that?"

No answer came from the sleeper. The crucial test had come. The contest of wills. The Doctor, however, was determined to succeed. Success meant a great deal to him, for he must either kill this man, or else control him. He did not consider the first expedient. Murder was not even in his thought. He stepped up to Barnes and took his two hands.

"You will forget that you followed me?"

Still no reply. The Doctor gently closed the open eyes of the sleeper, and rubbed them with a rotary movement of the thumb. Again he ventured:

"You will forget that you followed me? You—will—forget—that—you—followed—Dr. Medjora?" A pause, a quiver of the released eyelids, which opened slowly, allowing the eyes to gaze at the Doctor; then the lids closed again, a shiver passed over the sleeper's body, and the voice spoke:

"I will obey! I will forget!"

"You will forget that you followed me?"

"I will forget!"

"Repeat what I say. You will forget that you followed me?"

"I will forget that I followed you!"

"You will forget that you saw me and heard me speaking to a woman?"

"I will forget that you were speaking to a woman!"

"You will forget that there was a fire?"

"I will forget the fire!"

"You will forget the secret staircase?"

"I will forget the staircase!"

"The secret staircase!" The Doctor was determined to take no risk.

"I will forget the secret staircase!" said the sleeper.

"You will forget this room?"

"I will forget this room!"

"Finally, you will forget that you have been asleep?"

"Finally, I will forget that I have been asleep!"

"Good! That ought to be safe enough!" This the Doctor said to himself, but the sleeper replied:

"Good! That ought to be safe enough!"

"Pah! He is a mere automaton," said the Doctor.

"A mere automaton!" repeated Barnes.

At this last sally the Doctor burst out into uncontrolled laughter, so much heartier than before that it was plain that his previous laughing had been but a part of his scheme to overawe the strong young will of his companion, by raising up the affrighting echoes. The sleeper joined in with this laughing, imitating it almost note for note, and the answering echoes adding to the bedlam, made the place indeed like some dwelling-place of evil spirits. The Doctor's hilarity passed, and placing one hand upon Barnes's shoulder, in a voice of command he cried!

"Silence!" At once the stillness of death ensued, as though each gibbering demon had scurried back into his hiding-place. The Doctor took the young man's head in both hands, the palms open against the temples, and a thumb over each eye. Rubbing the closed lids gently, at the same time pressing the temples, he spoke in deep resonant tones.

"Sleep! Sleep more deeply! Sleep unconscious! Sleep oblivious! Sleep as though dead, but awaken when I call upon you to awaken!"

He continued his manipulations a few moments, and then removed his hands. The eyelids released, slowly opened, and the sleeper gazed at him. Then as slowly they closed again, and being shut, twitched and fluttered as the heart of a dying bird might do. More and more quiet the movements became, till at length all was still. Then the erect head sank gently down, until it rested upon the breast, and the body swayed, and slipped by easy stages from the stone to the floor, where, as it turned over and lay prone upon the face, a long-drawn sigh escaped, and Barnes lay as one dead. The Doctor gazed silent, satisfied, yet as though awed by his own work. Then he lost himself in reverie.

"And this thing is a man. A strong healthy body encasing a powerful will. Yet where now is that will? What has become of the soul that tenants this shell, which now seems empty, dead. Escaped, gone, and at my bidding! 'He sleeps, he is not dead,' says the scientist. What wily excuses men make for their ignorance. If he sleeps, he is dead, for sleep is death, different only because there is an awakening. Yet in the true death is there not an awakening? All analogy cries out 'Yes!' Now this man sleeps, and I have made him thus temporarily dead. Except at my bidding there can be no awakening on this earth. Then if I do not bid him rise, am I a murderer? The law would say so. The law! The law! Pah! The law that says that, is but a written token of man's ignorance. For if I leave him here, he still must awaken. And who can say that if I leave him to awaken in another world he might not thank me so much, that his spirit in gratitude would become my attendant guardian, until his foolish fellow-men, having hanged my body to a gibbet, by a rope, should send my soul into eternity beside him. My soul! Have I a soul? Yes! and not yet is it prepared to pass beyond the limit of this life. No, despite the laws, and the minions of the laws, I will live to reap the harvest which my great ancestor has garnered here. So this fellow must be awakened and restored to his place amongst his kind! Will it be safe? I have made his mind a blank. But will it so remain? His will is strong. He offered more resistance than any upon whom I have tried my power. Had I not first numbed his brain by twisting it into knots, I doubt that I should have controlled him. So if I release him, to-morrow in his waking senses he will perceive that several hours of his life are as a blank. He will realize that during that time something must have occurred that he has forgotten, and all his energy will be aroused to force remembrance. There is a vivid danger should he recall his experience, before my trial occurs and ends. And with our stupid laws who may say when that may be? Ah! I have the trick. His mind is now a blank, and these few hours will be a void. I have charged him to forget. Now I must bid him to remember, and furnish him with the incidents with which to account for the lapse of time. I will take him near the truth. So near that fluctuating recollection will be unable to disentangle fact from fiction. Thus what he recalls will bear no menace to my safety, and yet will so satisfy his will to know what has passed, that no great effort will be made to delve deeper into the records of this day. But first I must take him from this sacred place. It will be safer."

He opened the iron door, lifted the body of the sleeper in his arms and bore it into the passage at the foot of the stairs. Immediately opposite, there was another door, dimly shown by the light from the swinging lamp. This he kicked open with his foot, without dropping his burden. He walked straight across, through the darkness of this old wine cellar, towards a dim ray of light which penetrated at the opposite end, presently coming to a low arch through which he passed with lowered head, emerging into a greater light. They were now in an old cistern, and a circular opening above permitted the moonlight to enter. Here the Doctor laid the sleeper gently down, and retraced his steps. Re-entering the domed chamber, he extinguished the lamp, and then again emerged, closing the door behind him. From a corner under the stairway he procured a long-handled, heavy, iron hammer, such as men use who break large rocks. He next went into the wine cellar, closing the door behind him, and thence passed on through the archway into the cistern. Taking one glance at the still sleeping form of Jack Barnes, he threw off his coat, and attacked the brick-work of the arch, raining upon it heavy blows, each of which demolished a part of the thick wall. At the end of half an hour the opening was choked with fallen debris, and the entrance into the wine vault thus effectually concealed.

This task accomplished, the Doctor resumed his coat, and turned to examine the sleeper. He raised him up, and stood him against that side of the wall upon which the most light was shed. As the body was thus supported, the head hanging, and the weird half-light making the face more ghastly, one might readily have supposed that this was a corpse. But the Doctor presently cried out:

"Awaken! Awaken! not entirely, but so that you may hear and speak!"

In an instant the head was lifted, the eyes opened, and the voice said:

"I am awake! I can hear and speak!"

"Good!" exclaimed the Doctor. "Tell me, what do you remember?"

"You commanded me to remember nothing!"

"True! I commanded! But do you remember?"

"You are the master! I have forgotten!"

"I am the master. Now I tell you to remember!"

"It is impossible! I cannot remember what I have forgotten, unless you tell it to me again!"

"Very true. I will tell you what you have forgotten, and you will then remember it. You will remember even after you are awakened!"

"I will obey. I will remember what you tell me!"

"You left your office this afternoon to follow Dr. Medjora?"

"Yes! I followed Dr. Medjora!"

"He took a car, and you took another?"

"He took a car, and I took another!"

"He left the car, and you followed him to a house and saw him enter?"

"I saw him enter a house!"

"Then there was a fire and you watched the house burning?"

"I saw the house burning!"

"Then you rushed forward and fell into this well?"

"I rushed forward and fell into the well!"

"You will remember all this?"

"Yes, I will remember!"

"Everything else you have forgotten? Nothing else occurred?"

"Nothing else occurred!"

"Now sleep!" The Doctor passed his hands over the eyes and the deep sleep was resumed. The Doctor pressed his lips near the sleeper's ears, and said:

"You will awaken completely in two hours, climb out of this place, and return to your home!"

To this there was no reply, but the Doctor had no doubt that the injunction would be followed. He laid Barnes down upon the bottom of the cistern so that his opening eyes would gaze directly at the orifice above, and then, climbing upon a lot of loose rubbish, he easily reached the edge of the hole, and clutching it with his strong hands drew himself out.

Exactly two hours later, Barnes opened his eyes and slowly awakened to a sense of stiffness and pain in his limbs. He staggered up, and soon was sufficiently aroused to see that he must climb out of the place where he was. This he did with some difficulty, and after wandering about for nearly an hour he found his way to the bridge and crossed the river. Thence he went home, threw himself on his bed, and was soon wrapped in deep, but natural slumber.

In the morning he wondered why he had slept in his clothing. His head ached, and his limbs felt bruised. Slowly he seemed to recall his following Dr. Medjora, his tracking him across the bridge, the house afire, and his tumble into a well, from which he had climbed out late at night. In fact nothing remained in his recollection except what had been suggested by Dr. Medjora whilst he had been hypnotized. Still in a vague way he half doubted, until at breakfast he found seeming corroboration in the newspaper account, which told that the suspected man had been burned to death. How could he reject so good an authority as his morning paper?

CHAPTER IV
DR. MEDJORA SURRENDERS

Madam Cora Corona watched the destruction of the old mansion in which she had last seen her lover, with mingled feelings of horror and of hope. At one moment it seems impossible that the Doctor could find a means of escaping from the flames, whilst at the next she could but remember the manner of man that he was, and that having told her of his intention to surrender to the police, he would scarcely have chosen so horrible a death whilst immediate safety was attainable by simply opening the door of the passageway before the flames enveloped the whole building. Besides, how did the fire occur? He must have started it himself, and, if so, with what object, except to cover up his escape? But love, such as she bore this man, could never be entirely free from its anxiety, until the most probable reasoning should become assured facts. So, with a dull pain of dread gnawing at her heart, she drove her horses home, holding the reins herself, and lashing the animals into a swift gait, which made their chains clank as they strained every nerve to obey their mistress's behest.

Reaching her sumptuous home on Madison Avenue, she hurried to her own room, passing servants, who moved out of her way awed by her appearance, for those who dwelt with her had learned to recognize the signs which portended storm, and were wise enough to avoid the violence of her anger.

Tossing aside her bonnet and mantle, regardless of where they fell, Madam Corona dropped into a large, well-cushioned armchair, and gazed into vacancy, with a hopeless despair depicted on her features. The death of Dr. Medjora would mean much to this woman, and as the minutes sped by, the conviction that he must have perished, slowly burned itself into her brain.

She was the widow of a wealthy Central American. Her husband had been shot as a traitor, having been captured in one of those ever-recurring revolutions, whose leaders are killed if defeated, but made governors if they succeed; rulers until such time when another revolutionary party may become strong enough to depose the last victors. Thus the chance of a battle makes men heroes, or criminals.

She had never loved her husband, and, with a sensual, passionate temperament, which had never been satisfied by her marriage, she welcomed her freedom and her husband's wealth as a possible step towards that love for which she longed. Exiled from her own country, because of the politics of her dead husband, she had come to the United States, the home of all aliens. Her estates had not been confiscated, for fear that the fires of the revolution, smothered but not quenched, might have been again stirred by a seeming warring against the woman. But the President had said to his council:

"Madam Corona is too rich, and she talks too much." So the hint had been given to her to depart, and she had acquiesced, glad enough to retain her fortune.

In New York she had been welcomed amidst the Spanish-Americans, and with a different temperament might readily have endeared to herself a host of true friends. But her selfish desire for a despotic sway over all who came near, and her extreme jealousy of attentions to others, imbued those who made her acquaintance with an aversion which was scarcely concealed by the thin veneer of the polite formalities of social life. So she knew that in the new, as in the old home, she had no friends.

One day she was taken ill, and sent for Dr. Medjora, of whom she had heard, though she had not met him. His skill brought about her rapid recovery, and, being attracted by his fine appearance, she invited him to visit her as a friend. He availed himself of this opportunity to become intimate with a wealthy patron, and called often. Very soon she became aware of the fact that here was a man over whom she could never hope to dominate, and so, as she could not make him her slave, she became his. Her whole fiery nature went out to him, and she courted him with a wealth of passion which should have melted ice, but which from the Doctor earned but little more than a warm hand-clasp at parting. Finally, to her utter amazement, as she was about to despair of ever attracting him, he came to her and asked her to marry him. She consented joyously, and for twenty-four hours lived in rapture.

Then her morning paper told of the death of Mabel Sloane, and connected the Doctor with the tragedy. She hurried to his office and heaped upon him vituperation and reproach, such as only could emanate from a heart capable of the deepest jealousy. He met the storm unflinchingly, and turned it away from himself by reminding her that he would probably be tried for murder, and that thus she would be rid of him. At once she changed her threats to entreaties. She begged him to fly with her. Her wealth would suffice, and in some other clime they could be safe, and she would forget, forgive, and love him.

He appeared to yield, and bade her be ready to come to him at his bidding. She returned home, only to write him a long urgent letter, containing money; the letter to which the Doctor had alluded during the conversation overheard by young Barnes. Then she had been summoned and had gone to him. And now? Now the longer she thought, the more certain did it appear to her, as the hours went by, that her lover was dead. And such a death! She shuddered and closed her eyes. But she could not shut out the vision of her beloved Doctor standing bravely, with folded arms, as the flames crept upon him, surrounded him, and destroyed him. She could not shut out the sound of a last despairing cry wrung from his unwilling lips, as with a final upflaring of the flame, the whole structure fell in.

Maddened by her thoughts, at length she started up and turned towards her basin, intending to lave her fevered brow, when with a cry she sprang back, for there, in her room, with arms folded as in her vision, stood what she could but suppose to be the wraith of the dead. She shrieked, and fell forward in a swoon, to be caught in the arms of Dr. Medjora, who had admitted himself, unknown to the sleeping servants, by a latch key furnished to him by her, when she had begged him to join her in flight.

When she recovered consciousness and realized that this was no spectre which had intruded upon her, she lavished upon him a wealth of kisses and caresses, which should have assured him of the intensity of her love and joy. She laughed and cried alternately, petted him and patted his cheeks, kissed him upon the hands, upon his face, his hair, his lips. She threw her arms around him and pressed him to her palpitating heart, the while crying:

"Alive! Thank heaven! Alive! Alive!"

"And did you think me dead, Cara mia?" He folded his arms about her, touched by the evident genuineness of her feelings, and moved to some slight response.

"Yes! I thought so! No! I did not! I knew you were too clever to die so. But then the flames! They ate up the whole building, and I did not see how–I could not imagine–and I was afraid! But now you are safe again! You are with me, and I love you a million times more that I have mourned your death!"

"Come, come, dear heart! I am alive and unhurt. I never was in danger. I would not kill myself, you know. I love my life too well! And it was I who set the fire!"

"I thought that too at times! You did it to baffle the police! I see it all! Oh, you are so clever! Now they will think you dead, and we can go away together and live without fear! Is it not so?"

"No, Cora! As I told you this afternoon, I shall give myself up to the police!"

"No, no, no! You must not! You shall not! What, risk your precious life again? You will not, say that you will not! If you love me, say it!"

She twined her arms about his neck, and held him tight as though he meditated going away at once. In the fear of this new danger, an agony welled up about her heart, and tears choked her utterance. But the Doctor remained impassive. He gently, but forcibly, disengaged himself from her embrace, and seating himself, drew her down to her knees beside him. Then he took her head in his hands, compelling her to look at him, and spoke to her in measured tones.

"Cora! Calm yourself! You are growing hysterical. You know me too well, to suppose that I would swerve from a fixed purpose. I will not leave this city. As I have told you, all my hopes for the future bind me here. Elsewhere I should be as nothing, here I will grow into greatness,–greatness which you shall share with me, if you be but brave!"

"But this trial! Suppose–suppose–oh! The horror of it!" She dropped her head upon his lap and wept. He stroked her beautiful black hair, which had become disengaged and now fell down her back, completely covering her shoulders. Presently when she was more quiet, only an occasional sob indicating that she was yet disturbed, he spoke to her, soothingly, caressingly, so that under the magic of his tones she gradually recovered her self-possession.

"My little one, have no fear! This trial is but an incident which scarcely gives me a troublesome thought. The worst is that I shall probably be in prison for some time awaiting trial. A meddlesome interference with the liberty of a man, which the law takes, offering no recompense when the accused is proven to have been innocent. This is one of the anomalies of a system which claims to administer equal rights and justice to all. I am accused of a crime. I am arrested and incarcerated for weeks, or months. I am tried and acquitted. I spend thousands of dollars in my defence. When I am released, I am in no way repaid for my loss of liberty and money. Indeed, innocent though I be, I am congratulated by a host of sympathizers because I was not hanged. But I have had full justice. I have been accorded an expensive trial, with learned talent against me, etc., etc. The law is not to blame, nor those who enforce the laws. I am the victim of circumstances, that is all. Well, so be it. A stupid doctor has warned the authorities that a woman has died of morphine poisoning, despite the fact that a more competent man has signed a certificate that she died of a natural disease. So I have been accused, and will undoubtedly be indicted and tried. But do you not see, that I have but to show that diphtheria caused death, and my innocence will be admitted?"

"Yes, but—!"

"No! There is no but? Now show me to a room, where I may rest unobserved, until the day after to-morrow. We must not rob the public of its sensation too soon. Think of it, I read my own holocaust in an afternoon paper!"

Madam Corona shivered at this, not yet fully unmindful of her own recent forebodings. Obediently she took him to a room, and left him, the single comforting thought abiding with her, that she would have him all to herself during the whole of the following day.

When Messrs. Dudley and Bliss learned from Barnes that he had followed Dr. Medjora, and had seen him go into the building which had been destroyed by fire, their hope that possibly the newspaper accounts were erroneous, was dissipated.

"I knew it!" began the junior member. "I knew that it was too good to be true. Think of that man's permitting himself to be burned to death just as we were about to get our chance. It's too exasperating."

"It is annoying, Robert, of course," said Mr. Dudley. "Yet there is some comfort in the thought that he had the courtesy to pay us a retainer. That five hundred is most acceptable."

"Oh! certainly, the money will come handy, but what is five hundred dollars to an opportunity such as this would have been?" Mr. Bliss was in a very bad humor.

"Robert," began his partner, speaking seriously, "you must not be so impatient. We are no worse off, at any rate, than before the man called upon us, so far as our profession goes, and we are better off than we would be if he had not called at all. You should be grateful for the good received, and not cry after lost possibilities."

"Oh! well! I suppose you are right!" and throwing up both arms in a gesture of disgust, he went to his desk and began writing furiously. A long silence was maintained. These two men contrasted greatly. They had met each other during their law-school days, and were mutually attracted. Mr. Dudley was a hard student who had realized early in life that the best fruit comes to him, who climbs, rather than to him who shakes the tree; whilst that man who lies at ease, basking in the sunshine and waiting for ripe plums to fall into his mouth, is likely to go hungry. He was methodical, persistent, patient, energetic. He wasted no time. Even during his office hours, if there were nothing else to occupy him, he would continue his studies, delving into the calf-bound tomes as though determined to be a thorough master of their contents.

Mr. Bliss was his antithesis, and yet he had just those qualifications which made him complement his partner, so that he strengthened the firm. He was a brilliant, rather than a deep student. He read rapidly, and had a remarkable memory, so that he had a superficial comprehension of many things, rather than a positive knowledge of a lesser number. He could be both rhetorical and oratorical, and, at a pinch, could blind a jury with a neat metaphor, where surer logic might have made a smaller impression, being less attractive. When addressing the jury, he would become so earnest, that by suggesting to his hearers that he himself was convinced of the truth of his utterances, he often swayed them to his wishes. He was quick, too, and keen, so that he eventually became justly celebrated for his cross-examinations. But at this time his greatness had scarcely begun to bud, and so he sat like a schoolboy in the dumps, whilst his graver partner, though equally disappointed at the prospect of losing a good case, showed not so much of his annoyance.

Presently Barnes entered with a telegram, which Mr. Bliss took, glad of anything to divert his thoughts. A moment after reading it he was greatly excited, and handing the message to his partner, exclaimed:

"Mortimer, in heaven's name read that!"

Mr. Dudley took the despatch and read as follows:

"Be at office District Attorney to-morrow ten o'clock. I will take your advice and surrender. Medjora."

"Well, Robert, what of it?"

"What of it? Has the Western Union an office in the other world now, that dead men may send telegrams?"

"Certainly not. Therefore this was sent before he died."

"Before he died!" This unthought-of possibility shattered the rising hopes of Mr. Bliss. He made one more effort, however, saying:

"What is the date?"

"Why, the date is to-day!" said Mr. Dudley, slowly. "Singular! But it is an error, of course."

"Why do you say 'of course'?" asked his partner, testily. "You seem to be anxious to lose this case. Now, how do you know that Medjora is dead after all?"

"Why Barnes saw him go into the building, and he could not have escaped, for the place was surrounded by the police."

"There is no telling what that man can do. I verily believe that he is more than human, after the way in which he read my thoughts yesterday. I am going to probe this thing to the bottom." And before his partner could detain him, he had taken down his hat and rushed off.

Two hours later, he returned discouraged. At the main office he had been referred to a branch, far uptown. Arriving there he found that the operator who had sent the despatch had gone off duty. The original blank upon which the message had been written was undated. So he learned practically nothing.

"Never mind," said he, doggedly, after relating his ill-success, "I will go to the District-Attorney's office to-morrow, and wait for that man whether he come, or his ghost. I firmly believe that one or the other will do so."

"I will go with you," said Mr. Dudley. "Only promise me to say nothing, unless our man turns up."

At half-past nine on the next morning, both of the young lawyers were at the appointed place. Mr. Dudley sat down and read, or appeared to read, the paper. Mr. Bliss walked about impatiently, leaving the room occasionally to go out into the hall and stand at the main doorway, looking into the street.

A few moments before ten o'clock the District Attorney himself arrived and nodded pleasantly to the young men, with whom he was acquainted.

"Waiting for me?" he asked of Mr. Dudley.

"No! I am waiting for a client," was the quiet rejoinder. Mr. Bliss started to speak, but a signal from his partner reminded him of his injunction.

"Strange news in the morning paper," remarked the District Attorney, evidently full of his topic. "That man Medjora, the fellow who poisoned his sweetheart you know, was burned to death trying to escape the detectives. Served him right, only it is a great case missed by us lawyers, eh?"

"Why do you say it served him right?" asked Mr. Bliss, quickly. He still hoped that the Doctor would appear, and it occurred to him instantly, that he might learn something from the prosecution, thus taken unawares, supposing the case to be ended.

"Oh, well!" said the old lawyer, careful of speech by habit rather than because he saw any necessity for caution in the present instance; "had the case come to trial, we had abundant evidence upon which to convict, for Medjora certainly murdered the girl."

"Your are mistaken!" said a clear voice behind them, and as the three men turned and faced Dr. Medjora, the clock struck ten. Without waiting for them to recover from their surprise the Doctor continued: "Mr. District Attorney, I am Emanuel Medjora, the man whom you have just accused of a hideous crime; the murder of a young girl, by making use of his knowledge of medicine. To my mind there can scarcely be a murder more fiendish, than where a physician, who has been taught the use of poisons for beneficent purposes, prostitutes his knowledge to compass the death of a human being; especially of one who loved him." He uttered the last words with a touch of pathos which moved his hearers. Quickly recovering he continued: "Therefore, both as a man, and as a physician, I must challenge you to prove your slanderous statement. I have come here to-day, sir, to surrender myself to you as the law's representative, that I may show my willingness to answer in person the charges which have been made against me. Messrs. Dudley Bliss here, are my counsel."

The District Attorney was very much astonished. Not only was he amazed to see the man alive, when he had been reported dead, but he was entirely unprepared to find this suspected criminal to be a man of cultured refinement, both of speech and of manner. He was thus, for the moment, more leniently inclined than he would have been, were he alone considering the mass of evidence which his office had already collected against the Doctor. Turning to him therefore he said:

"So you are Dr. Medjora! Well, sir, I am delighted to see you. That you have voluntarily surrendered yourself will certainly tell in your favor. You must pardon my hasty remark. But I thought that you were dead, and——"

"And as you could not hurt the dead, you saw no harm in calling an unconvicted man a murderer. I see!" There was a vein of satirical reproach beneath the polished manner of saying these words, which stung the old lawyer, and restored him at once to his wonted craftiness.

"Perhaps you are right, Doctor, and I ought not to have used the words about you, dead or alive. Of course, in this office the prisoner is only the accused. Never more than that, even in our thoughts. That is an imperative injunction which I place upon all of my assistants. You see, gentlemen," he addressed them all collectively, with the purpose of bringing the Doctor to the conclusion that he was not specially thinking of him. Thus he prepared to spring a trap. "You see, the District Attorney is a prosecuting officer, but he should never persecute. It is his duty to represent and guard the liberties of the whole community. He should be as jealous of the rights of the accused, as of the accuser. More so, perhaps, for the prisoner stands to an extent alone, whilst the whole commonwealth is against him. And so, Dr. Medjora, if you are an innocent man, as you seem to be, it would be my most pleasing duty to free you from the stigma cast upon you. And should you come to trial, you must believe that the more forcible my arguments may be against you, the more do I espouse your cause, for the more thorough would be your acquittal if you obtained the verdict." Then having, as he thought, led his man away from his defence, he asked quickly, "But tell me, why have you not surrendered before?"

If he hoped to see the Doctor stammer and splutter, seeking for some plausible explanation, he was doomed to disappointment. Dr. Medjora replied at once, ignoring a signal from Mr. Bliss not to speak.

"Mr. District Attorney, I will reply most candidly. Whilst, as you have just said, it is your duty to guard the interests of the accused as well as of the commonwealth, I regret to be compelled to say that such is not your reputation. People say, and I see now that they must be wrong,"–the Doctor bowed and smiled most politely,–"but they do say that with you it is conviction at any cost. Thus even an innocent man might well hesitate to withstand the attacks of so eminent and skilful a jurist as yourself. Circumstantial evidence, whilst most reliable when thoroughly comprehended, may sometimes entrap the guiltless. So whilst my blood boiled in anger at the disgraceful charges which were made against me, my innate love of liberty, and my caution, bade me think first. Not satisfied with my own counsel, I deemed it wise to consult legal authority, which I did two days ago. Messrs. Dudley Bliss advised me to surrender, confident that my innocence will be made so apparent that I do not materially jeopardize my life. In compliance with the understanding entered into two days ago, as these gentlemen will testify, I am at your service."

"But why did you not come here two days ago?"

"Because I had some affairs of a private nature to arrange."

"What about the incident of the fire reported in the papers?"

"Why, I see nothing in that but poor reportorial work. I did not choose to be arrested when I had decided voluntarily to surrender, as such a mischance would have injured my case. I therefore escaped during the confusion. That I was unobserved, and was reported to have perished, is not my fault certainly."

"Very well, Doctor. You have not been indicted, and there is no warrant out for your arrest; still, as you have surrendered, are you willing to be taken to prison?"

"That is what I expect. I am entirely ready."

"May I ask," said Mr. Dudley, addressing the District Attorney, "in view of the fact that our client has voluntarily surrendered himself, that his confinement in prison may be as brief as possible? We claim that the Doctor is an innocent man, deprived of his liberty whilst awaiting trial, through the blundering accusations of a stupid physician. We venture to suggest that common justice demands that his trial should be as soon as possible."

"I shall arrange to have the trial at as early a date as is consistent with my duty to the commonwealth!"

"And to the accused?" interjected Dr. Medjora, with a twinkle in his eye.

"And to the accused, of course," said the old lawyer, with a smile, unwilling to be outdone.

And so Dr. Emanuel Medjora was taken to prison to await his trial, and the public was treated to another sensation through the newspapers.

CHAPTER V
FOR THE PROSECUTION

In spite of the promises of the District Attorney, several months passed before the great murder trial was commenced.

The public at last were delighted to hear that their love for the harrowing details of a celebrated crime was to be satisfied. A few of the newspapers of the sensational stamp announced that they, and they only, would have the fullest accounts, illustrated with life-like portraiture of the accused, the lawyers, the judge, the jury, and the chief witnesses. This promise was so well fulfilled that on the opening day there appeared several alleged portraits of Dr. Medjora, which resembled him about as little as they did one another.

Several days were consumed before the jury was impanelled, and then at length the prosecution opened its case, which was mainly in charge of Mr. George Munson, a newly appointed Assistant District Attorney, the very man of whom Mr. Dudley had spoken, when his partner had bewailed their unfortunate lot, because they had never been intrusted with a criminal case.

Mr. Munson was a rising man. He had attracted attention, and was receiving a reward of merit by his promotion to the office which he now filled. It was hinted somewhere, that his appointment had been largely dependent upon his conduct of that murder case, during which he had shown a wonderful knowledge of chemistry, for one not actually a chemist. And his having charge of this most important case, in which chemical expert testimony seemed likely to play an important part, substantiated the statement.

He was well versed in law, was keen and quick at cross-examination, and merciless in probing the private lives of witnesses, when such action promised to aid his cause. He was not, however, a very brilliant speaker, but it was expected that the District Attorney would himself sum up. Thus the prosecution seemed to be in able hands. Opposed to them were Messrs. Dudley Bliss, two young, unknown men, and people wondered why the Doctor, reputed to have wealth, had not engaged more prominent counsel.

Mr. Munson's opening speech was not lengthy. He confined himself to a brief statement of his case, summarizing in the most general fashion what he expected to prove; in brief, that Mabel Sloane had died of morphine poisoning, and not of diphtheria, that the poison had been administered by Dr. Medjora, and that his object had been to rid himself of a woman who stood in his path, an obstacle to the advancement of his ambition. Mr. Munson thus avoided the mistake so often made by lawyers, where, following the temptation to make a speech, they tell so much that they weaken their cause, by affording their opponents time to prepare a more thorough defence.

A few witnesses were called to establish in a general way the death of the girl, her place of residence, and such other facts as are essential in the preparation of a case, in order that no legal technicality may be neglected. But as it is manifest that I cannot, in the scope of this narration, give you a full account of the trial, I shall confine myself to compiling from the records just so much of the evidence as shall seem to me likely to attract your interest, and to be necessary to a full comprehension of the Doctor's position, and relation to this supposed crime.

The first important witness, then, was Dr. Meredith, the physician who had aroused suspicion by reporting to the Board of Health that the girl had, in his opinion, died of opium narcosis. It was apparent, when he took the stand, that he was extremely nervous, and disliked exceedingly the position in which he found himself. Indeed it is a very trying predicament for a physician to be called upon to testify in a court of law, unless he is not only an expert in his profession, but also an expert witness. He finds himself confronted by an array of medical and legal experts, all conspiring to disprove his assertions, and to show how little his knowledge is worth. Generally, he has little to gain, whereas he may lose much in the estimation of his patrons by being made to appear ridiculous on the stand.

After taking the oath, Dr. Meredith sat with his eyes upon the floor until Mr. Munson began to question him. Then he looked straight at the lawyer, as though upon him he relied for protection.

"You attended Miss Mabel Sloane in her last illness, I believe?" began Mr. Munson.

"I did."

"How were you called in to the case?"

"I was called in consultation by Dr. Fisher."

"You were sent for by Dr. Fisher! Then I am to understand that you and he were good friends?"

"The best of friends."

"And are so still?"

"I think so. Yes."

"And Dr. Medjora. Did you know him before your connection with this case?"

"Only slightly."

"Were you present when Miss Sloane died?"

"I was present for half an hour before she died."

"Exactly! And you remained with her until she was actually dead?"

"Yes, sir. I saw her die."

"Of what did she die?"

"I object!" cried Mr. Bliss, springing to his feet and interrupting the prosecution for the first time.

"State your objection," said the Recorder, tersely.

"Your Honor," began Mr. Bliss, "I object to the form of the question. The whole point at issue is contained in it, and I contend that this witness is not qualified to answer. If he were, the trial might end upon his doing so."

"The witness is only expected to testify to the best of his belief," said the Recorder.

"Very true, your Honor. I only wish it to go to the jury in the proper form. If they understand that this witness does not know of what Miss Sloane died, but simply states what he thinks, I shall be perfectly satisfied."

"You may as well modify your question, Mr. Munson," said the Recorder. Thus Mr. Bliss scored a little victory, which at once convinced the older lawyers present that, though young, he would prove to be shrewd to grasp the smallest advantage. His object had evidently been to belittle the value of the answer, before it was made, by thus calling attention so prominently to the fact that Dr. Meredith could not know positively what he was about to charge.

"In your opinion, what caused the death of Miss Sloane?" This was the new question formulated to meet the objection raised.

"She died of morphine poisoning!" replied Dr. Meredith.

"You mean you think she died of morphine poisoning?" interjected Mr. Bliss.

"Kindly wait until you get the witness before you begin your cross-examination!" said Mr. Munson, with a touch of asperity.

Mr. Bliss merely smiled and kept silent, satisfied that he had produced his effect upon the jury.

"Will you state why you conclude that Miss Sloane died of morphine poisoning?" continued Mr. Munson.

"I observed all the characteristic symptoms of morphine narcosis prior to her death, and the nature of the death itself was consistent with my theory."

"Please explain what the symptoms of morphine poisoning are?"

"Cold sweat, slow pulse, stertorous breathing, a gradually deepening coma, contracted pupils, which, however, slowly dilate at the approach of death, which is caused by a paralysis of the respiratory centres."

"Did you observe any of these symptoms in Miss Sloane?"

"Yes. Practically all of them."

"And would these same symptoms occur in any other form of death, except from morphine poisoning?"

"They would not. Of course they do not apply to morphine only. They are generally diagnostic of opium poisoning."

"But morphine is a form of opium, is it not?"

"Yes. It is one of the alkaloids."

"Now, Doctor, one more question. You have testified that you attended this girl in her last illness; as a physician you are familiar with death from diphtheria; you have stated what are the symptoms of morphine, or opium poisoning, and that you observed them in this case; further, that an identical set of symptoms would not occur in any other disease known to you; now, from these facts, what would you say caused the death of Miss Mabel Sloane?"

"I should say that she died of a poisonous dose of some form of opium, probably morphine."

"You may take the witness," said Mr. Munson, as he sat down. Mr. Bliss spoke a word to Doctor Medjora, and then holding a few slips of paper, upon which were notes, mainly suggestions which had been written by the prisoner himself, and passed to his counsel unperceived by the majority of those present, he faced the witness, whose eyes at once sought the floor.

"Doctor," began Mr. Bliss, "you have stated that you are only slightly acquainted with Dr. Medjora. Is that true?"

"I said that I was only slightly acquainted with him prior to my being called to attend Miss Sloane. Of course I know him better now."

"But before the time which you specify, you did not know him?"

"Not intimately."

"Oh! Not intimately? Then you did know him? Now is it not a fact that you and Dr. Medjora were enemies?"

"I object!" exclaimed Mr. Munson.

"I wish to show, your Honor," said Mr. Bliss, "that this witness has harbored a personal spite against our client, and that because of that, his mind was not in a condition to evolve an unprejudiced opinion about the illness of Miss Sloane."

"I do not think that is at all competent, your Honor," said Mr. Munson. "The witness has testified to facts, and even if there were personal feeling, that would not alter facts."

"No, your Honor," said Mr. Bliss, quickly, "facts are immutable. But a prejudiced mind is as an eye that looks through a colored glass. All that is observed is distorted by the mental state."

"The witness may answer," said the Recorder.

At the request of Mr. Bliss the stenographer read the question aloud, and the witness replied.

"Dr. Medjora and myself were not enemies. Certainly not!"

"Had you not had a controversy with him upon a professional point?"

"I had an argument with him, in a debate, just as occurs in all debates."

"Precisely! But was not this argument, as you term it, a discussion which followed a paper which you had read, and in that argument did not Dr. Medjora prove that the whole treatment outlined by you was erroneous, unscientific, and unsound?"

"He did not prove it; he claimed something of the kind!"

"You say he did not prove it. As a result of his argument, was not your paper refused publication by a leading medical journal?"

"I did not offer it for publication."

"I think this is all incompetent, your Honor," said Mr. Munson.

"You may go on," said the Recorder, nodding to Mr. Bliss.

"Is it not customary for papers read before your societies to become the property of the society, and are they not sent by the society to the journal in question?"

"Yes, I believe so."

"Was not your paper sent to the journal as usual, and was it not rejected by the journal?"

"I do not know that it was."

"Well, has your paper been published anywhere?"

"No."

"You said that you were present when Miss Sloane died. Now how did that happen. Were you sent for?"

"No. I had seen the patient with Dr. Fisher during the day, and she seemed to be improving, so much so that Dr. Fisher decided that we need not see her until the next morning. Later I thought this a little unsafe, and so I called during the evening."

"Oh! Dr. Fisher thought she was well enough, but you did not. Was that why you called at night?"

The witness bit his lip with anger at having made this slip.

"I live near, and I thought it would do no harm to call."

"Now when you called, you have stated that you were with her for half an hour before she died. Did she die a half hour after you entered her room?"

"In about half an hour."

"How soon after you saw her, did you suspect that she had been poisoned?"

"Immediately."

"Oh! Immediately! Then of course you made some effort to save her life, did you not? You used some antidotes?"

"It was difficult. At first of course there was merely a suspicion in my mind. I tried to have her drink some strong coffee, but deglutition was almost impossible. This is another evidence of the poison."

"Now, Doctor, be careful. You say that impaired deglutition was due to poisoning. But do you not know that deglutition is most difficult in cases of diphtheria?"

"The patient swallowed very well in the afternoon."

"But if she had grown worse, if the false membrane had increased, would she not have had greater difficulty in swallowing?"

"Yes, but—"

"Never mind the buts. Now, then, when you found that she was too ill to swallow, what else did you do?"

"I injected atropine, and sent for Dr. Fisher."

"Oh! Then you did send for Dr. Fisher?"

"Yes."

"Did he arrive before she died?"

"Yes. About five minutes."

"Did you suggest to him that the patient was dying of poison?"

"I did, but he would not agree with me. Therefore I could not do anything more, as he was the physician in charge."

"Is Dr. Fisher a skilful man?"

"Yes."

"As skilful as you are yourself?"

This was a hard question, but with Dr. Fisher present, only one answer was possible.

"Certainly, but we are all liable to make a mistake."

This was a bad effort to help his cause, for Mr. Bliss quickly interposed.

"Even you are liable to make a mistake, eh?"

"Of course, but in this instance I saw more of the case than Dr. Fisher did."

"Still, Dr. Fisher was present for several minutes before this girl died, and though you suggested that she had been poisoned, and proposed taking some action to save her from the poison, he disagreed with you so entirely that he made no such effort. Is that right?"

"Well, there was very little that he could have done anyway. It was too late. The drug had gone too far for the stomach-pump to be efficacious; the atropine had had no beneficial result, we had no means of applying a magnetic battery, and no time to get one. Artificial respiration was what I proposed, whilst waiting for a battery, but Dr. Fisher thought it a useless experiment, in presence of the diphtheria. He offered to perform tracheotomy, but as I considered that the respiratory centres had been paralyzed by morphine, I could see no advantage in that."

"So whilst you two doctors argued, the patient died?"

"It was too late for us to save her life. The coma was too deep. It was a hopeless case."

"Now, then, Doctor, let us come to those symptoms. You enumerated a list, and claimed that you observed them all. The first is cold sweat. Did you notice that specially?"

"The cold sweat was present, but not very marked. It would be less so with morphine than with other forms of opium."

"Oh! So there was not much sweat after all? Now was there more than would be expected on a warm night such as that was?"

"I think so. It is only valuable as a diagnostic sign in conjunction with the other symptoms."

"Next we have slow pulse. This was a half hour before death. Does not the pulse become slow in many cases just before death?"

"Yes."

"Very good. Not much sweat, and slow pulse does not amount to anything. What next? Oh! 'stertorous breathing.' That is not uncommon in diphtheria, is it, Doctor?"

"No."

"Just so. Now then, 'gradually deepening coma.' That is to say, a slow sinking into unconsciousness. Or I might say, dying slowly. Is a slow death of this kind only possible where opium poisoning has occurred?"

"No."

"Lastly we have the contracted pupils. That is your best diagnostic symptom, is it not, Doctor?"

"Yes. It is a plain indication of opium."

"Now then, Doctor, admitting that the contracted pupils are a sign of morphine, how did you determine, in that darkened room, that there was a contraction of the pupils?"

"I passed a candle before her eyes, and they gave no response, whilst the pupils were contracted minutely."

"How small?"

"As small as a pin's point."

"Now then, Doctor, you answered a lengthy question for Mr. Munson and you told us that these symptoms, that is, all of them occurring together, would not be found in any other condition than that which in your opinion would be the result of opium poisoning. Please listen to this question and give me an answer. Suppose that a patient were suffering with diphtheria, and were about to die of that disease, and that some time before she died morphine were administered in a moderate, medicinal dose, would it not be possible to have the contracted pupils such as you have described as a result of the morphine, whilst death were really caused by diphtheria?"

"I object!" cried Mr. Munson, quick to see the ingenuity of this question, which if answered affirmatively by the witness would leave the inference that Miss Sloane might have taken a non-poisonous dose of morphine and still have died of diphtheria.

"The question seems to me to be a proper one," said the Recorder.

"Your Honor," said Mr. Munson, "this witness is here to testify to facts. He is not here as an expert. That is a hypothetical question and does not relate to the facts in this case."

"It is no more a hypothetical question than one which the prosecution asked, your Honor. He asked if the described symptoms could occur in any other disease. The witness was allowed to answer that."

"Yes," said the Recorder, "but you made no objection. Had you done so, and claimed that this witness could not give expert testimony, I would perhaps have sustained you. I think you may leave your question until the experts are called, Mr. Bliss."

"Oh! Very well, your Honor. I should prefer to have an expert opinion upon it. If this witness is not an expert, of course his opinion would be of no value to us."

This was a rather neat manoeuvre, tending to further discredit the witness, without placing himself in opposition to the Judge, an important point always. Mr. Bliss then yielded the witness, and the Assistant District Attorney asked a few more questions in re-examination, but they were mainly intended to re-affirm the previous testimony, and so obtain a last impression upon the minds of the jury. Nothing was brought out which would add to what has already been narrated. Court then adjourned for the day.

CHAPTER VI
DAMAGING TESTIMONY

On the following day the newspaper accounts of the trial, and especially of the sharp cross-examination of Dr. Meredith, attracted a tremendous crowd, which assailed the doors of the court-room long before the hour for opening. Every conceivable excuse to gain admission was offered. Men claimed to be personal friends of the prisoner, and women brought him flowers. Some essayed force, others resorted to entreaty, whilst not a few relied upon strategy, appearing with law books under their arms, and following in the wake of counsel. Thus when the Recorder finally entered, and proceedings were begun, every available seat, and all standing room was fully occupied by the throng, which, without any real personal interest in the case, yet was attracted through that curious love of the sensational, and of the criminal, which actuates the majority of mankind to-day.

The first witness was called promptly. This was Dr. McDougal, the Coroner's physician, to whom had been intrusted the autopsy. He gave a full account of the operations performed by himself and his assistants upon the body of the deceased. He described in detail each step of his work, and exhibited a thoroughness and caution which more than anything demonstrated that he was the expert pathologist which the prosecution claimed him to be. Indeed, it would be well in great trials, if those having charge of autopsies would emulate the example of Dr. McDougal. He explained how, before opening the body, it had been thoroughly washed in sterilized water, and placed upon a marble slab, which had been scrubbed clean and then bathed in a germicidal solution. Next new glass cans, absolutely clean, had been at hand, in which the various organs were placed as they were removed from the body, after which they were hermetically sealed, and stamped with the date, so that when passed into the hands of the analytical chemist, that gentleman might feel assured that he received the identical parts, and that nothing of an extraneous nature, poisonous or otherwise, had been mixed with them. It was evident that this careful man made a deep impression upon the jury, and that his statements would have weight with them, not alone as to his own evidence, but by strengthening the chemical report, since he had made it apparently assured that if poison had been found, it had not reached the body after death. Finally, Mr. Munson brought his witness to the point of special interest.

"From what you observed, Doctor," said he, "are you prepared to assign a cause of death?"

"I should conclude that she died of coma!" was the reply.

"Can you state whether this coma had been produced by a poisonous dose of morphine?"

"I should say that it was very probable that opium in some form had been exhibited, in a poisonous dose."

"State specifically why you have adopted that opinion!"

"I found the brain wet, the convolutions flattened; the lungs, heart, liver, and spleen, distended and engorged with dark fluid blood. The vessels of the cerebro-spinal axis were also engorged with black blood, and the capillaries of the brain, upon incision, vented the same fluid."

"And these signs are indicative of opium poisoning?"

"They are the only evidences of opium poisoning that can be discovered by an autopsy. Of course a chemical analysis, if it should show the presence of the drug, would go very far to corroborate this presumption."

"Then if the chemical analysis shows the actual presence of opium, would you say that this patient died of opium poisoning?"

"I would!"

"Doctor, it has been suggested that she died of diphtheria. What is your opinion of that?"

"I found evidences in the throat and adjacent parts, that the woman had had diphtheria, but, from the total absence of false membrane, I should say that she was well on the way to a recovery from that disease, at the time of her death."

"Then from these facts do you think that she died of opium poisoning?"

"I think it most probable, judging by what I found after death."

"It has been testified by the physician in charge of the case, that the symptoms of morphine poisoning were sufficiently marked for him to deem antidotes necessary prior to death. Would not that corroborate your own conclusions?"

"If correct, it would substantiate my opinion."

Considering the very positive and damaging nature of this evidence, it was thought that the cross-examination would be very exhaustive. To the surprise of all, Mr. Bliss asked only a few questions.

"Dr. McDougal," said he, "did you examine the kidneys?"

"I did."

"In what condition did you find them to be?"

"They were much shrunken, and smooth. Non-elastic."

"Is that a normal condition?"

"No, sir. It is a morbid condition."

"Morbid? That is diseased. Then this woman had some kidney disease? Do I so understand you?"

"Unquestionably!"

"Can you state what disease existed?"

"I should say Bright's disease."

"Might she not have died of this?"

"No. There was evidence of the existence of Bright's disease, but not sufficient to adjudge it a cause of death."

"But you are certain that she had Bright's disease?"

"Yes, sir."

"That is all."

Professor Orton then took the stand for the prosecution. Under the questioning of Mr. Munson, he described himself to be an expert analytical chemist and toxicologist. He said that he was a lecturing professor connected with the University Medical College, and clinical chemist for two other schools, besides being president of several societies, and member or honorary member in a dozen others. Then, proceeding to a description of his work on this particular case, he explained in almost tedious detail his methods of searching for morphine in the organs taken from the body of the deceased. Some of these tests he repeated in the presence of the court, showing how, by the reaction of his testing agents upon the matter under examination, the presence or absence of morphine could be detected. Having thus paved the way towards the special evidence which he was expected to give, his examination was continued as follows:

"Now then, Professor," said Mr. Munson, "you have proven to us very clearly that you can detect the presence of morphine in the tissues. Please state whether you examined the organs of the deceased, and with what result?"

"I made a most thorough examination and I found morphine present, especially in the stomach and in the intestines."

"Did you find it in poisonous quantities?"

"The actual quantity which I found, would not have been a lethal dose, but such a dose must have been administered for me to have found as much as I did find."

"Well, from what you did find, can you state what quantity must have been administered?"

"I cannot state positively, but I should guess—"

"No! No! I object!" cried Mr. Bliss, jumping up. "You are here to give expert testimony. We do not want any guess-work!"

"Professor," said the Recorder, "can you not state what was the minimum quantity which must have been administered, judged by what you found?"

"It is difficult, your Honor. The drug acts variably upon different individuals. Then again, much would depend upon the length of time which elapsed between the administration, and the death of the individual."

"Then in this case your opinion would be a mere speculation and not competent," said the Recorder, and Mr. Bliss seated himself, satisfied that he had scored another point. But he was soon on his feet again, for Mr. Munson would not yield so easily.

"Professor," said he, "you said in reply to his Honor, that you could not answer without knowing how long before death the drug had been administered. Now with that knowledge would you be able to give us a definite answer?"

"A definite answer? Yes! But not an exact one. The drug is absorbed more rapidly in some, than in others, so that one person might take two or three times as much as another, and I would find the same residuum. But I could tell you what was the minimum dose that must have been administered."

"Well, then, supposing that the drug had been administered about three hours before death, how large must the dose have been, or what was the minimum quantity that could have been given, judging by what you found?"

"I must object to that, your Honor!" said Mr. Bliss.

"Your Honor," said Mr. Munson, "this is a hypothetical question, and perfectly competent."

"It is a hypothetical question, your Honor," replied Mr. Bliss, "but it contains a hypothesis which is not based upon the evidence in this case. There has been absolutely no testimony to show that morphine was administered to this woman about three hours before death."

"We have a witness who will testify to that later," replied Mr. Munson, and this announcement created no little sensation, for here was promised some direct evidence.

"Upon the understanding," said the Recorder, "that you will produce a witness who will testify that morphine was administered three hours before death, I will admit your question."

"We take an exception!" said Mr. Bliss, and sat down.

"Now please answer the question," said Mr. Munson, addressing the witness.

"Under the hypothesis presented I should say that the minimum dose must have been three grains."

"That is to say, she must have had three grains, or more?"

"Yes, sir; three grains or more."

"What is a medicinal dose?"

"From a thirty-second of a grain to half a grain, though the latter would be unusual."

"Unusually large you mean?"

"Yes. It would be rarely given."

"Then would you say that three grains would be a lethal dose?"

"It would most probably prove fatal. One sixth of a grain has been known to produce death."

"One sixth of a grain has proven fatal, and, from what you found, you conclude that three grains had been given to this woman?"

"Yes, provided your hypothesis as to the time of administration is correct."

"Oh, we will prove the hypothesis."

"Then I should say that three grains had been administered."

"Three grains or more?"

"Yes, three grains or more."

"You may take the witness," said the Assistant District Attorney, and Mr. Bliss at once began his cross-examination.

"Professor, as an expert toxicologist now, leaving analytical chemistry for awhile, you are familiar with the action of drugs in the human body during life, are you not?"

"Of poisonous drugs. Yes, sir."

"Of poisonous drugs of course. Of opium and its alkaloids especially, is what I mean?"

"Yes, sir. I have studied them minutely."

"Now then in regard to morphine. You said to his Honor, awhile ago, that this drug acts variably upon different individuals. Is it not true that it also acts differently upon the same individual at various times?"

"Yes, sir, that is true."

"And is its action affected by disease?"

"It might be!"

"Supposing that the drug were administered continuously, might it not occur, that instead of being absorbed, the morphine would be retained, stored up as it were, so that the quantity would accumulate?"

"Yes, the records contain reports of such cases."

"Well, now, suppose that a patient had some kidney trouble, such as Bright's disease, would not morphine be retained in this way?"

"I have never seen such a case."

"Never seen it! But you have read, or heard of such cases?"

"Yes, sir. That is the claim made by some authorities."

"By good authorities?"

"Yes. Good authorities."

"And these good authorities claim that morphine, administered to one who has Bright's disease, might accumulate until a poisonous dose were present?"

"Yes, sir!"

Thus was made plain the object of the line of cross-examination that had been followed with Dr. McDougal. It became evident that the defence meant to claim that if Mabel Sloane died from morphine it was because it had been stored up in her system, in consequence of the diseased kidneys. Satisfied with this admission from the prosecution's expert, Mr. Bliss yielded the witness, and he was re-examined by Mr. Munson.

"Professor," said he, "supposing that in the case of this girl, morphine had been retained in the system, suddenly destroying life because a poisonous quantity had been thus accumulated, would you expect to find it, after death, in the stomach?"

"No, sir, I would not."

"How long a time would be required to eliminate it from that organ?"

"Ordinarily it should be eliminated from the system entirely within forty-eight hours. Certainly after that length of time, it should not appear in the stomach."

"And yet in this case you found morphine in the stomach?"

"Yes, sir."

"So that to be there, it must have been administered within two days, and could not have been there as a result of accumulation beyond that time?"

"I should say that the presence in the stomach proves that the administration must have occurred within two days."

Upon re-cross Mr. Bliss asked a few questions.

"On your original examination, Professor, you said that you found morphine in the intestines and in the stomach. Where did you find the greater quantity?"

"In the intestines!"

"If, because of kidney disease, morphine were retained in the system, where would you look for it after death?"

"In the intestines."

"That is all."

The next witness was a young woman. Her examination proceeded as follows, after she had given her name and occupation.

"Now, Miss Conlin, you say you were engaged in your capacity of professional nurse, to care for Miss Sloane. Were you on duty on the day of her death?"

"Yes, sir. Day and night."

"You were present when the doctors called in the afternoon then. What did they say of her condition?"

"That she was very much better. The membrane had entirely disappeared. Dr. Fisher thought she would be up in a few days."

"Did Dr. Medjora call during the afternoon, or evening?"

"Yes, sir. He called about five o'clock."

"Did you remain with your patient throughout his visit?"

"No, sir. Dr. Medjora said that he would stay until nine o'clock, and that I might go out for some fresh air."

"Did you do so?"

"Yes, sir. I was glad to go."

"Did you not consider it wrong to leave your patient?"

"Why, no, sir. She was getting better, and besides, Dr. Medjora being a physician could care for her as well as I could."

"When you went out did you state when you would return?"

"Yes. I said I would be back at nine o'clock."

"As a matter of fact, when did you return?"

"About half-past eight. It was eight o'clock when I left my home."

"Did you go at once to your patient's room?"

"Yes, sir."

"And enter it?"

"Yes, sir."

"What did you see when you entered?"

"I saw Dr. Medjora bending over Miss Sloane, giving her a hypodermic injection of morphine!"

"How could you tell it was morphine?"

"He washed out the syringe in a glass of water, before he put it back in his case. I tasted the water afterwards, and distinguished the morphine in that way. Besides, I found several morphine tablets in the bed."

"What did you do with these tablets?"

"At first I placed them on the mantel. Afterwards, when Dr. Meredith said that Miss Sloane was dying from morphine, I put them in a phial and slipped that into my pocket."

"Was that the same phial which you brought to me?"

"Yes, sir."

"Is this it?" He handed up a phial containing four pellets, which was admitted in evidence, and identified by Miss Conlin.

"Did you tell Dr. Medjora that you had seen him administer the morphine?"

"No, sir. At the time I thought it must be all right, as he was her friend, and a physician."

"Did he know that you had seen him?"

"No, sir. I think not."

The witness was then given to Mr. Bliss for cross-examination.

"Miss Conlin," he began, "who engaged you to attend Miss Sloane?"

"Dr. Medjora."

"What did he say to you at that time?"

"That a very dear friend of his was ill, and that he would pay me well for skilful services."

"Did he pay you?"

"Yes, sir."

"During her illness what was the general behavior of Dr. Medjora towards her. That is, was he kind, or was he indifferent?"

"Oh! very kind. It was plain that he was in love with her."

"I move, your Honor," said Mr. Munson, "that the latter part of that answer be stricken out, as incompetent."

"The motion is granted," said the Recorder.

"You said that the Doctor was always kind," said Mr. Bliss, resuming. "So much so that you would not have suspected that he wished her any harm, would you?"

"I object!" said Mr. Munson.

"Objection sustained!" said the Recorder.

"Now, then, we will come down to the administration of the hypodermic," said Mr. Bliss. "You testified that you saw Dr. Medjora administer the hypodermic. Are we to understand that you saw Dr. Medjora dissolve the tablets, fill the syringe, push the needle under the skin, press the piston so that the contents were discharged, and then remove the instrument?"

"No, sir. I did not see all that."

"Well, what did you see?"

"I saw him taking the syringe out of Miss Sloane's arm. Then he cleaned it and put it in his pocket, after putting it in a case."

"Oh! You did not see him push the syringe in, you only saw him take it out. Then how do you know that he did make the injection, if one was made at all?"

"Why, he must have. I saw him take out the syringe, and there was no one else who could have done it."

"Then you saw him put the syringe in a case, and place the case in his pocket, I think you said?"

"Yes, sir."

"What sort of case was it?"

"A metal case!"

"Was it a case like this?" Mr. Bliss handed her an aluminum hypodermic case, which she examined, and then said:

"It looked like this." The case was then marked as an exhibit for the defence.

"In what position was Miss Sloane when you saw the Doctor leaning over her?"

"She was lying across the bed, with her head in a pillow. She was crying softly!"

"I think you said that this occurred at half-past eight o'clock?"

"Yes, sir. About that time."

"At what hour did Miss Sloane die?"

"At eleven thirty!"

"That is to say, three hours after you supposed that you saw Dr. Medjora make the injection."

"Yes, sir!"

"Did you leave the room again during that time?"

"No, sir."

"Not even to get the coffee which Dr. Meredith had ordered?"

"No, sir. I made that on the gas-stove in the room."

"Well, then, during that last three hours did you, or any one else, in your presence, inject, or administer morphine in any form to Miss Sloane?"

"No, sir; positively not."

"Such a thing could not have occurred without your knowledge?"

"No, sir."

"Now, your Honor," said Mr. Bliss, "I would like to ask the prosecution whether this is the only witness upon whom they depend to prove the hypothesis that morphine was administered within three hours prior to the death of Miss Sloane?"

"That is our evidence on that point," replied Mr. Munson.

"Then, if it please the court, I move that all that testimony of Professor Orton's following and dependent upon the hypothetical question, shall be stricken from the records."

"State your grounds," said the Recorder.

"Your Honor admitted the question upon the express understanding, that the hypothesis that morphine had been administered within the specified time should be proven. The prosecution's own witness tells us that no such administration occurred during the last three hours of the life of the deceased. The proposition then hinges upon what this witness claims to have seen as she entered the room. She admits that she only saw Dr. Medjora remove a syringe. She did not see him insert it, and she could not possibly know what the contents of that syringe were."

"I think," said the Recorder, "that the question whether or not her testimony shows that Dr. Medjora administered a hypodermic of morphine is a question for the jury. The evidence may stand."

"We take exception," said Mr. Bliss. After a few moments consultation with Mr. Dudley he said to the witness: "That is all," and she was allowed to leave the stand. This ended the day's proceedings.

CHAPTER VII
THE PROSECUTION RESTS

The first witness called, on the resumption of the trial, was a druggist, named Newton, who qualified as an expert pharmacist and chemist. He examined the pellets contained in the bottle identified by the professional nurse as the one which she had given to Mr. Munson. These he dissolved in water, and then submitted to chemical tests, from the results of which he pronounced them to be morphine. He testified that he recognized them as the usual pellets carried by physicians for hypodermic use. He was not cross-examined.

The next witness was Prof. Hawley, an expert pathologist. He swore that he had assisted at the autopsy, and in the main substantiated the evidence of Dr. McDougal, the Coroner's physician, agreeing with him, that from the physical appearances, the probable cause of death had been morphine poisoning. He was asked the hypothetical question and answered as did the other witness, that at least three grains must have been administered. Up to this point the evidence was merely cumulative, but Mr. Munson then essayed another line of inquiry.

"Professor," said he, "from your examination of this body can you tell us whether or not the deceased had been a mother?"

"I object!" cried Mr. Bliss springing to his feet, with more energy than he had yet exhibited. It was plain that though heretofore his objections to the admission of evidence may have been suggested rather by his desire to fully protect his client, than because he feared the testimony, this time he fought to exclude this evidence because of some vital interest, as though, indeed, this point having been foreshadowed in the early newspaper accounts, he had been fully instructed by Dr. Medjora. This became the more apparent, when Mr. Dudley himself took part in the argument, for the first time bringing the weight of his legal knowledge to bear upon the case publicly. For when the court asked for a cause of objection, it was Mr. Dudley who replied.

"May it please your Honor," said he, "it seems to us, that the fact which counsel here endeavors to introduce, is entirely irrelevant. Whether or not Miss Sloane was a mother, can have no possible connection with our client's responsibility for the crime of which he is accused. It is no more against the law to kill a mother, than to slay any other woman. We hope that your Honor will see the advisability of shielding the name of the dead from any such imputation as the guesses of even this celebrated expert might cast upon her."

"I really cannot see the bearing of this evidence," said the Recorder, addressing Mr. Munson.

"If it please your Honor," said Mr. Munson, "we wish to show that this girl was an unmarried woman; who nevertheless bore a child to the prisoner. Further, we will show that Miss Sloane was a poor girl, seeking to earn her living as a music teacher. Now the accused suddenly finds the opportunity to marry a wealthy woman, and the poor musician, with her claim upon him as the father of her child, becomes an obstacle in his path. Thus, your Honor, we supply a motive for this crime."

"But, your Honor," said Mr. Dudley, "there has not been a particle of evidence to prove any of these assertions, so glibly put for the benefit of the jury, and therefore we must contend that this evidence is entirely incompetent."

"As tending to explain the motive, I must rule that counsel may examine fully into the relations that existed between the prisoner and the deceased," said the Recorder.

"But," persisted Mr. Dudley, "even granting that this expert can say whether a woman has borne a child, which is a question of grave uncertainty, assuredly it cannot be claimed that he can testify as to the father of the child. Therefore he can throw no light whatever upon the relation which existed between the dead girl and our client."

"The question is admitted. The witness may answer!" replied the Recorder, upon which the defence entered an exception. The expert then answered:

"It was positively discernible that the deceased had been a mother."

"Can you state how long ago?"

"It is understood, your Honor," said Mr. Dudley, "that we take exception to this whole line of examination?" To this the Recorder nodded in assent, and the witness replied:

"Not within a year, I should say."

The witness was then yielded to the defence, but the cross-examination was confined entirely to the condition of the kidneys, thus making the prosecution's expert once more add to the evidence in favor of the defence, by admitting the diseased condition of organs, which it was claimed would materially affect the action of morphine in the system.

Next followed several witnesses, all of them boarders in the house where the deceased had dwelt. The object of their testimony was to show that the deceased passed in the house as a single woman, and that Dr. Medjora appeared in the light of an accepted suitor. They all denied that the girl had ever claimed that she was married, or that she had ever worn a wedding-ring. Under cross-examination they all admitted that they had never heard of, nor seen a child. It transpired that she had lived in the house a little more than a year, and that Dr. Medjora had been a visitor for less than half of that period.

Mrs. Sloane, the mother of the dead girl, then took the stand. She was dressed in deep mourning, and wept frequently. She testified that her daughter had always been of an unruly, headstrong disposition, and fond of enjoying herself. That she had been disinclined to work at home, and appeared to feel herself better than her own kith and kin. She had met Dr. Medjora at some musical party several years before, and the Doctor had become a constant visitor. "But I never liked the man. Somehow I knew that he was a cruel, dangerous man for a poor girl, with high ideas, like my Mabel." These remarks offered voluntarily, and delivered so rapidly that she could not be prevented from having her say, were objected to, and promptly ruled out, the Recorder agreeing with Mr. Dudley, that personal impressions could not be received in evidence against a man's character. Coming down to a later period, she explained that she and her daughter had "had some words about her going with that man," and the girl had suddenly left home. "Of course I knew she had been lured away by that black-hearted villain," ejaculated the witness, half sobbing. This was also ruled out, and the witness was admonished to restrain herself, and to confine her remarks to answering questions of counsel. She went on to say that she had received letters from time to time from the girl, post-marked from New York, but she had never discovered her address, nor seen her alive after they separated. In these letters, Miss Sloane had told her mother "not to worry," that she was "doing very well and hoped soon to do better;" that "my friend, the Doctor, has been very kind to me," and other passages of this nature. But there was never any allusion to a marriage, nor to Dr. Medjora as intending to marry her.

Under cross-examination, which was rather brief, she admitted that since her daughter left home, she had had no knowledge of her except through those letters, and that therefore she did not know, positively, that the girl had not been married. It was also made to appear that the girl had never been very happy in her home, and had frequently, even before her acquaintance with Doctor Medjora, expressed her determination to "leave home at the first chance." She also admitted, reluctantly, that she knew nothing, positively, against the character of the accused, "except that it was plain to be seen that he was a villain with no respect for a woman." This, of course, was stricken out.

The undertaker, who had originally taken charge of the body, was placed upon the stand, and testified that he had not removed the body from the house, when he was notified by the Coroner to retire from the case. Neither he, nor his assistants, had used any embalming fluid, nor had they injected any fluids whatever into the body before they gave it into the care of the Coroner's physician. He swore that it was the same body which had been shown to him as that of Mabel Sloane, that he had given to Dr. McDougal.

A few more witnesses were called in corroboration of minor details, and to protect the case of the prosecution from technical flaws of omission, and then Mr. Munson announced that their side would rest.

The crowd in the court-room leaned forward, as Mr. Dudley arose, eager to hear him open for the defence, as they supposed that he was about to do. Instead of this he addressed the court as follows:

"May it please your Honor, we must request you, before permitting the prosecution to rest, to instruct that Dr. Fisher be called as a witness."

"Dr. Fisher, your Honor," said Mr. Munson, "is not our witness. He is not named in the indictment. There is no reason, however, why the defence should not call him if they wish him."

"Upon what ground, Mr. Dudley," asked the Recorder, "do you make this motion?"

"Upon the ground, sir, that Dr. Fisher is an important witness to material facts connected with the demise of Miss Sloane. He was the senior attending physician, whilst Dr. Meredith had only been called in consultation. The prosecution have called Dr. Meredith, recognizing that as an attending physician his knowledge of the facts is material to the cause at issue. We claim that the testimony of Dr. Fisher, the other physician in attendance, and present at the death-bed, is equally material, and that the prosecution have no right to choose between the two men, selecting one as their witness, and rejecting the other. The fact that they have done so, would warrant the imputation that the prosecution are seeking for a conviction of our client, rather than looking for justice, in a thorough sifting of all available facts. I am sure that the honorable council on the other side will be only too glad to avoid such an imputation in the public mind, now that their attention has been called to the omission."

"Counsel is very generous," said Mr. Munson, with much sarcasm. "His solicitude for the reputation of the district attorney's office is very touching, but at the same time entirely misplaced. In this matter, those who have charge of the case of the commonwealth, feel that they can safely permit the conduct of this case to meet the most searching criticism. We decline to call Dr. Fisher, unless ordered to do so by the court."

"Then we move that the court so order," snapped back Mr. Dudley.

"It certainly seems to me," said the Recorder, "that the testimony of this physician is very material, and that he should have been included among the witnesses for the people. Have you any arguments against this view, Mr. Munson?"

"Only this, your Honor, that it was considered that the testimony of one witness would suffice. The selection was made without regard to known opinion, for none had been expressed prior to the issuance of a subpoena calling Dr. Meredith into the case. We decided to have but one witness, merely to save unnecessary costs. Now so far as this motion is concerned, we maintain that it comes too late. Counsel was served with a copy of the indictment, which contained a list of our witnesses upon the back. Thus they had ample notice of our intention not to call Dr. Fisher, and if they desired that we should do so, the motion should have been made earlier, and not at the end of our case."

"What have you to say in reply, Mr. Dudley?" asked the Recorder.

"Your Honor," said Mr. Dudley, showing by his bearing an assurance of gaining the point for which he contended; "the excuse that the name of Dr. Fisher does not appear among the list of witnesses for the prosecution, is entirely aside from the issue. It is a claim that has been made and rejected more than once. I need only remind your Honor of the Holden case, to bring it to your Honor's immediate recollection. That case was very similar to this one. Three surgeons had examined the body of the deceased, and but two of these had been called by the prosecuting attorney, counsel refusing upon the identical ground that his name had not appeared in the indictment. The presiding judge, Paterson, ruled that as a material witness, he must be called. That is precisely the condition here and I hope your Honor will see the justice of calling Dr. Fisher."

"I am decidedly of the opinion, Mr. Munson, that counsel is in the right. This man is a witness material to the cause of justice!"

"Oh, certainly, if your Honor thinks so, we will call him. He was omitted under the presumption that his evidence would be redundant, and add unnecessarily to the costs." Mr. Dudley sat down much pleased at his victory, and older lawyers nodded approvingly at his skilful presentation of the law. Dr. Fisher, being in court, was then asked to take the stand. Mr. Munson examined him with evident reluctance.

"You attended Miss Sloane in her last illness, Doctor?" he began.

"Yes, sir!"

"From what disease was she suffering?"

"Diphtheria."

"Any other disease?"

"Not to my knowledge."

"Then of course you saw no symptoms of Bright's disease?"

"Well, my attention was not called to any such trouble."

"Be kind enough to give us a direct reply. Did you, or did you not, discover symptoms of Bright's disease?"

"I cannot say that she did not have that disease, but she made no complaints which made me suspect it."

"Exactly! You did not suspect that she had Bright's disease, until you heard it suggested here during this trial. Is that about it?"

"I did not consider it at all."

"Now, then, I believe that you called Dr. Meredith into the case?"

"Yes, sir."

"Why did you do that?"

"Because, despite the efforts of myself and Dr. Medjora, the girl did not improve."

"That is to say, you found yourself incompetent to control the disease?"

"I felt that I should have assistance. It is common practice to call a physician in consultation when a disease becomes uncontrollable."

"He is usually a man who has special knowledge, is he not?"

"Yes, sir."

"And you considered Dr. Meredith such a man?"

"Yes, sir."

"That is to say, he had more knowledge of this disease than you yourself?"

"Not that precisely. But he has made a special study of the disease, and I knew that he could give us valuable advice."

"After Dr. Meredith came into the case the patient began to improve, did she not?"

"Yes, sir."

"On the last day of her life, you met Dr. Meredith at the house, and you decided that it would be safe to leave the patient until the following day, I believe. You found her much improved?"

"Yes, sir."

"The membrane had all disappeared, had it not?"

"Very nearly."

"So much so that she could swallow without difficulty?"

"She swallowed very well."

"In fact you concluded that she would recover?"

"I thought that she had passed the crisis, but I did not deem her to be entirely out of danger."

"Did you, at any time during this illness, prescribe or administer opium in any form?"

"No, sir."

"Did you see any evidence of that drug exhibited by her condition, lethargic sleep, contracted pupils, or any other diagnostic symptom?"

"No, sir."

"Now, then, you left this girl in the afternoon, recovering from her attack of diphtheria and able to swallow, and you were hurriedly called back in the evening, and found her dying. Did not that surprise you?"

"Yes. I had not expected the disease to take a fatal turn, at least not so rapidly."

"Yet she was in such a condition that she could not even swallow coffee?"

"No, but that—"

"Never mind the reasons, Doctor. The fact is all that we want. Shortly after your entrance into her room she died, did she not?"

"Yes, sir, at eleven thirty. About five minutes after."

"Now, Doctor, notwithstanding the fact that in the afternoon you thought this girl practically out of danger, and notwithstanding the sudden and alarming change which you saw in her that night, and in spite of the fact that the specialist whom you yourself had called into the case, reported to you that he suspected morphine poisoning, you signed a death certificate assigning diphtheria as the cause of death. Now why did you do that?"

"Because it was my opinion!"

"Oh, I see. It was your opinion. Then you did not actually know it."

"Not actually of course. We never—"

"That is all!" exclaimed Mr. Munson, cutting off the witness at the point in his reply most advantageous to his side, and the Doctor remained silent, but appeared much annoyed.

Mr. Bliss smiled at the old legal trick, and in taking the witness began at once, by allowing him to finish the interrupted speech.

"Dr. Fisher," said he, "you had not quite ended your reply when counsel closed your examination. What else was it that you wished to say?"

"I wished to say that I could not actually know the cause of death, because medicine is not an exact science. It is rarely possible to have absolute knowledge about diseased conditions. No two cases have ever been seen that were precisely identical."

"But you judged that this girl died of diphtheria from your experience with such cases, is that it?"

"Yes, sir."

"How much experience have you had!"

"I have been in practice nearly forty years."

"And Dr. Meredith, although a specialist, has had less experience than you, has he not?"

"I object," cried Mr. Munson, "Dr. Meredith was not an expert witness in the first place, and it is too late to try to impeach his ability now."

"The objection is sustained," said the Recorder.

"Now, Dr. Fisher, as you signed a death certificate naming diphtheria as a cause of death, of course that was your opinion at that time. You have been present throughout this trial, and have heard all of the evidence, I believe?"

"Yes, sir."

"Have you heard anything which has made you alter your opinion?"

"No, sir."

"Then tell us, please, in your opinion what was the cause of death."

"I still think that the girl died of diphtheria."

"Despite all the testimony as to finding morphine in the body, and despite the condition of the kidneys, you still think that this girl died of diphtheria?"

"I do."

Mr. Bliss was taking full advantage of his victory over the prosecution, in compelling them to call this witness, who was now giving evidence so damaging to their side.

"Now, then, Doctor, we would like a little more light upon the facts from which you make this deduction. It has been testified and admitted by you, that in the afternoon the membrane had nearly all disappeared, and that the crisis had passed. Yet the girl died a few hours later, and you still attribute it to the original disease. How do you come to that conclusion?"

"Diphtheria causes death in several ways. Commonly the false membrane grows more rapidly than it can be removed, and the patient is practically strangled, or asphyxiated by it. It is in such a condition that tracheotomy is essayed, affording a breathing aperture below the locality of the disease. It is not uncommon for the patient apparently to combat the more frightful form of the disease, so that the false membrane is thrown off, and the parts left apparently in a fair state of health, so far as freedom to breathe and swallow is concerned. But then it may happen, especially in anæmic individuals, that this fight against the disease has left the patient in a state of enervation and lowered vitality, which borders on collapse. The extreme crisis is passed, but the danger lurks insidiously near. At any moment a change for the worse might occur, whilst recovery would be very slow. When death comes in this form, it is a gradual lessening of vital action throughout the body; a slow slipping away of life, as it were."

"Exactly! So that such a condition might readily be mistaken for a gradually deepening coma?"

"Yes, sir. Whilst the term coma is applied to a specific condition, the two forms of death are very similar. In fact, I might say it is a sort of coma, which after all is common in many diseases."

"So that you would say that this coma, did not specifically indicate morphine poisoning?"

"No, sir, it could not be said."

"How was the pulse?"

"The pulse was slow, but that is what we expect with this form of death."

"So that the slow pulse would not necessarily indicate poison?"

"Not at all."

"Was the breathing stertorous?"

"Not in the true sense. Respiration was very slow, and there was a slight difficulty, but it was not distinctly stertorous."

"How were the pupils of the eyes? Contracted?"

"No, they were dilated if anything."

"Now then, Doctor—please consider this. Dr. Meredith told us that a symptomatic effect of morphine death, would be pupils contracted and then dilating slowly as death approached. Now did you observe the contracted pupils?"

"No, sir."

"What effect does atropine have upon the pupils?"

"It dilates them."

"Dr. Meredith admitted that he injected atropine. In your opinion would that account for the dilatation of the pupils just previous to death, which you say that you yourself observed?"

"I should say yes."

"I will only detain you another minute, Doctor." Mr. Bliss then asked for and obtained the aluminum hypodermic case and handed it to Dr. Fisher. He asked:

"Doctor, do you recognize that?"

"Yes, it is mine."

"How long has it been out of your possession?"

"I missed it on the day of Miss Sloane's death. I think now that I may have left it there by accident."

Mr. Bliss then yielded the witness, and Mr. Munson began a re-direct examination, which was practically a cross-examination, because this witness, though technically for the prosecution, was in effect a witness for the defence. The lawyer tried with all his cunning to confuse the old doctor, but the longer he continued the more he damaged his own cause. About the only thing which he brought out that might help him, was the following in relation to the hypodermic case.

"How do you know that this case is yours?"

"Because it is made of aluminum. I had it made to order. I do not think that such another is yet on the market, though the house that made mine for me, has asked permission to use my model."

"So this is certainly yours?"

"Yes, sir."

"If you did not make any injections, as you have testified that you did not, how is it that you could have left this at the house?"

"I probably took it out of my bag, when getting out my laryngoscope and other instruments to treat the throat."

"I see that this case not only contains the syringe, but also some small phials filled with tablets. What are those tablets?"

"They are various medicines used hypodermically."

"Was there any morphine in this case when you last saw it?"

"Yes, sir."

"How much?"

"There was a phial filled with tablets. Altogether eighty tablets, of one eighth of a grain each."

"Please count the tablets remaining, and state how many there are?"

"I find forty-eight."

"That is to say thirty-two pellets have been taken out?"

"Yes, sir."

"Now, then, supposing that this is the identical syringe which the nurse saw Dr. Medjora using, and deducting the four pellets which she found in the bed, how large a dose must have been administered at that time?"

"I object!" said Mr. Bliss.

"It seems to be a mere matter of arithmetic," said the Recorder.

"No, your Honor. That question supposes that the tablets missing from the phial were administered to the patient. Now there is no evidence whatever as to that?"

"Whether the missing tablets were administered or not is a question for the jury to decide. You may state, Doctor, how much morphine was contained in the missing tablets."

"As there are forty-eight here, thirty-two are missing. Deducting four, that leaves us twenty-eight, or a total of three and a half grains."

This was a corroboration of the estimate made by the experts, that three grains must have been the minimum dose administered, and if the jury should believe that these missing tablets had been given by the prisoner, it was evident that they must convict him. So that after all the prosecution did gain something out of the witness who had been forced upon them. They then rested their case, and court adjourned, leaving the opening for the defence until the following day.

CHAPTER VIII
FOR THE DEFENCE

When Mr. Dudley arose to open the case for the defence, the crowded court-room was as silent as the grave, so intense was the interest. He spoke in slow, measured tones, with no effort at rhetorical effect. Tersely he pictured the position of his client, assailed by circumstantial evidence, and encircled by a chain which seemed strong enough to drag him to the dreadful doom which would be his upon conviction. But the lawyer claimed that the chain was not flawless. On the contrary he said that many of the links had been forged, and he dwelt upon the word with a significant accent, as he glance towards the prosecuting counsel; forged from material which was rotten to the core, so rotten that it would be but necessary to direct the intelligent attention of the jury, to the inherently weak spots, to convince them that justice demanded a prompt acquittal of Dr. Medjora.

A part of his speech is worthy of being quoted, and I give it *verbatim*:

"This case has aroused the interest of the entire community. Prior to the beginning of this trial the people, having heard but the distorted reports of the evidence against our client, were wondering what the defence was to be. I do not mind confiding to you now that we, the counsel for the defence, wondered also. It had been told in the newspapers, that Dr. Meredith, one of the attending physicians, had suspected morphine poisoning, before the death of Miss Sloane. We were informed that the autopsy, made by most eminent and skilful pathologists, had revealed evidences of this deadly drug. We heard later, that the chemical analysis had proven the actual presence of the poison itself. What defence could we rely upon to refute such damning evidence as that? We were in a quandary. We went to our client and revealed to him the gravity of his position, and we begged him to suggest some way out of the dilemma. What was his reply? Gentlemen of the jury, he said to me: 'I cannot invent any defence. I would not if I could. I would not accept my life, or my liberty, by means of any trick. But I know that I am innocent. Moreover, as a member of the medical profession, and as an acquaintance of the experts who have been at work for the prosecution, I rely upon their integrity and skill, to discover the true secret of this death, which was as shocking to me, as to the community.' Thus we were told by our client to formulate no defence in advance, but to wait for the evidence of the prosecution's expert witnesses, and from the very source from which conviction would be expected, he bade us pluck his deliverance. At the time, it seemed to us a hazardous dependence, but, gentlemen of the jury, it has proven better than we had reason to expect, for it will be upon the testimony of the prosecution's witnesses, almost exclusively, that we will look to you for an acquittal. In evidence of what I have told you, I will ask you to recall the testimony of the first witness, Dr. Meredith. He claimed that the characteristic symptoms of morphine poisoning could alone indicate that death had been due to morphine. Then you will remember that my associate, in cross-examination, formulated a hypothetical question in which he asked if it would not be possible for a patient dying of diphtheria to take morphine, and whilst exhibiting symptoms of that drug, still to die of diphtheria. I submit it to you, gentlemen, was not the hypothesis suggested by that question an ingenious one? I think so, and as such I think that my associate is entitled to credit. But, gentlemen, it was the invention of a lawyer, conscientiously seeking for a loophole of escape for his client; it was not the true, the only proper, defence in this case. And it is this that explains the fact that the question has not been propounded to the other experts. It was, nevertheless, a shrewd guess on the part of Mr. Bliss, though being only the guess of a lawyer groping blindly amidst the secrets of medicine, it does not include the whole truth. But now, our defence has been made plain, illuminated, as it were, by the statements of the experts, who have testified, until even the minds of plain lawyers, like myself and my associate, have grasped it. Then, and not until then, did our client give us information, which he will repeat to you presently, and which corroborates the view which we shall ask you to accept. The simple facts in this case are: Miss Sloane suffered terribly from Bright's disease, until through pain she was driven to take morphine, finally becoming addicted to it. Then came the attack of diphtheria, throughout which Dr. Medjora nursed her, procuring skilled physicians, and a competent nurse, until the arrival of the tragic day which ended her life. When the doctors believed that the worst phase of diphtheria had passed, but when, as you have heard, she was still in danger from exhaustion, she experienced a severe attack of pain caused by the Bright's disease, and to relieve that, morphine was given as you shall hear. That night she died, whether of exhaustion from diphtheria, or whether, because of Bright's disease, morphine had been stored up in her system, until a fatal dose had accumulated, none of us will ever know. But that is immaterial, for in either case, she died a natural death, and thus our client is entirely blameless in this whole affair. The Doctor will now take the stand in his own behalf."

Dr. Medjora did as he was bidden by his counsel, and thus became the cynosure of all eyes. Mr. Dudley took his seat and Mr. Bliss conducted the examination.

"Dr. Medjora," he began, "will you please state what relation you bore to the deceased, Miss Mabel Sloane?"

"She was my wife!" he replied, thus producing a startling sensation at the very outset.

"When were you married, and by whom?"

"We were married in Newark, by the Rev. Dr. Magnus, on the exact day upon which Miss Sloane parted from her mother and left her home in Orange. The precise date can be seen upon the certificate of marriage."

Mr. Bliss produced a marriage certificate, which was admitted, and identified by Dr. Medjora, Mr. Bliss explaining that the clergyman who had signed it would appear later and testify to the validity of the document.

"Did you and your wife live together after marriage?"

"Yes. For more than a year. Then I had occasion to go to Europe for several months, and she went to live at the Twenty-sixth Street house."

"How was it that at that place she passed as a single woman?"

"Because before I went away, I took from her the marriage certificate, and her wedding-ring. I then instructed her to keep our marriage a secret, threatening to abandon her if she did not obey me."

"What explanation have you to make of such conduct?"

"Shortly after our marriage, I discovered that my wife was afflicted with Bright's disease, for which I treated her with much apparent success. Unfortunately, however, previous to our marriage, she had become addicted to the use of morphine for relief until she had almost become an *habitué*. I used every effort to cure her, and thought that I had succeeded, when, just before my departure for Europe, I found her one day with morphine tablets and a new hypodermic needle, in the act of administering the drug. In despair I simulated great rage, took away her marriage certificate and ring, and threatened that if during my absence she should use the drug, I would never acknowledge her as my wife. Thus, my apparent cruelty was intended as a kindness. I knew that she loved me, even more than she did morphine, and I hoped to compel her to abandon the drug, by causing her to fear the loss of her love."

"Did you take any further steps for her safety!"

"Yes. I confided her secret, and mine, to a dear friend and skilful physician, who promised to watch over her, and shield her from pain or other harm during my absence."

"Will you state who this friend is?"

"Was, you mean. He no longer is my friend, if he ever was. He proved himself to be a traitor to friendship, for he tried to alienate my wife's affections from me, in which, however, he failed utterly. That man was Dr. Meredith, the false friend who charged me with this crime."

Here was a sensation so entirely unexpected, and the situation became so intense, that people held their breaths, awed into silence. Dr. Meredith, who was in court, held his eyes down and gazed steadfastly at a knot in the floor, whilst those nearest to him saw that he trembled violently. Mr. Bliss, quick to recognize that his client was making a most favorable impression, with true dramatic instinct, paused some time before continuing. Finally he asked:

"Then Dr. Meredith knew that Miss Sloane was your wife?"

"He did."

"Also that she was addicted to morphine?"

"I told him so myself."

"That she had Bright's disease?"

"Yes."

"How soon after your return did you learn that he had been too attentive to your wife?"

"I must object, your Honor," interjected Mr. Munson. "Counsel is again endeavoring to impeach our witness, and I must once more maintain that it is too late to do so."

"The question is allowed," replied the Recorder.

"But, your Honor," persisted Mr. Munson, "you ruled yesterday that questions of this nature could not be asked."

"I know very well what I ruled, Mr. Munson," said the Recorder, sharply. "You objected yesterday to evidence against Dr. Meredith's ability as a physician, and I sustained you. This is a different matter. As I understand it, counsel is now endeavoring to show that Dr. Meredith was a prejudiced witness. I shall allow the fullest latitude in that direction."

"We thank you very much, your Honor," said Mr. Bliss, and then turned to his client saying: "Please answer my question."

"I knew of it before I returned. In fact, it was because of letters from my wife, complaining of this man, that I shortened my trip abroad."

"What happened between you after your return?"

"I charged him with his unfaithfulness to his trust, and we quarrelled. Had he been a larger man, I should have thrashed him!"

"Was it after this that you attacked one of his papers in debate?"

"Yes, immediately afterwards. In fact I think that the quarrel between us had much to do with it. He must have been in a very disturbed frame of mind, to have written such a blundering thesis, for ordinarily he is a skilful physician."

"Then, on the whole, Dr. Meredith was inaccurate when he said that you and he are not enemies?"

"He simply lied."

"You must not use such language," said the Recorder, quickly.

"I must apologize to your Honor," replied Dr. Medjora. "But when I think of what this man has done to me, it is difficult to control myself."

"But you must control yourself," said the Recorder.

"Now, then, Doctor," said Mr. Bliss, "please tell us of your acquaintance with your wife prior to marriage." Thereafter Mr. Bliss always spoke of the dead girl as the wife, thus forcing that fact upon the attention of the jury. Dr. Medjora replied:

"I met my wife when she was scarcely more than a school-girl, and I became interested in her because, as her mother hinted, she was above her people, being far superior to them in intelligence and demeanor. I cannot say when my friendship increased to a warmer feeling, but I think that I first became aware of it, by seeing her mother beat her!"

"You saw your wife's mother beat her, you say?"

"I called one evening, without previous warning, and the door of the cottage being open, I felt privileged to walk in. I saw the girl down on her knees, before the mother, who held her by the hair with one hand, whilst she struck her in the face with the other."

"Did you interfere?"

"I was much enraged at the cruel exhibition, and I took the girl from her mother forcibly. After that I went to the house oftener, and we became more closely attached to one another. The mother never spoke civilly to me after that occurrence."

"Mrs. Sloane testified that she had had a quarrel with her daughter, shortly after which she disappeared. What do you know of that?"

"Mabel wrote to me that her mother had again undertaken to beat her. I use the word advisedly, because it was not a chastisement such as a parent may be privileged to indulge in. Mrs. Sloane would strike her daughter with her fists, bruising her face, neck, and body. Besides, Mabel was no longer a child. When I heard this, I sent a message instructing Mabel to meet me in Newark. There we were married."

"Now, Doctor, we will go back to Dr. Meredith. Will you explain how it happened that, although you and he were enemies, he should have been called into the case?"

"When the attack of diphtheria presented, I undertook to treat it at first. Two days later I became ill myself, and called in

Dr. Fisher. I did not tell him that Mabel was my wife, but let him think, with those in the house, that she was merely my *fiancée*. I gave the case entirely into his care. During my sickness Dr. Fisher became alarmed, and called in Dr. Meredith, of course not suspecting that there existed any ill feeling between him and me. That Dr. Meredith should have accepted the call under the circumstances, was contrary to medical etiquette, but he did so, and I found him attending my wife when I recovered. I could not interfere very well, without creating a scandal, and, besides, though I despise him as a man, I know him to be one of the best specialists in the city." Dr. Medjora accorded this praise to his rival with every appearance of honest candor, and it was evident that his doing so was a wise course, causing the jury to receive his other statements with more credulity. If he was playing a part he did so with marvellous tact and judgment.

"Between the time of your return from Europe, and this attack of diphtheria, do you know whether your wife took any morphine?"

"Upon my return I did not question her at all. I had made the threat of abandoning her, with no intention of course of carrying it into effect, for whilst I hoped that it would act as a deterrent, stimulating her will to resist the attraction of the drug, I knew from my professional experience that she would not be able to withstand it entirely. Thus if I had questioned her, she must have confessed, as she was strictly truthful. This would have placed me in an awkward predicament, compelling me to admit that my threat had never been seriously intended, and thus I should have lessened my influence over her for the future. However, not long before her last illness, I found a syringe in her room as well as some tablets. These I appropriated and took away without saying anything to her."

"How long before the attack of diphtheria was this?"

"Two or three days."

"Supposing that she had been taking morphine prior to that time, do you think that it might have accumulated in her system, finally producing death?"

"I object!" said Mr. Munson. "The witness is not here as an expert."

"He is the accused," said the Recorder, "and as the party having the greatest interest at stake I will allow him to answer.

He simply expresses his opinion. The jury will decide whether it is worthy of credence."

Mr. Bliss smiled with satisfaction, but was a little surprised at the answer, though later he understood better that the Doctor appreciated what he said. The answer was:

"Considering the length of time which elapsed from the moment when I took away the syringe, to the day of her death, I cannot believe that morphine taken previously could have accumulated, and have caused death ultimately."

Mr. Bliss was puzzled and paused a moment to think, whilst Mr. Munson, much pleased at this apparently damaging testimony given by the prisoner himself, wore a pleased expression. Mr. Bliss scarcely knew what to ask next. He glanced at a list of notes supplied by Dr. Medjora and read this one. "Ask me about retained morphine. Go into it thoroughly." The latter part of this sentence convinced him that Dr. Medjora must have conceived his defence along this line, and, therefore, though doubting the propriety of doing so, he ventured another question.

"It has been admitted," said he, "by the expert witnesses that morphine may be accumulated in the system, finally resulting fatally. How does that occur, and why do you think it did not occur in this case?"

"I have not said that it did not occur. You asked me whether morphine taken prior to her illness, may have caused her death, and I said no, to that. I did not say that she did not die from morphine, because I do not know that. As I understand it, when morphine acts fatally by accumulation, it is where it is administered continuously. Part of the dose is eliminated, and the rest stored up. Finally this stored up quantity amounts to a lethal dose. In this case, as far as we know, there was a suspension of the administration. The accumulated quantity, when the drug was stopped, could not have amounted to a lethal dose, or death would have ensued. The dosing being discontinued, the stored-up quantity must have grown less and less, day by day, by gradual elimination."

This interested the jury very evidently. They could not but decide that this man was honest, to offer such evidence as seemed against his own interests. Mr. Bliss, still puzzled, ventured another question.

"You said that your wife may have died of this drug, or words to that effect. How can you think that?"

"Whilst, as I have said, the accumulated drug was lessening in quantity daily, by elimination, nevertheless death by poisoning would have ensued at any time, if a dose of morphine had been administered, of sufficient size, so that when added to that still in the system, the whole would have amounted to a lethal quantity."

"Miss Conlin, the nurse, testified that she saw you administer a dose of morphine. She afterwards admitted that she had only seen you remove a syringe. Did you at that time administer a dose of morphine, a dose large enough to have caused death in the manner you have described?"

"I did not."

"Then as far as you know, your wife did not take any morphine on the day of her death?"

"On the contrary, she did take some!" This was a tremendous surprise.

"How did it occur?" asked Mr. Bliss, still following his notes and at length seeing the point to which Dr. Medjora had been leading.

"She administered it to herself." The Doctor paused a moment as though to allow his startling statement to be digested. Then he continued: "As the nurse testified, I gave her permission to go out. I sat and chatted with my wife a few moments, and then bade her be quiet, lest talking should injure the throat. She obeyed, and after a time seemed to be asleep. I sat over by the lamp reading, and, thinking that my patient was asleep, became absorbed in my book, until I was attracted by an ejaculation from my wife. I went to her, and to my surprise found that she had just administered a dose of morphine to herself. I snatched her hands away, and withdrew the instrument whilst there was yet a little of the solution in it. Miss Conlin came in at the moment. I knew that she had seen me, and not wishing to arouse her suspicions as to the truth, I preferred to let her think that I had given the injection myself. Therefore I washed out the syringe, and placing it in my pocket, took it away with me."

"So that there was sufficient morphine solution left in the syringe, to have enabled Miss Conlin to taste it, as she claims to have done?" Mr. Bliss asked this question, because at last he had discovered the full intentions of the Doctor. It is very often the case in great criminal trials, that, either upon advice of counsel, or by direction of the accused, vital points are left unexplained, or else related with variations which convince the jury that a lie is told. The prisoner having heard all of the evidence, sees that certain acts of his have been viewed, and accepted as proof of his guilt. He becomes afraid, and when asked about these, he denies flatly that they have occurred. Then the prosecution, in rebuttal, brings cumulative testimony to support its first witnesses, and the jury, seeing that the prisoner has lied, conclude that he is guilty of the crime charged. Yet it may be that a man may lie in following a badly conceived line of defence, even though he be an innocent man. Still, it takes a brave man, and a cool one, to go upon the stand and admit damaging circumstances as Dr. Medjora was doing. But Dr. Medjora was undoubtedly courageous, and not one to become confused. Therefore Mr. Bliss, admiring his coolness, decided to give him a chance to relate the very occurrences which when told by the nurse had seemed so conclusive of guilt. Dr. Medjora replied:

"I have no doubt that she could have tasted the morphine in the water in which I washed out the syringe."

"Can you tell how your wife obtained possession of the hypodermic syringe, and the morphine?"

"I did not know at the time. But as it was the aluminum case which has been placed in evidence, it must have been left by Dr. Fisher, unless she abstracted it surreptitiously from his bag."

"Do you know how much morphine she took at that time?"

"No, not positively, but I have no doubt that the estimate made regarding the missing tablets closely represents what she took."

"You mean three and one half grains?"

"She probably took between three, and three and a half grains, as some was left in the syringe."

"Then that self-administered dose was sufficient to cause death?"

"Oh, no. I have known her to take twice that quantity." This statement was also received with much surprise.

"The experts told us, Doctor," said Mr. Bliss, "that a sixth of a grain has caused death."

"Has been known to cause death. Yes. But that does not prove that it will always do so. The *habitué* becomes wonderfully tolerant of it. The records are replete with histories of from twenty, to even a hundred grains of morphine without fatal result."

"Then you do not think that three, or three and a half grains of morphia would have caused the death of your wife?"

"Not of itself. But if a quantity of the drug was in her system, this added dose may have contributed to her death."

"In such a case where would the morphine be chiefly found after death, by chemical analysis?"

"In the intestines mainly, because there the stored quantity would have been. But also in the stomach, because of the recent administration." This view was entirely agreeable with the expert evidence.

"In your opinion then, your wife died from the accumulation of morphine, all of which was self-administered?"

"Certainly all the morphine that she took was administered by herself."

"But you are charged with having administered morphine, or other form of opium, which caused death. What have you to say to that?"

"I deny that during this last illness, or at any time, any such drug was administered to my wife, Mabel Medjora, by me, or at my order!"

The last speech was electric, partly from the manner of its utterance, and especially because, for the first time during the trial, the dead girl was called by the name of the prisoner. Mr. Bliss felt assured that he had won his case, and yielded the witness for cross-examination with a smile. Mr. Munson begged for an adjournment, that the cross-examination might be continuous, and not interrupted as it would necessarily be if begun late in the afternoon. This request was granted, and the shrewd lawyer thus obtained time to read over the Doctor's evidence, and be better able to attack him.

CHAPTER IX
THE DEFENCE CLOSES

The next day's proceedings began promptly, Dr. Medjora taking the stand for cross-examination. His evidence in his own behalf, it was generally conceded, had materially weakened the prosecution's case, and it was with much interest that the lawyers watched the outcome of his cross-examination. Mr. Munson began:

"You have testified that Miss Sloane was a morphine *habitué*." Before he could propound a question based upon this statement, the Doctor replied quickly:

"I have not so testified."

"You have not?" asked the attorney, with much surprise.

"No! I said that she had taken morphine, for pain from Bright's disease, until she had almost become an *habitué*."

"That is practically the same thing," said the lawyer, testily.

"Pardon my disagreeing with you. Had she become a confirmed user of the drug, for the drug's sake, she would probably have been suspected by those who lived in the house with her, and thus it would be easy for us to produce witnesses in corroboration of my assertion. But as she used it merely to soothe pain, even though she did take large doses, it was at such intervals, that symptoms of morphine were not sufficiently marked to attract the attention of an ordinary observer."

Messrs. Dudley and Bliss were delighted at this early proof that the Doctor would be a match for the astute attorney, who was about to endeavor to entangle him in contradictions, or damaging admissions.

"Oh! Very well!" said Mr. Munson. "You say that she took morphine in large doses. You knew this, and also that she had a serious disease, and yet you left her alone in a strange boarding-house, whilst you went away to Europe?"

"I left her under the medical care of one who certainly possessed skill, and who pretended to be my friend. I went to Europe, in the cause of humanity, to prosecute studies which I yet hope to make a benefit to my fellows." Thus the Doctor confidently predicted his acquittal. This was most shrewd, for it not infrequently occurs that men may be moved by suggestion, even when not in the hypnotic state. Dr. Medjora was a past master in psychological science.

"How long had you been married, at this time?"

"Eighteen months."

"Then, when you left this woman, she was not only suffering from disease, and the dangers of morphine, but she was grieving for her dead child, was she not?"

This was a neat trap, sprung without warning, but the game was shy and wary. The Doctor replied sternly:

"I have not testified either that she had a child, or that, if so, she had lost it."

"Well, did she have a child?"

"You have had expert testimony upon that point. Why ask me?"

"That is my affair. Answer my question."

"I must decline to do so!"

"I appeal to the court to compel the witness to answer."

"Your Honor," cried Mr. Dudley, rising, "we object. Counsel, for some undiscoverable reason, seems determined to probe the private affairs of our client. We think that this question is irrelevant and incompetent."

"What is the object of this, Mr. Munson," asked the Recorder.

"Your Honor has ruled, and a million precedents uphold you, that we may examine into the relations that existed between the accused and the deceased."

"Your Honor," interjected Mr. Dudley, "you allowed a similar question yesterday, because counsel argued, that if he could prove the existence of a natural child, he would show that the deceased through the child had strong claim upon our client. I will also call your Honor's attention to the fact, that at that time allusion was made to another visionary claim on the part of the prosecution. This was that Dr. Medjora was in the position to marry a wealthy woman, and that the poor musician, with her child, became an obstacle in his way. Now, not a scintilla of evidence has been brought out, in substantiation of that claim, which as I said, at that time, was made merely to affect the jury. Moreover, since then, we have shown that this woman was the lawful wife of Dr. Medjora, and, therefore, her having, or not having a child, can have no possible bearing upon the issue. I hope that the question will not be allowed."

"I cannot see," said the Recorder, "what is to be gained by this, Mr. Munson?"

"Oh, very well, your Honor," said Mr. Munson, "if you think that it is unnecessary to the case of the people, I will withdraw it. We only seek for justice, despite the aspersions of counsel."

"I have no doubt whatever of your conscientiousness," said the Recorder, to mollify the rising anger of Mr. Munson. The examination then proceeded.

"You told us yesterday, that you had received a letter whilst in Europe, in which Miss Sloane wrote that Dr. Meredith was persecuting her with his attentions. Of course you have that letter?"

"No! It has been lost, unfortunately!"

"Unfortunately lost! I should say most unfortunately lost, since it is the only corroboration you had of your remarkable statement. How did you happen to lose this precious document?"

"I think that it was stolen when my office was searched by detectives, who were accompanied by Dr. Meredith."

The insinuation deftly concealed in this statement, that either Dr. Meredith had taken the paper, or that the District Attorney had suppressed it, had a visible effect upon the jury, who looked from one to the other significantly. Mr. Munson was chagrined to find what he had thought a good point in his favor, thus turned against him so quickly. He attempted to repair the damage.

"You say you think this. Do you not know, that what a man thinks is not admissible in evidence?"

"I did the best that I could to answer your question." This reply, in the humblest of tones, caused a smile.

"You have no positive knowledge that it was stolen, have you?"

"I know that it was locked in my desk, that during my absence the desk was forced open, and that upon my return the paper was gone. Whether it was stolen, or whether it forced its way out of my desk, you may decide for yourself."

"You have no evidence, beyond your own word, that Dr. Meredith acted as you have charged?"

"None!"

"You never told any friend, before the death of this girl, that Dr. Meredith had persecuted her?"

"No. I had no confidants."

"Not even when you found that he had been called in to attend Miss Sloane? You did not explain this to Dr. Fisher?"

"No. Dr. Fisher was comparatively a stranger to me. I knew him by association in societies only."

"You could have spoken to him however, and so have had Dr. Meredith dismissed from the case."

"I considered the matter, and decided not to do so."

"Why did you come to so singular a conclusion?"

"Because, as I have already testified, despite my animosity, I concurred with Dr. Fisher's estimate of his skill. I thought him the most valuable consulting physician to be had, and, in a case of life and death, I believed that personal antagonisms should be forgotten."

"You say Dr. Meredith was the most valuable consulting physician to be had. Do you mean that he is the most skilled expert that you know?"

"No. But he is skilful and his office is very near to the house where the patient was. That fact was of importance in deciding whether to retain him or not."

Mr. Munson seemed to strive almost in vain to outwit the witness who adroitly parried every attack.

"You have claimed," continued the lawyer, "that Miss Sloane administered morphine to herself?"

"I assert it."

"Then at least you admit that a dose, a large dose, was taken by the deceased in your presence, on the day of her death?"

"Yes."

"And though you, as a physician, were conversant with her troubles and aware of the danger of such a dose, you did not prevent her from taking this dangerous poison?"

"I endeavored to do so. I took the syringe away from her."

"You took it away from her after she had taken nearly all of the dose?"

"She had taken all but five minims before I could reach her."

"It was you who sent the nurse away, I believe?"

"I gave her permission to go out."

"You told her to remain until nine o'clock?"

"I told her that she might do so."

"And this syringe incident occurred at eight o'clock?"

"At eight thirty."

"That is, half an hour before you expected to be interrupted by the return of the nurse?"

"You do not word your questions justly. I did not expect to be interrupted by the return of the nurse. To be interrupted, one must be occupied with some special work. I was not specially engaged."

"You were supposed to be specially engaged watching your patient, in place of the nurse, with whose services you had dispensed. Had you done your full duty, that is, had you done what the nurse would have done, kept your patient under surveillance, she would not have had a chance to take the morphine, would she?"

"It may be that I was grievously at fault, not to observe her more closely. But I thought that she was asleep. An error is not a crime."

"There are errors that are criminal. Your jury will judge in this case. Now, if you please, answer my question without further evasion. Did not the nurse return half an hour sooner than you expected her?"

"She returned half an hour earlier than the time up to which I had given her permission to be away."

"Exactly. Now, had she remained the full time, she would not have known anything about this morphine incident?"

"Of course not."

"In which case, you would have kept it a secret."

"Most probably."

"But, as she did see you handling the syringe, you knew that she would be in the position to testify to the fact that you yourself administered the morphine?"

"It is not a fact that I administered the morphine, but I supposed that she would so testify, judging from what she saw."

"Judging honestly?"

"Yes. Judging honestly."

"So that this professional nurse, accustomed herself to using hypodermic syringes, had a right, as you admit, to judge from what she saw, that you administered morphine to the patient?"

"She saw me taking away the syringe, and of course could conclude that I inserted the needle myself. Nevertheless her opinion was only an opinion; it was not knowledge."

"Very well. You admit that she had a right to her opinion, and that you suspected what that opinion would be. Now, of course you realized, being an intellectual man, that such evidence would weigh against you?"

"I fully appreciated the gravity of the situation."

"And that if not refuted, this testimony almost alone, would tend towards a conviction?"

"Yes."

"Therefore you decided to claim that the drug was self-administered, knowing that the administration would be proved?"

"I knew that the administration of the drug would be proved. But my reason for saying that it was self-administered, is because it is the truth."

"That will be for the jury to decide!" With this parting shot the lawyer dismissed the witness, and his own counsel decided to ask no further questions.

The clergyman who had performed the marriage ceremony, then took the stand, and testified to the validity of the marriage. He was not cross-examined.

Then a celebrated expert toxicologist was called, Professor Newburg. He testified in corroboration of the claims of the defence, and especially to the large doses of morphine, which he had known to be tolerated by persons accustomed to it by habit. It also was claimed by him, that persons who had been known to take as much as four and five grains per day without ill effect, had suddenly died from so small a dose as half a grain. He thought that in these cases the drug had accumulated in the system, and the whole quantity stored up, was made active by the assimilation of the last dose, which of itself would not have been poisonous. Cross-examination did not materially alter his testimony.

Next a pathologist was introduced, and in answer to a long hypothetical question, based upon the testimony of Dr. Fisher and the experts for the prosecution, he said that in his opinion the deceased died from anæmia, following diphtheria. The symptoms of morphine poisoning observed were probably due to the morphine which she had taken, but under the conditions described, he did not think that even three and a half grains would have caused death. He came to this conclusion, arguing that the condition of the kidneys showed that they were diseased, and the tendency would have been to store up this last dose, just as previous doses had probably been retained. In that event only a small portion would have become active, and whilst it might have caused contracted pupils, it would not have caused death. All things duly considered, therefore, he thought that death was attributable to diphtheria.

Under cross-examination he admitted the postulate of the previous witness, that a small dose, following retained larger doses, might cause death, but still he adhered to his opinion that it had not occurred here. A long series of questions failed to shake his opinion, or cause him to contradict himself.

Several other witnesses were called, but I need scarcely introduce their evidence here, as much of it was of small importance, and none of it could have materially affected the verdict. The defence then rested.

Mr. Munson called several witnesses in rebuttal, but to so little effect that Mr. Bliss did not even cross-examine them, considering his case practically won. He did interfere, however, when Mr. Munson at last called Madame Cora Corona.

"I must ask your Honor, what counsel expects to prove by this witness, and moreover, your Honor, I will ask that the jury be sent from the room, before any discussion of this subject be allowed."

This request was granted, and the jury went into an adjoining apartment. Mr. Munson then explained:

"We have been trying for a long time to summon this witness, your Honor, but she has skilfully avoided the court officers, so that it was only this morning that we found her. She will testify to the fact that Dr. Medjora has been courting her, and seeking a marriage with her, even previous to the death of the woman who he claims was his wife."

"That is the most extraordinary expedient I have ever heard of, your Honor," said Mr. Bliss. "Counsel certainly knows better, than to suppose that at this late hour he can introduce new evidence. He certainly cannot claim that this is in rebuttal!"

"But I do claim that!" said Mr. Munson.

"What does it rebut?" asked the Recorder.

"This man claims that he was a true and loving husband to his wife, and denies that he contemplated such a marriage as this one, by which a wealthy wife would aid him to accomplish his ambitions."

"That claim, Mr. Munson, was made by counsel for the defence," said the Recorder. "It has not come out upon the witness stand. You cannot introduce a witness to rebut a statement of counsel. If you wished to introduce this evidence you should have questioned the prisoner upon these points when on the witness stand. Had he denied the desire to marry again, I would have allowed you to disprove his assertion by this witness. As it is, I must rule out the evidence offered."

Mr. Munson bit his lip in mortification, when the Recorder pointed out to him the serious omission made in the examination of the accused, but of course he was powerless to do anything. Having no other witness to call, when the jurors had returned to their seats, Mr. Bliss arose and addressed the jury.

CHAPTER X
MR. BLISS MAKES HIS SPEECH

"May it please your Honor and gentlemen of the jury," began Mr. Bliss, amidst an impressive silence, "in a few hours you will be called upon to act in a capacity which has been delegated to you by your fellow-men, but which finally is the province of our heavenly Father alone. You are to sit in judgment upon a human being, and accordingly as ye judge him, so shall ye be judged hereafter. I have not the least doubt of the integrity of your purpose; I fully believe that such verdict as you shall render will be honestly adopted, after the most thorough weighing of the evidence which has been presented to you. All I ask is that you form your final opinion with due recognition of the fact, that if a mistake is to be made, far better would it be that you release our client, if he be guilty, than that you should send him to the hangman, though innocent. I beg of you to remember that great as is the majesty of the law and the rights of the people, yet more must you respect the rights of this man, who stands alone, to defend himself against such an array of witnesses and lawyers, as the wealth of the whole commonwealth has been able to summon against him. The very weakness of his position, as compared with the forces against which he has to contend, should excite your sympathies. If there be any doubt in your minds, it becomes, not your privilege, but your sworn duty to accord it to him. For, as his Honor will undoubtedly explain to you when expounding the law, the prosecution must prove the charge beyond all doubt.

The burden of proof is upon them. They claim that the deceased came to her death by poison administered by our client. They must therefore prove that she died of poison, and that the poison was given by Dr. Medjora. But they must prove even more than that, for they must show that it was given with intent to destroy life. Thus, if you decide that she died of diphtheria, of Bright's disease, of poison retained in the system, or even of the last dose which was taken by her, you are bound to acquit our client, unless indeed you should adopt the extraordinary conclusion, that the final dose of morphine alone produced death, and that Dr. Medjora himself administered it, intending that it should destroy his beloved wife, for whom he had retained skilled medical service and nursing, and at whose bedside he even tolerated the presence of his bitterest enemy, because he knew that the man possessed the greatest skill available in the vicinity of the house where the poor girl lay ill. Had he intended to injure his wife, had he premeditated poisoning her, do you think that he would have allowed a man to be nigh, who would be only too glad to find a pretext upon which to charge him with a crime, but who, moreover, was possessed of exactly the experience and ability needed to detect the symptoms of a deadly poison? The proposition is preposterous, and I am sure that such intelligent gentlemen as yourselves will cast it aside from you. But if the prosecution fail to prove that the girl did not die from natural causes, then they fail utterly to make out their case. Upon this point the law is most explicit. In fact in one of our great text books, a work recognized by the entire legal profession as the highest authority, I find a passage which seems almost to have been written for your enlightenment in this very case. I will read it to you:

"It does not follow that because a person is wounded and dies, the death is caused by the wound; and the burden in such cases is on the prosecution to show beyond reasonable doubt that the wound in question produced death. It may happen also, where poison has been administered, that death resulted from natural causes. The presence of poison may be ascertained from symptoms during life, the *post mortem* appearances, the moral circumstances, and the discovery of the existence of poison in the body, in the matter ejected from the stomach, or in food or drink of which the sufferer has partaken. But to this should be added proof that the poison thus received into the system was the cause of death.'

"I think that passage most clearly indicates to you the task which the prosecution have undertaken. Upon what do they rely for the accomplishment of their purpose? Two things mainly. Circumstantial evidence, and expert testimony. And now, if I may hope for your close attention, I will say a few words upon both of these classes of evidence, in general.

"Circumstantial evidence, I need hardly tell you, is most delusive in its character. Analyzed, what do we find it to be? It has been truly argued that there is, and can be, no cause without an effect. In considering circumstantial evidence, the mind of the investigator is presented with the relation of a number of facts, or effects, and he is asked to deduce that they are all attributable to a stated cause. For example, a peddler is known to have started out upon a lonely road, and to have in his pack certain wares, a given amount of money in specified coins and bills, wearing a watch and chain, and he is subsequently found murdered, by the wayside. Later, a tramp is arrested upon whose person is found the exact missing money, and many of the articles which were known to have been in the pack. He is charged with the crime, and the evidence against him is circumstantial. His possession of these articles is an effect, which is said to be attributable to a cause, to wit, the killing of the peddler. But strong as such evidence may appear, as I have said, it is delusive. For just as the prosecution ask you to believe that a number of effects are traceable to a single cause, the crime charged, so also it is possible that all of the effects may have resulted from various causes. Thus in the case cited, the tramp may have been a thief, and may have stolen the articles from the peddler after some other person had killed him. And if it could be shown that the watch and chain were missing, and yet were not found upon the tramp, that would be as good evidence in his favor, as the other facts are against him. So that in circumstantial evidence the chain must be complete. If a single link be missing, or have a flaw, the argument is inconclusive, and a doubt is created, the benefit of which must invariably be given in favor of the accused.

"If this be true where there is a single link that has a flaw, what are we to say when we find that the entire chain is composed of links which are faulty? You are asked to decide that from this fact, and that fact, and the other fact, the accused is guilty of a crime! Suppose that we show that from either the first, or the second, or the third fact, we can trace back to other causes as producing the result? Why, then, the prosecution's case is rendered so fragile that the gentlest breath of a zephyr must blow each separate link to a different quarter of the globe. Now, that is what I shall endeavor to demonstrate; that, from the chief facts claimed by the prosecution, you may deduce innocence rather than guilt.

"First, we have the accuser, Dr. Meredith. He aids the prosecution's claim of poison by relating the symptoms of poisoning, which he says he observed before death. Now, even granting that this is a true statement of facts, observed by an unprejudiced mind,—of which, gentlemen, you can readily judge, when you recall the abundant testimony as to an existing animosity,—but, even granting its absolute truth, what does it show? Simply that morphine had been administered, in a dose large enough to have produced *ante-mortem* evidences of its presence. But what of that? Does it show that the drug was administered by any particular person? By Dr. Medjora, as the prosecution have claimed? If so then I am ignorant, and ill informed as to all the rules of logic. It shows that morphine was present, and it shows no more, and no less. Now that fact we freely admit. The Doctor himself told you how the drug was taken, and there has been nothing whatever offered, that even tends to disprove his assertion. Thus, as his testimony is all that we have upon the subject, and as it has been unimpeached, you are bound to accept it as the only evidence available. I may also remind you at this point, that in this country, where the God-given liberty of one man is as much cherished as that of the whole people, a man is to be considered innocent until after he has been adjudged guilty. He therefore goes upon the witness stand, as unsullied as any other witness, and his evidence is entitled to the same credence. I may also interject a momentary remark as to the difference between juridical and common judgment. You may see a man commit a crime and if accepted upon the jury which tries him, although you know that he is guilty, you are bound to bring him in innocent, unless the evidence introduced against him proves his guilt, entirely aside from your own prejudices or prejudgment. You must give a juridical opinion only. So that if you have imbibed any prejudices against Dr. Medjora,–which is scarcely probable, for he must have impressed you as favorably as he has every one else who has seen him in court,–but if so, you are to set that all aside, and accept his unimpeached evidence upon this point, relative to the administration of the morphine, as the only available evidence upon which to base an opinion. And if you do adopt that, and decide, as you necessarily would, that self-administered morphine cannot implicate Dr. Medjora in this crime, why the case is ended at once, and need scarcely go any further.

"However, merely as a matter of form, I will take up one or two more points. The second link in this circumstantial chain is that evidences of morphine were found at the autopsy. But, gentlemen, what of that? You and I know how it entered the system, and of course we expect that eminent specialists, such as the gentlemen who performed the autopsy, must necessarily recognize the recent presence of the drug. It forms no particle of proof whatever against Dr. Medjora. That we see clearly enough, when we eliminate the bare facts from the fog of misinterpretation. But I may casually remind you of another fact, which these same eminent specialists told us about. They found that the kidneys were atrophied, an evidence of disease, and later we learned that if the kidneys are diseased morphine is retained in the system, until a poisonous dose may accumulate. So we see that even if the deceased was poisoned to death, it was only by the retention of many doses, due to a diseased condition, and in no way attributable to criminal interference.

"The next link is the actual presence of the drug, as testified by the expert chemists. They tell us that they found morphine. Why of course they did. It was in the system; we knew that it was there; and we are not at all shocked by the discovery.

"But I need not take up any other of these forged links, for, as you plainly see, the principal ones are so very faulty that as they are the mainstay of the bonds that bind our client, we break them asunder with scarcely an effort.

"Now, I will say a few words relative to expert testimony, and I beg of you to understand throughout, that however I may attack this sort of evidence as a class, I speak in general terms only, and in no way cast any imputations against the scientific gentlemen who have appeared upon the stand, except as they come within the limitations of their class, as I am about to explain to you.

"When expert testimony was first introduced it was received with marked respect. The expert witness was counted as a professor in his specialty, and his word was almost final. Experience, however, has materially altered all this. The field from which the expert may be cited has been vastly broadened, whilst at the same time his testimony is accepted with much more caution, and less credence. The causes which have operated towards this state of things are manifold, but I need not explain them here. Wherever there is any sort of specialty, from the blacking of boots, to the highest scientific pursuits, we now have experts who go upon the stand, and dogmatically inform us that their opinions are the true and only accepted finality upon the subject presented. But we have found, that however positive one, or two, or three experts may be in asseverating what they claim to be a fact, an equal number, of equally scientific, equally experienced, and equally trustworthy experts, may be found whose testimony will be equally as positive, though diametrically opposed. Indeed, so true is this, that I may quote the wise words of that eminent jurist Lord Campbell, who says: 'Skilled witnesses come with such a bias on their minds to support the cause in which they are embarked, that hardly any weight should be given to their evidence.' These are strong words, but what does Lord Campbell mean? That an eminent scientist would go upon the witness stand, and perjure himself merely because he has been engaged to substantiate a given proposition? Not at all. Of all experts, I may be permitted to say perhaps, that the most eminent are those connected with the professions, for we must rank the professions higher than the arts, just as the arts are above the trades. We have three great professions, to wit, the Ministry, Medicine, and Law. If we could have before us the most prominent Minister, the most celebrated Physician, and the most eminent Lawyer, we would probably have three men standing equally high in public esteem. Then let us suppose that this most eminent lawyer were engaged as counsel in some great suit. Suppose that some intricate technicality of law should arise, upon which the presiding judge should ask for argument and precedents. Suppose, then, that associate counsel should place this most eminent lawyer upon the stand as an expert witness? Remembering that he had been paid for advocating the cause in behalf of which he was testifying, how much weight would his evidence have? I think you will agree that it would be very slight indeed! Yet is it not the same with the expert physician? Is not the skilled medical witness hired, and paid for his advocacy, just as that eminent lawyer was? Then why should we discard the evidence of the one, and accept the other? Neither of these gentlemen commits perjury. What they tell, is honestly told. But–and, gentlemen of the jury, I now come to the vital point of this argument–the expert does not give us an unbiased opinion. The reason is plain. As experts can be found with varying opinions, so those are sought whose opinions agree with the position which they are called to sustain. To be more definite, the experts called by the prosecution in this case, were called, because it was known in advance what they would testify, and because said testimony would be favorable to the hypothesis of the prosecution. Though, I may say parenthetically, in this case it has proven otherwise. But, stated on general principles, that is the fact. The prosecution chooses experts, whose views can be relied upon to support the charge against the prisoner. And I must candidly confess that the defence is actuated similarly. Surmising in advance what the opposing experts would tell us, we went about amongst equally eminent men, and found no difficulty in selecting those who could with equal positiveness, with equal authority, and with equal experience and knowledge, support our hypothesis. Had we found a gentleman who entertained views similar to those of the prosecution's witnesses, do you suppose, for one moment, that we would have engaged such a man to aid us? Of course not! Then are the lawyers for the prosecution any more human than we? Do you suppose that they would call an expert, if they knew that his honest opinions would controvert their claims? Certainly not. Were they not loath to call Dr. Fisher? Thus, gentlemen, have we discovered, by analytical reasoning, the cause of the bias existing in the mind of an honest man. His opinion is sought in advance. If favorable he is engaged. When engaged he becomes a hired advocate, as much as the lawyer. Moreover, unlike the witness of facts, his testimony is tinged by a personal interest. He knows that celebrated experts will oppose his views. His reputation is on trial, as it were. If the verdict is for his side, it is a sort of juridical upholding of his position. He is therefore arrayed against his antagonists, as much as the lawyers of the opposing sides. In short, having once expressed an opinion, he will go to any extreme almost, to prove that he is right. The questions asked by the counsel for his side, the majority of which he prepares or dictates himself, are glibly and positively answered. But when the cross-examination begins, what do we see? An interesting spectacle from a psychological standpoint. We see a man, honest in his intentions, standing between two almost equal forces; the love of himself and of his own opinions, on the one side, and upon the other the love of scientific truth which is inherent in all truly professional men. When a question is asked, to which he can reply without injury to his pronounced opinion, how eagerly he answers. But when a query is propounded, which his knowledge shows him in a moment, indicates a reply which his quick intelligence sees will be against his side, what does he do? We find that he fences with the question. As anxious not to state what he knows to be false, as he is not to injure his side of the case, he parries. He tells you in hesitating tones, 'It may be so, in rare cases,' 'Other men have seen and reported such instances, but I have not met them,' 'It might be possible under extraordinary circumstances, but not in this case,' and so on, and so on, reluctant to express himself so that he may be cited afterwards. You have witnessed this very kind of evasion in this case, so that you readily grasp my meaning. When I asked Professor Orton, whether the action of morphine is modified by disease, his answer was, 'It might be'; and when I asked him whether, from continual dosage, it could accumulate in the system, he said, 'The records contain reports of such cases.' When I asked him if morphine would not be so retained where Bright's disease were present, he tried evasion again by saying, 'I have never seen such a case,' after which he admitted that he had read of them in good authorities.

"As I have told you, speaking generally, this sort of evasion under cross-examination is a peculiarity common to nearly all experts, so that in singling out Professor Orton as an example, I do so with no intention of attacking his honesty of purpose. He was simply defending himself, and upholding the side which pays him for his advocacy. But I choose this testimony because if we analyze it I think we will find more, much more than appears at a glance; and I can at the same time show you how all expert testimony should be received. I will exemplify the amount of caution to be displayed in accepting what a skilled witness tells. I will show you principally, that what the expert testifies under cross-examination is more likely to be true, than what he tells the friendly lawyer on his own side.

"Now, when I asked Professor Orton whether Bright's disease would act as a cause to facilitate the accumulation of morphine in the system, he answered, 'I have never seen such a case.' That, gentlemen, is the set of words which I beg of you to analyze. Why did the Professor use just this language? For, mark you, it is a well-studied answer. Let us suppose that this eminent toxicologist had made an exhaustive series of experiments, which had proved, beyond all cavil, that the commonly accepted idea among physicians is wrong, and that Bright's disease will not effect an accumulation of morphine. How gladly would he have said 'No' to my question! How positively would he have asserted that Bright's disease would not have the effect which we claim! Therefore, that he does not use any such dogmatic denial shows logically and conclusively that he has no such knowledge. He does not know, beyond all doubt, that Bright's disease will not modify the action of this poison. But we can see more in this answer. Suppose that, lacking absolute knowledge, he had still a firm conviction. He would then most probably have said, 'It is my opinion that Bright's disease does not modify the drug's action.' But, gentlemen, he had not even a conviction of this kind. On the contrary, he must either have known, or else have leaned towards the belief that such an accumulation is possible, otherwise he would not have said just what he did say: 'I have not seen such a case.' 'I have not seen such a case'! Why, the very words suggest that such a case has existed. More–that the Professor had heard of such cases, and believed in them. Perhaps he hoped that this evasive answer would be accepted as final. In that case, gentlemen, it might have served, in your minds, as well as a negative reply. But, gentlemen, a lawyer's mind is necessarily trained to the quick appreciation of situations like this. As soon as he had said that he had never seen such a case, I was prompted by intuition to ask if he had not heard of them. Then the fat was in the fire, and we had an admission, however reluctantly given, that he had heard of them, and from competent authority. But the very attempt on the part of this witness to parry the question, and evade a full and truthful reply, carries a conviction with it, that he recognized immediately the importance of our claim, and the possibility that it is a true explanation of the sad death of this young wife. He saw at once that all the damning evidences of the presence of poison, are explainable by this simple hypothesis, that Bright's disease might cause otherwise proper doses of morphine to accumulate until a lethal dose be present, and then act to destroy life. He therefore attempted to belittle the hypothesis. He could not refute it; he scarcely dared to deny it as a possibility, and therefore he essayed evasion.

"Thus we may deduce more from the reluctant admission of an expert, than from their glibly-told tales which have been rehearsed in the office of the District Attorney. So that, after all, expert testimony is valuable—most valuable—if we but consider it with caution, and analyze it, until bereft of bias and prejudice, the grain of truth stands out, as truth ever will, conspicuous midst the mass of extraneous matter surrounding it, much of which is introduced for the express purpose of befogging your minds, and leading you away from the facts.

"Thus, gentlemen, upon closer examination we find that just as their circumstantial evidence was faulty, so the prosecution's experts prove a boomerang. For it is upon their evidence that we mainly rely for acquittal. Dr. McDougal, the Coroner's physician, examined the kidneys at the autopsy, and freely expressed the opinion that Bright's disease had been present. Of course he denied that this disease had caused death, but there we have the opinion of an advocate. Next we have Professor Orton, who, as I have shown, practically testifies that Bright's disease may cause morphine to accumulate in the system until a poisonous dose has resulted. Is not that enough, gentlemen, to satisfy you that, if this girl died of morphine, she died a natural death, and was not murdered? At least, does it not raise a doubt in your minds, which must be credited to Dr. Medjora, and which would deter you from sending him to the hangman? I am so

positive that it must, that I will close this appeal, without calling your attention to the evidence, which has been abundant,
and which indicates that death was not the result of poisoning
at all, but of diphtheria, as indeed was certified in the burial
permit. I could go over all the evidence in greater detail, but I
am so strongly impressed with the innocence of our client, and
so firmly confident that you are as capable as I am of reaching
a proper conclusion in considering the evidence, that I will not
take up more of your time, but leave our cause now in your
care, satisfied that, regardless of the able rhetorical ability of the
gentleman on the other side, you will be guided by Providence,
and your own hearts, to aid the cause of justice and release Dr.
Medjora from his present trying situation. And as you deal
justly with him now, so may you receive your reward in the life
hereafter."

CHAPTER XI
TERMINATION OF THE GREAT CASE

The District Attorney himself arose to speak for the commonwealth. "May it please your Honor and gentlemen of the jury,"
he began, "you have just heard an able argument in behalf of the
prisoner. Counsel has told you truly, that in this free Republic,
which has become the refuge and asylum for the oppressed of all
nations, the liberty of one man is as sacred as the rights of the
whole people. He has also used the well-worn argument that the
prisoner should have your sympathy, because of the weakness of
his position. By this is meant, that the State; having wealth, can
engage prosecuting officers of ability, whilst the prisoner, thrown
upon his private resources, may be compelled to intrust his cause
to the care of inferior counsel. But, gentlemen, you must see at
a glance that our learned opponent has weakened his own argument by the unusual display of ability which he has exhibited in
this case. Surely in his hands the cause of the prisoner is eminently safe! The commonwealth, with all its resources, cannot
summon greater legal ability to its aid. Therefore you may relieve
your minds of any idea of pity for the prisoner, and omitting
all thought of him personally, decide this case entirely on the
evidence.

"But if you find it difficult to disregard the fact that here is a man, whose liberty or life is at stake, then I bid you remember, that whilst it is true that his rights are equal to those of the State, they are no greater. The commonwealth must have equal place, in your judgment, with the prisoner.

"As the prosecuting attorney I stand in a somewhat peculiar position. In ordinary lawsuits, opposing counsel are retained by the various sides, and are arrayed against each other solely. Under such circumstances the able arguments of Mr. Bliss would hold sway. I am alluding now to his attack upon expert witnesses. Let us suppose that a suit is brought to overthrow a will, the plaintiff arguing that the signature has been forged. Experts in chirography are called by both sides. It is manifest, as Mr. Bliss has said, that the opinions of experts will be sought by the contending counsel, and at the trial we would have those favoring the theory, forgery, testifying to that effect, whilst the others would support the genuineness of the signature. Undoubtedly, also, had either of these gentlemen expressed a different opinion prior to the trial, he would have been found upon the opposite side. Or, in plainer words, the men are hired to testify, because, previous to the trial, they hold an opinion favorable to the side which pays them. Thus, as has been shown to you at some length, eminent jurists now accord but cautious credence to expert testimony, because of the bias which must attend paid advocacy. But, gentlemen of the jury, as logical as all this is, when applied to a civil suit, it becomes but the most specious reasoning when introduced into a criminal case, such as this.

"We are often led astray by arguments, which contain analogies which are but apparently analogous. In this case there is a flaw at the very root of the argument, and therefore the very flower and fruit of the whole beautiful array of words must wilt and fail.

"This flaw is easily pointed out. In the civil case, as I have said, and as you know, opposing counsel defend but the side that pays them. In a criminal case it is entirely different. The District Attorney is engaged, not for a special case, against a special prisoner, but by the whole community, for the protection of all the people. Now the prisoner is himself one of these, and his rights are ever in the minds of the very men who prepare the arguments against him. Let us glance for a moment at the *modus operandi*. Suspicion is aroused against a man. If sufficiently grave, the first bits of evidence attainable are presented to the Grand Jury, and perhaps they find an indictment. This gives the State authority to hold the prisoner by arrest, until such time when he may be tried. But, gentlemen of the jury, are all indicted men tried? Not at all. The District Attorney not infrequently, in the course of preparing a case, finds that an error has been made: that the man is the victim of circumstances: in short that he is innocent. What occurs then? Does he act the part of the hired lawyer and proceed, merely that he may collect a fee? Not at all. He protects the rights of the prisoner, as one of the people, and by due process of law the man is released from custody, free from even a stain upon his character.

"Now let us for a moment suppose that the charge is one of murder; of murder by poisoning, let us say. The first step is to place the medical investigation of the facts into the hands of eminent experts. Here we find that the very resources of the commonwealth become the prisoner's greatest safeguard. The State having abundance of money, places this investigation into the care of the very ablest men to be obtained. It is not at all true, that these experts are retained because of their known opinions. When they are retained, they have no opinions whatever, because they are engaged to pursue an investigation, and their opinions are non-existent until after the conclusion of their analyses. Now, gentlemen, imagine that the commonwealth's counsel would be base enough to dispense with an expert witness, because his testimony would be detrimental to the hypothesis of the prosecution, would such a course be possible? Not at all. In the first place, the autopsy and the chemical analyses have been made upon the tissues of the body of the deceased. In the course of this work these tissues are rendered useless for any further analyses. Therefore, the only investigation possible is the original one, and the only expert opinions obtainable are those of the men, who, as I have shown, are engaged long before they have any opinion to express. If these men were omitted from the case then no experts could be called to replace them; but what would be worse, these very witnesses, discarded by the prosecution, would immediately be retained by the defence. For,

as Mr. Bliss has candidly admitted, the defence only engages
experts whose opinions are known to be favorable. That is the
difference between the paid experts of the defence, and those
engaged by the prosecution. The one is an advocate for a fee,
whilst the other is merely an independent outsider, who relates
the medical facts which he has found upon examination of the
body of the deceased, and then explains the scientific deductions
which he makes from these facts. The witness of the defence is
biased; the witness of the prosecution is not. No, gentlemen of
the jury, when the experts for the prosecution form opinions
which oppose the idea of a crime, the District Attorney has but
one course which he can pursue. He must protect the prisoner,
as it is his sworn duty to do, and obtain his release.

"But *per contra*, when these eminent medical men discover,
within the tissues of the deceased, plain evidences of the fact
that a crime has been consummated, it then becomes the duty of
the District Attorney to prosecute the accused, and to produce,
before a jury of his countrymen, the evidence which these gentlemen of science have discovered. And this class of evidence is not
only valuable, and pertinent, but it is indispensable. Without the
assistance of experts, it would be almost impossible to convict a
man of murder, by the use of poison. The pistol, the knife, and
other weapons, all leave wounds discernible by the eyes of all.
But poison works insidiously, and is unseen. As deadly as the
bullet, it operates not only without noise, but in skilful hands
the death may simulate that caused by known diseases, so that
even eminent physicians might sign a burial permit, as did Dr.
Fisher in this case, without a suspicion of the presence of the
poison. But suspicion having been aroused, by the aid of science
it is now possible to search microscopically into the tissues of
the victim, and find every trace of poison if one has been used.
And if, gentlemen, able men of science, prominent in their spe-
cialties, and honored by their professional brethren as well as by
the community in which they dwell, make an impartial investigation of this nature, and report to you that they have found
poison actually present, and in quantities which would have
proved fatal, I submit it to your intelligence, gentlemen, is not
that expert testimony of the most important character? Can we
assail such evidence with the cry of bias, merely because it comes

within the general category of expert testimony? Certainly not. You will therefore forget entirely the anathema which Mr. Bliss has delivered against experts, for though true enough against the class, it does not apply in this instance.

"Before dismissing this phase of the subject, I must say a few words in defence of Professor Orton. Mr. Bliss pointed out to you that when an expert is replying to direct examination he answers readily, whereas, when answering the cross-examining lawyer, he is more cautious. This is true; but, gentlemen, what does that signify? Simply that having told the truth, the witness is compelled to defend himself against the traps that will be set for him by the opposite side. He knows in advance that he will be assailed by hypothetical and ambiguous questions, worded to confuse him, and to mystify the jury. Under these circumstances, therefore, he must necessarily think well, before replying. He is in a court of law, under oath, and his professional reputation is at stake. If he were not cautious in his replies he would be worthless as a witness. He is justified, too, in parrying questions which he knows are introduced merely to disguise the truth, or to lead the minds of the jury into wrong channels. Mr. Bliss has made much, or thinks that he has made much, of the answers which Professor Orton gave. By specious reasoning he tries to prove that Professor Orton believed that this woman died of an accumulation of morphine, caused by a diseased condition of the kidneys. Mr. Bliss tells us that he rests his case upon the evidence of our witnesses, and largely upon this admission from Professor Orton. Now, as a matter of fact, what Professor Orton did say cannot help the prisoner. He admitted that other men have held the opinion that diseased kidneys may cause an accumulation of morphine. But, gentlemen, how does that effect this case? This very witness, upon whom Mr. Bliss is willing to rely, tells us that whatever the possibilities might be in other cases, it is his positive belief that this particular woman did not die as claimed by the defence. He found poison in the stomach in considerable quantities, whereas, where death occurs by a slow accumulation, the drug would have passed beyond that organ, and none would have been found there. So that we see, that what might be, and what perhaps has been in the past, has no bearing on this case even inferentially, because the same expert who says it is possible in other cases, tells us plainly that it did not occur in this instance.

"And now, before speaking of the actual evidence in this case, let me say a few words in regard to circumstantial evidence. It has been common practice for counsel defending criminal cases to inveigh against circumstantial evidence, until a suspicion has been engendered in the public mind, that it is of dubious value. Indeed, the people, knowing a little law, and understanding that all reasonable doubt must be accorded to the prisoner, and, further, having imbibed the idea that all circumstantial evidence contains a doubt, have come almost to feel that a conviction obtained by such means is a miscarriage of justice.

"This is entirely erroneous. All evidence is divided arbitrarily into two great classes, direct and circumstantial. I do not here allude to documentary evidence, which is somewhere between the two, the validity of the document being necessarily proved by one or the other. This classification, as I say, is arbitrary, for he would indeed be a wise man who could tell us exactly where direct evidence ceases to be direct, or where circumstantial evidence becomes solely circumstantial. The two are so interdependent, that it is only by extreme examples that we can dissociate them. All direct evidence must be sustained by circumstances, whilst all circumstantial evidence is dependent upon direct facts.

"Let me give you an example of each, that this may be more clear to your minds. Let us suppose that several boys go to a pool of water to swim. One of these is seen by his companions to dive into the water, and he does not arise. His death is reported, and the authorities, later, drag the pool and find a body. This is called direct evidence. The boy was seen to drown, you are told, and your judgment concedes the fact readily. But is the proposition proved, even though you have these several witnesses to the actual drowning? Let us see. The body is taken to the morgue, and the keeper there, an expert in such matters, makes the startling assertion that instead of a few hours, or let us say a day, the body must have been immersed for several days. This is circumstantial evidence. The keeper has no positive knowledge that this particular body has been under water so long. Still he has seen thousands of bodies, and none has presented such an appearance after so short an interval. How shall we judge between such conflicting evidence? On the one side we have direct evidence which is most positive. On the other we have circumstantial evidence which is equally so. Is the original hypothesis proven? Does not the circumstantial evidence raise a doubt? Certainly. Now let us take another step. The witnesses to the drowning are called again, and view the body, and now among ten of them, we find one who hesitates in his identification. At once we find another circumstance wanting in substantiation of the original claim. Now we see, that all that was really proved was, that a boy was drowned, and not at all that it was this particular boy who was found. But is this even proved? How can it be, in the absence of the drowned body? Now suppose that, at the last hour, the original boy turns up alive, and reports that he had been washed ashore down the stream and subsequently recovered. We find that our direct evidence, with numerous witnesses to the actual fact, was entirely misleading after all, because we had jumped to a conclusion, without duly considering the attendant circumstances of the case. So it is always. This is no case manufactured to point an argument. There is no such thing as positive proof, which does not depend upon circumstances. The old example may be cited briefly again. If you see one man shoot at another and see the other fall and die, can you say without further knowledge, that one killed the other? If you do, you may find later that the pistol carried only a blank cartridge, and that the man died of fright.

"It is equally true of circumstantial evidence, that without some direct fact upon which it depends it is worthless. As an example of this, I may as well save your time by introducing the case at issue. If we could show you that the prisoner desired the death of this girl; that he profited by her death; that he had a secret in connection with her child which he can keep from the world better, now that she is dead; that she died under circumstances which made the attending physician suspect morphine poisoning; that as soon as the suspicion was announced, the prisoner mysteriously disappeared, and remained in hiding for several days; that he had the opportunity to administer the poison; that he understood the working of the drug; and other circumstances of a similar nature, the argument would be entirely circumstantial. All this might be true and the man might be innocent. But, selecting from this array of suspicious facts, the one which indicates morphine as the drug employed, and then add to it the fact that expert chemists actually find morphine in the tissues of the body, and you see, gentlemen, that at once this single bit of direct evidence gives substantial form to the whole. The circumstantial is strengthened by the direct, just as the direct is made important by the circumstantial. The mere finding of poison in a body, though direct evidence as to the cause of death, neither convicts the assassin, nor even positively indicates that a murder has been committed. The poison might have reached the victim by accident. But consider the attendant circumstances, and then we see that a definite conclusion is inevitable. It is from the circumstantial evidence only that we can reach the true meaning of what the direct testimony teaches.

"So we come at last to find that evidence is evidence, and that all evidence is important, and may prove convincing. This is true, without regard to the technical classification. Leave classification to the lawyers, gentlemen. You have but to weigh all that has been offered to you as relevant, and bearing upon the issue. Be assured, the Recorder would not have admitted any extraneous matter. You are not to cast aside anything that you have heard, merely because Mr. Bliss tells you that it is delusive. It is not delusive. On the contrary, all is very clear, as I shall now demonstrate to you.

"I will take up the chain of evidence much in the same order as did Mr. Bliss. First, then, we have Dr. Meredith. Mr. Bliss hints to you that he is a prejudiced witness, but whilst I might argue that a man must be more than a villain to falsely accuse another of murder, I need go into no defence of this witness, because it has been freely admitted that his testimony is true. Mr. Bliss argues that all that can be deduced from what Dr. Meredith tells us, is that morphine was present in quantity sufficient to show toxic symptoms. Now that is all that we care to claim from this witness. He recognized morphine poisoning prior to death, but Mr. Bliss attempts to belittle the value of this by the hypothesis that the drug was self-administered. He calls your attention to the statements of the prisoner to this effect, and tells you to believe him. On this subject I will speak again in a moment. The principal thing at this point is, do they ask us to believe that the girl died from diphtheria, or did she die of poison, regardless of how she received it? They do not choose between these two queries, but ask you to say either that she died of diphtheria, or, if of poison, that it was self-administered. It rests with you, gentlemen, then, to decide this weighty point. As to diphtheria, we have the report of the experts against it. Dr. Meredith declared, even before her death, that she was dying from poison. The autopsy showed that the cause of death was poison. The chemical analysis shows morphine in a poisonous dose, which is declared to be more than three grains. True, Dr. Fisher, a witness who was forced upon the prosecution, declares that diphtheria caused the death, but this is in contradiction to the opinion of all the others, and though honestly offered, no doubt, may be accounted for by the natural desire to substantiate the statement made in the death certificate. But this same witness tells us later that exactly three and a half grains of morphine is missing from his medicine-case, the one from which the defence admits that the morphine was taken. We find also that the defence seem to lay more stress upon explaining the death by morphine, than upon any effort to prove that diphtheria killed this girl.

"I think, then, that, with no injustice to the accused, you may adopt the pet theory of the defence, and conclude that this girl died of morphine poisoning. But, gentlemen, I shall now even admit more than that. Let us grant that a diseased kidney will cause accumulation of morphine, and that this girl had such a disease. More than that, let us admit that she had taken a considerable quantity of morphine prior to her illness, and that a large portion of it was held secreted in some part of her body. Now, what is the situation on that last evening of her life? She has been ill for several days with diphtheria, but she is recovering. She is so far convalescent that the senior physician deems it unnecessary for him to see her again that night. She also has slight kidney trouble, and she has some morphine stored up in her system; an amount, however, which has been tolerated throughout the attack of diphtheria, when vitality was at its lowest ebb, but which has neither acted fatally, nor even affected her so that symptoms of its presence attracted the attention of the doctors.

"Gentlemen of the jury, now follow me closely if you please. We can often bring witnesses to a murder where a weapon is used, but rare indeed is it that the poisoner is actually seen at his deadly work. But, by a singular act of Providence, that is what happened here. The prisoner arrived at that house that night, and dismissed the trained nurse. Observe that this occurs precisely upon the night when the patient has been declared to be convalescent. Here, then, is this man, a physician himself, alone in the presence of a weak woman. Does not this surely indicate to you that he had the opportunity to commit the foul deed? Supposing that he wished to rid himself of this girl, how gladly would he have awaited for her death by natural causes? How willingly have seen the dread diphtheria remove her from his path, and save his soul from the stain of crime? But no! It was not to be! On this night, his skilled eye saw what the other doctors had seen. The girl would recover! If she was to die, it must be by his hand. Now how should he accomplish it? By what means rid himself of the girl, and be safe from the hangman himself. Here the diabolical working of a scientific mind reveals itself. As he has told us he well knew her condition. He knew that she had kidney disease. He knew that she had been taking morphine, and readily guessed that some of the deadly drug was still stored up in her system. If he administered morphine to this poor woman, infatuated alike with the drug and with him, she would not offer the slightest remonstrance. No cry would escape her lips as the deadly needle punctured her fair flesh. Loving him and trusting him, she would yield to his suggestion, and so go into the last sleep. But what of the after effects? He certainly would think of that? Why, certainly! The girl would die of coma, and the attending physicians, if summoned in time, would say that she died of anæmia caused by diphtheria. Or, even if suspicion were aroused, it might be claimed afterwards, just, gentlemen, as it has been claimed, that the drug was self-administered, and was not enough in itself to have proven fatal. He knew that the autopsy would substantiate his claim of kidney trouble, and that the toxicologists would admit the effect upon morphine. But more than all, being himself something of an expert in all branches of medical science, and especially in chemistry, he could almost to a nicety gauge the quantity of the drug which would be required, which of itself might not prove fatal to a morphine *habitué*, but which would compass her death when added to what was already in her system. Chance seemed to favor his horrible design, for Dr. Fisher had left his syringe and a supply of the drug. See this fiend, this scientific wife murderer, measure out and prepare the lethal dose! See him pierce the yielding flesh and inject the deadly drug, and then, lo! Providence brings upon the scene a witness to the deed! The nurse returns unexpectedly and sees, gentlemen, mark my words, actually sees this man in the act of using the hypodermic syringe!

"What can he do? He knows that it would be hazardous to deny the testimony of this trained nurse. Therefore he admits what she tells us, and then ingeniously invents the explanation that he was removing the syringe, but had not made the injection. But I submit it to you, gentlemen, is that a probable tale? If this girl had time to prepare the drug, to fill the syringe, to pierce her flesh, to inject the drug, would she not have been able to remove it herself? Does it take ten minutes to withdraw a needle? Or five minutes, or one minute? Or one second, gentlemen? Can you even compute the brief moment of time in which the withdrawal could have been effected? Mr. Bliss told you that the testimony of the accused must be final on this point. That until he is convicted of crime his word is as acceptable as that of any other witness. This may be a presumption of law, gentlemen, but it is a still greater presumption on the part of counsel to ask such intelligent men as you are, to believe that a murderer, or even an innocent man, would not perjure himself to save his life! Such things are told in romance, but we know that in actual life the most scrupulous of us all, will lie unhesitatingly if life itself be the stake.

"Thus, gentlemen, the whole thing comes to this. It matters not how much morphine this woman had taken herself, prior to her illness; it matters not how diseased were her kidneys: the cause of her death was that last dose of morphine, and you have to decide whether this man administered it as the nurse tells us, or whether the weak convalescent mixed and prepared the drug, and then injected it herself. We claim that Dr. Medjora administered that last dose, and that by that act he committed the crime of murder. And remember this, that if you decide that he administered that morphine, your verdict must be murder in the first degree, for having denied that he gave the drug at all, he cannot claim now that he gave it with no intention to destroy life. Gentlemen, you are the final arbiters in this matter."

The Recorder immediately charged the jury, but though he spoke at considerable length, I need scarcely give his speech here, as it was chiefly an explanation of the law. He was eminently impartial in all that he said, and it was surprising, therefore, how many objections and exceptions were entered by the defence. At last the jury was sent out, and the long wait began. The hours passed slowly and still those present remained in their seats, loath to risk being absent when the verdict should be announced.

It was nearly ten o'clock at night, and the jury had been out five hours, when word was sent in, that a verdict had been found. The Recorder a few moments later resumed his seat, and the jury filed in. After the usual formalities, the foreman arose and announced the following verdict:

"We find the prisoner, Dr. Emanuel Medjora, not guilty."

The words were received almost in silence by all present. Above the stillness a deep sob was heard at the farther end of the room. This had escaped from the tightly compressed lips of Madame Cora Corona.

BOOK 2

CHAPTER I
ONE NIGHT

"Leon! Leon!"

The cry was low and weak, and the suffering woman fell back upon her pillow. The youth, though asleep, heard, and quickly responded to the call. He had been sitting in the large arm-chair, beside a rude wooden table, upon which stood a common glass lamp, with red wick, whose flickering flame shed but a dim ray across the well-thumbed pages of a book which lay open. While reading under such unfavorable circumstances, the boy had slumbered, his mind drifting slowly toward dream-land, yet not beyond the voice of the sufferer. She had scarcely repeated his name, when he was kneeling beside her, speaking in a voice that was tender and solicitous.

"What is it, mother?" he asked.

"Nothing," was the reply.

"Do you wish to drink?"

"No."

"Are you in pain?"

"Yes. But no matter."

"Will you take your medicine?"

"No. Leon, I want to tell you something."

"Not to-night, mother. You must sleep to-night. To-morrow you may talk."

"Leon, when I sleep to-night, it will be forever."

"Do not talk so, mother. You are nervous. Perhaps the darkness oppresses you. I will turn up the light."

He did so, but the lamp only spluttered, flaring up brighter for a moment, only to burn as dull as before.

"You see," said the old woman, with a ghastly smile, "there will be no more light in my life."

"Indeed there will be."

"I tell you no!" She spoke fiercely, and summoned all her waning energy to her aid, as she struggled to raise herself upon her elbow. Then, extending a bony finger in his direction and shaking it in emphasis of her words, she continued: "I tell you I am dying. Death is here; in this room; I see his form, and I feel his cold fingers on my forehead. Sh! Sh! Listen! Do you not hear?

A voice from the darkness is calling–'Confess! Confess!'" Then with a feeble cry she dropped back, moaning and groaning as in anguish.

"Mother! Mother! Lie still! Do not talk so." Leon was much agitated by the scene which had just transpired. The woman was quiet for a time, except that she sobbed, but presently she addressed him again.

"Leon, I must talk. I must tell. But don't call me mother."

"Why not?

How frequently in life do we thus rush ruthlessly upon unsuspected crises in our fates? Leon said these words, with no thought of their import, and with no foreboding of what would follow. How could he guess that from the moment of their utterance his life would be changed, and his boyhood lost to him forever, because of the momentousness of the reply which he invited?

When the woman spoke again, her voice was so low that the youth leaned down to hear her words. She said:

"Leon, you have been a good son to me. But–I am not your mother." Having spoken the words with a sadness in her heart, which found echo in the cadence of her voice, she turned her face wearily away from the youth, and waited for his reply. And he, though astounded by what he had heard, did not at the time fully connect the words with himself, but recognized only the misery which their utterance had caused to the suffering woman. With gentleness as tender as a loving woman's, he turned her face to his, touched her lips with his, and softly said:

"You are my mother! The only mother that I have ever known!" Oh! The weakness of human kind, which, at the touch of a loving hand, the sound of a loving voice, yields up its most sacred principles! This dying woman had lived from birth till now in a secluded New England village, and, imbibing her puritanical instincts from her ancestry, she almost deemed it a sin to smile, or show any outward sign of happiness. She had been a mother to this boy, according to her bigoted ideas; she had been good to him in her own way; but she had kissed him but once, and then he was going upon a journey. Yet now, as overcome by his intense sympathy, his long-suppressed love welled out from his heart toward her, with a happy cry she nestled close within his arms, and cried for joy, a joy that was hers for the first time, yet which might have illumined all her declining days, had she not brushed it away from her.

A long silence ensued, presently broken by the woman, as she slowly related the following story.

"Years ago, no matter how many, I was a pretty woman, and a vain one. I had admirers, but I loved none as I loved myself. But at last one came, and then my life was changed. I loved him, and I began to despise myself. For the more I saw and loved him, the less likely it seemed that he could love me. I used all my arts in vain. My prettiest frocks, my most coquettish glances, were all wasted on him. It seemed to me that I had not even made him see that I might be won, if he would woo. He went away, and I thought that I would never meet him again, for he had been but a summer visitor. My heart was broken, and besides my pride was hurt, for I suffered the bitterness of being taunted with my failure by my sisters. A year later, he came to me again. Several months before, I had gone to live in Boston, but in some way he had found me out. To my surprise, he told me that he knew that I loved him. He said that he had not offered me his love, because he was already married. Then he asked me to do him a favor. I gladly assented, without knowing what he would ask, for I would have sacrificed anything for him, I loved him so. The next day he brought me a beautiful baby boy. He told me it was his, that his wife was ill, and that he wished me to care for the baby for a year, whilst he went to Europe. I undertook the charge, without considering the consequences. I returned to the farm, bound to secrecy as to the child's parentage. Very soon I discovered that my friends shunned me, and then I learned that by taking you, Leon, I had lost my good name. Well! I did not care. You were his baby! You had his eyes, and so my heart grew hard against the world, but I determined to keep the baby whose fingers had already gripped my heart. Then, shut out from all friendships, scorned even by my sisters to whom I had refused to make any explanation, I began to pray that something, anything, would happen so that you should not be taken from me. My wicked prayer was answered, for later I learned that the young mother had died, and I was to continue caring for you. At first my joy was very great, but soon I recognized, that you were mine only because I had prayed for the death of your mother. The Lord had granted my wish, as an everlasting punishment for my sinful longing. Thenceforward, however much I yearned to press you to my heart, I have not dared to do so. I have tried to accept the chastisement of the Lord with meekness of spirit. And so I have had my wish! I have kept you with me, ever to be a reproach for my sin. But I thank the Lord, that at the end he has allowed me to have one full moment of happiness. He has granted me the boon to see that my boy has learned to love me in spite of all my harshness. You have kissed me, Leon, and called me mother. Oh! God! Thy will be done!"

Then with a smile almost of beatitude, she sank down lower, and nestled closer to her long-denied love. Leon stooped and kissed her again, but did not speak. His heart was full, and his emotions rose within his breast, so that he felt a curious sensation of fulness in his throat, which warned him not to essay speech.

In silence they remained so for a time, not computed by either. She was lost in thoughts such as have been aroused in many hearts by the poet's magic words, "It might have been!" This boy was his, and might have been hers, if—! Ah! What chasms have been bridged by these two letters, which form this little, mighty word!

Leon began to grasp, but slowly, all that the future would hold for him with the added knowledge granted to him this night. He pondered over the past, and remembering how stern had been his life, and how austere had been the manner of this woman who had been his mother, and adding up the sum of all, he wondered that he had found such love for her within his heart. For his love had been recognized by himself as suddenly as he had given fervent expression to it, when he embraced that mother who denied her motherhood. If the poet's words which I have quoted conceal a thought of sadness within their meaning, what woe resides within the thought encompassed by those other words, "Too late!" To both of these, the woman and the boy, the recognition of the joys of love, had come too late. As this thought at last penetrated the mind of the dreaming youth, he started, awakening from his abstraction. At the same moment, the lamp flared up, flickered, and went out. Then as darkness enshrouded him, so deep that he almost felt it touch his brow, he shivered, and a long moan escaped him followed by an anguished cry:

"Mother!"

At last he realized what he had heard. In two ways was he to lose what all good men hold dearest on this earth: a mother. First, she denied the relationship; second, she had told him that she was dying. No answer came back to his cry. The woman in his arms made no sound. She did not stir. He leaned his ear against her heart. It had ceased to beat. She was dead. Her spirit had slipped away, unnoticed by the loving boy whose arms encircled her shrivelled form, but whose love full surely lighted her way up among the stars! Up, to that mysterious realm, too vast for human thought, too limitless for human mind; where the sinning and the sinless meet their deserts. However much of wrong or of error there had been in her life, in the moment of death she found true happiness; and I am grateful to her for arousing the thought, that we may all end our lives in peace. And so I leave her.

But the boy? The youth now left to buffet with the world alone? I will ask you to follow him as, with a heart crowded with anguish and resentment, he rushed bareheaded out into the night, and swiftly sped through the wood. For he is well worth following. He has reached an important epoch in his life, a turning point at which he abandons his boyish past and becomes a man.

Could he have been asked why he ran, or whither, he would have found himself bewildered and at a loss for a reply. Yet it is easily explainable. His home-life had never been attractive to him, nor in any way satisfying to his temperament, which, indeed, as we shall see, was such that he was ever in ill-concealed rebellion against the restraints of his surroundings, which threatened to crush his intellectual yearnings. Nevertheless, it was his home, so endeared to him by long association, that the sudden realization of the complex idea, first, that he did love this home, and second that he would now lose it forever, coming to him instantaneously, overwhelmed him.

He felt a dull pain in his breast, which made him almost imagine that some heavy body had been thrust within his bosom, and weighed heavily against his heart, interfering with that vital organ, so that the blood coursed sluggishly, and the lungs were loath to do their duty. Thus stifling, though only in imagination, he was instinctively compelled to rush out into the air, which cooled the fever in his veins. He ran, impelled by a mysterious feeling akin to fear, yet not fear, which exists within the breasts of all mankind, however loudly one individual may declare himself exempt, and which is aroused when one is suddenly brought into the presence of the dead, alone, and for the first time. Leon had never seen death before, although he had of course seen the dead, coffined and made ready for the grave. But he now passed through an entirely new experience. In one moment he held within his arms a living, breathing being whom he loved; and in the next he gazed upon a voiceless, senseless, shocking thing, and loathed it. It was from this thing, and from the house where this thing now lay, that he was running. But, as I have said, he did not know it at the time, and probably would have spurned the suggestion a day later. But, the fact remains that it was true.

Where he was going, is explainable by a simpler course of analysis. He was going to the lake. He was going to his boat. He was going out upon the water away from the companionship of that dead thing on land. He was going out upon the water, to be alone, and to find solace in his loneliness. In this, he but followed involuntarily a habit which he had practised for several years. When his home-life had pressed most hardly upon him at times, he had slipped away from the little farm, and rowed his boat out upon the lake, for self-communion and comfort. So now, without realizing that he had chosen any special direction in his flight, or that he had any fixed purpose in his mind, he ran swiftly along the wood-choppers' path, until at length he stopped panting on a bit of narrow beach. He stood silent for a moment, and then concluded to get his boat and go out upon the lake. Or rather, he thought that he formed this decision at that moment, but really it originated when he turned towards the lake, rather than towards the next neighbor. It was therefore not companionship, but solitude which he sought.

Within five minutes he was rowing lustily across the mirror-like surface of Massabesic, out towards the widest portion. The day had been insufferably warm, it being mid-summer, but in this region the nights are usually cool. This night was balmy.

Mars had appeared, a glowing red ball, above the eastern horizon, early in the evening, and an hour later the almost full moon had climbed up high enough to shed her silver rays across the waters. Later still the breeze had died away, and slowly the bosom of the lake grew quiet, as though even the waters had drifted into slumberous repose. When Leon started out in his boat, almost immediately his ruffled soul recognized the influence of the deadly calm surrounding him, for though at first he dipped his oars deep, and rowed vigorously, making the light bark leap upward at every pull, before he had gone a quarter of a mile, he stroked his oars with lessening vehemence, and presently, as though thoroughly awed by the stillness, and fearful of creating the noise even of a ripple, he was straining every nerve to dip and withdraw his oars, and to move his boat along without a sound. After a few minutes of this, he slowly raised both oars, letting them rest across the gunwales until the last drop of water had dripped off, and the last series of circles caused thereby had disappeared, and then, with the care and delicacy of one who moves about a chamber where some loved one is asleep who must not be disturbed, he placed his oars gently in the boat, and sat motionless.

Already Mars had almost reached the tops of the trees along the western banks, and, attracted by it, Leon gazed upon the planet until it disappeared. He had been still for ten minutes, and having recognized that all was quiet about him, and having abandoned his rowing, he was now mildly surprised to observe that his boat was in a totally different position; that in fact he had drifted a long distance. This awakened him slightly from his reverie, for here was a new bit of knowledge about a body of water with which he had been acquainted since his earliest recollection. He had never known, nor even suspected, that in a calm there could be a current. He endeavored to calculate by observation how fast he was moving; but the task was difficult. He could readily discern that since abandoning his oars he had moved a hundred yards, but, however intently he gazed upon the shores, he could not detect that he was moving. He pondered over this for a time, and being of a philosophical turn of mind, and fond of speculating, he likened his position at the moment, to life in general. However little we suspect it, there is an unseen but potent energy which urges us forward towards—the grave, and—whatever follows death.

This idea pleased him for a moment, for the analogy was a new one and original with himself, in so far, that he had never head it from another. Quickly, however, returning to the more practical problem, he determined to find a way to ascertain the rapidity with which his boat was moving. Placing a fishing-rod upright before him, and then closing one eye, gazing with the other at a conspicuous object along the horizon, immediately he could see, not only that he was moving, but that the motion was more rapid than he had suspected. Having thus satisfied the immediate and momentary questioning of an inquiring mind, his previous mental state, his loneliness and desolation, returned upon him with redoubled force. A moment later, Nature offered him another abstraction. Looking into the water he saw mirrored there the reflection of the moon. Not the stream of undulating silver over which poets have raved these many years, and which painters have fruitlessly essayed to convey to canvass, but the glorious, full, round orb itself. This he had never seen before, and he wondered why it should be. Almost as though in answer to his thought, a faint zephyr breathed across the surface of the waters, and beginning near the shores, the ripples rolled towards him, and with them brought the shimmering moonlight until all in a moment, the reflected orb had disappeared, and the usual silvery line of light replaced it. Thus he saw, that only water in motion will show the moonbeams, whilst a mirror, whether it be of glass, or the still bosom of the lake, reflects but the moon itself.

Again he returned to the bitterness of his night's experience, and now, no longer attracted by the moon, and not caring how fast or whither he drifted, he lay back in his boat, pillowing his head upon a cushion on the seat in the stern, and gazed up into the sky thus oblivious of the landscape and so without an indication of his progress.

His mind reverted to the house, and the dead woman. She was not his mother. Then who was she? Or rather who was he? She was, or had been, Margaret Grath, and he had thought that he was entitled to the name Leon Grath. But if she was not, or had not been, his mother, then plainly he had no right to her name. On considering this, he concluded that it was his privilege to call himself Leon, but the last name Grath, being obtainable legally only by inheritance, he must abandon. When the word "inheritance" crossed his thoughts, involuntarily a loud mocking laugh escaped him. And when the sonorous echoes laughed with him, he laughed again, and again. The drollery which aroused his mirth, was that, if a name might be inherited, why might not Margaret Grath have bequeathed hers to him? Perhaps she might have mentioned it in her will? But no! A name is a heritage acquired at birth, whilst only chattels are included in an inheritance which follows a death. Evidently he was nameless, except that he might be called Leon, just as his collie answered to the name Lossy. This made him laugh again. For now he thought that his dog had fared better than himself, for he was called "The Marquis of Lossy," after MacDonald's Malcolm. Thus the collie was of noble blood, whilst he was—only Leon, the child of nobody. As he reached this point, the moon dipped down below the western hill, the upper edge shedding its last rays across the boy and his boat, after which he was indeed enshrouded by the night. It seemed colder too, now that the orb had gone, and insensibly he felt in some way more alone. True, there were the stars, still twinkling in the firmament, but they seemed far away, like his own future. Still Leon dreamed on.

As he could not lift the veil which parted him from what was to be, he wandered back in thought, recalling what had been.

The Theosophist says that man has lived before upon this planet, inhabiting many corporeal forms, and drifting through many earthly existences. The Sceptic cries: "Ridiculous! but, granting the postulate, of what advantage is it to have lived before, or to live again, if in each earth-life I cannot recall those that have gone before?" Yet, without arguing for Theosophy, might I not remind this sceptic that he enjoys his life to-day, even though he might find it difficult to recall yesterday, or the day before, or a week, a month, a year ago? How many of us in looking backward over life's path, can summon up the phantoms of more than a few days? Days on which occurred some events of special moment?

The first landmark along his life's path, which stood out conspicuous among Leon's garnered memories, was his first visit to the church. Margaret Grath had dressed him in his brightest frock, curled his hair, and placed upon his head his newest bonnet. His heart had swelled with pride, as he trotted beside the tall, gaunt, New England woman, who walked with long strides, and held his hands, lest he should lag behind. But though his legs grew tired, he offered no rebellion, for he had often looked upon the red brick building, with wondering eyes, and his ears had oft been mystified at the tolling of the bell which swung and sounded, though moved by no hand that he could see, nor means that he could understand. He marvelled at the outside of the building, its steeple marking it a house apart from every other in the village, and he long had yearned to see it from within. On this day, to which his thought now turned, he had his wish. He followed Miss Grath down the aisle, clinging to her skirts, a little frightened at the people sitting straight and stiff, and he was rejoiced when he found himself at last on a comfortable cushion in the pew. The cushion was a treat; being his first experience with such luxury, and confirmed his idea that the church was better than other houses. Presently he began to be accustomed to his surroundings, having viewed all the walls, the roof, the organ, and the pulpit, until his active mind was satisfied so far as concerned the building itself. Then he began to feel the silence, and he did not like it. He longed to speak, but did not dare, because when he timidly looked up, Miss Grath, catching his glance, scowled reproachfully, and looked straight before her. Small and young as he was, he had learned to know this woman with whom he lived, and he needed no more explicit warning to hold his tongue. So he sat still, adding to the silence which oppressed him.

It was with a sigh of relief that he saw the preacher rise, and heard him speak; and it was with a throb of intense joy that his heart warmed as the notes of the organ reached him for the first time in his life. Thenceforward he was interested up to the point where the sermon began. The tiresome monotone in which this was delivered, and the impossibility of his comprehending what was said, soon fatigued his little brain, and then lulled him to sleep.

I may mention parenthetically, what of course did not now enter Leon's mind, for he never knew the subject of that first sermon which had been preached at him. If it had been incomprehensible to the child, the woman had understood well enough, for it had been aimed at her especially. The preacher, I cannot call him a minister, for he truly ministered unto none except himself, the preacher then, was a cold, hard Scotchman, High Church of course. He firmly believed in the damnation of infants, and a Hell of which the component parts would be brimstone and fire in proper proportions. He also believed in the efficacy of prayer, especially of his own. Therefore, it not infrequently happened, that when any one incurred his ill will, which was not difficult, he would offer up a prayer, consigning said individual to the hottest tortures of the world below. He did this so adroitly, that, while there were no plain personalities in his words, his description of the sinner would be so specific, that the party of the second part readily identified himself as the central figure of the excoriation.

Now this saintly preacher had at one time demeaned himself, or so he thought, sufficiently low to offer himself in marriage to Miss Margaret Grath. She had declined the honor, and he had hated her ever after. Like all true women, however, she had kept his secret, so that none of the congregation knowing the relation which existed, or which might have existed, between them, none could read between the lines of his sermons, when he chose to lash her by a savage denunciation of any mild backsliding, of which she might have been guilty, and himself cognizant. Her return to the village with the child, who had no visible father, and no mother, unless the guesses of the gossips were correct, had afforded him opportunity for a most masterly peroration. But he belched forth his greatest eloquence on that Sunday morning, when she had the temerity to bring into the sacred confines of his sanctuary this fatherless boy, for whose sake she had chosen to live a lonely life. If his prayer of that morning proved efficacious, then surely the infant was damned, and the woman's soul consigned to endless Purgatory. Thus the day to which Leon recurred in thought, was a landmark in another life beside his, and I have turned aside for a moment to relate this incident, that the character of Miss Grath may be better comprehended, for in spite of all that she had suffered through the animosity of the preacher, she had never omitted attendance at church, when it was a physical possibility for her to get there. It must be true that some of her determination and will descended from her to the boy, because association means more than heredity.

The next occurrence in his life, which now occupied his thoughts, was a day long after, when he was nearing his twelfth year. He was off on a hunting expedition, and had climbed a mountain. Careless in leaping from crag to crag, he landed upon a loose boulder, which rolled from under his feet, so that he was thrown. In falling, his foot twisted, and a moment later, intense pain made him aware that he could not walk upon it. For four hours he slowly, but pluckily, dragged himself down the mountain, and at last reached home. It so chanced that a celebrated physician from New York was spending a vacation in the neighborhood, attracted perhaps by the brooks, which were full of fish. This man was Dr. Emanuel Medjora, and having heard of the boy's hurt, he voluntarily visited the lonely farm-house, and attended upon him so skilfully that Leon soon was well.

Just why the thought of Dr. Medjora should come to him at this time was a problem to Leon, but one upon which he did not dwell. After that summer, he had seen the Doctor again at various times, two or three years apart, always at vacation-time. But it was now three years since they had met.

Swiftly his thoughts passed along the years of his life, until they stopped for a moment, arrested by an incident worthy of being chronicled. I have said that Leon lay in his boat, face skyward, and allowed his bark to drift whither it would. Thus he had not noted his progress until a crunching sound startled him, and he became aware that his boat had found a landing-place, having grounded amidst the sands of a little cove, sheltered by a high rock and overhanging shrubbery. Forced thus from his abstraction into some cognizance of his whereabouts, Leon, without raising his head, merely became aware of the branches and leaves overhead, and peered through them. Almost in the midst of the green, he saw what seemed to be a brilliant but monstrous diamond, pendent from a branch. In the next instant he recognized that he was gazing upon Venus, the morning star, which had risen during his reverie, and now shone resplendent and most beautiful. It was just at this moment, that the incident occurred to which I have alluded. Suddenly it seemed to him that the whole of his surroundings were familiar. Everything had occurred before. His boat drifting into the cove, the shrubbery overhead, and Venus in the sky; all that he now realized, in the most minute detail, had held a place in his experience before. Such a phenomenon is not uncommon. All of us have been impressed similarly. Indeed, some Theosophists, trying to prove a previous life for man, have reverted to this well-known feeling, and have claimed that here is a recollection of a former visit to this earth. But Leon, young philosopher though he was, would have laughed in scorn at such an argument. He had considered this problem, and had solved it satisfactorily for himself. His explanation was thus. Man's brain is divided into two hemispheres. Usually they act co-ordinately, but it is possible that, at least momentarily, they may operate independently. It is a fact that the phenomenon under consideration seldom, or never occurs, except when the mind is greatly interested or occupied. Something, perhaps in itself the merest trifle, diverts the mind from the intensity of its attention. This diversion leads by a train of circumstances to a long-forgotten memory, and one hemisphere of the brain reverts to a moment in the past, the other continuing intent upon its surroundings. Within an infinitesimal period of time, a period too brief to be calculable, both hemispheres are again acting in unison. The abstraction has been so brief, and the cause of it is so dimly defined, that the mind is oblivious of what has occurred, except that, as the diverted hemisphere again takes cognizance of its previous thoughts, and again recognizes the environment of the present, the phenomenon of a dual experience is noted. Of course the scene is identically the same as that which is remembered, because it is the same scene. And the previous experience will impress the individual as having occurred long ago, in exact proportion to the date of that circumstance to which one hemisphere has reverted.

Therefore, Leon did not, at this time, speculate upon the mystery, which he thought he understood, but he welcomed the advent of a long-sought opportunity, to trace out the cause of such an abstraction, so fleeting in its nature.

He was occupied thus, for half an hour, but at length believed that he had analyzed the experience. The turning-point, at which he had been diverted, was when he first recognized Venus. And now he remembered that occasion when he had gone upon a journey. Away from his home for the first time in his life, he felt many sensations which I need not record here. But one amusement had been to sit at night studying the stars, and from them fixing the position of the buildings on the home farm, in relation to those where he was then abiding. One evening, when watching Venus, then the evening star, he was looking across a pool of water, and trying to imagine himself back on Massabesic, with the same planet setting behind the western hill, when, turning his head, he saw a young and beautiful girl standing near him. As his eyes abandoned the planet for the woman, he was startled by the thought that the goddess had been re-embodied. A moment later, the girl asked him for some information relating to the nearest way to her home, which he gave, and she walked on. He had never seen her since, nor had he thought of her again. But now, having analyzed his thoughts and traced them back from the star to that girl, her face thus summoned seemed to take the place of the planet in the heavens, and to gaze down upon him with an assuring smile, which somehow made him feel that the future might hold something for him after all.

What that something might be, he did not even try to guess. Therefore, you must not adopt the conclusion that Leon thus suddenly fell in love with a girl whose face had been seen by him but once. No idea within his mind, connected with that face, was now coupled with a thought of her as an earthly being. He merely summoned up the image of a lovely being, and felt himself refreshed, and hope returning.

A few moments later the twilight brightened and the first red border of the sun, peeping over the tops of the trees, shed a warming ray upon Leon, thus awakened from his dreamy night into the first day of his manhood.

CHAPTER II
A FRIEND IN NEED

On a bright, warm morning, a week later, Leon had already arisen, though it was barely past five o'clock, and having wandered off into a secluded spot in the woods, lay on the ground, his head pillowed against a tree trunk. Margaret Grath had been laid away beneath the sod, and the old home was no longer homelike to him, since her two sisters had moved in, to take possession until "the auction" which was to occur on this day.

He had never liked these women, and they had lavished no affection upon him. Consequently he was uneasy in their presence, and so avoided them. They had plainly told him that he was no kith nor kin of theirs, and that though he might abide on the farm till the auction, after that event he would be obliged to shift for himself. They also volunteered the advice that he should leave the town, and added that if he did so it would be a good riddance. To all of these kind speeches Leon had listened in silence, determined that he would earn his living without further dependence upon this family, upon whom he now thought that he had already intruded too long, though unknowingly.

Now, as he lay among the fresh mosses, and inhaled the sweet scents of surrounding blossoms which lifted their drooping heads, and unfolded their petals to the kisses of the newly risen sun, he was musing upon the necessities of his situation, while in a measure taking a last farewell of haunts which he had learned to love.

Presently, a sound of rustling twigs arrested his attention, and he saw a tiny chipmunk looking at him. He smiled, and pursing up his lips emitted a sound which was neither whistle, nor warble, but a combination of both. The little creature flirted his head to one side, as though listening. Leon repeated the call a little louder, and with a sudden dash the chipmunk swiftly sped towards him, as suddenly stopping about ten yards away. Here he sat up on his haunches, and, with his forefeet, apparently caressed his head. Now Leon changed his method, and sounded a prolonged and musical trill, like the purling of a brook. The chipmunk came nearer and nearer, his timidity gradually passing away. And now, in the distance, another rush through the shrubbery was heard, and another chipmunk swiftly came out into the open, presently joining his mate, and approaching nearer and nearer to Leon, in short runs. At length they were quite close to him, and he took some peanuts from his pocket. One at a time he threw this tempting food to the little animals, who quickly nibbled off the outer shell and abstracted the kernels, sitting up, their tails gracefully curled over their backs. As Leon continued his chirping to his wild pets, two searching eyes were gazing with intense interest upon the scene. And the man who owned those eyes thought thus of what he saw:

"He has inherited the power. It is untrained at present, but it will be easily developed."

A few moments later, Leon waved his hand and the chipmunks scurried off, leaving the youth once more to his meditations. But soon again he was interrupted. This time the noise of the approaching creature was readily discernible even while he was yet afar off, and in a few moments there came bounding through the brush a magnificent collie, sable and white, and beautifully marked. This was Lossy, or, rather, "The Marquis of Lossy," to give him his full title. Lossy was truly a perfect collie, with long pointed nose, eyes set high in the forehead, and beaming with human intelligence and a dog's love, which, we all know, transcends the human passion which goes by the same name; his ears were small and, at rest, carried so close to the head that, buried in the long fur they were scarcely discernible, yet, they pricked sharply forward when a sound attracted, giving the face that rakish look so peculiar to the species; and besides a grand coat of long, fine hair, and a heavy undercoat for warmth, he had a glorious bushy tail, carried at just the curve that lent a pleasing symmetry to the whole form. In short, Lossy was a collie that would prove a prize-winner in any company.

But what was better than mere physical beauty, he was an exception in intelligence, even for a collie, and lavished a wealth of love upon his young master. On this morning, Leon had purposely stolen away without the dog, for the pleasure of what now occurred. Lossy, finally awakening from his morning nap, and missing his master, had started after him taking almost the same course pursued by Leon. And now, after his long run, he bounded forward, landing upon Leon's breast with force enough to roll him over, and then, whining with joy at the reunion, the dog kissed his master's face and hands again and again.

This display of affection delighted Leon, and he returned it with unusual demonstrativeness. Rising from the ground, he snapped his fingers, and at the sound Lossy bounded into the air, to be caught in the arms of his master, hugged close to his bosom, and then dropped to the ground. This trick was repeated again and again, the dog responding with increasing impatience for the signal. Sometimes it was varied. Leon turning his back, and bending his body at a slight angle, would give the signal, whereupon Lossy would spring with agility upon his back and climb forward, until, by holding the shoulders with his forepaws, he could reach his head around, seeking to kiss Leon's face. Here the fun was, for as the dog's head protruded over one shoulder, Leon turned his face away, whereupon Lossy would quickly essay to reach his goal over the other. In the midst of this sort of play, Leon was surprised to hear his dog growl. Then Lossy leaped to the ground, his hair rose almost straight along his spine, his ears pricked forward, and again he growled ominously. Before Leon could step forward to investigate, the man who had been silently observing the whole scene stepped out, and Leon recognized Dr. Medjora.

While the two men gaze silently upon each other, I may take the opportunity to say a few words about Dr. Medjora.

Immediately after his trial he left New York for a brief period, very much against the wishes of Madam Corona. She pleaded with him for an immediate marriage, but he firmly adhered to his own plans. The wedding occurred, however, a year later, and he resumed the practice of his profession in the Metropolis. Nineteen years later, at the time when Margaret Grath died, he was counted one of the most eminent practitioners in the country. He had steadfastly declined to adopt surgery, that most fascinating field wherein great reputations are frequently acquired through a single audacious operation, happily carried to a successful termination; but instead, he remained the plain medical man, paying special attention to zymotic diseases. Within this sphere he slowly but no less surely acquired fame, as from time to time the dying were plucked almost from the arms of death, and restored to health and usefulness.

Attracting the admiration and esteem of his patients in a most remarkable degree, he nevertheless aroused in them a certain feeling of almost superstitious awe. People did not say aloud that Dr. Medjora was a partner of the Evil One, but many whispers, not easily traceable, finally resulted in his being commonly known as the "Wizard Doctor" or simply the "Wizard."

On this morning, having come into the vicinity during the week for some trout fishing, and then having learned of the auction sale about to take place, he had determined to be present. He was early on his way to the farm, when, crossing the strip of wood, he had first observed Leon with the chipmunks. Now having shown himself he spoke:

"You are Leon Grath, I believe?" said he.

"If you do, your belief is ill founded," replied Leon, speaking with no ill temper, but rather with a touch of sadness.

"Surely you are Leon—"

"I am Leon, but not Grath. You are Dr. Medjora?"

"Ah! Then you remember me?"

"Certainly! I remember all men, friend or foe. You have been more the former than the latter. Therefore the remembrance is quite distinct."

Hearing the sound of his master's voice, untinged by anger, the collie evidently decided that the newcomer was no enemy, and strolling off a short distance, turned thrice, and lay down, resting his nose between his two forepaws, and eying the twain, awaited developments.

"I am glad that you have pleasant recollections of our brief acquaintance. But now, will you explain what you mean by saying that you are not Leon Grath. I thought that Grath was your name?"

"So did I, Doctor, but I have learned that I was mistaken. I was with Margaret Grath when she died, and she told me—" He paused.

"She told you what?" asked Dr. Medjora, with apparent eagerness.

"That Grath is not my name."

"What then is it? Did she tell you that?"

"No! I am Leon, the nameless!"

There was a touch of bitterness in Leon's voice, and, as he felt a slight difficulty in enunciation caused by rising emotions, he turned away his head and gazed into the deepest part of the wood, closing his jaws tight together, and straining every muscle of his body to high tension, in his endeavor to regain full control of himself. Dr. Medjora observed the inward struggle for mastery of self, and admired the youth for his strength of character. Without, however, betraying that he had noticed anything, he said quietly:

"What will you do about it?"

"I will make a name for myself," was the reply given, with sharp decisiveness of tones, and a smile played around the corners of Leon's mouth, as though the open assertion of his purpose was a victory half won.

Oh, the springtime of our youth! The young man climbs to the top of the first hill, and, gazing off into his future, sees so many roads leading to fortune, that he hesitates only about the choice, not deeming failure possible by any path. But, presently, when his chosen way winds up the mountain-side, growing narrower and more difficult with every setting sun, at length he realizes the difference between expectation and fulfilment. But Leon was now on the top of his first hill, and climbing mountains seemed so brave a task that he was eager to begin. Therefore, he spoke boldly. Almost at once he met his first check.

"You will make a name for yourself!" repeated Dr. Medjora. "How? Have you decided?"

Leon felt at once confronted with the task which he had set himself. Now, the truth was that he had decided upon his way in life; or, rather, I should say he had chosen, and, having made his choice, he considered that he had decided the matter permanently. Yet, the first man who questioned him, caused him to doubt the wisdom of his choice, to hesitate about speaking of it, and to feel diffident, so that he did not answer promptly. Dr. Medjora watched him closely, and spoke again.

"Ah, I see; you think of becoming an author."

"How did you know that?" asked Leon, quickly, very much perplexed to find his secret guessed.

"Then it is a fact? You would not ask me how I know it, were it not true. I will answer your question, though it is of slight consequence. You are evidently a young man of strong will-power, and yet you became awkwardly diffident when I asked you what path in life you had elected to follow. I have observed that diffidence is closely allied to a species of shame, and that both are invariable symptoms of budding authorship. To one of your temperament, I should say that these feelings would come only from two causes, secret authorship and love. The latter being out of consideration, the former became a self-evident fact."

"Dr. Medjora, you seem to be a logician, and I should think that you might be a successful author yourself."

"I might be, but I am not. I could be, only I do not choose to be. But we are speaking of yourself. If you wish to be a writer, I presume that you have written something. Does it satisfy you; that is to say, do you consider that it is as excellent as it need be?"

"I have done a little writing. While thinking, this week, about my future, somehow there came to me a longing to write. I did so, and I have been over my little sketch so many times, that I cannot see wherein it is faulty. Therefore, I must admit, however conceited it may sound, that I am satisfied with it."

"That is a very bad sign. When a man is satisfied with his own work he has already reached the end of his abilities. It is only continual dissatisfaction with our efforts, that ever makes us ambitious to attain better things. You have said that, in your opinion, I could be a successful writer. Then let me read and judge what you have written. You have it with you, I suppose?"

Leon was much embarrassed. He wished that he could say no, but the composition was in his pocket. So he drew it out and handed it to Dr. Medjora, without saying a word. The Doctor glanced at it a moment and then said encouragingly:

"There is a quality in this, as excellent as it is rare. Brevity."

"Ah, Doctor!" said Leon, eagerly. "That is what I have aimed at. I have but a single idea to expound, and I have endeavored to clothe it in as few words as possible. Or, rather, I should say, I have tried to make every word count. Please read it with that view uppermost."

The Doctor nodded assent, and then read the little story, which was as follows:

IMMORTALITY.

I am dead!

Have you ever experienced the odd sensation of being present at your own funeral, as I am now?

Impossible! For you are alive!

But I? I am dead!

There lies my body, prone and stiff, uncoffined, whilst the grave-digger, by the light of the young moon, turns the sod which is to hide me away forever.

Or so he thinks.

Why should he, a Christian minister, stoop to dig a grave?

Why? Because minister though he be, he is, or was my master; and my murderer.

Murderer did I say? Was it murder to kill a dog?

For only a dog I was; or may I say, I am?

I stupidly tore up one of his sermons, in sport. For this bad, or good deed, my master, in anger, kicked me. He kicked me, and I died.

Was that murder? Or is the word applicable only to Man, who is immortal?

But stay! What is the test of immortality?

The ego says, "I am I," and earns eternity.

Then am I not immortal, since though dead, I may speak the charmed words?

No! For Christianity preaches annihilation to beast, and immortality for Man only. Man, the only animal that murders. Shall I be proof that Christianity contains a flaw?

Yet view it as you may, here I am, dead, yet not annihilated.

I say here I am, yet where am I?

How is it that I, stupid mongrel that I was, though true and loving friend, as all dogs are; how is it that I, who but slowly caught my master's meaning from his words, now understand his thoughts although he does not speak?

At last I comprehend. I know now where I am. I am within his mind. His eagerness to bury my poor carcass is but born of the desire to drive me thence.

But is not mind an attribute of the human soul, and conscience too? And are not both immortal?

Thus then the problem of my future do I solve. Let this good Christian man hide under ground my carcass; evidence of his foul crime. And being buried, let it rot. What care I though it should be annihilated?

I am here, within this man's immortal mind, and here I shall abide forever more, and prick his conscience for my pastime.

Thus do I win immortality, and cheat the Christian's creed.

Having read to the end, Dr. Medjora nodded approvingly to Leon and said:

"For a first composition, you may well rest satisfied with this. It is very subtile. Indeed I am surprised at the originality and thought which you have displayed here. I should like to discuss with you some of the points. May I?"

"With pleasure," Leon replied with ardor, delighted to find his little story so well received.

"The first thought that occurs to me is, that there is a certain amount of inspiration about your essay. I say essay because it is that rather than a story. From this, I deduce a fact discouraging to your ambition, for inspirations are rare, and it is probable that were you to succeed in selling this to some magazine, you would find it difficult to produce anything else as good."

"Why, Doctor," said Leon, anxious to prove his ability, "I wrote that in a few minutes."

"By which statement you mean that with time for thought, you might do better. But your argument is in favor of my theory. The more rapidly you wrote this, the more difficult will it be for you to write another. Let me tell you what I read between the lines here. Miss Grath having died, you were left alone in the world. Her two amiable sisters coming to the farm, probably made your loneliness intensified, and whilst depressed by your mood, your dog showed you some affection, which reaching you when your heart was full, caused it to spill over, and this was the result. Am I wrong?"

"No! You have guessed the circumstances almost exactly. As you say, I was feeling lonely and depressed. I came here for solitude, which is something different from loneliness, and which is as soothing as loneliness is depressing. I was sitting under that tree, thinking bitter things of the world in general, and of the people about me more especially, when without my having heard him approach, my dog, Lossy, dear old brute, pushed his head over my shoulders, placed his paws around my neck, and kissed me. It affected me deeply. It was as though I had received a message from Providence, telling me not to despair. Then like a flash it came to me, that if love is an attribute of the soul, and a dog's love is the most unselfish of all, it must follow logically that a dog has a soul."

"Your deduction is correct, if there be any such thing as soul. But, for the moment, I will not take that up. You have told enough to show that I am right as to the origin of your tale. It is also evident that you cannot hope to be under such emotional excitement at all times, when you might be called upon to write; to write or go without a meal. However, I have faith in you, and do not doubt that we shall find a way for you to earn as many meals as you shall need."

"Do you mean that you will assist me?"

"I will assist you, if I am correct in my present opinion of you. Young men who need and expect assistance, are rarely worthy of help. But I wish to talk about your essay. I like the line 'Was it murder to kill a dog?' and the one which follows, 'For only a dog I was; or may I say, I am?' Of course the word murder, strictly applied, means the killing of a man by his fellow. I think I comprehend what you mean here, but I would like you to explain it to me."

"Doctor, you compliment me by taking this so seriously. There is a deeper meaning in the words than might be detected by a superficial reader. As you say, the word murder applies only to the killing of a man, by a man. Or I might change the wording and say, the killing of a human being. Here, human implies the possession of those higher attributes, the aggregate of which is the soul, which by man is arrogantly claimed to exist exclusively in man. And it is the violent separation of this soul from its earthly body, which makes it the heinous crime, murder; while the beast, not possessing a soul, may be killed without scruple, and without crime. Hence I say, 'Was it murder to kill a dog?' and at once, in so few words, I raise the question as to whether the dog has not a soul."

"I follow you. Your explanation is only what I expected. I said that I liked the next line: 'For only a dog I was; or may I say, I am?' This time I will show you that I comprehend you. The question here implies much. If the dog is annihilated at death, then this dog ceased to exist when his master slew him. But he is speaking; he realizes that he continues to exist. Therefore, he says most pertinently, 'or may I say, I am?' The question carries its own affirmative, for what is not, cannot question its own existence. The subtilty here is very nice. You convince your reader by presenting what seems to be a self-evident proposition, and if he admits this, he must accord immortality to the dog, for he that after death may say 'I am' is immortal. But the flaw, which you have so well hidden, lies in the fact that you have started with the assumption of that which you have essayed to prove. You make the dead dog speak, which would be an impossibility had he been annihilated."

"I am delighted, Doctor, at the way in which you criticise me. But I am contending that the dog is immortal, hence my assumption at the very start, that though dead, he may record his sensations. I do not really mean to discuss the point, nor to prove it. I merely mean dogmatically to assume it. I picture a dog, who in life believed that death would be his total extinction, but who, when suddenly deprived of life, finds that he is still in existence, and endeavors to analyze his condition. If you will overlook the seeming egotism of pointing out what I think the most subtle idea, I would call your attention to the line where, concluding that he is immortal, he says 'Here I am,' and instantly asks 'Where am I?'"

"Yes. I had already admired that and what follows; but I will ask you to expound it yourself."

"You are very kind," said Leon, pleased, and eager to talk upon his subject. "He asks where he is, and after a moment decides that he is in his master's mind. Then he argues truly that, as mind is but a part, or attribute of the soul, if the soul be immortal, the mind and all that it contains must live on, also. Therefore, being in the man's mind, he needs only to stay there, to escape annihilation. Then he adds, that he will prick the man's conscience forever. Here is something more than a mere dogmatism. None will deny that the wanton killing of a dog can never be forgotten, and if the dog remains in one's mind, is not that a sort of immortality?"

"Sophistry, my boy, sophistry; but clever. The idea is original, and well conceived for the purpose of your narrative. But, like many deductions assumed to be logical, it is illogical, because your premises are wrong. It is not the dog, nor his spirit, that abides in the mind and assails the conscience. What the man tries in vain to forget is the thought of killing the beast, and thought, of course, is immutable; but it does not at all follow that the thing of which we think is imperishable."

"I see your meaning, Doctor, and of course you are right. But do you side with the Christian, and claim that the dog is annihilated, while man is immortal?"

"A discussion upon religious topics is seldom profitable. In reply to your question, I think that you will be satisfied if I admit that the dog is as surely immortal as man. No more so, and no less. The Christian hypothesis, in this respect, is a unique curiosity to a thinking man, at best. We are asked to believe that man is first non-existent; then in a moment he begins to exist, or is born; then he dies, but, nevertheless, continues to exist endlessly. Now it is an evident fact that birth and death are analogous occurrences, and related only to existence on this planet. The body of a man is born, and it dies. It begins, and it ends. As to immortality, if you contend that something abided in that body which continues to exist after death, then it is necessary to admit that it had an existence previous to its entrance into the body, at birth. Nothing can continue to exist in all future time, which began at any fixed moment; it must have being, whether we look forward or backward. Form is perishable. It had a beginning, birth; and it will have an end, death! But the intelligence which inhabits all form will live forever, because it has forever lived. So I repeat, the dog is as immortal as the man."

There followed a silence after this speech, the two men gazing upon one another intently, without speaking. Leon was deeply affected. He felt almost as though listening to himself, and there is no human being who does not find himself entertaining. Leon had grown up without human companionship, for, in his environment, there was no one of temperament congenial to his. But he had not lacked for company. He found that within the covers of those books which he had begged, borrowed, or bought with hard-earned, and more hardly-saved, pennies. Miss Grath had never encouraged him to waste his time "reading those wicked science books," when he should have been studying his Testament. But he had sat alone in his garret room, on many a night, reading by a candle, for he dared not use the oil, which was measured out to last a given time. Thus he had become infatuated with works of divers kinds: Mythology, Sociology, Theology, Physiology, Psychology, and other kindred but difficult subjects. Difficult indeed to the student who is his own teacher. He had come to read his books, imagining that he listened to the authors talking, and, not infrequently, carried away by his interest in his subject, he had caught himself addressing questions aloud to the writer, whom his fancy pictured as present. Now, for the first time, he had heard a man "talk like a book." When he recovered from his pleasurable surprise, he said with emotion and ardor:

"Doctor, if I could be where I might hear you talk, or have you to teach me, I would be the happiest boy in the world."

"Are you in earnest, Leon, or are you merely carried away by an emotion, aroused by something which I have said?"

"I am in earnest, but—" here his voice dropped and his tone became almost sad, "of course I have no right to ask such a favor. Pardon my presumption."

"Leon, if you mean what you have said; if you will be happy with me; if you will accept me as your teacher, and endeavor to learn what I can teach you, your wish shall be gratified."

"What do you mean?" cried Leon, renewed hope stirring within his breast.

"You know me as a doctor, by which you understand that I physic people when they are sick. But the true meaning of doctor, is teacher. I am willing to be that to you, and I know much that I can teach; very much more than other men. I will take you as my student, if you will come."

"You are very kind, Dr. Medjora, and I could wish for no greater happiness than the chance to learn. Knowledge to me is God, the God whom I worship. But I could never repay you for the time and trouble that it will entail."

"Indeed you can. Knowledge is power, but the knowledge of one man has its limitation, for the man will die. I have two things that I must leave at death, money and knowledge. The former I may bequeath to whom I please, and he will get it, unless others squabble over my will until the lawyers spend the estate. With my knowledge it is different. I must impart it to my successor during my life, or it will perish with me. I have labored long and hard, and I have accumulated knowledge of the rarest and most unusual kind. Knowledge which makes me count myself the wisest physician in the world to-day. Knowledge which I can transfer to you, if you will accept it as a sacred trust, and use the power which it will confer upon you for the benefit of your fellows. Have you the courage and the energy to accept my offer? If so, do not hesitate, for I have been seeking for the proper man during several years. If you be he, I ask no other reward for what my task will be, than to see you worthy. Will you accept?"

"I will!"

Leon placed his hand in that of Doctor Medjora, and thus made a compact with one, to whom were attributed powers as potent as Satan's. Side by side, and deeply absorbed in earnest conversation, they started to walk to the farm, to be present at the sale. Lossy, although for the moment forgotten by his master, was on the alert and jumped up to follow, as soon as they started away. For the dog is a faithful friend, and the collie perhaps the most faithful of all dogs, if indeed there be any choice in that respect between purest bred and mongrel.

CHAPTER III
SELLING A NEW ENGLAND FARM

All the neighboring towns-people knew that the Grath farm was to be sold on this day. The "bills" had been "out" for over two weeks. These were announcements, printed in large letters, on bright-colored paper, and hung up in barber-shops, grocery stores, post-offices and even nailed on trees. One might be driving along an almost deserted road, several miles from any habitation, and suddenly find himself confronted by one of these yellow and black "auction bills," which would notify him that upon the stated date a homestead would be "sold out," in the next county.

Therefore it was not surprising that when Leon and the Doctor reached the farm, several "teams" were already "hitched" along the stone wall that surrounded the orchard.

The auction was advertised to begin at eight o'clock, and by seven over a hundred persons had already arrived, and were "rummaging" about the premises. An auction of this kind differs greatly from an art sale at Chickering Hall. There is no catalogue, numbering the various lots to be offered; nevertheless there is nothing so small, so worthless, so old, so broken, or so rusty, that it will not be put up, and bid for too. Many of the prospective buyers come many miles to attend, and as the sale usually lasts all day, it is expected that the owner will serve dinner promptly at noon, to all who may wish to partake of his hospitality. As these dinners, save in rare cases, usually amount to nothing better than a luncheon, many bring viands with them, thus reinforcing themselves against contingencies of hunger.

By the time that the auction was to begin, the Grath farm looked like a veritable picnic-ground; teams tied to every place that offered, one old man having "hitched" his horse to a mowing-machine, which caused some merriment when that article was sold, the auctioneer announcing that he would "throw in the critter leaning against the machine"; whilst here and there some of the bolder visitors had gathered together tables and chairs, and were keeping guard over them until the eating hour.

One old woman approached Leon and sought information, thus:

"Be you the boy that Marg'ret Grath took offen the county farm?" To which Leon vouchsafed no reply, but turned and walked away. This at once aroused the anger of the irascible old party, who followed him speaking loudly.

"Hoity! Toity! What airs for a beggar's brat! I'd have you to know, young man, that when I ax a civil question, I cac'late to git a civil answer!" Which calculation, however, miscarried.

Over near the barn he met another woman who asked:

"I say! You be the boy as lives here, be'ant you?"

"Yes, I live here," replied Leon.

"Well! I hearn as how Miss Grath hed some white ducks, so nigh as big 's geese, thet a body couldn't tell one from t'other. Now I've sarched the hull place lookin' fer them ducks, but bless me ef I kin find a feather on 'em. I seen a fine flock o' geese in the orchard, but I want you to show me them ducks. I'm jest achin' to see em."

"The flock in the orchard are the ducks; we have no geese," explained Leon.

"You don't mean it!" rejoined the woman, much astounded. "So them geese is the ducks! Land alive! And I took 'em for geese. Well, I never! To think I couldn't tell one from t'other! I mus' git another peak at 'em." Then she hurried away towards the orchard.

Over by the barn a man was coming out from the horse stalls, with an old leather strap in his hand, when he was suddenly confronted by the stern visage of Miss Matilda Grath, spinster.

Before he found words of greeting, she burst forth in wrathful tones:

"Jeremiah Hubbard, whatever do you mean by stealin' other folks' property, right before their very eyes?"

"Stealin', Miss Grath? Me steal? You mus' be losin your senses. Hain't ye?"

"No, I hain't!" snapped back Miss Grath. "An' ef you an't stealin' that strap, I'd like to know what you're doin', takin' it outen the barn, before it's sold?"

"Gosh! Ye don't mean you're goin' to sell this strap?"

"An' why not, I'd like to know? It's mine, an' I kin sell it, I spose, 'thout gittin' your permission?"

"Why, sartin! But 'tain't wuth nothin'."

"Ef 'tain't wuth nothin', I'd have you tell me what you're takin' it for?"

"Well, you see,"—Mr. Hubbard was embarrassed by the question—"it's this way. A bit o' my harness is a leetle weak, and I thought this'd come handy to brace it up till I get to hum."

"Jes' so," answered Miss Grath, with gratification, "an' as 't would come handy, you jes' took it, French leave. Well! Ef you stay till the end o' the auction, mebbe you'll git a chance to buy it. Meanwhile, Mr. Hubbard, it might be 's well to keep your hands offen what don't belong to you."

Mr. Hubbard threw the old piece of strap back in the stall, and pushing his hands deep into his pockets, snarled out:

"I reckon I'll put my hands in my pockets, where my money is, an' keep 'em there too!" With which he strode away, a very angry man. He stayed to the end of the auction, but Miss Grath noticed with regret that he did not bid on anything all day, and she wondered if she had not "put her foot in it," which she undoubtedly had. But there are many, many people, in this curious little world, who hold a penny so close to their eyes that they lose sight of many dollars that might come their way were they not blinded by the love of small gains. Mr. Hubbard, too, was troubled as he rode home, that night; for, aside from the fact that he had been accused, of stealing, and that the stolen property had been "found on him," because of his determination not to let "the old hag" get any of his money he had lost several good opportunities to secure tempting "bargains";

and there is nothing that a true New Englander loves so much as a bargain.

At last there was a commotion in the crowd. Some one had recognized the auctioneer's team approaching, and presently he jumped out of his light wagon, greeting the men and women alike, by their first names, for there were few who did not know Mr. Potter, and there was none whom Mr. Potter did not know.

Mr. Potter himself was a character of a genus so unique that he was perhaps the only living example. If it be true that poets are ever born, then Mr. Potter was born a poet. It was only by the veriest irony of fate that he was an auctioneer, although undoubtedly it is probable that he made more money by the latter calling, than he ever would have gained by printer's ink. And as for fame, that he had, if it please you. For be it known that no farm of consequence in New Hampshire hath passed under the hammer these five and twenty years, but Mr. Potter hath presided at the obsequies. I use that word advisedly, for, truly, though they make a picnic of the event, the selling of an old homestead is a funereal sort of pleasure.

The cause of his success lay in the fact that, with wisdom such as no professional poet has been known to possess, Mr. Potter had combined his business and his pleasure, so that he became known as a poetical auctioneer. Gifted with the faculty of rhyming, and well versed in the poets, he readily would find a couplet to fit all occasions. Sometimes they were quoted entire, sometimes they appeared as familiar lines with a new termination, and not infrequently the verse would be entirely original, provoked by the existing circumstances.

As to his personality, I need but a few adjectives to give you his picture. He was a large man, and a hearty one. Witty, genial, and gallant to the ladies. Above all things, he possessed the rare faculty of adapting himself to his surroundings. Add to this that he was scrupulously honest and fair in his dealing, and you will readily believe that he was popular. His name on a "bill" always assured a large crowd. On this occasion more than the usual throng surrounded him, as he climbed up into an ox-cart and opened the sale with these words:

"My friends, we will begin the morning services by quoting a verse from Dr. Watts, junior:

"Blest is the man who shuns the place Where other auctions be, And in his pocket saves his cash To buy his goods of me."

Then, when the laugh had died away, he offered for sale the cart upon which he stood, reserving the right to stand upon it during the balance of the day. The bidding was spiritless at first, and the cart went for two dollars. Mr. Potter remarking, as he knocked it down:

"Thus passeth my understanding!"

And so the sale progressed, Mr. Potter finding many opportunities which called forth some selection from his store of poetry. There were many sharp sallies from the crowd, for the New Englander is keen of wit, but the auctioneer ever had a ready rejoinder that turned the laugh away from himself, without causing ill-feeling.

After a couple of hours, during which Leon saw many things sold which were associated in his mind with what were now sacred memories, he turned away from the crowd, and went off towards the barn. Lost in thought, he did not notice that the collie followed at his heels, until presently, walking between the bales of new hay, and finding one upon which he could throw himself, Lossy jumped up beside him and kissed him in the face.

"Poor doggy," said the lad; "you know that I'm in trouble, don't you, old boy?" He paused as though he awaited a reply, and the dog, seeming to understand that something was expected of him, sat back on his haunches and offered his paw, tapping his master's arm again and again, until it was taken. Then Leon turned so as to face the dog squarely, and retaining the proffered paw, he spoke again.

"I wonder, Lossy, how you will do in a great city? Will you miss the old place, as I suppose I shall? Will you mind being penned up in a little yard, with strict orders not to come into the grand house? Will you miss going after the cows, and the sheep? Will you miss your swims in the lake?" He paused again, but Lossy was looking away much as a human being would who tried to hide his feelings. For there is little doubt that when a dog acts thus, in some mysterious way he comprehends his master's trouble, and shares it. "Never you mind, old fellow," Leon continued, "you sha'n't be entirely forgotten. I'll look out for you. The nights will be ours, and what fun we shall have. We'll go off together on long walks, and if there is any country near enough, why we'll go there sometimes on Sundays. For we don't care about church, do we, old boy? No, sir! The open fields, with the green grass, and the trees, and the birds, and the bright sunlight is all the church we need, isn't it, old doggy?" He stopped, and as his voice had grown somewhat more cheerful, the dog vouchsafed to look at him timidly. Seeing encouragement, he wagged his tail a few times. "Come, sir," said Leon, "I am talking to you. Don't you hear? Answer my question. Speak, sir! Speak!" "Whow! Whow! Whow-Whow!" answered Lossy, barking lustily. But Leon held up his finger in warning, and he ceased. "What do you mean by all that noise?" said Leon. "Don't you understand that this is a confidential conversation? Now, sir! Answer me again, but softly! softly!"

"Woof! Woof! Woof!" answered Lossy, in tones as near a whisper as can be compassed by a dog.

"Very well, sir!" said Leon. "That's better. Much better. We don't want to attract a crowd, so the less noise we make the better for us."

But, alas! The boy's warning came too late. Miss Matilda Grath had seen Leon go towards the barn, and when she heard the dog's loud barking, a sudden idea had come to her, which thrilled her cruel heart with anticipation of pleasure. So much so indeed, that she at once left the vicinity of the auctioneer, where her interests were, and hurried out to the barn, surprising Leon by her unwelcome presence.

"What are you doin' out here all by yourself?" she asked.

"I am not doing anything, Miss Grath!" replied Leon mildly, hoping to mollify her. A vain hope!

"Miss Grath!" she repeated sneeringly. "Don't you Miss Grath me. I an't to be molly-coddled by the likes o' you. I wanter know what you're doin' out here, when everybody's to the auction. You an't up to no good, I'll warrant. Now up an' tell me! An' no lies, or it will be the worst for you."

"I don't know what you're aiming at. I came out here to be alone, that is all!"

"Oh! You wanted to be alone, did you? Well, that's the right way for you to feel, anyway. The company of decent folks an't for the likes o' you." She paused, expecting an angry retort, but

failing to obtain the desired excuse for proceeding in the diabolical design which she was bent upon executing, she continued in
a worse temper. "You needn't think you kin fool me with your
smooth talkin'. I know you, and I know what you're up to!"

"Well, if you know, why did you ask me?" said Leon, stung
into something like anger.

"I don't want none o' your impudence. I'll tell you mighty
quick what you're up to. You're plannin' to steal that dog, that's
what you're after!"

"Steal Lossy! Why how could I do that? He is mine!" Leon
did not yet fully grasp what was coming, but the vague suspicion conveyed by the woman's words aroused a fear in his
breast.

"Oh! He's your'n, is he. We'll see 'bout that. How did he
come to be your'n? Did you buy him?"

"Why, of course not. He was born right here on the farm,
and, when he was a puppy, mother gave him to me."

"Don't you dare to call my sister mother, you impudent
young beggar. You never had no mother, and your scoundrel of
a father foisted you onto my innocent, confidin' sister, who took
you out o' charity, like a fool. I wouldn't 'ave done it."

"I have not the least idea that you would, Miss Grath. You
never did any one a kindness in your life, if what people say is
true."

"People say a deal sight more 'n their prayers. But that
an't to the p'int now. We're talkin' 'bout this dog. You say
he's your'n; that my sister gin him to you. Now kin you prove
that?"

"Prove it?" repeated Leon, at last fully comprehending that
his dog might be taken from him. "Prove it! Why, how can I?"

"Jes' so. You can't. My sister's dead, and an't here to contradict you, so in course you kin claim the dog. But that's all talk,
an' talk 's cheap. The dog's mine."

"He is not yours."

"An't he? We'll see 'bout that mighty quick." And before
either Leon or the dog understood her purpose, she had grabbed
Lossy in her arms, and was striding away towards the crowd
around the auctioneer. Leon jumped down and followed her, his
pulses beating high.

Reaching the cart where Mr. Potter was standing, she threw the dog towards him, saying:

"Here, sell this dog next. He's named Lossy. He's a right smart beast. Goes after the cows, kin tend sheep, and run a churn. He's wuth a good price. Sell him for what he'll fetch."

Mr. Potter stooped and patted the dog, who was trembling with fear, for ordinarily a collie is easily alarmed, and not very brave except when guarding his sheep, when he has the courage of a lion.

"Well," began Mr. Potter, "what'll you give for the dog. Come! speak, and let the worst be known, for speaking may relieve you. If it don't, I'll relieve you of the price of the dog, and you can take him with you."

"Dollar!" cried a voice in the crowd succinctly.

"'n' quarter," said another.

"Stop," cried Leon, fully aroused, now that his pet was actually offered for sale. "Mr. Potter, you shall not sell that dog. He is mine."

"It's a lie!" cried Miss Grath. Then pointing her bony finger at Leon, she continued: "Look at that ungrateful wretch. Look at him. You all know who he is, and where he came from. My sister nussed him, and fed him, and gin him his clothes all these years, and now arter she's dead, he's tryin to defraud me by claimin' my property, 's if he an't had enough outer my family a'ready."

"I've never had anything from you, and would not accept it if it was offered and I was starving," cried Leon, white with anger. But as just as the words were, they rather injured his cause, for most of those present held ideas not very dissimilar from Miss Grath's, and they accepted her version and believed him ungrateful. The prejudice against him was not lessened by the intuitive knowledge that, poor though he was, he was better than they. So those who heard him did not hesitate to speak against him, and such phrases as "Nuss a serpent and 'twill sting you," and "A beggar on horseback," reached his ears, and despite their inaptness, they wounded him.

Mr. Potter, seeing the rising storm, essayed to stem the torrent, and exclaimed:

"Don't show temper, friends; anger and pride are both unwise; vinegar never catches flies."

"Ther' hain't no flies on Potter," cried a voice, and a general laugh followed. Then, in spite of his protest, Leon saw Lossy offered again for sale.

Mr. Potter lifted the dog in his arms and said:

"Now here's a dog, by name of Lossy. Just feel his fur, so fine and glossy. I'm told that twixt his loud bow-wows He often fetches home the cows. Besides that, he can tend the sheep, And bring the butter in the churn. So buy him dear, or buy him cheap, He'll eat no more than he can earn.

"How much for the dog?"

The competition excited by the occurrences, and the verses, was now so great, that the bidding was spirited until fifteen dollars was reached, to which sum it had mounted by jumps of fifty cents. Then a man said quietly but distinctly:

"Twenty dollars," and a glad cry escaped from Leon, as he recognized Dr. Medjora's voice, and knew that his purpose was to restore his dog to him. But at the same instant Miss Grath also comprehended the situation, and determined that Leon should not have Lossy. She cried out to Mr. Potter:

"The dog's wuth twice as much. You kin stop sellin' him. I'll keep him myself."

At this Leon's hopes fell, only to be revived again by the auctioneer's words. Mr. Potter knew Miss Grath thoroughly, and he readily appreciated the fact that she was selling the dog to spite the lad, and that, in withdrawing him, she was actuated by some sinister motive. Sympathizing with Leon, against whom he had none of the prejudices of the neighborhood, he turned now to Miss Grath and said:

"You told me to sell him for what he would fetch. It's too late now to draw back."

"It an't too late," screamed the infuriated woman; "it's my dog, and I sha'n't sell him."

"Oh, you won't," said Mr. Potter. "'The best-laid plans of mice and men aft gang aglee.' Dr. Medjora gets the dog at twenty dollars."

"It's no sale! It's no sale!" cried out Miss Grath. "'T ain't legal to sell my property agin my word."

"Now, look here, Miss Grath," said Mr. Potter; "I'm here to sell, and whatever I sell is sold. That dog's sold, and that settles it.

If you dispute it, you jes' say so, right now, and you kin sell the rest of this farm yourself. Now decide quick! Is the sale of that dog all straight?"

Miss Grath, despite her anger, was shrewd enough to see that her interests would be ruined if she suspended the sale. She could never hope to get the crowd together again, and no other auctioneer would obtain such good prices. So she was obliged to yield, though she did so with little grace.

"Oh! I 'spose ef you choose to be ugly 'bout it, I hain't got nothin' more to say. Dr. Medjora kin have the dog, an' much good may it do him. I hope he'll regret buyin' it, some day."

And so, through the cleverness of Mr. Potter, the poet-auctioneer, when Dr. Medjora and Leon started for New York on the following morning the collie went with them.

CHAPTER IV
AN OMINOUS WELCOME

Leon at this time was about twenty years old, but, as we have seen, he had already passed the crisis in his life which made a man of him. He was a curious product, considered as a New England country boy. Despite the fact that all of his life had been passed on the farm, except a brief period when he had been sent to another section, equally rural, he had adopted none of the idioms peculiar to the people about him. Without any noteworthy schooling, he could boast of being something of a scholar. I have already mentioned his predilection for the higher order of books, and by reading these he had undoubtedly obtained a glimpse of a vast field of learning; but one may place his eye to a crack in a door and see a large part of the horizon, yet the door hides much more than the crack reveals, and the observer sees nothing except through the crack. So Leon, knowing much, knew less than he thought he did; and many ideas which he believed to be mature, and original products of his own brain, were but reflections of the authors whose works he had read, and whose deductions he had adopted, because he had read nothing by other writers contradicting them. Therefore he was exactly in that mental condition which would make him a good pupil, because he would be a disputative one. The student who accepts the teaching of his master without question, will acquire but a meagre grasp of knowledge, while he who adopts nothing antagonistic to his own reason, until his reason has been satisfied, may be more troublesome, because less docile, but his progress will be more real.

That Leon had very decided convictions upon many topics, and that he would argue tenaciously in defence of his views, would not at all militate against his learning. Those ideas which were most firmly fixed in his mind, could readily be dislodged, if erroneous, for the very reason that they were not truly original with himself. Having adopted the teaching of one book, he could certainly be made to accept opposite theories, if another book, with more convincing arguments, should be brought to his notice.

For these reasons, it might be said that his mind was in a plastic condition, ready to be moulded into permanent thoughts. With such a teacher as Dr. Medjora, he would learn whatever the Doctor taught; he would adopt whatever theories the Doctor wished. Under the control of another master he might become the antithesis of what the Doctor would make of him. Therefore it may be truly said that when he accepted Dr. Medjora's offer, he sealed his fate, as surely as when Faust contracted with Mephisto.

Just as he had gleaned the ideas of authors, so also his conception of cities, and city life, had been taken from books. He had read works of travel, and thought that he was quite familiar with travelling. He was consequently astonished to find how much at variance with the real, were his notions. When he found himself aboard of *The Puritan*, that palatial steamboat of the Fall River line, he was dazed by the magnificence and luxury, thus seen for the first time in his life. But later in the night, when he and the Doctor sat upon the upper deck, as they swiftly glided through the moonlit waters of Long Island Sound, he was so enraptured at this broader view of the Universe, that he felt a distinct pain as his thoughts recurred to Lake Massabesic, which now seemed so diminutive, and which only a few days before had been an ocean to him. Yet there was still the real ocean which he had not yet seen, and which would render the Sound as diminutive in comparison, as the lake. And so, also, we arrogant inhabitants of this planet may presently come to some other world so much greater, so much larger, so much more grand, that we will not even deign to turn a telescope towards the little world which we have left behind. In some such manner, Leon was leaving his little world behind him, and even already he was abandoning all thought of it, as his heart welled up and his soul expanded towards the greater world looming up before him. In that little town behind him he had lost his name, which indeed had never been his. But in the great city which he approached, was he not destined to make a new name for himself? He was young, and in answer to this mental question his answer was–"Certainly!" All young men see Fame just there–just ahead of them! They need but to stretch out a hand, and it is within their grasp. Yet, alas! How few ever clutch it!

Dr. Medjora sat beside Leon for a long time in silence. He noticed the lad's absorption, and readily comprehended the mental effects produced. It suited his purpose to remain silent. He wished his companion to become intoxicated by this new experience, for, in such a mood of abstraction, he hoped for an opportunity to accomplish a design which was of great importance to himself. He wished to hypnotize Leon. Why, I will explain later, but the chief reason at the present moment was this:

Dr. Medjora had, as you know, observed Leon feeding the chipmunks, and had said to himself, "He has inherited the power." By this he meant Leon possessed that temperament which is supposed to render the individual most capable of controlling others. And let me say at once that I do not allude to any occult power. There is nothing whatever in connection with this history, which transcends known and recognized scientific laws. But, to express myself clearly, I may say that all persons are susceptible to impressions from suggestion. Those who fall asleep, because sleep has been suggested, are said to be hypnotic subjects; while he who can produce sleep by suggestion in the greatest number of persons, may be said to have "the power" in its most developed form. But it is a power thoroughly well comprehended by scientists of to-day, and may be acquired by almost any one to some extent, just as any one is susceptible to hypnotic influence, to a greater or less degree according to the conditions. I believe that there is no person living who cannot be hypnotized, by some living person, however well he may resist all others. Or in other words, there be some individuals so little susceptible to outside suggestions, so self-reliant, and so strong in their own ego, that it would be extremely difficult to produce true hypnosis in them. Yet the phenomenon is possible with even these, provided the hypnotizer be one who is a past-master in methods, and possesses the most effective power of conveying suggestion.

Such a man was Dr. Medjora. Never yet had he met a human being who could resist him, if he exerted himself. He was a master of methods, possessing a knowledge of the minutest details of the psychological aspect of the subject, and therefore the most powerful hypnotizer of the age, perhaps. One fact he had long recognized. That just as one individual is more susceptible than another, so an individual who might resist at one time, would be perfectly docile at another. So much depends upon the mental attitude of the subject. One of the favorable states is abstraction, for in such a condition the mind is off its guard, so to speak, and it may be possible that, by a sudden shock, the suggestion to sleep, might be conveyed and be obeyed.

Thus he was glad to note that Leon was losing himself in thought, because it would give him an opportunity to hypnotize the lad, and if he could once be thrown into that state, hypnosis could be re-produced thereafter very readily. It would only be necessary for the Doctor to suggest to Leon, while asleep, that he permit himself to be hypnotized in the future, and the possibility of resistance would be destroyed.

Therefore the Doctor watched Leon, as a cat does a bird when seeking a chance to seize and destroy it. Several times he was about to make the attempt, but he hesitated. That he did so annoyed him, for it was a new experience to him to doubt his ability to accomplish a purpose. But, truly, he questioned the wisdom of what he meditated, in spite of the fact that he knew this to be a rare opportunity, which would never occur again. The boy would never, after this night, be so intoxicated by Nature as he was at this time. Even though Leon were, as the Doctor believed, one of those exceptional individuals who could successfully resist him, his will-power was for the time in abeyance, and a well-directed effort to throw him into hypnotic slumber promised success. Yet he could not overlook the other fact, that, were the attempt to prove a failure, it would render all future experiments doubly difficult.

Thus an hour passed. There was no one on the upper deck besides these two. Leon had remained so still, so motionless for many minutes, that he might have been a corpse sitting there and gazing into the line of foam which trailed in the wake of the boat. He was fascinated, why might he not be hypnotized? Still, the Doctor was loath to take a risk. He called the lad's name, at first very softly. But he repeated it again, and again, in louder tones. Leon did not reply. His abstraction was so great that he did not hear. It was certainly a favorable moment. The Doctor rose slowly from his chair; so slowly that he scarcely seemed to move, but in a few moments he stood erect. Then he paused, and for some time remained motionless. With a movement that was more a gliding than a step, one leg crept forward towards Leon, and then the other was drawn after it, thus bringing the Doctor nearer. Again he stood motionless. Again the manoeuvre was repeated, and now, still unnoticed, he stood beside the lad. The approach more than ever reminded one of a cat, only now one would think of a tiger rather than of the little domestic animal. For the Doctor looked tall and gaunt in the moonlight. Now he stooped slowly forward, bending his back, as the tiger prepares to spring upon its prey, and now his mouth was near Leon's ear.

The final moment had come; the experiment was to be tried. But even now the Doctor had devised a scheme by which he hoped to lose nothing, even though he should fail. His first intention had been to cry out, "Go to sleep!" a command which he had often seen obeyed instantly. This time the formula was changed. In a loud tone, which, however, was mellifluous and persuasive, he uttered these words:

"You are asleep!"

He paused and anxiously awaited the result. For a brief instant success poised upon the verge of his desire. Leon's eyes closed, and his head drooped forward. Then, like lightning, there came a change. The lad jumped up, and started back, assuming an attitude of defiance, and a wrathful demeanor. He was entirely awake and in full control of his senses as he cried out:

"You tried to mesmerize me!"

As swiftly the Doctor was again master of himself, and, recognizing defeat, he was fully prepared to assume control of the
situation and twist circumstances so that they should culminate
in advantage to himself. In the very moment of his first failure,
his quick mind grasped at the hope that was offered by Leon's
words. He had said "mesmerize," and this convinced Dr. Medjora
that the word "hypnotize" was as yet unknown to him, and that
all the later discoveries in psychical science must be as a sealed
book to him. So with perfect calmness he replied:

"I fail to see upon what you base such a senseless deduction.
You have sat motionless for half an hour. I called you three or
four times, and you did not reply. Then I came here and stood
beside you, but you took no notice of me. Finally I said what I
thought was true, 'You are asleep!' Instantly you jump up like a
madman and accuse me of trying to mesmerize you. Now, why?
Explain!"

How could this youth cope with the skill of such a man?
He could not. As he listened to the Doctor's words and heard
his frank and friendly speech, his fears were banished, his suspicions lulled, and he felt ashamed. Being honest, he expressed his
thoughts:

"I beg your pardon, Doctor. I think now that I must have
been sleeping. Your words startled me, and, as I awoke, I spoke
stupidly. Will you forgive me?"

There was a shade of anxiety in his tones, which demonstrated to the Doctor that he valued his friendship, and feared to
alienate his good will. Thus he knew that he had deftly dispelled
doubt, and that nothing had been lost. Indeed, something had
been gained, for he knew now what he had only before suspected;
that Leon could not be hypnotized. Or, rather, not by any one
else in the world besides himself, for he by no means abandoned
his design. Only, when next he should make an attempt, he
would take better precautions, and he would succeed. So he
thought. Now, it would be as well to continue the conversation,
by discussing the suggested topic, for it would strengthen the
lad's confidence, if he did not appear to shun it.

"Forgive you, my boy," said the Doctor, "there is nothing to
forgive. It was I who was stupid, for I should not have disturbed
you so unexpectedly. But I am fond of studying human beings,

and you have been very entertaining to me to-night. I have been observing the effect that Nature can produce upon a virgin mind, such as yours. You have been drinking in the grandeur of the world about us, until you were so enthralled that you had forgotten all except the emotions by which you were moved. You were not asleep, but you were in an abstraction so deep that it was akin to sleep. I yielded to the temptation of saying what I did, merely to see what effect it would produce. I was certainly surprised at the result. That you should have been startled is natural enough, but how the idea of mesmerism occurred to you, bewilders me. What do you know about that mysterious subject?"

"Not very much," said Leon, with some diffidence. "As you may imagine, Doctor, I have not had a large library from which to choose. But I have read a translation of a work by Deleuze, which appears to discuss the subject thoroughly."

"Ah! I see. You have read Deleuze. I am familiar with the work. Well, then, tell me. After weighing the matter thoroughly in your own mind, do you believe it is possible for one person to mesmerize another?"

"I do not. Most emphatically I do not," said Leon.

"Most emphatically you do not. A strong way to express your views, for which you must of course have convincing reasons. But if so, why were you afraid that I would do what you emphatically believe to be an impossibility?" The Doctor smiled indulgently as he asked this embarrassing question.

"Because, as you have said, I was only half-awake," replied Leon, apologetically.

The Doctor was now assured that Leon, even when he should come to think over the occurrences of the night when alone, would harbor no suspicion against him. So all would be safe.

"Well, then," continued the Doctor, "tell me why you are so sure that mesmerism is not possible. You say you have read Deleuze. He claims that wonderful things may be accomplished."

"So wonderful that a thinking man cannot believe them to be true."

"But surely Deleuze was honest, and he relates many remarkable cases which he assures his readers occurred within his own cognizance."

"That is very true. No one who reads the author's book could doubt the sincerity of his purpose and the truth of what he relates. Or rather I should say, one must believe that he does not wilfully deceive. But it must be equally evident that the man was deluded."

"Why so?"

"It is difficult to tell exactly. But I know this, that after reading his work, which is intended to convince the skeptic, not only did his words leave me unconvinced, but a positive disbelief was aroused. There are places where he makes assertions, which he admits he cannot explain. He tells of wonderful occurrences which he cannot account for, while, in spite of that, he does not hesitate to attribute them to mesmerism. Such teaching is unsatisfactory and unscientific."

"Very true, but because Deleuze did not understand a phenomenon, does it logically follow that there is no explanation of it to be had?"

"Why, not at all, Doctor. But the explanation must eliminate it from the realm of the mysterious, and make it acceptable to the reason. In its present form it is utterly unacceptable. I cannot believe that one individual may possess a power by which he may control his fellow-creatures. The idea is repugnant in the extreme. It lessens one's self-dependence. Do you believe in mesmerism?"

This was a direct question, and the Doctor thought that the subject had been pursued far enough. He had no desire to approach a point where he might be compelled to give this inquiring youth an insight into the scientific side of hypnotism. He preferred to leave him wallowing in the mire of mesmerism. Consequently, he did not hesitate to reply:

"No, Leon. I do not believe in mesmerism. Mesmer himself was a very erratic, unscientific man, who either did not or would not arrange his observations into scientific order, from which logical deductions might have been made. Therefore, his whole teaching may be counted rather among the curiosities of literature, than as having any value to the mind of one who seeks the truth. Life is too short to waste much time upon such fruitless speculations."

"I am glad that you agree with me," said Leon. "I was afraid from what you said that you might believe in that sort of thing."

To this the Doctor made no reply, the words "that sort of thing" threatening to lead him upon dangerous ground again. He essayed, by a gentle digression, to divert the conversation into another direction.

"Speaking of mesmerism, Leon, I suppose that you know that its advocates likened it to the power which reptiles are said to have over birds and small animals, whom they fascinate first, and then devour. Now I was much interested to note the familiarity with which the little chipmunks approached you this morning."

"Did you see them?" Leon was surprised, for he had not known how long the Doctor had been present.

"Yes," replied the Doctor; "I watched you for some time. How is it that these little wild animals would come to you? Disbelieving in mesmerism, have you yourself the power to charm or fascinate the lower animals?"

"Why, not at all, Doctor. Let me explain. First, as to the chipmunks. There was nothing wonderful about that, for though they are wild, they know me as well as though they had lived in the house with me. One day I found a dead chipmunk, and later I found the nest of young ones in a tree. I took food to them from day to day, and they grew to know me. Were it not that I have not been in the woods since the funeral until this morning, so that it is several days since the little fellows last saw me, they would have shown even greater friendliness than they did. I have often had them run up to my shoulders, and perch there eating what I would give them."

"But what you tell me only makes me believe the more that you exert some power of fascination," said the Doctor, laughing jestingly. "You must teach me the secret of charming animals, Leon. Really you must."

"I will do so gladly. It is very simple. The animals, the little ones I mean, are afraid of us. Banish their fear, and at the same time excite their instinct to take food where they can find it, and your desire is accomplished. For example, take the fish. If I go to the edge of Lake Massabesic at a certain spot, the fish will jump out of the water in their anxiety to receive food from my hands. I can even take the little fellows out of the water, and when I drop them in again, they pause but a few moments before venturing within my reach again. How did I train them to this?

I noticed that from my habit of throwing the old bait out of my boat when landing, the fish had made the spot a feeding place. I threw them some crumbs of bread, and they hurried to the surface to snatch it, diving swiftly down again to eat. I tried an experiment. Holding the bread in my hand, I dipped my arm deep into the water, and allowed it to remain motionless. For a long time the fish were very shy. They stood off at a distance, and gazed longingly, but they did not approach this strange object. I crushed the bread into small bits and withdrew my arm. In a moment they were all feeding. After doing this a number of times on successive days, at last one fellow, more venturesome than the others, made a swift dash forward, and grabbing a bit of the bread from my hand as quickly swam off with it. Others, observing his success, followed his example. Within a few more days, they did not hesitate, but approached as soon as my hand appeared below the water, and presently they were not alarmed if I moved my hand about among them. The first time that I attempted to take hold of one, I created a disturbance which made them shy for a few days; but after a time they learned that I would not harm them, whereas I always brought them food. Why should they not trust me? So you see, Doctor, there is no witchcraft about it."

"No! Your explanation of how you charm fish removes it from the region of the mysterious, and I have no doubt that what Mesmer observed, could be as satisfactorily explained if we only knew how."

So the subject was dropped, and both retired to their state-rooms, as the hour was late. Dr. Medjora, when alone, occupied himself with the serious problem before him. He had undertaken a charge,—the education of a youth endowed with unusual intelligence. To teach him all that he wished him to know, it became an essential part of his plan that Leon should be hypnotized. How should he accomplish it?

Leon slept soundly, or if he dreamed at all, it was of the name which he would make for himself.

Early on the following morning the steamboat landed her passengers, and Leon set foot upon the shores of New York City. He had sat upon the deck for more than an hour, marvelling at the extent of the two cities between which they passed down the East river; he had gazed with wondering eyes upon the great bridge, astonished that the name of the engineer was not known to him; and the thought hurt, for if one might build such a structure and not be more widely known to fame, how was he, a poor country boy, to earn distinction? He had admired the beautiful Battery, the Statue of Liberty, the lovely bay, the tall buildings, and had felt that he was almost approaching Paradise. But at last he was ashore, and in New York, the Mecca of all good citizens of the New World, and he felt correspondingly elated.

Cabs and carriages were offered by shouting hackmen, with stentorian voices, and insinuating manners, but the Doctor pushed through the throng, and crossed the street to where two magnificent black horses, attached to a luxurious carriage, tossed their heads and shook their silver chains. A man in livery opened the door, and Dr. Medjora made a sign to Leon to get in, which he did, for the first time beginning to realize that his newfound friend was a man of wealth.

The drive seemed endless, and if Leon was surprised at the length of the city as he viewed it from the river, he was more amazed now, as the carriage rolled rapidly through continuous rows of houses built up solidly on each side. In reality they drove almost the entire length of the Island, for their destination was that same place where the Doctor had once set fire to his house.

Everything, however, was changed. Where once was an old dwelling on a rugged lot of land, there was now a royal mansion within a spacious park. This was the home of Dr. Emanuel Medjora and his wife. They had no children. But a retinue of servants, and frequent arrivals of company, kept the two from feeling lonely.

The Doctor ushered Leon into a cosy reception-room, made pleasant by sunshine, and the light morning's breeze, and there bade him wait a moment, while he summoned his wife. But Leon was not left to himself long, for within a few moments a door opened and Madame Medjora entered. She insisted that she should always be called Madame, and therefore in deference to her nationality, as well as to her wishes, I give her that title.

Hearing the carriage, she had hurried to meet her husband, but by accident they had not met, and she was surprised to see the stranger of whom she had heard nothing, and whose arrival was therefore entirely unexpected. Leon arose and bowed to her, in courteous and graceful greeting, but, angered because she had not been advised of his coming, she asked with brusqueness.

"Who are you?"

"I came with Dr. Medjora," replied Leon, somewhat startled by the unfriendliness of her manner.

"But who are you? What is your name?"

Alas! The inconvenience of having no name. In a moment Leon was all embarrassment.

"My name?" He paused and stammered. "My name is— Leon—" Here he stopped, blushed, and looked away.

"Leon! Leon what?" asked Madame Medjora, in tones far from conciliatory. Leon did not reply. She continued, now thoroughly aroused. "You are ashamed of your name, are you? What is your name? I will know it! What is your last name, your full name?"

"Leon Grath is his name!" said a voice behind, and, turning, they both saw Dr. Medjora.

CHAPTER V
A FACE FROM THE PAST

Madame Medjora turned at the sound of her husband's voice with mingled emotion,—pleasure at seeing him at home again, for she still loved him with the passionate ardor of those earlier days, and anxiety, because her keen ear detected a tone of reproval in his words. Had she been a thoroughly wise woman that note of warning would have served to make her desist, but she was not to be baffled, when once she had determined to learn the meaning of anything that had aroused her curiosity or excited her suspicion. So instead of abandoning the subject, and welcoming her husband with an effusiveness which would have smoothed the wrinkles from his forehead, she turned upon him almost angrily, and said:

"Why do you prompt him? Is he an idiot that he cannot tell his name?"

"Not at all," said the Doctor, hopeful of dispersing the threatened storm, and therefore becoming slightly explanatory and conciliatory. "You have evidently confused Mr. Grath by your manner of questioning him, that is all. He is a country boy, unused to city ways, and you must excuse him if he is not as ready with an answer, as he will be after we make a citizen of him."

"He must be from the country indeed," was the sneering reply. "He must have been raised in a forest, to be so confused because I ask him his name." Then altering her tone, and speaking more rapidly, she continued: "Do not think that your wife is a fool, Dr. Medjora. Even a dog knows his name. There is something about this that you wish to hide from me. But I will not submit to it. You shall not bring any nameless beggars into my house!"

Leon uttered a cry as though wounded, and started to leave the apartment, but the Doctor, livid with anger, detained him by clutching his arm, as he would have passed, and turning upon his wife uttered but one word:

"Cora!"

That was all, but his voice implied such a threat, that the woman shrunk back, awed, and frightened, and utterly subdued, she merely murmured:

"Emanuel, forgive me!"

"Go to your room!" ejaculated the Doctor, sternly, and after one appealing glance at him, which he ignored, she swiftly glided through the door, and closed it softly after her. Thus the two men were left to themselves. Leon was the first to speak:

"Dr. Medjora," he began, "I thank you most heartily for what you have intended to do for me, but we have made a mistake. I cannot enter your home now. I can never hope that your wife will forget what has occurred to-day. Therefore were I to remain, my presence must become intolerably obnoxious to her; and her unhappiness would be but a blight upon your own peace."

"Perhaps you are right," said the Doctor quietly, and as though meditating upon the affair. "It is possible that you would not be as happy here as I would wish you to be. But if you go away from me, what will you do?"

"Work!" answered the youth, succinctly.

"Well answered," said the Doctor. "But, my boy, that is more easily decided upon than accomplished. You are a stranger, not only in the city, but to city manners and city methods. You would start out with determination to succeed, and in the first day you would apply at many places. But at them all you would be met with such questions as 'Where did you work last?' 'What experience have you?' 'What references can you offer?' You would answer them all unsatisfactorily, and you would be dismissed with a shrug of the shoulders."

"I have no doubt, Doctor, that it will be hard to obtain a place; but, as ignorant as I am, I have formed an idea upon this subject. I believe that in this country, where surely nine tenths of all men earn a livelihood, the small proportion of idlers have themselves to blame for their condition. Of course there must be a meritorious few who are unfortunate, but I speak of the greater number. Therefore I think that if I seek work, without any scruples as to what work it may be, I shall not starve."

"But are you ready to go right out into the world, single handed? Do you mean that you would begin the battle at once, to-day?"

"I do!"

"You do? Then I have faith in you. I, too, believe that you will succeed. I wish you God speed!"

Leon said "Thank you," and then there was a pause. In a moment, however, Leon started towards the front door, and the Doctor followed him in silence. The youth took down his hat from the jutting spur of a gnarled cedar stump, which, polished and varnished, served as a hat-rack, and a moment later stood upon the stoop extending his hand in farewell.

"Dr. Medjora," said Leon, "you must not think that I am ungrateful, nor that I am too proud to accept your aid. I am only doing what I deem to be my duty after—after what has passed. Good-by."

"Good-by, Leon," said the Doctor, shaking his hand warmly.

Leon started away, and, passing along the path, was nearing the gate that led to the street, when suddenly he paused, turned, and quickly retraced his steps. He found the Doctor standing where he had parted from him. Rushing up the steps, he essayed to speak, but a sob choked his utterance, and it was with difficulty that he said:

"Lossy!" Then he stopped, looking anxiously at the Doctor. It was surely a pretty picture. The lad had not hesitated to cast himself against the rude pricks of Fate, but the recollection of his dog made him tremble.

"Lossy will be brought here this afternoon," said the Doctor. "I have already sent my man down to get him out of his box, and bring him. What do you wish me to do about him?"

"Oh, Doctor," exclaimed the boy, appealingly, "if you would only keep my dog! You were kind enough to buy him for me. But now—now—unless you will keep him awhile—why—why—" Here he broke down utterly and ceased to speak, while a tear-drop in each eye glistened in the sunlight which crossed his handsome features, illuminated by the love that welled up from his heart; love for this dumb beast that had been his friend for so long a time.

"I will keep Lossy for you, Leon," began the Doctor, but he was interrupted by Leon, who grasped his hand impulsively, crying:

"Heaven bless you, Doctor!"

"But, I will keep you, also, my boy," continued the Doctor, tightening his grasp of Leon's hand, so that he could not get away.

"No! No!" cried the lad.

"Yes! Yes!" said the Doctor. "Now come back into the house and let me explain myself." Half forcibly he drew the youth after him, and they returned to the room where they had first been. Then the Doctor resumed:

"Leon, did you suppose that I meant to let you go away? That I would bring you so far and then abandon you to your own resources? Never for one instant did I harbor such a thought. But when you spoke as you did, I determined to try you; to see whether you were speaking in earnest, or for effect. Therefore I seemed to acquiesce. Therefore I let you go without even offering you some money, or telling you to come back to me if in distress. My boy, you stood the trial nobly. I was proud of you as you walked down the path, and I was about to follow you when I saw you pause and turn back. For an instant I feared that you had wavered, but I was more than gratified that it was to plead for the dog, and not for yourself that you returned."

"But Doctor, how can I remain?" asked the lad, helplessly, for already he began to feel the necessity of submitting to the domination of this man, as so many others had experienced.

"How can you remain? Why, simply by doing so. You mean, what will my wife think? She will think just what I wish her to think. It is a habit of hers to do so." Here he laughed significantly. "But you need not fear Madame. You believe that she will resent what she would term an intrusion. But you are mistaken. You will meet her next at dinner, and you will see that she will be quite friendly. In fact, she did not understand matters this morning. She was angry with me because I had not notified her that I would bring home a guest, but when I shall have talked with her that will be all changed."

So the matter was determined, and, as usual, Dr. Medjora's will decided the issue. Meanwhile, Madame had ascended to her room in high dudgeon. Since the day when we last saw her she had altered very little. Her most prominent characteristics had not changed, except as they had become more fully developed. But in many ways this development had been deceptive, for, whereas many who knew her believed that certain unpleasing features had been eliminated from her character, the truth was that she had merely suppressed them, as a matter of policy.

The union of such a woman with a man like Dr. Medjora, was an interesting study in matrimonial psychology. In all marriages one of two results is usually to be anticipated. The stronger individuality will dominate the other and mould it into submission, or the two characters will become amalgamated, each altering the other, until a plane is reached on which there is possible a harmony of desires. In this case neither of these conditions had been fulfilled, although nearly all who were acquainted with the Doctor and his wife supposed that the husband was the ruling spirit. The truth, however, was that while Dr. Medjora controlled his wife in important matters, he had by no means succeeded in merging her character into his own. Where contention arose, she obeyed his commands, but she never submitted her will. She surrendered, like a wise general, to superior force, but she secretly resented her defeat, and sought a way of retreat by which in the end she might compass her own designs.

By these means, she had deceived all of her acquaintances, and she enjoyed the idea that she had also deceived her husband. In this she was mistaken. Dr. Medjora understood thoroughly that his wife only yielded to him under protest, and in many instances he had refrained from making a move, when by doing so he could have thwarted her subsequent efforts to have her own way. Thus he adroitly avoided open warfare, satisfied that in secret strategy he was his wife's equal, if not her superior. In this manner they had lived together for so many years, enjoying their relationship as much as is usual with married folks, and keeping up an outward show that caused all to believe that, with them, matrimony was a great success. And so it was, if one could only overlook the fact that beneath this semblance of happiness there smouldered a fire, which might at any time be aroused by a chance spark, and grow into a blaze which would consume the whole fabric of their existence. The embers of this fire were, jealousy and suspicion on the side of the woman, and secretiveness in the man. Madame Medjora had never forgotten that her inquiry as to whether her husband had had a child by his previous wife had been unanswed; nor had she quite abandoned the hope of satisfying herself upon the subject.

During the later years, she had much regretted to see what she considered one source of power slowly slipping away from her. In the beginning, her husband had not hesitated to call upon her for funds with which to advance his interests, but as the years passed his own resources had increased so rapidly, that he was now entirely independent of her, and, indeed, owing to shrinkages in the values of her property, he was really richer than she. The house in which they lived had been rebuilt by him, and by degrees he had paid off the mortgages out of his earnings, until he owned it freed from debt.

So, as she sat in her room and meditated upon the fact that she had said that Leon should not be admitted to the house, she remembered with a feeling of bitterness that she was the mistress in the house only by right of wifehood, and not because she held any privileges arising from proprietorship.

She had been anticipating pleasure from the reunion with her husband, and now, because of "that country boy," she had received only unkind words from the Doctor. Naturally, she exonerated herself from all fault, and, because of her love, she would not blame her husband. There was no other course but to attribute the whole trouble to Leon. But for him, she argued, all would have been pleasant, therefore he must bear the brunt of her resentment. Already she began to hate him. To hate him as only a tropical temperament can hate. She was in this mood when the Doctor entered. At once she arose to greet him. In an instant she hid within the depths of her bosom all emotions save those of love, and any one, other than the Doctor, would have believed that she harbored no unpleasant recollections or ill feeling because of the recent scene. He was not deceived. He had lived with her for more than fifteen years, and in that time he had appraised her correctly. Now, however, it suited him best to accept her caresses, and to return them with a show of warmth, which made the blood course faster through her veins, the more so because she had expected him to be angry, and because he rarely exhibited much feeling. This wily man well knew the weak spot in this woman's armor, and when he most desired to sway her actions, he first touched her heart.

"Well, *cara mia*, are you glad to have me with you again?" He folded her close to his breast, and kissed her lips. She nestled within his arms, and returned the salute rapturously. Presently he spoke again. "You were naughty, down stairs, little one?"

There was scarcely a reproach in his voice; he spoke rather as an indulgent parent chides an erring, but beloved child. She looked up into his eyes and merely murmured,

"You will forgive me?"

Some may doubt that the warmer demonstrations of love could survive the destroying influences of a companionship covering so many years, and be still expressed with the fervor of youth. To such I say, what has not come within your own experience is not necessarily false. Love, especially in woman, is a hardy plant and will blossom and flower, long after its earlier excitations have ceased to exist. The beauty of form, and attractiveness of manner, which first arouses the tender passion within our breast, may pass away from the object of our admiration, and yet our love may be deeper, fuller, and wider than at its inception. Yea, it may even retain its fullest demonstrativeness. In many cases it thrives most by harsh treatment, where it might expire by over-tending. Madame Medjora's affection was of this sort. Had her husband yielded to her all that she demanded, she would long ago have been surfeited, and not improbably she would have left him. This, however, he had never done. She had always feared that he did not love her as she yearned to be loved, and therefore she was ever ready with cajolery, flattery, and other means familiar to women, to win from him a fuller responsiveness.

At this moment, intoxicated by his caresses, she spoke from her heart when she asked him to forgive her. The slight reproof of his words, however gently spoken, was the tiny bit of cloud upon her present clear sky of joy. She wished to dissipate it utterly, and then bask in the full sunshine of his love, as dear to her to-day as before her nuptials. But by no means did she regret the act which had called forth his speech, except as it affected her momentary happiness. She was ready to yield outwardly to anything that he might demand of her in such a mood, but, later, she would return to her purpose with zeal. That purpose, in this instance, would be to make Leon as miserable as she could if he remained, but to have him out of the house if possible. The game was now worth watching, for both players were very skilful, and each was intent upon carrying the day eventually. Each was as patient as persistent.

"You ask me to forgive you, Cora," was the Doctor's reply. "Do you admit that you behaved very badly?"

"Now you are going to scold," said his wife, in a demure tone that sounded odd from one of her years. But Madame often assumed the airs of youthfulness, without realizing how poorly they suited her.

"I would never scold you, Cora, if you would only think always before you act. You have been both unwise and unreasonable."

"I would not have been if you had informed me in advance that the boy was coming. But you never tell me anything, Emanuel."

"Perhaps I should have done so in this case. But I only decided yesterday, just before I left the country. A letter would not have reached you, and I would not telegraph, because you are always frightened by a despatch."

"The horrid things! I hate telegrams!"

"Exactly! It was from consideration for you that I did not notify you. As soon as I reached home I came here to find you and explain, but you had run down the other stairway, and so unfortunately you met Leon before I intended you should."

"Leon Grath?" There was an accent upon the last name, and an inflection of the voice very delicately expressed, which intimated that there was a doubt. Madame could not resist speaking thus quickly, hoping that a glance, an expression, however fleeting, might cross the Doctor's face, which would be a clue upon which she might base her future investigation. But she gained nothing by the manoeuvre, and the Doctor continued, as though unsuspicious of her intent.

"Yes, Leon Grath. Sit down and I will tell you about him. Some years ago I first met Leon, while hunting in the vicinity of his home, he had broken his leg, and I set it for him. Subsequently in succeeding years we have hunted together. This summer I was intending to look him up, as a companion on a fishing excursion. Arriving in his neighborhood, I learned that his mother had just died, leaving no will, and that the farm would be sold and the boy left penniless, through a technicality which made the small estates revert to the surviving sisters. These old hags hated Leon, and, consequently, from a comfortable home, he was about to become an outcast. I therefore decided to bring him home with me. He will now live with us."

"Forever?" gasped Madame, surprised to learn that, instead of a guest, the lad was destined to be a permanent addition to their household.

"Forever!" replied the Doctor, with just a little severity; enough to check the expression of resentment which he saw rising. Then in order to give her time to regain control of herself he went on. "Yes! I have long needed an assistant, and I am sure that Leon will prove an apt pupil and rapidly learn enough to become useful to me. However, I may be mistaken. He may prove a failure, and then I should find him a position elsewhere." This was offered as a sort of compromise for her acceptance. He held out the possibility that Leon would leave them. Madame was in nowise deceived. She had appreciated the tone of her husband's voice as he uttered the word, "Forever," and she knew that Leon would never leave them on account of proving a failure as a student. However, she accepted the situation, and assumed a satisfaction which was mere dissembling.

"Now that I understand the facts, Emanuel, I shall do all in my power to make the boy happy while he is here, even though it be only for a short time." The last words were in response to her husband's suggestion, but he understood her motive as well as she had comprehended his. Thus they fenced with one another.

"I knew that you would do so, Cora," replied the Doctor. "Will you come down now and speak to Leon before I take him out with me? I must have some clothing ordered for him."

Together they descended to where Leon sat awaiting them, and the youth's fears were set at rest, for the time being at least. Madame approached him with her most alluring manner, and welcomed him, in words, to his new home. She even asked him to forget her brusqueness at their first meeting, and then, suggesting that he must be hungry, rang a bell and ordered light refreshments.

The Doctor sat apart from them, apparently looking over his letters, but in reality observing closely all that transpired, and while Leon was thoroughly charmed by the altered manner of his hostess, Dr. Medjora decided, within his own mind, that in relation to this boy his wife's actions would require the closest scrutiny.

Presently a gong sounded, and a few moments later a servant announced:

"Judge Dudley. Miss Dudley."

The Judge came in with extended hand, and was warmly greeted by the Doctor, while the young lady went up to Madame, who kissed her on her cheek, and received her with an outward show of cordiality, which a close observer might have seen was but a polite veneer. The Doctor hastened to bring Leon forward, and presented him first to the Judge, and then to Miss Agnes Dudley.

The young people bowed their acknowledgments, and as they raised their heads, so that their eyes met, both started slightly. Leon was astonished to recognize the face of the girl whom he had met when studying Venus, and whose image had recurred to him that night on Lake Massabesic.

CHAPTER VI
AGNES DUDLEY

After the trial of Dr. Medjora, the young men who had so successfully defended him became rapidly prominent. Within six months they were retained in another celebrated case, and won new laurels. Within five years they were counted among the first lawyers of the Metropolis, and had already a practice which assured them ease and comfort for their declining years.

Mr. Dudley continued to be the ardent student that he had always been, and those who knew how well versed he was in law, were not at all surprised when he was eventually made a judge, a position which at this time he had held with honor for five years. He had achieved well-deserved fame. Aside from his undoubted probity, he really graced his position, for it was very seldom that any of his rulings were reversed by the higher courts.

I may mention here, parenthetically, that Mr. Bliss had also risen in his profession, and had just been elected District Attorney, having previously acquitted himself well as an assistant to his predecessor.

Agnes Dudley, the Judge's daughter, was eighteen years of age, having been born about a year after the Medjora trial. Indeed, Dr. Medjora always called her his godchild, because he had been present at her birth, and had enjoyed an intimate acquaintance with her and her parents throughout the years that followed. Judge Dudley had not merely defended Dr. Medjora as a matter of business. Having no positive opinion at the beginning of the trial, he had become convinced during its progress, and especially while his client was on the witness-stand, that Dr. Medjora was entirely innocent of the crime with which he was charged. This feeling was intensified when the jury showed an agreement with him, by acquitting the Doctor, and, as a result, an intense sympathy was aroused in his breast for one who seemed to have wrongfully undergone such an ordeal. For a man must suffer in reputation when once the finger of suspicion is pointed in his direction, and it is out of the power of the State to repair the harm which has been done. Thus, from the position of client, Mr. Dudley elevated the Doctor into that place in his regard occupied by his warmest friends.

Dr. Medjora had been quick to appreciate the affiliation of a man of brains, such as he recognized Judge Dudley to be, and, therefore, the friendship had thriven. None exalted the legal ability of Mr. Dudley higher than did the Doctor, and no one valued Dr. Medjora's professional skill more than did Mr.

Dudley. Under these circumstances, of course the Doctor was intrusted with the medical care of the lawyer's family, and thus it was natural that he should feel a paternal regard for his friend's daughter.

If he loved Agnes, she returned his affection in full measure. She used to say, even when a little tot, that she had two papas, and if asked which she loved best, she would reply: "Bofe of 'em."

As she grew older, of course she discriminated between her father and the Doctor, but if Judge Dudley received the greater share of her demonstrations of affection, the Doctor was more than satisfied with what was allotted to him.

In proportion as the Doctor loved the child, so his wife disliked her, though she never exhibited her feelings openly. Indeed, in this one matter she had succeeded in deceiving her husband, who, astute as he was in all other things, had never suspected that Madame harbored any ill-feeling against the girl. But Agnes herself was not very old when she began to understand, and as her wisdom increased with her years, she became less and less demonstrative towards the Doctor when the wife was present. Women detect these hidden heart-throbs with an instinct which is peculiar to their sex, and which transcends reason, in that it is unfailing, however illogical it may seem to a man.

Agnes was a rare child, a rarer girl, and one of the rarest of women as she matured. Without having a beautiful face, measured by the rules of high art, she was endowed with a countenance which might escape notice, but which, having once attracted observation, was never to be forgotten. Hers was a face that the least imaginative could readily recall in a dark room, and by an operation of the mind which produces images subjectively, summon up a hallucination of the girl, as distinct in lineament as though she were present in the flesh. An artist had proven this by sitting in his studio, lighted only by a candle, that he might see his drawing-board, and he had succeeded in producing a portrait of Agnes, as true to life as was possible. He claimed afterward that, without difficulty, he had projected his mental image of her against the dark background of his room, and that he had seen her as clearly as though she had sat for him.

From one point of view, then, it might be said that she had a strong face, by which I would mean that it would make an indelible impression upon the mind that observed her closely. There is a psychological reason for this, which I must ask you to look at with me if you wish to know Agnes. One dead face differs from another merely in the outlines of form. A living face differs from all others, and is different itself in varying moods, because there is something within the form which animates it. This is intellect. Some are poor in this, while others are richly endowed. The greater the intellect, the more distinctively individual will be the face, and it is this individuality which marks the features, differentiating the countenance from all others about it, so that it leaves a deeper impression upon the brain, just as a loud noise is heard, or a bright flash seen, the more intensely.

Agnes's pre-eminent characteristic was her intellectuality. She absorbed books, as a sponge does water, without apparent effort, and as a sponge may be squeezed and made to yield up nearly as much as it had drawn in, so Agnes, if catechised, would show that she had a permanent grasp on what she had studied. She developed a fondness for the classics, and for law, which delighted her father, and as her mother died when she was nearing her fifteenth year, they grew to be very close companions. The father, deprived of the support and encouragement always afforded by a true and well-beloved wife, gradually leaned more and more upon his daughter, who showed herself so worthy of affiliating with him mentally. It was therefore not very long before her services became indispensable to him in finding references in his law library, and in many ways connected with his profession.

Of two other things in connection with Agnes I must speak. Physically she was the perfection of ideal womanhood. She was strong in limb and body, yet possessed all the grace of contour essential to the feminine scheme of beauty. She had never been corseted in her life, and yet her figure was superb, being well rounded and full, yet so supple that every muscle was obedient to her will. She could ride a horse, leap a fence, swim, fish, and row a boat as well and untiringly as a man, yet in nothing was she masculine. She had cultivated all of those physical possibilities of her body, which it should be the privilege of all women to do, without transgressing some rule of society which has been fashioned to protect the weaker specimens of the sex, rather than to develop the dormant energies of womankind. It was her constant boast that neither rain nor sun, nor any untoward freak of the elements, could deter her from pursuing a pre-arranged purpose. She never "caught cold." In truth she had never been ill one whole day since her birth.

The other matter may seem a slight one, as I describe it, but were you to meet the girl, you would notice it very quickly. I allude to her manner of speech. We all of us, when writing, are careful in forming our sentences. We spell all words in full, avoiding abbreviations. But note well the speech of even the most liberally educated and carefully nurtured, and what do we discover? That our English is sadly defective, not merely in grammatical construction, but, more particularly, in pronunciation, and in enunciation. We slur many letters, and merge many words, the one into the other. We are so pressed for time that we cannot pause to breathe between words; our sentences have no commas, and sometimes not even periods, that can be recognized as such. In our hurry we use abbreviations whenever possible. We say "don't," "won't," "can't," and many others that we "shouldn't."

Agnes never did this. Her language was always as correct, her pronunciation as perfect, and her enunciation as distinct, as though she were constantly studying to be a purist. You say that she must have been affected! But you are wrong. Not for an instant did she make such an impression upon any one. In this, as in all things, she was merely her natural self. It was a charm to the ear to hear her in conversation. Her voice was so musical, and her intonation so pleasant. I remember how attractive to me it was to listen to her as she would say "I shall let you, etc." pronouncing the "t" and the "y" without effort and yet each distinctly. How much prettier than the "let chou" which so commonly assails the ear! Ah! You are saying that you do not so merge words; but be honest, and observe when next you essay such a phrase.

It was by the merest chance that the Judge and Agnes called on the very day of Leon's arrival. They were *en route* for the race-track, and passing near the Doctor's home, the Judge turned his horses in the direction of his friend's house to inquire when he was expected to return. He was delighted to meet him.

Greetings having been exchanged they began a general conversation.

"What have you been doing up in the country, Doctor?" asked the Judge. "Fishing, I suppose?"

"You might say," answered Dr. Medjora, "that I have been a fisher of men. I brought one back with me, you see." He indicated Leon by a wave of his hand. The Judge glanced at the youth, and awaited a further explanation.

"Leon and I are old friends," continued the Doctor. "I met him first when he needed my services to help him with a broken leg. But I have accepted his assistance many times since, when, without him, I might never have found my way back to civilization from the jungles into which I had strayed. For the future I need him so much that I have brought him home with me, to remain permanently."

"Indeed!" said the Judge, much interested, for if Leon were to be always with his friend, it was of more than passing moment to himself. "In what way do you need him?"

"Judge, as you know, my good wife here has not given me the son that I have longed for." Madame scowled, enraged by the speech which however had not been meant to wound her. The Doctor had not thought of her at all, but merely mentioned what was a fact. "Therefore I have no heir. I do not mean in connection with my worldly goods. I speak of my profession. I wish a student to whom I may impart my methods, so that after my day has passed my people may still have some one to depend upon. You see, I look upon my practice, much as a shepherd would consider his sheep. I am responsible for them. They depend upon me to keep them out of danger. I consider it a duty to supply a successor to myself."

"And this young gentleman is to be he?" asked the Judge.

"Leon is my choice before all whom I have known. Above all others I have decided that he is the most worthy of the trust that I shall impose in him." The Doctor spoke feelingly.

"Young man," said the Judge, addressing Leon, "I hope you appreciate the rare opportunity offered to you by my friend. If you are really capable of becoming his successor, then you are destined to be a power in the community, as he is to-day."

"Judge Dudley," said Leon, "I know that I am most fortunate. Dr. Medjora has taken me from beggary, and placed before me a future which would tempt any young man. But, to me, it means more than a salvation from drudgery; it means more than a high-road to fortune. I feel that I am destined to realize the hopes of my life, the yearnings of all my past days. I shall have a chance to acquire learning, to cultivate my intellect, to gain knowledge, which in my mind is the supremest power."

The Judge was somewhat surprised to hear such words from a country lad, still habited in clothing more suited to a farmer than to one with such aspirations. He said: "Young man, you interest me. Evidently you have learned to think for yourself. Come, tell me! Why do you lay such store by knowledge, when the rest of mankind are crying for money?"

"Money! Money! Money!" repeated Leon with a contemptuous curl of the lip. "Judge Dudley, I am nearing my majority, and I can say, that in all my life I do not think that I have owned more than fifty dollars. My food, clothing, and a home, have been provided for me, but aside from that I have not spent more than the sum named, and most of that went for books. So, you see, one may live without wealth, if enough to cover actual necessities be his. Without knowledge, a man would be an idiot. I think that is a logical proposition. If you grant that, then the less knowledge one has, the nearer he must be to the imbecile, and the more he acquires, the closer he approaches the highest stage of existence. Money we leave behind us at death. Knowledge, on the contrary, not only goes with us, but is really the only guarantee the individual has of a continuance of existence beyond the grave."

The Judge became more and more interested, and Dr. Medjora, observing the good impression which his *protégé* was making, was content to remain silent and listen.

"Your last statement indicates that you have formulated some mode of reasoning, upon which to base your convictions," said the Judge. "Will you take us a little further into your doctrine?"

"I am afraid that my ideas are rather crude, sir. I have had access to few standard works, and have been compelled to think out things for myself. But if I do not bore you, I shall be only too willing to continue. Indeed, it is a great treat to me, to speak with some one who may contradict me where I fall into error."

"You are a modest young man, Mr. Grath. Please continue. You were saying that one's knowledge might assure him a life hereafter."

"So I believe. Of course it is almost impossible, if not quite so, to prove anything in connection with the great future. But it is the prerogative of man to reason upon all subjects, and it is eminently fitting that he should study that one which most nearly affects himself. In the absence of absolute proof, I claim that one may adopt any theory that appeals to him as reasonable and probable. Now in relation to knowledge. I say it is more important to amass knowledge than to hoard up wealth. Money belongs to the material plane, and, having no relation to any other, it is as perishable, as far as it affects one individual, as is the human body. Money buys luxuries and comforts for the body only. It can add nothing to intellectual attainment. You may say that with it one may purchase books with which to improve the mind. That is true, but does not invalidate my argument, for it is not the book which is pabulum to our intellect, but only the thoughts which have been recorded upon its pages. Money procures us the possession of the book, whereas if we borrow it, and return it again, in the interval we may receive all the mental benefit which it can bestow upon the owner. Knowledge, on the other hand, is immaterial. It is an attribute of what has been called the soul. It is potent while being invisible, and though invisible it has a market value as well as things material. All the wealth of the world may not suffice to make one man wise, while all the wisdom in the world would surely make its possessor wealthy, but for the fact that he would probably be too wise to wish for riches. If, then, knowledge is such a potent factor in the world's affairs, can it be that it ceases to exist when a man dies? It is reasonable to suppose that it does not: then what becomes of it? The man cannot leave it to his heirs, as he does his chattels. Therefore it must continue where it has always been, and that is within the mind, which must have a continuance of existence to retain its knowledge."

"Ah! Very good! But Dr. Medjora has just announced that he is preparing to bequeath his knowledge to you, who are to be his heir in that respect. How do you make that conform to your curious theory?"

"You misapprehend the true condition. Dr. Medjora does not purpose giving me his knowledge, as one gives money, thereby lessening his own store. He merely intends to cultivate my own intellect, training it in grooves parallel with those which he himself has followed. He might live until I know as much as he does now, yet he would be no less wise than he is. Rather, he would have grown wiser himself in having acquired the experience of teaching another."

"You should study law instead of medicine. If you grow tired of the Doctor, you must come to me. Only, let me ask you one more question. If, according to your tenets, the wisest man is most certain of a future life, what of the most idiotic?"

"He is most apt to meet with annihilation. But he would cease to exist, only as to his individuality. I have not thought very deeply in that direction, but as my mind cannot conceive of the actual annihilation of anything that is existent, I have surmised that perhaps the minds of many idiots may become coalescent, so that a new individual might he created, who would possess sufficient intellectuality at birth in the world, to realize the importance to himself of mental cultivation."

"Ha! Ha! Doctor," said the Judge, laughing. "If two idiots may eventually be rolled into one, there is some hope for you and me. We may be joined together in the next world, and what a fellow we would be on our next trip to this old-fashioned planet! But seriously, Mr. Grath, your theories interest me. We will talk together again. You must come to our house some day. But I have not time for theology now. My daughter has a little bet on the first race, and if I delay longer she will miss seeing it. She has been making impatient signs to me for some time."

"Father!" exclaimed Agnes, deprecatingly; then turning to Leon, she continued: "Mr. Grath, you must not lay too much stress upon what my father says, when he is not upon the bench. When acting in his official capacity, his word is law, but at other times—"

"My daughter's is," interrupted the Judge, with a good-humored laugh.

"At other times," Agnes resumed, "he often prevaricates. He is constantly endeavoring to impress people with the idea that I am only a child, and not capable of comprehending serious conversation. Let me assure you that I have been highly entertained and edified by what you have been saying."

Leon bowed gravely without a suspicion of a blush, or embarrassment of manner, at thus receiving a compliment for the first time in his life from the lips of beauty. He was very self-reliant, though never obtrusively so. What he said was very simple.

"That you have been pleased to listen to me with attention, was sufficient proof to me, Miss Dudley, that at least I was not trying your patience too far by my speech."

"Come, Agnes, or we will miss that race, and whether you care or not, I confess that I do."

Then adieux were made and Dr. Medjora accompanied his guests to the door, where he paused a moment to say a word to the Judge, Leon having remained behind.

"What do you think of the lad?" he asked.

"A promising pupil, Medjora," replied the Judge. "He has brains, an uncommon endowment in these days. He is worth training. Do your best with him."

"I will!" answered the Doctor.

As the carriage bore the Judge and Agnes towards the race-track, the former asked his daughter this question.

"Agnes, what do you think of Mr. Grath?"

"He is bright," she replied, "but what he was saying impressed me from the fact that he seems to have convinced himself of the correctness of his theories, rather than from any argument which he offered, which would satisfy another's mind. Nearly all of it I have read."

When the Doctor returned to the room, he found Leon looking at a book on the table, whereas he had expected to see him at the window watching the departing girl. Therefore he asked:

"What do you think of Miss Dudley?"

"Miss Dudley?" repeated Leon. "Oh! She has a face which one would not easily forget. I met her once, some years ago, but only for a few minutes. Long enough only to answer some question which she asked, yet also long enough to impress her face upon my recollection indelibly. But I suppose you mean the girl herself, and all I can say is, that I should never form an opinion after an interview so brief. I would add, however, that she seems to be intellectually superior to her sex."

He spoke entirely dispassionately, and Dr. Medjora said no more.

Madame Medjora had quietly left the room while Leon was expounding his views to the Judge.

During the afternoon, the Doctor took Leon down into the city, to show him about, and more especially to have proper clothing prepared for him. They returned to the Villa Medjora, as Madame called their home, just in time to hear the voice of the Doctor's wife raised in anger. She was enraged because the butler had opened a box and released Lossy.

"It is bad enough to have the beggar boy thrust upon me," she had exclaimed. "I will not tolerate the nuisance of having a pest like this about the premises. Put him back in his box, and take him away from here instantly. Do you hear?"

The butler heard, but did not heed. He had learned that the Doctor was the master, and having received explicit orders in relation to the dog, he proceeded to put them into effect, despite the protests of Madame. Thus Lossy was bathed, combed, dried, and fed, Madame watching the performance from a window, and continuing her violent tirade, becoming more and more angered as she realized the impotency of her wrath.

As the Doctor and his *protégé* entered the grounds, Lossy bounded along the walk, barking delightedly at the sight of his master. For one moment the lad's cup of happiness was full, but in the next a dread entered his heart. He distinctly heard Madame say:

"I'll poison that beast!" With which she closed the window and disappeared. Leon looked appealingly at the Doctor, whose brows were knit together in an ominous frown.

"Do not be alarmed, Leon," said he, "I will guarantee that Madame will not carry her threat into execution. She is a woman of hasty temper, and often speaks without reflection. She is annoyed because the dog has come, but when she learns that he will not disturb her in any way, her resentment will pass. Lossy is safe. Let your mind rest easy on that point." He placed his hand upon Leon's shoulder and looked at him with reassuring kindliness. Leon felt slightly relieved, but when he retired to rest that night, in the room allotted to him, he secretly carried Lossy with him, and the dog slept at the foot of his master's bed.

CHAPTER VII
A WIZARD'S TEACHING

During the six months which followed, Leon advanced rapidly in his studies. His regular routine was to spend a specified number of hours each day in the magnificently appointed chemical laboratory; to accompany the Doctor upon many of his professional rounds, especially to hospital cases, and to the tenements of the poor; and in the evening it became usually their custom to spend an hour together, during which the Doctor gave his pupil oral instruction, rehearsed him in what he had already learned, and set new tasks for him to master. This hour was generally the last before bedtime. After dinner the Doctor's habit was to yield himself to the demands of his wife, who delighted to carry him off to social functions, or to the theatres. Leon very rarely accompanied them. He remained at home to study, and was ready to meet his teacher at the appointed hour, which was seldom later than eleven o'clock. Dr. Medjora was a great disciplinarian, and had Leon been differently constituted, he might have rebelled at the amount of work which he was expected to accomplish each day. But he never uttered complaint of any sort. Indeed, he seemed to have an unlimited capacity for study, so that his assiduity, coupled with a marvellous memory, rendered his progress very rapid. Nevertheless the Doctor was not satisfied. He was impatient to see the day arrive when Leon should reach the same pinnacle of knowledge which he himself had attained, in order that thereafter they might traverse the road to fame hand in hand, leaning upon and assisting one another.

At last the day, the hour, arrived, beyond which the Doctor had decided to pursue their sluggish method no further. He knew how to teach Leon in one year, all that he had learned by weary plodding throughout the greater part of his life. But it was essential to his scheme, that he should be able to hypnotize Leon, and in this he had made one trial which had failed. During the months which had passed since then, he had matured a plan which he was sure would prove successful, and now he entered his pupil's presence prepared to carry it into execution.

Leon was reading, but instantly closed his book and laid it aside, greeting the Doctor, not as the foolish schoolboy afraid of his master, but as the ardent student eager for learning. The Doctor seated himself in a comfortable Turkish chair, and began as follows:

"Leon, are you tired? Could you prolong the hour a little to-night if I should not otherwise find time for what I wish to say?"

"I will gladly listen to you till morning, Doctor," replied Leon.

"You have been taking every night the draught which I prescribed?"

"Yes, sir. There on the table is the potion for to-night."

"You do not know what it is, Leon, and the time has not yet arrived when I can explain its decoction to you. Suffice it for me to tell you, that this colorless liquid is practically the Elixir of Life, for which the ancients sought in vain."

"The Elixir of Life? Why, that is a myth!" Leon almost smiled. But he did not quite, because the expression on the Doctor's face was too serious.

"I said that it is practically the magic fluid. It has the property of supplying the body in twenty-four hours, with the vital energy which it would otherwise need several days of rest and recreation to recover. That is why I prescribe it to you, while you are engaged so arduously upon your studies. Do you not find that you are less easily fatigued?"

"I do, indeed. It is certainly a wonderful invigorator!"

"Leon," said the Doctor, after a slight pause, "I believe that I have your confidence and trust?"

"Absolutely, Doctor!"

"Would you take any drug that I might administer, without knowing its effects, and without questioning my motive, so long as I assure you that you would be benefited?"

"I would!"

"I will put you to the test, but, in exchange for your trust, I will tell you in part what I mean to do." He took a small phial from his pocket, a tiny tube containing less than five minims of a clear colorless liquid. "In this little bottle, Leon, there is a medicine of frightful potency. One drop would suffice to destroy a human life. But mixed with your nightly draught, a new chemical compound is produced, which, though harmless, will so energize the brain-cells that the powers of recollection will be more than trebled. By this means, your progress can be very much enhanced, for instead of receiving what I offer to you each night, and assimilating a part of it, you will find in the future that all my words will be indelibly imprinted upon your mind."

"I would have taken the drug without your explanation, Doctor, but now I am eager for the experiment."

"This is no experiment, Leon. Beware of operating upon a human being when your knowledge is so meagre that you must resort to experimental tests." There was a touch of deep feeling in the Doctor's tones, as though he might at some time have made the error against which he admonished the lad. Leon, however, did not observe anything out of the common. He was intent upon what the Doctor was about to do. Dr. Medjora carefully removed the tiny glass stopper from the phial, and, holding it in his left hand, took up the glass from the table with his right. Pausing a moment he exclaimed:

"Watch!"

Then with a quick movement he poured the contents of the phial into the liquid in the glass. Instantly there was a commotion. There was a sound of water boiling, and a sort of steam arose.

"The poisonous properties are thrown off, you see, in the form of gas," said the Doctor.

The liquid in the glass, from having been colorless, was now converted into a bright green, but as Leon watched he was astonished to see this emerald hue gradually fade, until within a minute it had disappeared, and the fluid was as colorless as before.

"Observe, Leon," said the Doctor, "how easily I could have administered the added drug without your knowledge, for just as you see no difference that the eye can detect, so also will your potion be as tasteless as before. Will you drink it?"

Leon took the glass and drank, without hesitation.

"I thank you for this evidence of your faith in me," said the Doctor, and pausing awhile, presently spoke again: "Leon, you were probably surprised when, as a part of your task for to-night, I told you to read a portion of the book of Genesis, in the Bible. I had a special purpose in view, which I will now explain. I have a sort of story to tell, which at first may seem entirely unconnected with our work, but bear with me, be closely attentive, and you will soon discover that all I shall say has an important bearing. The beginning of the Bible of the Jews should make all who study it pause to consider a singular circumstance. The creation of the world, and all that occurred up to the time of the Flood, is narrated in seven short chapters, the end of the seventh recording the Flood itself, and the almost total annihilation of all the creatures of the earth. But from the Flood up to the nativity of the Christ, we find the historian well stocked with facts, and hundreds of pages are filled with his narration."

"Was it not because Moses, or the author of the earlier books, had more data concerning the events following the Flood, than those which preceded it? Indeed, it is probable that the Flood itself obliterated the records of previous times."

"A good argument, my boy, if we consider the Bible as a mere history. But does not the religious world claim that it is an inspired work? If the Creator actually revealed the past to Moses, then there was no reason why he could not have been as explicit about the occurrences before the Flood, as after? But your explanation is the true one. The author of Genesis did not have access to actual records, but could merely generalize from the legends then in existence. There are two events in the history of the world which stand out pre-eminently important. First, the Flood, which destroyed mankind, and second, the discovery of America, which restored a lost continent. That these two events have a very close relationship is suspected only by a few scientists."

"How are they connected? A great period of time separates them."

"True. But let me tell you the real story of the Flood, and you will comprehend my meaning. I shall not stop to give you arguments to substantiate what I say, because that would take too long, and would lead us away from what I am aiming at. However, while my own knowledge of the facts was received from other sources, when you have the time you will find the whole subject ably expounded in a work in my library, entitled *The Lost Histories of America*, by Blacket.

"At the time of the Flood, or just prior thereto, the highest civilization in the world existed in Mexico. There, a vast empire flourished. The arts and sciences had received much attention, and beautiful cities, populated by cultured people, abounded everywhere in the land. Navigation was well understood, and colonies from Mexico had made new homes for themselves on the western coast of Africa, in Ireland and England, along the Mediterranean, and, in the opposite direction, they had even penetrated Asia, crossing the vast Pacific. Then came that great convulsion which all peoples, in all climes, remember to-day through legends of waters rising and submerging the whole surface of the earth. It is probable that a great tidal wave narrowed the continents of North and South America along both shores, eating away the central portion more extensively, the complete division of the two being prevented only by the mountainous character of the region. In South America, we find the southermost part narrowed to a point."

"Do you mean that South America was once wider?"

"The proof of my assertion lies in the ruins and monuments still to be found buried beneath the waves, hundreds of miles from the shore, though some were undoubtedly on islands which also sunk at this time. What would be the first effects of a cataclysm of such magnitude? The ships at sea, if they escaped at all, would sail for home. Arriving where the original shores had been, and finding nothing for even fifty miles beyond, the survivors would imagine that the whole country had been lost, and so would turn towards those other shores which their race had colonized. They would carry with them the story of the Flood which had submerged the whole of the western continent, and from this account we would finally inherit our version of the awful event. Having accepted the theory of the destruction of their home-land, and being thus compelled to adopt permanently their new abiding-places, would not these colonists immediately set about making their new home to resemble as much as possible the old? Undoubtedly! Hence we find them building the tower of Babel, in which project they were foiled by the confusion of tongues. Would it surprise you, however, to know that a similar legend is found in Central America?"

"I am ignorant, Doctor, of all that pertains to the subject. Therefore, of course, I should be surprised, but I am deeply interested."

"The legend is still current among the natives dwelling near the pyramid of Cholula, to which it alludes, but I will give you a version of it which is recorded in a manuscript of Pedro de Los Rios. It is as follows:

"Before the great inundation, which took place four thousand eight hundred years after the creation of the World, the country of Anahuac was inhabited by giants. All those who did not perish were transformed into fishes, save seven, who fled into caverns. When the waters subsided, one of these giants, Xelhua, surnamed the Architect, went to Chollolan, where, as a memorial of the mountain Tlaloc, which had served for an asylum to himself and his six brethren, he built an artificial hill in form of a pyramid.... The gods beheld with wrath this edifice, the top of which was to reach the clouds. Irritated at the daring attempt of Xelhua, they hurled fire [lightning?] on the pyramid. Numbers of the workmen perished; the work was discontinued."

"Indeed, Doctor, the two traditions are similar. How is that to be understood, since certainly from the time of the Flood, until the discovery by Columbus, there was no communication between the Old and the so-called New World?"

"Wherever, in two places devoid of communication, similar occurences are recorded, they have a common inspiration. So it was in this instance. The colonists built the temple to their God whom they had worshipped in Mexico. The Mexicans did likewise, moved to the action by the destruction of all their places of worship, because of the great inroad made by the sea, and the consequent narrowing of the land. In both instances, we can understand the desire to attain a great height, in order to have a place of safety if a second flood were to supervene. Now let me call your attention to a little coincidence. You observe in the Mexican story that seven giants were saved. This number seven has always been considered a numeral of great significance, by all the religionists of olden times. Thus the author of the book of Genesis so divided the beginning of his narration, that the creation of the world and all that occurred up to the Flood, is told in seven chapters. Depending upon legends for his facts about that period, which the Mexican story says covered forty-eight hundred years, he condenses it all into the mystic number of seven chapters."

"From all this, then, I am to believe that the story of the Flood is true in the main? I had always supposed that it was either a myth, or an exaggeration of some local inundation?"

"Undoubtedly the great Flood occurred. But now I come to the object which I had in telling you all this. The great pyramids in Mexico, or *teocali* as they were called, were temples, places of worship consecrated to the god Tesculipoca. Would it surprise you to hear that this Mexican deity is no other than Æsculapius, commonly called the father of medicine?"

"It would, indeed!"

"Yet it is true. Like many other of the mythological gods of Europe, he really existed in Mexico. The quickest manner of recognizing him, is by his name. Let us place the Mexican and the European, one under the other:

TESCULIPOCA AESCULAPIUS

"Now, if we remember that the presence of a diphthong in the transformation of names implies a lost consonant, we see that the names are virtually the same, the O C A being the Mexican suffix, and the I U S the Greek. To go a little further in our identification, mythology informs us that Æsculapius is the son of Apollo. We are also told that the Tower of Babel was consecrated to Bel, but that the upper story was devoted to Æsculapius. This is significant, from the fact that Apollo and Bel are forms of the same deity. Thus we find that immediately after the Flood, those who escape on one side of the great Ocean proceed to build a temple to Æsculapius, while on the other, in the home country, they build a new pyramid, a *teocali*, in which to worship Tesculipoca. Are you satisfied that Æsculapius was originally an inhabitant of this continent?"

"It certainly seems so."

"Seems so? It is so! And in that fact, Leon, abides a secret which has been of vast importance to me, and shall be to you. Few men know what I am, or whence I came. Let me tell you that the high priests of these *teocali* were all lineally descended from the great physician, and to this day there are many who still blow upon the embers of the old faith, down in the forest fastnesses of Mexico and Central America, secure from the prying eyes of white men. I inherited the right of priesthood at my birth."

"You? You a Mexican priest?" Leon started up amazed.

"By inheritance, yes! But early in life I made a discovery of vast importance. By deciphering some old hieroglyphical writings, I learned that, somewhere in the North Country, the first *teocali* had been built. That in the topmost chamber of it, as in the tower of Babel, the god himself had dwelt. In the dome which surmounted that temple, he had sculptured hieroglyphics, which recorded all the vast knowledge which he possessed. I even found some fragmentary copies of these sculptures, and I learned enough to make me determined to seek, and to find that lost temple."

"You succeeded!" ejaculated Leon, much excited.

"I always succeed," said the Doctor, with significant emphasis. "It has been the rule of my life, from which I have never deviated. Yes! I succeeded! I discovered the dome of the temple, buried beneath the earth. For years I have spent many hours of otherwise unoccupied time, deciphering the sculptured records of the lost past. Lost to the world, but found by me, Emanuel Medjora, whom men call Wizard!" There was a flash of triumph in the Doctor's eye, as he uttered these words. Leon looked at him, but did not speak.

"Yes! The knowledge garnered by Æsculapius has been inherited by me. This it is, that I mean to bequeath to you. Is it not better than money?"

"You mean that you will take me into that chamber, which you have found?" Leon was incredulous, yet hopeful of receiving an affirmative reply.

"That is what I will do, but not to-night. The hour is now late. You must retire to rest. To-morrow night, I will give you proof of what I have told you. Now, good-night, and remember that I have intrusted you with a secret more valuable than all the world. Beware of betraying me."

"Doctor!" expostulated Leon, much hurt.

"You need not speak so, Leon. If I doubted you, I would never have confided in you. Once more, good-night."

"Good-night!" And Leon turned to leave the room.

"Pleasant dreams," said the Doctor, and Leon had no suspicion that there was a studied purpose in the utterance.

After the lad's departure, the Doctor sat alone, musing upon the situation. He did not go to rest, because his work was not yet complete. He recalled the night on the Fall River boat, when he had endeavored to hypnotize Leon, and had failed. To-night he would try again. For months he had been arranging all the preliminaries, and now he was confident of success. The object which he had in view was this: He desired to teach Leon more rapidly than the lad could learn in his normal condition. This he hoped to accomplish with the aid of hypnosis. By gaining control of Leon, in this manner he expected to utilize the marvels of suggestion. He would instruct him, and then charge him to remember all that he had been taught, and the result would be that the mind would obey the injunction, and thus acquire knowledge more rapidly than by ordinary study.

But, for the present, he believed it to be of vital importance that Leon should not suspect what he was doing. To this end he had arranged his mode of procedure with the caution of a master of psychology. In the first place, he had prepared Leon's mind for the rapid progress of the future, by telling him that the drug administered would increase his mental powers. This was false. What he had added to the usual tonic draught, was not a poison, as he had claimed, but a powerful narcotic. In order, however, to make an impression upon his mind, he had relied upon the chemical reaction, and the changing color, which has been described.

Then he had related to him enough of the history of Æsculapius and of the secret chamber, so that if on the morrow Leon should remember the visit to the dome, where he meant to carry him presently, he would easily account for it to himself, as a dream. To make sure of this, he had suggested dreaming to him as they parted.

So, as he reviewed his arrangement, the Doctor was satisfied that he had taken all necessary precautions, and with patience he awaited the time which he had set for further action.

The minutes crept by, until at last a little door in the front of the great clock opened, and a silver image of Vulcan raised a tiny hammer and brought it down upon the anvil before him with force enough to draw forth a sharp ring from the metal. Then the door closed again. It was one o'clock.

The Doctor arose and went to a closet, whence he brought forth a pair of soft slippers which he put on instead of his shoes. Leaving the room, he climbed the stairway as noiselessly as a cat, not a board creaking as he slowly lifted himself from one step to the next. He had no fear of arousing Leon, but he did not wish to attract the attention of any other one in the house. Soon he was in Leon's room, standing beside the bed. Leon lay sleeping as calmly as a babe. Dr. Medjora knelt beside him, and listened to his heart beating. He felt his pulse, and seemed satisfied. From a couch he took a heavy slumber robe, and without hesitation lifted Leon from the bed and wrapped him in the robe. Next he raised him in his arms and carried him from the room. At the end of the hall he paused long enough to open the door which led to his laboratory, which occupied a wing of the building, and passing through he closed the door behind him, and laid his burden on the floor.

Next he lighted a small lamp which shed but a dim light, and stooping, felt along the floor until he found a secret spring which he released, and then slid aside a trap-door, exposing to view a flight of stairs. Down these he descended, the ruby-colored shade of his lamp throwing red rays upward as he disappeared. In a few moments he returned without the lamp, which, placed somewhere below, still lighted the opening with a dull glow. The Doctor took Leon in his arms, and carried him down the steps, until he reached the same door through which he had taken young Barnes on the memorable night of the fire. In rebuilding upon the property, the Doctor had purposely placed his laboratory over his secret underground chamber.

Having entered the remains of the temple of Æsculapius, he laid Leon upon a comfortable mass of rugs which covered the central stone. Taking from his pocket a small phial, he opened Leon's mouth and poured the contents into it, holding his nose until, in an effort to breathe, the drug was swallowed. This accomplished the Doctor retired behind a screen, which had been formed by him in such accurate reproduction of the walls of the chamber, that one would not readily suspect that it was not a part of the original structure.

"Within ten minutes he should awaken," mused the Doctor. "But when he does, and his eyes rest upon the scene about him, he will surely think that he is dreaming of the temple of Æsculapius. Then, while his brain is heavy with drugs, and his mind mystified, he will yield readily to hypnotic influences."

The ten minutes had barely elapsed, when the sleeper moved. A moment later, Leon opened his eyes, and as the dim light from the little lamp enabled him to see the dome above him, he lay still, regarding it with some surprise. A few moments more, and he rubbed his eyes with the knuckle of his forefinger, and the Doctor knew that he was wondering whether he were awake or dreaming. Not fully satisfied, Leon sat up, and gazed about him. He was becoming more thoroughly awake, and very soon he would know that he was not in dream-land. But the Doctor no longer delayed his plan of action. Ere Leon could recover from the surprise of his first awakening, and as he gazed directly in front of him, Dr. Medjora touched an electric button with his foot, and instantly a blaze of light appeared upon the wall. A hundred tiny incandescent lamps, arranged in the form of radiating spokes from a wheel, placed before a brightly burnished silver reflector, with thousands of facets upon its concaved surface, shed a light as dazzling as a sun. Leon closed his eyes to protect them from the glare, but when he opened them again another surprise awaited him. By touching another button, the Doctor had started a motor, which, with a dull humming sound, set the wheel of lights in motion, the reflector revolving rapidly in one direction while the fixture which contained the lamps turned swiftly the opposite way. The scintillating rays were so dazzling, that it was impossible for Leon to gaze upon it more than an instant. He turned his back upon it, bewildered, but immediately before his eyes there appeared on the wall confronting him another similar wheel of light, which began to revolve also. Again he turned his eyes away, and again, and again, and again; but wherever he looked, the rapidly moving electric suns burst forth, until a dozen of them surrounded him.

He stood a moment with his gaze upon the floor, trying to recover control of himself, for his astonishment was such that he felt as though he were losing his mind. But all in vain. As much as he dreaded those fiery suns, as well as he knew instinctively that to look upon them was to be lost, he could not resist the temptation. Slowly, as with an effort, he raised his eyes and stared at the scintillating suns before him. For a brief time his eyes turned from one to another, but finally they became fixed and he gazed only at one. In a moment all the others were turned out, and that one revolved faster and faster. Two or three times it seemed as though he tried to withdraw his gaze, but eventually all resistance to the influence of the dazzling light ceased. Leon sank back into a partly sitting posture upon the rugs, and in a few moments the eyelids closed heavily, the head sank upon the breast, the body quivered, and the limbs hung limp. Leon was passing into a hypnotic, sleep, caused by the ingenious mechanical device coupled with the skilfully prepared surprise which the mind had received.

The Doctor pressed a button, and the last wheel was extinguished and stood motionless. Once more the only light was from the little lamp, which now, by contrast with the recent glare, seemed like a glowworm. Dr. Medjora came forth and placed himself in front of Leon. With the palms of his hands on the lad's temples, he rubbed the eyeballs through the closed lids, with his thumbs. After a short time he spoke.

"Leon! Leon! Are you asleep?"

There was no reply.

"Leon! You are asleep, but you can speak!"

An indistinct murmur escaped from the sleeper.

"Leon! You are asleep! But you are also awake! Open your eyes, but do not awaken entirely! Open your eyes!"

In response to the command, authoritatively given, Leon's eyes opened slowly, and he stared before him, as though seeing nothing.

"Look! You can see me if you try! You can recognize me! You can speak! Speak to me!"

The sleeper gazed at the Doctor a while, but said nothing.

"Do you not hear me? I tell you that you can speak! You must speak! Speak! I command you! Speak!"

"Doc-tor Med-jo-ra!" was the reply uttered in separate syllables, with a pause between each, and in hollow tones.

"Good! You see you can speak if you will. You will find it easy enough directly. Look about you now, and tell me where you are."

"I think I am in the temple!"

"You are correct. You are in the temple of Æsculapius. Do you understand?"

"The temple of Æsculapius! I understand!"

"Do you know how you came here?"

"No!"

"Do you wish to know?"

"No!"

"I brought you here. Do you understand that?"

"Yes!"

"Are you glad or sorry?"

"Glad!"

"You are asleep! You know that, do you not?"

"I am asleep!"

"Do you wish to awaken?"

"I did at first! Now I do not!"

"Then you are happy in your present state?"

"I am with you! I am happy! I am with you!"

"Then you trust me?"

"I do, now!"

"You do now! Did you ever mistrust me?"

"Yes! Once!"

"When was that?"

"On the boat! You tried to make me sleep!"

"But I have made you sleep now. Do you still trust me?"

"Yes!"

"Why did you mistrust me before then?"

"I did not know how pleasant it is to sleep!"

"Then you are happy, when you are asleep like this?"

"I am with you! I am happy! I am with you!"

"Very well! In the future if I try to make you sleep, you will not resist me?"

"No!"

"Say, I will not resist you!"

"I will not resist you!"

"You will sleep, whenever I wish you to do so?"

"I will sleep, when you wish me to do so!"

"Now, if I ask you a few questions, will you answer me truthfully?"

"Yes!"

"I wish you then to tell me whether you are in love with Agnes Dudley?"

"What is love?"

"Do you not know?"

"Only what I have read!"

"You have not felt what it is to love a woman?"

"I have not!"

"Then you do not love Agnes Dudley?"

"I suppose not!"

"Have you thought of it at all, as possible?"

"I have not!"

"Not even for an instant?"

"Not even for an instant!"

"That is very strange. She is a magnificent girl. Beautiful, intellectual, and cultured. You have observed that?"

"Yes! I have observed all that!"

"Nevertheless, you have not thought of loving her?"

"Nevertheless, I have not thought of loving her!"

"Are you tired now of sleeping?"

"I would like to sleep the other sleep! I cannot explain! Yes, I am tired!"

"You need not explain. I understand. This is your first experience, and must not be continued longer. But you must promise me something."

"I will promise!"

"You remember all that I told you to-night before you went to sleep?"

"I do!"

"You must never forget any of it. You must remember it all. Not the words, but the substance. You will remember?"

"I will remember!"

"Now I will take you back to your bed. When you have been there ten minutes, you will awaken!"

"I will awaken!"

"You will remember this place, but only as though you had seen it in a dream!"

"I will remember the dream!"

"Then you will immediately fall into a natural sleep!"

"I will fall into a natural sleep!"

"In the morning you will either remember nothing, or if anything only that you have had a dream!"

"Only a dream!"

"Now sleep! Sleep deeply!"

The Doctor pressed Leon's eyes with his thumbs, and when he released them the lids remained closed.

"You cannot open your eyes!"

"No! I cannot open my eyes!"

"Now you cannot speak!"

There was no reply. Dr. Medjora wrapped the sleeper in the robe and carried him upstairs, and back to his own room again. He placed him in his bed, and covered him carefully, as a mother would her babe. Stooping over him he placed his lips close to Leon's ear and said:

"Can you hear me? If so, raise your arm," a feeble elevation of the arm was made in response. "Good, you hear! Remember! Awaken in ten minutes! Awaken from a dream! Then sleep again!"

The sleeper stirred slightly, and breathed a long sigh. Dr. Medjora leaned over him, and imprinted a kiss upon his forehead. Then he left the apartment, closing the door cautiously behind him, and sought his own room.

CHAPTER VIII
THE FAITHFUL DOG

On the following morning, when Leon entered the laboratory, he found Dr. Medjora busily engaged upon a chemical analysis. He, therefore, without interrupting him, went to his own table, and took up his morning's task. Half an hour passed in silence, and then the Doctor spoke:

"Good-morning, Leon," said he. "I hope that the late hour at which you retired last night did not interfere with your rest?"

"On the contrary, Doctor," said Leon, "I slept very soundly; so soundly that I did not awaken as early as usual this morning. Yet I am puzzled by one thing."

"And that is—?"

"A dream. I have a distinct recollection of a dream, and yet I am sure that I slept soundly until the very moment of my awakening. I have always thought that dreams come only when one dozes, or is half awake. Do you think that one might sleep soundly, and nevertheless dream?"

"It is a question much disputed. If you have done so, however, you have proven the possibility. Tell me your dream."

Thus adroitly did the Doctor avoid committing himself by a statement which would have lead to an argument, Leon's controversial instinct being a prominent characteristic.

"The dream was singular," replied Leon, "not so much because of what I dreamed, but rather because of the impression made upon my mind. As a rule, what one dreams is recalled as a dimly defined vision, but in this instance, I can see the temple of Æsculapius as clearly as though I had really visited the place."

"Then in your dream you imagined that you saw that wonderful place?"

"Yes. There is nothing odd about that, because you told me that you would take me into the chamber to-night. I went to sleep with the desire to see the temple prominently present in my thoughts, and consequently, in my dream, that wish was gratified. But now I am anxious to verify my vision, to note how much resemblance there will be between the real and the imaginary. It would be very curious if I should be able to recognize the place!"

Leon looked away off into space, as one gazes at nothing when deeply absorbed in the contemplation of some perplexing problem. The Doctor at once recognized the danger that presented. Leon's memory was more vivid than he had intended it to be. If taken into the crypt, in his present state of active inquiry into the phenomenon which his mind was considering, and if he really should become convinced that what he thought a dream was the exact counterpart of the real, it would not be improbable that his suspicion of the truth might be aroused. It was therefore essential that his mind should be led into a safer channel. The Doctor undertook to do this.

"Leon," said he, "you are always interested in psychological phenomena, and therefore I will discuss this with you. The action of the mind is always an attractive study; attractive mainly because man cannot thoroughly unravel the mysteries surrounding the working of a human mind. Ordinarily, what one cannot comprehend and explain, is written down as a miracle. There are no miracles, except as the words may be used to describe that which mystifies. But the mystification passes, as soon as the explanation is arrived at. Now it is manifestly impossible that you should dream of a place which you have never seen, and obtain an accurate mental image of it."

"I do not say that I have done so. I only wonder how much resemblance will exist between the dream and the chamber itself."

"True! But I should not be at all surprised, when I take you there, if you claim that it is the counterpart of your dream."

"Why do you think that, Doctor, when you have just said truly, that such a fact would be impossible?"

"It would be impossible that such a thing should be a fact, but it is not at all impossible that you should think it to be a fact. Let me explain myself more clearly. As I said before, one cannot produce in the mind an absolutely accurate image of a thing which he has never seen. But mental images may be created, not alone through the sense of sight, but also through the sense of hearing. Last night I told you the story of Æsculapius. I described to you the *teocali* which had been reared in his memory. I told you that at the very top a dome-like chamber was specially dedicated to Æsculapius. I also explained to you that in the dome which I have discovered the walls are covered with hieroglyphical sculpturing. With such a description of the place, meagre as it is, you could readily construct a mental image, which would be sufficiently like the original for you to believe it identical. A dome is a dome, and, in regard to hieroglyphical figures, in the books in my library you have seen many pictures of those found on this continent."

"Still, Doctor, that would only enable me to create an image which would be similar. It could not be identical."

"No! It could not be identical. But suppose that you enter the crypt! Instantly you look about you, and an image of the place is imprinted upon your brain. This is objectively produced. You compare it with the subjective image left by your dream, and you are astonished at the similarity. Note the word! You look around you again, and again an objective image is formed. Again you essay a comparison: but what happens now? As clearly fixed upon your brain as you believe your dream to be, it is but a shadowy impression compared to those which come to you when awake. So your subjective image of the place is readily displaced by that first objective impression, and when you compare the second, it is with this, and not with your dream at all. As both are identical, you form the conclusion that your dream and the actuality are identical. So your first idea that they are similar passes, and you adopt the erroneous belief that they are identical. You have compared two objective impressions, where you believe that one was the subjective image of your dream. Thus you are deceived into believing that a miracle has occurred. And thus have all miracles been accepted as such; thus have all superstitions been created, through the incorrect appreciation of events and their causes."

"I see what you mean, Doctor, and I recognize, now, how easy it is to fall into error. Few in this world have the analytical instinct possessed by yourself. Yet, I must confess, I am anxious for the test to-night. Now that you have warned me, I wish to see whether my first comparison will give me the idea that the two images are identical, or merely similar."

From this speech Dr. Medjora saw that the lad was not entirely convinced. He concluded therefore to risk a test, that would definitely settle the question.

"Leon," said he, "you are a good draughtsman. Draw for me a picture of any part of the hieroglyphical sculpture which is most distinct in your recollection!"

In this the Doctor depended upon the fact that Leon could have but an indistinct remembrance of the place itself, because, from the moment of his awakening in the crypt, his mind had been confused by the rapid series of surprises presented to his eyes. The revolving lamps, and the glare emitted by them, would have been sufficient to create such shadows, that the sculptured figures would have been distorted, the mind itself being too much occupied for more than a very cursory glance at the walls of the place. Leon, however, at once began to draw, and within a few minutes he handed the paper to the Doctor, who was pleased to find upon it a poor copy of some figures in *Kingsborough's Antiquities*. Thus the Doctor's speculation was vindicated, because as soon as Leon had endeavored to draw, he copied an image in his mind, made by a picture which he had had time to study closely, yet which in his thought replaced the indistinct impression obtained in the crypt.

"You are quite sure, Leon," asked the Doctor, "that this is a figure which you saw in your dream."

"Quite sure," answered Leon, promptly, "although, of course, there may be some slight inaccuracy in my draught of it."

The Doctor then went to the library, and returned with the volume of Kingsborough, in which was the picture which Leon had really copied. When he showed this to the lad, he convinced him of his original proposition, that the hieroglyphical sculptures of his dream were but recollections of what he had seen in books. Thus he averted the threatening danger, and once more proved that, through his knowledge of psychical laws, he was an adept in controlling the minds of men.

Later in the day, Leon called at the home of Mr. Dudley, having been sent thither by the Doctor.

Doctor Medjora had given Leon a letter, with instructions to take it to the house, and if Mr. Dudley should be out, to await his return to deliver it and obtain a reply. In this he was actuated by a motive. He chose an hour when he knew certainly that the Judge would not be at home, though Agnes would. He wished Leon to be thrown into her society more often than circumstances had permitted heretofore. In the future, he intended so to arrange that the young people should meet more frequently. Dr. Medjora was willing to abide by the acts of Providence, as long as they aided his own designs; when they failed to do so, then he considered it time to control Providence, and guide it to his will.

When Leon was admitted into the reception-room at Judge Dudley's, he found Agnes reading. She laid aside her book and arose to greet him cordially. He explained the object of his visit, and that he would like to await the return of the Judge. Agnes therefore invited him to be seated. His great fondness for books led him to utilize her reading as a starting-point for conversation.

"I am sorry, Miss Dudley," he began, "that I have interrupted your reading. May I be permitted to ask what book you have?"

"Certainly!" she replied. "I have been reading a novel!"

"Oh!" was all that Leon said, but the tone excited Agnes at once, for in it she thought she detected a covert sneer.

"Do you never read novels?" she asked.

"I have little time for anything but science. I think that I have read but two novels in my life."

"May I ask what they were?"

"George MacDonald's *Malcolm* from which I named my dog 'Lossy,' and a book called *Ardath*. I do not remember the name of the author."

"*Ardath*, and you do not remember the name of the author? She would feel quite complimented at the impression made upon you, I am sure. Perhaps you would like to refresh your memory?" Agnes spoke with a tone of triumphant satisfaction, as she handed to him the book which she held. He took it and read on the title-page, "*Ardath; The Story of a Dead Self*; by Marie Corelli."

"This is a coincidence, is it not, Miss Dudley," said Leon, returning the volume. "I suppose it was very stupid of me to forget the author's name, but really I am so much more interested in the world of science, that romance has little attraction for me. In the one we deal in facts, while the other is all fiction."

"Is that your estimate of the relation existing between the two," said Agnes, with a twinkle in her eye. She always delighted in an argument, when she felt that she held the mastery of the situation, as she did now. Therefore she entered the combat, about to begin, with a zest equal to the love of debate which Leon possessed.

"You say that science deals only in facts. If you remember anything of *Ardath*, which is not probable, since you forget the writer, you may recall that in his wanderings through the city, Al-Kyris, Theos meets Mira-Khabur, the Professor of Positivism. The description of this meeting, and the conversation between the men is admirable, as a satire upon the claims of the scientists. Let me read to you one of the Professor's speeches. Theos has said:

"Then the upshot of all your learning sir, is that one can never be quite certain of anything?"

"Exactly so!" replied the pensive sage, with a grave shake of the head. "Judged by the very finest lines of metaphysical argument you cannot really be sure whether you behold in me a Person, or a Phantasm! You *think* you see me,–I *think* I see you,–but after all it is only an *impression* mutually shared–an impression which, like many another less distinct, may be entirely erroneous! Ah, my dear young sir! education is advancing at a very rapid rate, and the art of close analysis is reaching such a pitch of perfection, that I believe we shall soon be able logically to prove, not only that we do not actually exist, but, moreover, that we never have existed."

"What have you to say to that?" asked Agnes closing the book, but keeping one finger between the leaves, to mark the place.

"Why," said Leon, smiling, "that it is a very clever paragraph, and recalls to my mind the whole scene. I think that, later, this same Professor of Positivism declares that the only thing he is positive of, is the 'un-positiveness of Positivism!'"

"Ah! Then you do remember some of the novel. That is a hopeful sign for novelists, I am sure. But, jesting aside, you have not defended your pet hobby, science, from the charge brought against her!"

"If you wish me to take you seriously, then of course I must do so. What you have read, is clever, but not necessarily true. It is good in its place, and as used by the author. It typifies the character of the man, from whose mouth the words escape. But, in doing this, it shows us that he is merely the disciple of a school which depends for its existence upon bombast rather than true knowledge; upon sophistical cloudiness of expression rather than upon logical arguments, based upon reason and fact."

"Ah! Now I have you back to your first statement, that science deals with facts. But is it not true, that by your logical arguments various and varying deductions are obtained by different students, all seeking these finalities, which you term facts? Then which of them all is the true fact, and which is mere speculation?"

"I am afraid, Miss Dudley, that you have asked me a question which I am scarcely qualified to answer. All I can say is, that so long as matters are in dispute, we can have no knowledge of what is the truth. In speaking of facts, I only alluded to those proven hypotheses, which have been finally accepted by all scientists. Those are the facts of which science boasts."

"Yes, many of them are accepted for a decade, and then cast aside as exploded errors. But come, I do not wish to argue too strongly against science. I love it too well. What I prefer to do, is to defend my other hobby, romance; that which you called fiction. I will give you a paradox. I claim that there is more fact in good fiction, and more real fiction in accepted fact, than is generally credited."

"I am afraid I do not comprehend what you mean," said Leon, very much puzzled. He was growing interested in this girl who talked so well.

"Good," said Agnes. "I will gladly expound my doctrine. The best exponent of so called fact which I can cite, is the daily press.

The newspapers pretend to relate actual events; to tell us what really occurs. But let us look into the matter but a moment, and we discover that only on rare occasions is the reporter present when the thing happens, of which he is expected to write. Thus, he is obliged to depend upon others for his facts. Each person interrogated, gives him a version of the affair according with his own received impressions. But occurrences impress different persons in very different ways. Thus Mr. Reporter, when he comes to his desk, finds that he must sift out his facts from a mass of error. He does so, and obtains an approximation of the truth. It would be erroneous enough if he were now to write what he has deduced; but if he is at all capable, as a caterer to the public taste, he is compelled to serve his goose with a fancy sauce. He must weave an amount of fiction into and around his facts, so that the article may have some flavor. And the flavor is sweet or sour, nice or nasty, in accordance with the known predilections of the subscribers. What wonder that one who truly seeks for the facts in the case, endeavoring to obtain them by reading several accounts, finally throws all the newspapers away in disgust!"

"Bravo, Miss Dudley! You have offered an excellent arraignment against the integrity of the press. But I am more curious than ever to hear you prove that fiction contains fact."

"It must, or it is essentially inartistic. The writer who seeks to paint the world, the people, and the events of the world, as they really are, sets up in his mind, as a subject for copy, the sum of his observation of the world and the people in it. First, we will imagine that he weaves a plot. This is the fiction of his romance. If he writes out this story, adhering closely to his tale, calling the hero A, the heroine B, and the villain C, he deals in fiction only. But even here it would have no material attraction, unless it is conceded to be possible; it need not be probable. But if it is a possible sequence of events, at once we see that the basis is in fact. But when he goes further, and calls A, Arthur, B, Beatrice, and C, Clarence, at once they begin to acquire the characteristics of real people, or else puppets. If the latter, there is no value to the conception, while if the former, then in dealing with these creations of his mind, the writer must allot to each a personality, emotions, demeanor, and morality, which must be recognizable as human. He must in other words clothe his dummies with the semblance of reality, and for that he must turn to the facts of life, as he has observed them. Thus good fiction is really all fact. Q. E. D."

"Your argument is certainly ingenious, and worthy of consideration. It is a new way to look upon fiction, and I am glad that you have reconciled me to the idea of reading novels, for I must confess that though, when reading *Ardath*, I felt guilty of neglecting more important studies, nevertheless I was very much entertained by the book, which contains many ideas well thought, and well presented. But to resume the argument, as to the facts of fiction, let me say this. Is it not true that the predominant theme with novelists is love? And would you contend that love is the most important fact in the world?"

"Unquestionably it is the predominant fact, to use your own word. All the joy and misery, good and evil, is directly traceable to that one absorbing passion."

"You speak with feeling. Pardon my asking if it is a predominant emotion with yourself?"

"It is not," answered the girl, quickly and frankly. "Of course I understand you to mean by love, the feeling which exists between two persons of opposite sex, who are unrelated by ties of consanguinity; or, where a relationship does exist, that sort of affection which is more than cousinly, and which leads to marriage. Such an emotion is entirely foreign to my nature, and therefore of course does not form a predominant characteristic of my being. But on this you cannot base an argument against what I claim, because I am an exception to the rule. With the vast majority, love is undoubtedly the leading motive of existence."

"Miss Dudley, if you find the study of mankind interesting in the form of novels, which you say record the impressions of the authors, then you must pardon my studying your character as you kindly reveal it to me. This must explain my further questioning. May I proceed?"

"Oh! I see! You wish to use me as the surgeon does the cadaver. You would dissect me, merely for the purposes of general study. It is hardly fair, but proceed." She laughed gayly.

"You said," continued Leon, "that love, such as you have described, is foreign to your nature. Am I to understand that you could not form an attachment of that kind which leads to matrimony?"

"Well, all girls say that. But I believe I may say so, and be truthful. I doubt whether any man will ever inspire me with that love, without which I would consider marriage a sin. I do not say this idly, or upon the impulse of the moment. While I have never felt those heart-aches of which the novelists write, yet I have considered the subject deeply, in so far as it affects myself. So I say again, love is foreign to my nature."

"It is very singular!" said Leon, and he spoke almost as though soliloquizing. "I have the same feelings. I have always thought that no one would ever love me; but, latterly, I have come to consider the subject from the other stand-point, and now I believe as you do that I shall never love any woman. If I may go further, I would like to ask you why you have adopted this theory about yourself? I will agree to explain myself, if you will reply."

"With pleasure! From childhood I have been thrown almost exclusively into the companionship of two exceptional men, my father, and Dr. Medjora. I have the sincerest affection for them both. I say this, for without loving them I would probably never have been so influenced by them as I have been. While they are very unlike in their personalities, yet they have one characteristic in common: a deep longing for intellectual advancement. Growing up in such an environment, I have acquired the same predilection, so that now my one aim in life is knowledge. I do not see how love could aid me in this, while I do see how it might prove a great obstacle in my pathway. Household cares, and with them the care of a man, are not conducive to the acquirement of learning. Now I will listen to you."

"In a measure our cases are similar. I too have always deemed the search for knowledge the highest aim in life, but I did not extract that desire from my surroundings, for there was no inspiration about me. What I have learned, prior to my companionship with Dr. Medjora, was rather stolen sweets, that I obtained only in secret. The ideas about love, however, probably did emanate from my environment, for while I believe that my adopted mother loved me, I did not discover it until the day on which she died. Because no one loved me, I believed that no one ever would. But in my later analysis I have come to believe, that after starving from the lack of affection for so many years, I have finally lost the responsive feeling that gives birth to the emotion. I think that no one can attract me to that extent necessary to enkindle in my heart the emotion called love."

He looked away in a wistful manner, and Agnes felt a slight pity for the lad who had never known the love of his parents.

"Does it sadden you to think that way?" she asked softly.

"You have detected that? Yes! It is very curious. Ordinarily I accept the idea calmly. But occasionally I seem to be two persons, and one, who recognizes the happiness possible from love, looks at the other with pitying sympathy, because he will never love. Then in a moment I am my single self again, but the momentary hallucination puzzles me. It is as though I had been in the presence of a wraith, and the name of the spectre, dead to me, were Love itself. It is not a pleasant thought, and you must pardon my telling you. Ah! There comes the Judge!"

He bowed his adieux and went out into the hall to meet Judge Dudley. Agnes took up her book and essayed to read again, but the spectre of love which he had described, danced like a little red demon with forked tail, up and down the pages, until she put the book aside and went up to her room, where she threw herself on her lounge and lost herself in thought.

When Leon reached his room, upon returning home, he was surprised to find his dog, Lossy, lying under his bed, growling ominously at Madame Medjora, who was poking at him with a broom handle. She was evidently disturbed at Leon's entrance, and turned upon him angrily.

"This dog of yours must not come in the house. I will not have it. I am mistress here, and dogs must be kept in the stable."

Without waiting for a reply she hurried out of the room. Leon, not comprehending what was the matter, but realizing that his pet was unhappy, stooped to his knees and coaxed him from his hiding-place. He was much astonished to find that Lossy held a letter between his teeth, which, however, he yielded readily to his master. When Leon had taken it from him, Lossy stood in the middle of the floor and shook himself, as a dog does after swimming, until his rumpled fur stood smooth and bushy. In the same moment his good temper returned. Leon recognized the letter, as one which he had read that morning, but though he perused it again mechanically, it did not explain to his mind the scene, of which he had witnessed only the end. Had he been able to comprehend the situation, much of what occurred later might have been avoided.

What had happened was this. In the morning's mail a letter had come for Leon, and he had read it at the breakfast-table. This excited the curiosity of Madame Medjora, because it was the first that had come to the boy since he had lived with them. She therefore had noted that he placed it in his pocket, and she studied how she might become possessed of it. No chance offered until Leon went out, to call at Judge Dudley's. Then he changed his coat, and he had scarcely left the house, before the woman entered his room and eagerly searched for, and found the letter. So engrossed was she in the perusal of it, that she did not notice that Lossy had followed her from his master's apartment into her own boudoir, whither she had gone, before reading it.

The letter was as follows. As a specimen of chirography, and an example of high grade orthography, it was worthy of a place in a museum.

"mister leon Grath, my Dare nevue have you forgot yore Ant Matildy I hav not hearn frum you in menny menny wekes an I mus say I have fretted myself most to deth abowt my Dare Sisters little boy leon all alone in this wide wide wurld A weke ago mister potter the man that ocshioned off the Farm Wuz up to owr plase and he tole us how you wuz makin lots of money in York along of Doctor mejory. Now ef its tru that you be makin so much money I think it only fare to let you know how much yore Ant Matildy who wus always gud an kined to you is now in knead of help the farm is goin to rack an ruin sence you lef and I want you to sen me a hundred dollars as sune as this reaches you as I knead it dredful It would be better for you and for Doctor Mejory too ef the money is sent rite off as if not I mite tell things I know wich wont be plessant Matildy Grath"

Unfortunately for Leon's future happiness later in the day Madame copied this letter carefully, and also noted the postmark on the envelope. Otherwise the action of Lossy would have left her dependent upon her memory, to do what she had immediately decided upon. It was while she was reading over her copy, that Lossy came stealthily forward, stood upon his hind legs and took the letter, which he had seen her steal from his master's coat. Before she fully realized her loss, the dog was scampering along the hall. She followed him into Leon's room, and used every means to get him from under the bed. Coaxing failed, and she tried the broomstick, which she was still using when Leon entered.

But of all this the lad knew nothing. He read the letter again; then tore it up and threw it into the fire, supposing that the matter ended there.

CHAPTER IX
A WIZARD'S KNOWLEDGE

During the next three months Madame Medjora waited and watched. She watched for another letter to Leon. She judged the writer by herself, and she decided that Matilda Grath would not abandon her project, having once decided that she possessed knowledge, by the judicious use of which she could extort money. She knew that Leon had no means of sending her such a sum, and she was sure that Doctor Medjora would never part with one penny under compulsion. He was a man who ruled others. He was never to be intimidated. Yet the woman had said that it would be better for the Doctor too, if the demand were satisfied. How to construe this she could not tell. Did Matilda Grath know a secret which the Doctor would wish to have suppressed? Or did the threat merely mean that the Doctor could be made to suffer through his affection for Leon? The mention of the Doctor's name in the letter had a twofold effect. It incited her all the more to carry out her project and ferret out the secret, if one existed; while on the other hand it made her hesitate to do that which might bring down the wrath of her husband upon her head. She did not openly admit it, but she feared him. Thus it was that she waited. Waited hoping that her watching might enable her to intercept the second letter from Matilda Grath, which she thought must inevitably follow, and which might give her a more definite due upon which to base her action.

But as the weeks went by and no letter came, she grew restive. In this mood one day she read of the remarkable capture of the true criminal, made by Mr. Barnes, in the Petingill case. She did not know that this detective was the office boy who, while in the employ of Dudley and Bliss, had had the temerity to shadow her husband, hoping to convict him of murder. Had she known, it is doubtful whether she would have visited him. As it was, she impulsively determined to engage him to unravel the mystery connected with Leon, and she decided to give him the copy of the letter which she had made, as a clue with which to begin.

Thus it was that Mr. Barnes, at the height of his ambition, the chief of a private detective agency, was astonished one morning to read the name "Madame Emanuel Medjora," upon a card handed to him in his private office. He pondered awhile, and searched his memory to account for the fact that the name sounded familiar, as he muttered it aloud. In an instant he recalled his first attempt at unravelling a great crime, and, with a feeling that chance was about to give him an opportunity to retrieve the bungling failure of that day, long ago, he invited the lady into his sanctum.

Once in the presence of the detective, Madame was half frightened at what she had undertaken, but it was too late to retreat. So in hurried words she explained her case, gave Mr. Barnes the letter, and engaged him to investigate the matter.

"Find out for me," said she, "who this Leon Grath really is. I will pay you well for the information. But understand this. I exact the utmost secrecy. You must not come to my house, nor write to me. When you wish to communicate with me, put a personal in the *Herald* saying "Come," and I will understand. Above all things, promise me that whatever you discover shall be known only to myself; that you will make no use of the knowledge except as I may direct."

"Madame may depend upon my discretion," answered the detective, and with a restless doubt in her breast, which was to gnaw at her peace of mind for weeks to come, Madame Medjora returned to the home of the husband whom she had promised to love, honor, and obey, and against whom she was now secretly plotting.

After the first time when Dr. Medjora had taken Leon into the temple of Æsculapius while asleep, and there hypnotized him, the two spent an hour together in the crypt nightly. The Doctor deciphered for his pupil the meaning of the hieroglyphics in the order in which he had studied them out for himself. His method was peculiar. On the second night, he revealed to Leon the secret approach, and took him into the buried dome whilst yet awake. Then before his astonishment and admiration for the place had subsided, and, therefore, while his mind was yet off guard, as it were, he suddenly commanded him to sleep, just as he had done on the Fall River steamboat, only this time he succeeded. With scarcely any resistance, Leon passed into a hypnotic trance, and while in that condition the Doctor began expounding to him the sculptured records of a forgotten knowledge. At first the tasks were brief, but they were increased, and more and more was accomplished each night as he acquired greater hypnotic control over his subject. At the end of each lesson, he would say to his pupil:

"Leon, to-morrow you will remember that we have been here together, that I have taught you a part of the knowledge inscribed upon these walls; you will forever retain a recollection of that knowledge which you have gained to-night; but you will imagine that you have been with me in your normal waking condition, and you will forever and forever forget that I have commanded you to sleep. Do you promise?"

"I promise!" would be the reply, and then, to assure success, he would awaken the lad and continue awhile his teaching, so that Leon would depart awake, as he had entered. Thus it was, that the Doctor's scheme for educating his *protégé* was meeting with marvellous success, and Leon was rapidly assimilating the wisdom which was offered to him. Already he knew more of diseases and their treatment, of the science of chemistry and bacteriology, than many graduates of medical schools. In addition to what may be termed his hypnotic education, he was acquiring practical experience through his daily work in the laboratory, so that at length Dr. Medjora thought that he could see a promise of fruition for his cherished scheme.

In one thing he was disappointed. It was his hope to effect a love match between Leon and Agnes, but his keen study of both of the young people convinced him that they were as indifferent to one another, after nearly a year's acquaintance, as they had been at first.

Dr. Emanuel Medjora, however, was not a man to be thwarted, and he had long decided upon a course of action, whereby he might further his design, if the current of ordinary events did not turn the tide in his favor. Finally he decided to act, and in furtherance of his purpose he invited Judge Dudley to spend an evening with him.

"Come promptly at eight o'clock," his note had said, "and be prepared to remain as long as I may require. The business is of great moment to us both, and to those whom we love."

In response to such a summons, the Judge reached Villa Medjora just as the clock chimed the appointed hour. He was conducted into the Doctor's study, which opened into the laboratory. When his guest was announced, Dr. Medjora rose at once to greet him. When the two men were seated comfortably, the Doctor opened the conversation at once.

"Judge Dudley," said he, "I have, as you know, a young man with me, in whom I have taken the deepest interest,—Leon Grath, my assistant and pupil. Let me tell you something of him."

"With pleasure," replied the Judge.

"You already know, that I look upon the knowledge which I possess as a sacred trust, which I must utilize for the benefit of my fellows. I have held that it is incumbent upon me to transmit this knowledge to some one younger than myself, that he may be my successor. I searched for years for such a lad. The exactions were great. He would need extraordinary endowments. He should be superior to his fellows, intellectually and physically. I decided that I had found such a man, when I selected Leon."

"I hope you have not been disappointed?"

"On the contrary. He has exceeded my expectations, though my estimate of his powers could not be far wrong, because I rarely make a mistake." The egotism of these words did not appear to effect the Judge. He was too well acquainted with Dr. Medjora, who continued:

"Leon has evinced such worthiness of the trust which I have reposed in him, that I know he will not only be a capable successor to me, but he will achieve that which I cannot hope to accomplish within the few years which are left to me."

"Come, my friend," said the Judge, "you must not talk as though you were nearing the end of life. You will be with us twenty years longer at least."

"They will not be twenty years of usefulness, if I should." The Doctor spoke as though in augury of his own fate. He continued:

"But it is not of myself that I desire to speak. Leon, I say, will be a wiser and a greater man than I. He will be beloved by his associates, and will be a blessing in the world."

"I do not doubt it!" said the Judge, impulsively, not knowing to what the words would lead him.

"I am glad you appreciate his worth," replied the Doctor, quickly. "I have already taught him much, and I will teach him more, if I am spared, but, even without my assistance, the fountain of knowledge from which he now draws will supply him amply. One thing he needs. A cloud hangs over his past, because he knows not who were his parents. He has no name, and that thought hangs as a millstone about his neck, and often weighs him down with discouragment, as he feels that he is alone in the world. I intend to remedy that. I shall bestow upon him my own name."

"Your own name?" ejaculated the Judge.

"My own name! I will formally adopt him, and he shall take my name. I wish you to aid me in the legal steps requisite."

"I will do so with pleasure. Medjora, you are a noble man. I honor you with all my heart." The Judge occasionally lost his usual dignified reserve, when his emotions were deeply touched.

"I thank you," said the Doctor. "But, Judge, if I am noble in doing what I purpose, you have the chance to be even more so."

"What do you mean?"

"Leon needs more than a name. As I have said, the past hangs over his heart like a pall. Even with my name, he will be a lonely man. He will continue his habits of studiousness, but he will become a recluse. He will shun his fellows, because of his sensitiveness upon one point. He will fear to intrude himself, where he might not be welcome. In such a life, he would be of little value to his fellows. The world will lose a great benefactor. There is but one salvation for him, from such a fate."

"And that is?"

"Marriage! Marriage with a woman of kindred spirit. Marriage with a woman, possessing equal intellect, and capable of spurring him to ambitious deeds, at the same time soothing his hours of fatigue. Marriage, in short, with your daughter."

"With Agnes!" exclaimed the Judge, almost horrified, so great was his surprise.

"With Agnes!" repeated the Doctor, calmly.

"Impossible! You are mad!" ejaculated the Judge.

"And yet, despite your protest, the marriage will occur," said Dr. Medjora, in tones so portentous, that the Judge paused and looked at him almost in fear. For one instant, the cry of the public that this man was a wizard flashed across his mind, but in the next he cast it aside with scorn, and again he said peremptorily.

"I tell you no! It is impossible!"

"Nothing is impossible," said the Doctor, impressively, "if I have decided in my own mind that it must be. I have never failed in any purpose of my life, and I will not fail in this. Judge Dudley, listen to me. I have a claim upon your daughter Agnes, equal to, yea greater, than your own."

"What!" exclaimed the Judge, more amazed. He sank back in his chair bewildered. How could this man have a claim upon his child greater than his own? It was an unsolvable riddle to him.

"You do not comprehend me," said the Doctor, "and to explain myself it will be necessary for me to speak at some length. Shall I do so?"

"You must do so! After what you have said, I must hear more. Go on!"

"Very well. If at first I seem to speak of matters unconnected with the subject, bear with me and listen attentively. I shall be as brief as possible, and yet give you a thorough insight into my meaning. As you are well aware, men call me a wizard. Now, what is a wizard? The dictionary says he is a sorcerer, and that a sorcerer is a magician. In olden times the magicians were of two kinds, evil and good, accordingly as they practised Black Art, or the reverse; which only means that they were men endowed with knowledge not shared by their fellows, and that, armed with the powers thus acquired, they used their abilities either for evil or for good purposes. Thus, if in this day of civilization I possess any knowledge in advance of other scientists, I suppose that I am as truly a wizard, as were the magicians of the ancients."

"Nonsense!"

"Not at all. I claim to have knowledge which is fully twenty years in advance of to-day, just as I know that the present generation is but slowly awakening to truths which were known to me twenty years ago. But before I speak of what I myself know, let me give you a summary of the advance which modern science has made in a specified direction. You have heard of what is commonly called the 'Germ Theory' of disease?"

"Yes! Certainly!"

"You say yes, and you add certainly, by which latter you mean that it was folly for me to ask you such a question. Yet how much do you really know of the great progress which has been made in mastering the secret causes of human disease? You are a learned Judge, and yet you know comparatively little of the subject which is of most vital interest to mankind. I mean no offence, of course. I am as ignorant of the Law, as you are of Medicine. Let me open a window that you may peep in upon the scientific students busy with their investigations. The 'Germ Theory,' briefly stated, is this. There are all around us millions of micro-organisms, parasites which thrive and grow by feeding upon the animal world. In proportion as these parasities infest, and thrive upon a given individual, so will that individual become diseased, and it has been shown that in many cases a special germ will cause a special disease. I could deliver you a lecture, hours long, upon the classification, morphology, and pathogenic action of bacteria, but I wish at present to lead your mind into a different channel. Undoubtedly the most important question in biology is the immunity from disease-generating germs, which is possessed by various animals."

"Do you mean that some animals can resist the attacks of bacteria?" asked the Judge. Anxious as he was to arrive at the point where his daughter's name would be again introduced, his natural love of knowledge caused his interest to be aroused as the Doctor proceeded.

"I do," continued Dr. Medjora. "It has long been known that certain infectious diseases, such as typhoid fever, are peculiar to man, while the lower animals do not suffer from them; and that, on the other hand, man has a natural immunity from other diseases which are common among the lower animals. Again, some species will resist diseases which become epidemic among others. In addition to an immunity peculiar to a whole race, or species, we have individual differences in susceptibility or resistance. This may be natural, or it may be acquired. For example, the very young are usually more susceptible than adults. But a difference will also be found among adults of a race. The negro is less susceptible to yellow fever than the white man, while, contrarily, small-pox seems to be peculiarly fatal among the dark-skinned races."

"Have the scientists been able to account for these phenomena?"

"They theorize, and many of them are making admirable guesses. They account for race tolerance by the Darwinian theory, of the survival of the fittest. Imagine a susceptible population decimated by a scourge, and the survivors are plainly those who have evidenced a higher power of resistance. Their progeny should show a greater immunity than the original colony, and, after repeated attacks of the same malady, a race tolerance would become a characteristic."

"That is certainly a plausible theory."

"It is probably correct. But acquired immunity, possessed by an individual residing among a people who are susceptible, is the problem of greatest interest. The difference between a susceptible and an immune animal depends upon one fact. In the former, when the disease-breeding germ is introduced, it finds conditions favoring its multiplication, so that it makes increasing invasions into the tissues. The immune animal resists such multiplication, and possesses inherent powers of resistance which finally exterminates the invader. But how can this immunity be acquired by a given individual?"

"Upon the solution of that question, I would say depends the future extermination of disease," said the Judge.

"You are right," assented the Doctor. "Ogata and Jashuhara have recorded some interesting experiments. They cultivated the bacillus of anthrax in the blood of an animal immune to that disease, and when they injected these cultures into a susceptible animal, they found that only a mild attack of the disease ensued, and that subsequently the animal was immune to further inoculation."

"Why, if that is so, it would seem that we have only to use the blood of immune animals, as an injection, to insure a person against a disease!"

"Behring and Kitasato experimenting in that direction, found that the blood of immune animals, injected into susceptible individuals, after twenty-four hours rendered them immune, but this would not follow with all diseases. In many maladies common to man, a single attack, from which the person recovers, renders him safe from future epidemics. The most commonly known example of this is the discovery by Jenner, who gave the world that safeguard against small-pox, known as vaccination. But the most important discovery in this direction yet made is one which is not fully appreciated even by the discoverer himself. Chauveau, in 1880, ascertained that, if he protected ewes by inoculating them with an attenuated virus, their lambs, when born, would show an acquired immunity."

"This is incredible!"

"I have now related all that the modern scientists have recorded up to the present date, and when I tell you that all of this, and very much more than is at present recognized, was known to me twenty years ago, you will see that my claim that I am twenty years in advance of my generation is well founded. I shall not enter into the many theories advanced to explain the phenomenon of acquired immunity from disease, because it would be unprofitable to take up such a discussion, while you are waiting to hear what concerns you more closely. Suffice it to say, that various scientists have learned that immunity may be produced in a previously susceptible animal by the injection of various preparations. But in each instance, the injection is expected to produce immunity from only one disease. My own studies were at first in this direction, and I have succeeded not only in learning how to prevent each malady separately, but what is far better, I have discovered a method by which I can render an individual immune to all zymotic diseases."

"Then, indeed, are you a wizard!"

"Yes, because I do that which transcends the powers and knowledge of my fellows! But mark my prophecy! Just so surely as the scientific investigators of to-day have learned what I knew twenty years ago, so will the investigators of the future master the secrets which now are known only to myself. I am a wizard, perhaps, but I am a modern wizard. There is nothing of the supernatural about my methods. But now let me be more explicit. What Chauvau did with sheep, I have done with the human being."

"What! You have dared to make such an experiment?"

"Dared? Emanuel Medjora dares all things, in the pursuit of knowledge!"

The man had arisen as he warmed to his subject, and now, as he drew himself up erect, he towered over the Judge as a giant might.

"Listen, and be convinced. I discovered a precious preparation, which, if injected at the proper time would, in my opinion, bring me the consummation of my dreams. A single fluid, which would produce immunity from all diseases. Just after you had procured my acquittal, and thus saved me and my learning for the benefit of the world, you were kind enough to intrust me with the care of your wife's health."

"I had no hesitation in doing so. I had faith in you."

"The result has shown that your faith was well founded. At the proper time, I injected the preparation which I had formulated, into the arm of your wife."

"You did that?"

"I did. You will recall the fact that from being feeble she began to gain strength. Periodically I repeated my injections, and renewed vigor coursed through her system."

"You certainly worked wonders. I distinctly remember that I marvelled at the improvement which followed your treatment."

"In due season you were presented with a daughter. A beautiful, baby girl!"

"My little angel Agnes!"

The Judge spoke softly, and with tenderness. In fancy he looked back to the day when the nurse brought him the little cherub, newly arrived, and he felt again the tightening of his heart-strings which told him that he was a father.

"You held the babe in your arms," said the Doctor, "and you, as well as all the others, recognized that it was an exceptional infant. But none of you guessed that a child had been born, who, like Chauvau's lambs, would be immune to all disease!"

"Do you really mean that you accomplished that almost incredible miracle?" exclaimed the Judge, as at last he perceived the nature of the claim upon Agnes, which the Doctor was endeavoring to establish.

"Do you doubt it? Glance back over her career. Remember the various climates that she has visited; the many epidemics which she has passed through in safety. Yellow fever in Memphis, small-pox in the Indies, and several seasons of diphtheria at home, here in New York. She has been near typhoid and scarlet fever; la grippe has visited us twice in epidemic form, and is carrying off hundreds at this very time. Can you recall a day in all her life, when Agnes has been ill? No! You cannot!" The Doctor's tone was triumphant. The Judge's reply was low.

"Providence has certainly blessed her with remarkable health," he murmured.

"Providence?" exclaimed the Doctor, passionately. "No! Not Providence, but I! I, Emanuel Medjora, the Wizard! I have blessed her with her wonderful health! To me she owes it all! I claim her! She is as much mine as yours!"

He was grandly dramatic as he uttered these words, but, marvelling as he did at what he had heard, the Judge was not yet ready to yield. This iteration of the fact that he claimed Agnes, aroused the father's antagonism, and, in an almost equally impe-rious tone, he sprang to his feet and cried:

"No! She is mine! I am her father, and she is mine! All mine! I deny your claim, and Wizard though you be, I defy you!"

The two men glared at each other for a moment, and then the Doctor spoke suddenly.

"You defy me! Ha! Ha! Ha!" His laugh rang through the chamber with a weird sound. "Agnes is yours! Ha! Ha! Ha!" Again the laugh, prolonged and piercing. In an instant his man-ner changed. Grasping the Judge by the arm, he said: "Come with me!" then half dragged him towards, and through the door that led into the laboratory.

CHAPTER X
THE BETROTHAL

The Judge offered very slight resistance as Doctor Medjora urged him forward, and even in the pitchy darkness of the labo-ratory he made no effort to free himself. He was no coward, and in defying this man whom so many feared, he showed that he feared no man.

The Doctor went straight to the trap-door, and began to descend the stairway. His reason for having no light in the laboratory was, that he did not wish the Judge to know by what way they went down. As the trap-door was open, he would not suspect its existence; all that he would be able to recall would be that they had descended a flight of stairs. Should he enter the laboratory, at some future time, he would be unable to discover the way to the crypt below.

But it was not to the temple of Æsculapius that the Doctor now led his companion. He had decided not to divulge that secret to any other person, besides Leon. Mr. Barnes, it is true, had been taken into the crypt, but by hypnotic suggestion the Doctor had eradicated all recollection of that visit. You will remember that on the night when the Doctor had controlled Mr. Barnes by making him sleep, he had subsequently taken him through an old wine cellar. This vault still existed, though it had been remodelled at the time when the new house was built.

It was into this secret chamber that the Doctor now took the Judge. Closing the door behind him, he touched a button, and an electric lamp illumined the apartment.

The chamber was comfortably carpeted and furnished, and in all ways presented the appearance of a luxurious living room, except that there were no windows. On this night, a silk curtain, stretched across from wall to wall, seemed to indicate that there was something beyond. What that was, at once arrested the attention of the Judge, but he exhibited no curiosity by asking questions, preferring to await the unfolding of events as they might occur.

"Now, Judge," said the Doctor, "I must ask you to pardon my having brought you here. I may also have seemed rude or brusque in manner, which you must set down to excitement, rather than to malicious intent. You understand that I would not harm my friend?"

"I have no fear!" replied the Judge, coldly.

"Be seated, please," said the Doctor, and then both took chairs. "Judge Dudley," continued the Doctor, "I have expressed to you my opinion that I have a claim upon your daughter. You have denied it. Or, rather, you have probably conceded in your mind that what I have done for Agnes creates an obligation, but you are not willing to admit that on that account I should have the privilege, of selecting her husband? Do I state the facts clearly?"

"Sufficiently so! Proceed!"

"Very well! I have brought you to this apartment to demonstrate to you, first, that the obligation is greater than you suspect, and secondly, that your daughter's fate is entirely in my hands. In fact that you are powerless to oppose my will."

"I have, perhaps, more determination than you credit me with. It will be difficult for you to swerve me from my purpose."

"Those men, who have the strongest wills, are the ones most easily moved. You are as just, as man ever is. When you learn that your daughter's happiness, after this night, will depend entirely upon her marriage with Leon, you will yield."

"I certainly would make any sacrifice for the happiness of my daughter. But I must be convinced."

"You see! Already you are amenable to reason. I will proceed. Judge Dudley, a while ago I told you something of the present theories concerning the existence of germs which affect physical life. I also explained to you, how, by using greater knowledge than has as yet been generally disseminated, I have succeeded in producing in the person of your daughter a physically perfect being; one who cannot be attacked by bodily ailments. I will now unfold to you some theories which are even more in advance of the thought of to-day. It has long been conceded that man is a dual creature; that is, there is a material and, I will say, another side, to every human being. What is that other side? It is immaterial; it is intangible but nevertheless we know that it exists. At death there remains everything of the physical body that existed a moment before. What then has departed? An instant before death, a muscle will lift a given weight, and a second after, long before mortification of the flesh could operate to disintegrate the fibres, we find that one tenth of that weight will suffice to tear the same muscle. What then is this potential power which has left the body? For the purposes of the present argument, I shall call it the psychical side of man. The physical and the psychical, dwelling in harmonious unison, produces a living creature. This much is plain, and of course presents no new thought to you."

"True, but I suppose you are leading to something else?"

"Yes! The introduction is necessary. Given then these two divisions of human life, and, I submit it to you, is it not curious that the physical has received a hundred times as much study as has the psychical? With myself it has been different. I have studied both together, because I have ever found them together. I argued that I could never fully comprehend the one, without an equal knowledge of the other. So I know as much about the psychical side of life as I do of the physical."

"Then you must know a great deal!"

"I do! In the beginning of my career I grasped one truth, which seems to have escaped the majority. The secrets of Nature are simple. We do not discover the mysteries, because we think them more mysterious than they are. The key to the knowledge of Nature's methods is in her analogies. All natural laws operate on parallel lines, because the aim of all is the same; evolution towards perfection. Thus, in studying the psychical, I had but to master the physical and then discover the analogy which exists between the two."

"And you claim to have done this?"

"In a great measure. Leon, before he dies, will achieve more than I, because he will begin where I shall be compelled to abandon my work. But I have accomplished more than any other mortal man, and that is a gratifying thought, to an egotist. There is but one phase of this subject which I wish to submit to you. I have explained the germ theory of disease. I will now announce to you the germ theory of crime."

"The germ theory of crime?" asked the Judge, utterly amazed. "Do you mean that crime is produced by bacteria? As a jurist, I certainly will be interested in your new doctrine."

"You do not yet grasp my meaning. It is manifestly impossible that bacteria, which are living parasites, could affect the moral side of a man. I have said that the secret is in analogy; the two germs, the physical and the psychical, are not identical. But I will start your thought in the right direction, when I say that all forms of vice and crime are diseases, as much as scarlet fever or small-pox. It is a curious fact that many great secrets which have escaped the individual have been recognized by the multitude. Many expressions in the language, which are counted as metaphorical, are truly exponents of unrecorded facts. One says that a girl has died of a 'broken heart,' without suspecting that disappointed love has been known to cause an actual heart rupture, demonstrable by *post-mortem* examination. So, to return to my subject, people say that an immoral man has 'a diseased imagination,' without realizing that they state the exact condition from which he suffers."

"Why, if such were the case, it would be improper to punish criminals!" Such an idea seemed rank heresy to the Judge.

"It is entirely wrong to punish criminals. We should however imprison them, because they are dangerous to the community. But their incarceration should be precisely similar to the forcible confinement of individuals suffering with diseases which threaten to become epidemic, and for very similar reasons. First, to endeavor to effect their cure, and second, and most important, to prevent the spread of the malady."

"You mean that jails should be reformatories?"

"Exclusively. Moreover, the length of the confinement should not be regulated by statute, but should depend upon the intensity of the attack of crime or vice, which has occasioned the arrest of the prisoner. He should be jailed until cured, just as a leper is, even though it be for life. However, I cannot now discuss that aspect of the question. I wish to more fully explain the germ theory of crime."

"I am impatient to hear you." In his interest in the subject the Judge had almost forgotten his recent feeling of animosity.

"The idea then is this. Suppose that a babe could be born, with a perfect psychical endowment. We would have a being in whom all the higher virtues would predominate, while the vices would be non-existent. But take such an individual and place him in an environment where he would daily be associated with vice in its worst form and it would be inevitable that he would become vicious, for crime is as contagious as small-pox. The germ of a physical disease is a parasite so small in some instances, that when placed under a microscope and magnified one thousand times, it then becomes visible as a tiny dot, which might be made by a very sharp pencil. The germ of crime is even more minute and intangible. It exists as a suggestion."

"A suggestion?"

"Yes! Suggestion is the most potent factor in the affairs of the world. There is never a suggestion without an effect. Wherever it occurs an impression is created. No living man is free from its influence. A common example which I might cite is the congregation of a crowd. Without knowing what he goes to see, a man crosses the street and swells a growing crowd merely because others do so. The idea is suggested, and the impulse becomes almost irresistible. Even if resisted, the temptation will be appreciated. The suggestion has produced an effect. To explain the specific growth of a crime by this means, I will remind you of the woman who, when leaving home, told her children not to go into the barn and steal any apples, but that if they did go, above all things not to lie about it when she should return. Of course they went, and of course they lied to her upon her return. She had suggested both actions to them. The child who sees theft for the first time, may look upon it with abhorrence, because home influence has suggested to it that stealing is wrong. But permit a daily association with theives, and the abhorrence will pass into tolerance, and thence into imitation."

"I begin to perceive your meaning, and after all it is only the old idea, that conscience is merely the result of education."

"Precisely so! But that very expression is but another example of the indefinite recognition of an important fact. You say my theory is old. Perhaps! But my utilization of it is new. Just as there are pathogenic bacteria which produce disease, so there are also non-pathogenic bacteria which not only do not cause bodily affliction, but which actually are essential and conducive to perfect health. The one takes its sustenance by destroying that which is needed by man, at the same time generating poisons which are deleterious, while the latter thrives upon that which is harmful to the human body. Analogously, just as there are germs, or suggestions which debase the morality, so also there are suggestions which produce the highest moral health."

"That seems probable enough!"

"By the means which I have explained to you, your daughter was born, immune to all diseases. You have heard that certain maladies, as consumption, can be transmitted, and are therefore inherited. This is not true. But a parent who has suffered with phthisis, may transmit to his progeny what is termed a diminished vital resistance. The child is not born consumptive, but he is poorly equipped to contend against the germ of that disease. If thrown into contact with it, consumption will probably follow. But it is possible that as he matures his environment may be such, that his vital resistance may increase, so that the time might come when he would not acquire the disease, even though brought into contact with it. The reverse follows as a logical deduction. Agnes was born with an enormous stock of vital resistance, which would operate to protect her from all diseases. But it would have been possible for her to degenerate as she matured. This I guarded against. By cultivating her companionship, and yours, I have had access to her at all times, and I have periodically supplied her with potions containing those germs which are conducive to health. In a similiar way, I have cared for her psychical life, by advancing her moral nature!"

"What is that? I do not comprehend your meaning!"

"I have said that no person is exempt from the influences of suggestion. But it has been demonstrated that, when hypnotized, an individual is singularly susceptible to suggestion, and many phenomena have been recorded. But as yet little practical use has been made of this knowledge. With me it has been an endless source of power. Especially have I used hypnotic suggestion for the moral advancement of your daughter!"

"You mean that you have hypnotized Agnes?" The Judge was stunned by the announcement.

"I began the practice when she was five years of age, and have continued it up to the present moment. By this means I have made her psychically as perfect as she is physically. I have inculcated in her the highest virtues, and I have taught her to love intellectuality above all things. Thus again I show you a claim that I have upon her. But the highest obligation is that which is based upon the good of the world, and the advancement of science. She is now so fond of knowledge that she would never marry any ordinary man. There is but one man living, to whom she can be united, and be happy, and as yet she does not suspect it. That one is Leon. Do you not see that you must consent to this union?"

"Not yet! I must be convinced of the truth of all the extraordinary things which you have told me."

"You ask for proof? You shall have it! For that I brought you here! Watch what you shall see, but stir not, however great may be the temptation. If you make an effort to interfere, it would be doubly useless, first, because I would restrain you by physical strength, and second, because though you will see your daughter, you will be unable to make her see or hear you. Beware how you trifle with what you do not understand! A false move on your part might mean a lifelong injury to Agnes. Behold!"

The Doctor touched a spring and the silk curtains parted. The Judge started forward with a cry, but the Doctor grasped him by the arm and cried "Beware!" upon which he subsided, but gazed with intense anxiety upon what followed.

Behind the curtains, there appeared a sort of stage, which was divided in half by yet another curtain. To one side, Leon lay reclining on a couch, as though asleep, his eyes closed. On the other side, Agnes lay in similar posture. The Doctor spoke:

"Agnes! When I command you to do so, you will open your eyes, and awaken enough so that you may speak to me! You will see me! You will hear my voice! But you will neither see nor hear any other person! Awaken!"

Agnes slowly opened her eyes, and gazed steadily towards the Doctor. Otherwise, she did not move.

"You see and hear me?" asked the Doctor.

"Yes!"

"Do you see any other person?"

"No!"

"Agnes, I wish to question you upon a very important subject. Will you reply truthfully?"

"I will reply. Of course it will be truthfully, because I do not know falsehood."

"Do you love any one, so that you would marry him?"

"I do not know what love is. I do not know what marriage means for me."

The Judge breathed a sigh of relief as he heard these words. He thought that his daughter was safe, but even yet he did not comprehend the power of the man beside him.

"I will now tell you what it is to love. Listen!"

"I will listen!"

"In heaven's name, Medjora," cried the Judge, "go no further!" He grasped the Doctor's arm as he made the appeal, but he might as well have addressed a thing of stone. He was unheeded. The Doctor proceeded:

"Somewhere in a secret corner of thy soul, as yet unreached, there is a spot more sensitive than all the rest. A single vibration penetrating there, if harmonious and according with thine own desires, would awaken a joyousness to which all other joys compare as the odor of the rankest weeds to the fragrance of the sweetest rose. A thousand, thousand dreams of happiness are insignificant to the thrill which courses through the veins when that centre of thy soul is touched by love. Forever and forever after, wilt thou be a different being; thine old self cast behind and buried in the oblivion of the past, whilst thy new existence will remain incomplete, until coupled with that other dear one, whose glancing eye hath pierced and found the deepest corner of thy heart. But this is not all. If the first recognition of the existence of thy love be delirious ecstacy, by what name shall I nominate that joy which issues from the consummation of thy heart's desire, when thy love is perfected by a union with one that loves thee better than he loves himself? This is love! Wouldst thou not taste it?"

The girl's lips quivered, and she spoke as one enraptured.

"I would! I would! O give me love! Love! Sweet, sweet love!"

"Thy wish shall be gratified. Look towards that curtain!"

She raised herself into a sitting position, and did as directed.

"Now sleep until I bid thee awaken into love! Sleep!"

The eyelids closed, and the bosom heaved gently as the girl slumbered. The Doctor addressed Leon.

"Leon! Awaken! I have promised you that you shall meet your future love. She will be life and love to you forever! Awaken!"

Leon stirred, opened his eyes, and looked at the Doctor.

"You cannot see anyone unless I tell you! Look towards that curtain!"

Leon obeyed, and he and Agnes were gazing towards each other, but the silk curtain divided them.

"Now sleep, and when you again awaken, your happiness will be complete!"

Leon's eyes closed. The Doctor touched another spring, and the curtain was drawn aside. At the same instant a fragrant aroma filled the apartment, as though the sweetest incense were burning. He stood a moment in silence, gazing upon the two figures who looked at each other, but did not see. The Judge was overcome so that he found it difficult to speak. He essayed to address the Doctor, but his tongue was heavy, and words were impossible. The Doctor looked towards him an instant, as a slight gurgling sound issued from his lips, and he saw the appeal in the father's eyes; but swiftly he turned away and spoke:

"Awaken! Awaken both! Leon and Agnes, awaken! Awaken and love!" Having reached the climax of his experiment, even the Doctor himself felt a twinge of anxiety lest he might fail. But, as the possibility flashed across his brain, he cast it out again and gazed the more intently at the scene before him. The Judge also watched in dread anxiety, and with waning strength. He hoped almost against hope that the trick would fail.

Leon opened his eyes, and instantly rested them upon Agnes. No sign of recognition appeared upon his face, but only admiration was pictured there. The girl awakened, too, and her eyes gazed upon Leon's face. Instantly there was a convulsive trembling, and she breathed heavily. Her lips parted and closed, again and again. It seemed as though a word sought utterance, but was restrained by some secret emotion. Leon began to move towards her, his eyes fixed upon hers, and an expression of ecstatic pleasure spreading over his features. Slowly but surely he advanced, and, as he approached, Agnes trembled more and more.

A swift alteration in the attitude of the girl then took place. In one instant she became thoroughly controlled; all quivering ceased. She stood erect, exhibiting to its fullest her marvellously attractive form. Then, with a bound, she sprang forward, and cast herself upon the breast of her dream-land lover, with a cry that went straight to the heart of her father.

"Leon! Leon! I love you! I love you!" she exclaimed, and as the youth folded her in an enraptured embrace, Judge Dudley fell to the floor senseless.

CHAPTER XI
THE GENESIS OF LOVE

I must explain more fully how the scene just related was pre-arranged. As Dr. Medjora told the Judge, it had been a common occurrence for him to hypnotize Agnes whenever favorable occasions presented. These had not been infrequent, because the girl had exhibited a great fondness for the study of chemistry, and therefore often visited the Doctor in his laboratory. Since the advent of Leon, this habit had been discontinued, or only rarely indulged, and the Doctor, appreciating the maidenly reserve which prompted her, had made no comment.

When, however, he decided that the time had arrived when it would be best for him to put his scheme into operation, he had one day invited Agnes to be present at some interesting experiments which he wished to show. Thus she had readily been enticed to the laboratory, and then the Doctor had hypnotized her, and subsequently led her to the chamber where he had arranged the paraphernalia for his little scene. Before this, he had commanded Leon to sleep, and in a similar condition the lad had been conveyed to the couch whereon he was afterward shown to the Judge.

The Doctor had calculated to meet opposition in the Judge, and his hypnotic *séance* had been conceived with the double purpose of convincing him of the uselessness of antagonism, while at the same time he would utilize the opportunity to suggest the idea of love to both of the young people.

Ordinarily, by which I mean with subjects having less individuality than these, he would have been content to operate upon one at a time; but with Agnes and Leon, he knew that he could succeed only by acting upon both simultaneously, and at the moment of suggesting love, to present them each one to the other, *in propria persona*, rather than through the imagination. He counted upon personal contact so to intensify the suggestion, that it would not be overcome by will power exerted in the waking state, which would ensue.

All had passed to his entire satisfaction, and he had little doubt that his experiment would succeed, but there was still much to do. First, he again commanded Leon and Agnes to sleep deeply, and then leaving them slumbering on their respective couches, he bore the body of the Judge to the floor above. Examining him closely he soon satisfied himself that his friend had only succumbed to emotional excitement, and that he would soon recover from his swoon. He then took him to the study and placed him in the chair which he had occupied earlier in the evening. Hastily returning to the secret chamber, he brought Agnes upstairs, taking her through the hall and down to the parlor.

Here he suggested to her that, when she awakened, she should think she had merely been visiting the house, but that it was then time to return to her home. In a moment more she opened her eyes, and in natural tones, which showed that she was devoid of any suspicion of what had transpired, she asked if her father was ready to take her home. The Doctor replied that the Judge would join her in a few moments, and returned to the study just in time to find Judge Dudley rubbing his eyes and staring about him bewildered. At sight of the Doctor much of what had happened recurred to him, though he doubted whether he had not been dreaming.

"Doctor Medjora," he exclaimed, "what has happened? Tell me! Tell me the truth!"

"All that is in your mind has occurred," replied the Doctor, calmly. "You have not been dreaming as you suppose, though you have been unconscious for a brief period."

"And my daughter?" asked the Judge, anxiously.

"Agnes is waiting for you to escort her home. As it is late, I have ordered my carriage to be at your disposal. It should be at the door now. Will you accept it?"

The quiet tone, and the commonplace words disconcerted the Judge. He would have preferred discussing what was pressing heavily upon his thoughts, but after gazing steadily at his host for a moment he decided to let the matter rest for a time. Thus he demonstrated the truth of the Doctor's suggestion theory, for the language used, and the manner adopted, had been chosen with the intention of producing this effect. The Judge, however, did not entirely avoid the topic. His reply was:

"Medjora, you have given me food for deep thought. I cannot at once decide whether you are the greatest charlatan, or the most advanced thinker in the world. I am inclined to give you the benefit of the doubt. The other affair shall have my consideration. Good-night!"

"I thank you, Judge," said the Doctor, suavely, "and believe me that I speak with sincerest truth, when I assure you that your daughter's happiness is now, as it has always been, the chief aim of my life. I will accompany you to the carriage."

Having seen his friends depart, the Doctor immediately sought the secret chamber again, and brought Leon up to the laboratory, thence taking him to his room, where he awakened him, and chatted with him for a few minutes, after which he left him to go to rest.

During the long ride home the Judge and his daughter were both silent, each being lost in thought. The Judge was endeavoring to disentangle from the maze of his recollection a history of the night's events which would appeal to his mind as reasonable. Had Agnes been asked to proclaim her thoughts she would have replied that she was "thinking of nothing special." Yet in a dim indefinable way she was wondering how a woman could become so attached to a man, that she would be willing to yield her whole life and independence to him. She was, therefore, a little startled, when just before reaching home her father suddenly addressed her, saying:

"Agnes, my daughter, I wish you to answer a question. Are you particularly interested in any young man? Are you in love with any one?"

"Why, what a question, father! Of course not!" She replied, with some asperity, the more so because she felt the blood mount to her face, and was annoyed at the idea that she was blushing. Her father did not pursue the subject, but leaned back in his seat, mentally relieved. He thought that he had received satisfactory proof that, whatever the Doctor might make Agnes say under hypnotic influence, his spells could not enthrall her during her waking hours. The Judge was not yet convinced of the Doctor's suggestion theory.

When Agnes retired to rest, as she lay in her luxurious bed, her head pillowed on soft down, with silken cover, she began to seek for an explanation of that blush in the carriage, which she was so glad that the darkness had screened from the eyes of her father. She argued to herself that, as she did not love any one, and never would or could do so, she had answered quite truthfully the question which had been put to her. Then why the blush? She had always understood a blush to be a sign of guilt or shame, and she was not conscious of either. She did not readily read the riddle, and while yet seeking to unravel it, she gently drifted away into dream-land. How long she wandered in this mystic realm without adventure worthy of recollection I know not, but at some hour during that night she experienced a sense of heavenly happiness.

It seemed to her that she was walking along a trackless desert. The sun beat down heavily, withering up the shrubbery, and drying up all the moisture in the land. Everything about seemed parched and dying except herself. She had a plentiful supply of water, and walked along without fatigue or suffering from the heat. Presently she came to a stone, upon which sat an old woman, who looked at her and begged for water. Agnes immediately took her water-bottle, and was about to place it to the lips of the old woman, when lo! she observed that the water had nearly all evaporated, so that only enough was left to slake the thirst of one person. At this she was surprised, having thought that there was a plenty, but not even for an instant did she consider the propriety of keeping the water for her own uses. Without hesitation she allowed the old woman to drink all, to the last drop. In a second, the woman had disappeared, and in her place there was a most beautiful being, a fairy, as Agnes readily recognized, from the many descriptions which she had heard and read. The fairy thus addressed her:

"My dear, you have a kind heart, and shall be rewarded. Presently you will leave this desert, and come into a garden filled with delicious flowers. Choose one, and the wish that enters your heart as you pluck it shall be gratified. But of two things I must warn you. The flowers are all symbolic, and your wish can only be appropriate to the blossom of your choice. Second, you can go through the garden but once; you cannot retrace your steps. So be careful how you decide."

As the last words were uttered, the fairy vanished, and Agnes walked on, hoping soon to enter the garden of promise. A mile farther, and the fragrance of many flowers was wafted towards her on a light zephyr which now tempered the heat of the sun. She hastened her steps, and very soon stood before a curiously carved gate made of bronze. As she approached, the gate opened, and admitted her, but immediately closed again behind her, thus proving the correctness of what the fairy had said. In all directions before her were rose-bushes in bloom, but she observed that the whole appeared like a huge floral patch-work quilt, because all of one kind had been planted together, so that great masses of each color was to be seen on every side. Just before her the roses were all of snowy whiteness. She moved along a glittering path, and admired the flowers, ever and anon stooping over one more exquisite than its neighbors, and pressing her face close against its petals, inhaling its sweet fragrance. When she thus stooped over the largest and choicest which she had yet seen, a tiny sprite appeared amidst the petals, and, stretching out his arms invitingly, addressed her in a voice which reminded her of a telephone.

"Maiden fair, choose this blossom. Pluck this bloom, and wear it in thy bosom forever. In return thou shalt be the purest virgin in all the world, for these roses are the emblems of Chastity!"

But, for reply, Agnes shook her head gaily, and merely said: "All that you promise is mine already," and then passed on.

The next were gorgeous yellow roses. They were rich in color and regal in form and stateliness, as on long stems each full-blown rose stood boldly forth above the bush of leaves below. Again a sprite popped out his head, and oped his lips:

"Stop here, fair girl. Pluck one of these, and thereby gain Wealth and all that wealth implies. These are the symbols of gold!"

"I want no more of wealth," said Agnes, and again she refused the tempting offer. The next were roses of a size as great as those just left behind. There was just as much of fragrant beauty, too, or even more, perhaps, in these most glorious roses, just blushing pink.

"Choose one of us, dear girl, and Beauty will adorn thy cheek forever more!" the little sprite invited, but once more Agnes would not acquiesce, and so went on.

What next appeared was somewhat puzzling. The bushes were filled with buds, but at first she could not find a single flower in full bloom. At last, however, she did espy just one, a rose of crimson color and luscious fragrance. With a strange yearning in her breast, she stooped, and almost would have plucked it, when, as she grasped the stem, a sharp pain made her desist. She looked at her hand and saw a drop of blood, of color which just matched the rose. A silvery laugh, like the ripple of a mountain brook, attracted her, and she looked up to see a little fellow, with bow and quiver, smiling at her from the centre of the flower.

"Fair maiden," said the sprite, "if thou wouldst taste the joy of paradise, the happiness which transcends all other earthly pleasure, choose one of these unopened buds. Take it with thee to thy home, and nurse it as thou wouldst care for thine own heart. Tend it, nourish it, and cherish it. Then, in time, it will expand and unfold, and from its petals you will see emerge, not a tiny sprite like me, but the spirit face of one such as thou, though of other sex, who will arouse within thy breast that endless ecstacy which men call Love. For these deep red roses are the emblems of Love!"

Without hesitation Agnes plucked the largest bud within her reach, unmindful of the pricking thorns which pierced her flesh, and then hurried on, passing the roses of Wisdom, and many other flowers of great attractiveness. And as she ran the wish that surged up in her soul was that the words of the sprite might prove true, and that she might see that face: the face of him who was born to be her master; the one for whom she would slave, and be happy in her slavery.

Then it seemed that she was at home again, in her own room, and that the cherished bud was in her most beautiful vase. She thought that she supplied fresh water, placed the vase where the sun would kiss the bud for one full hour every day and in every way did all that she could devise to hasten its maturing. At last one morning, a tiny bit of color gladdened her eyes as the first tips of the petals burst from their sheath and pushed themselves out into the great world. From that hour, as the bud slowly unfolded, she felt within her heart a sympathetic feeling which was a pleasure and yet was painful too. It seemed as though the fate of the flower was interlaced with her own so tightly, that if it should die, why then no longer would she wish to live. And so she waited and watched and tended the blooming rose with anxious patience, awaiting that hoped-for day when the promise of the fairy, and the sprite, would be fulfilled. But the days went by, and at last the rose began to fade, and as the petals dropped away one by one, she felt an answering throb as she thought that her hope would die. At length, when half of the rose lay a shower of dead petals on the table around the vase, it seemed as though she could no longer endure the suspense. She became desperate, and determined to end it all by destroying the rose which had caused her such sweet hope, and such bitter disappointment. She grasped the flower and took it from the vase, but, as she essayed to crush it, her soul was filled with remorse and she hesitated. She gazed at it for a time, as tears filled her eyes, and finally with a sob of pain she began to dismember the bloom, plucking the petals one by one and throwing them idly in her lap. At last, only a half dozen remained about the heart of the flower, when in an instant she was amazed and overjoyed to see a face slowly emerge from amidst the stamens. At the same moment an overpowering fragrance welled up and enthralled her senses, so that she almost sunk into unconsciousness. Then, as she knew that her hope was realized, that the fairy's promise was fulfilled, and that Love was within her grasp, she leaned forward eagerly, to scan the feature of the face before her. It was but a miniature, but after a very brief scrutiny she readily recognized it, and knew that it was Leon's. With a cry of surprise she awakened, while all the details of the dream were yet fresh within her mind.

As the morning sun shed a ray across the features of Agnes Dudley, now freed from the bondage of sleep, it illumined a puzzled countenance. Agnes could not quite understand the feelings which swayed her heart. The sense of gladness was new, as was also a dread anxiety which rose up, and almost suffocated her as she thought, "It is only a dream!"

She had dreamed of love, and she had coupled Leon with that idea in some way, but why should it disturb her to find that it was but a dream? Surely she could not be in love with Leon? Of course not! The very thought was preposterous, even coming to her as it had, while she was asleep. Springing out of bed she was astonished to find that it was already nine o'clock, for usually she was an early riser. She began dressing hurriedly, and rang for her maid. When the girl came she brought with her a beautiful bunch of red rosebuds, half blown. Instantly Agnes was reminded of her dream, but when she noted that a card was attached, and read upon it the words, "With the compliments of Leon," she felt a blush creep over her face, neck, and shoulders, which made her for the first time in her life feel ashamed. She was ashamed because she thought that the maid might observe and understand her confusion, and she was very angry with herself to find that so simple a gift should so disturb her. She sent the maid away that she might once more be alone. Then she read the card again, and noted the signature more closely. Why should he sign only his first name? That was a privilege accorded only to very close friendship. It seemed presumptuous, that the first note received by her from this young man should be so signed. She certainly would show him that she resented what he had done. Indeed she would! Then, with an impulse which she did not analyze, she crushed the buds to her lips and kissed them rapturously. In another moment she realized what she was doing, and again a blush colored her fair skin, and as she observed it in her mirror, she exclaimed, half aloud:

"A red blush, the symbolic color of love!" She paused, retreating before her own thought. But there was no repressing it. "Do I love him?" She did not reply to this aloud, but the blush deepened so that she turned away from the glass, that she might hide the evidence of her own secret from herself.

If the Judge could have guessed what was passing through the mind of his daughter, he might have more fully respected the suggestion theory which Doctor Medjora had propounded to him. As it was, a night's sleep, and an hour's consideration of the matter on the following day, enabled him to conclude that there was nothing about which he need disturb himself. He had come to admit, however, that assuredly Agnes was a wonderfully healthy and intellectual girl, and he was willing to accord some credit therefor to her association with his friend, the Doctor. Feeling consequently indebted to Dr. Medjora, he hastened to write to him that he would immediately take the steps necessary for his legal adoption of Leon, and for giving the lad the name Medjora. The receipt of this letter gratified the Doctor very much, and for the rest of the day he was in high spirits.

CHAPTER XII
THE MARQUIS OF LOSSY

With Leon, the Doctor's suggestion had worked differently, though none the less potently, despite the fact that the lad himself did not detect the symptoms, as did the girl. I think a woman's instincts are more attuned to the influences of the softer passions than are a man's. Certainly it has been often observed that she will recognize evidences of love, which man passes by unnoted and unheeded. If a girl is quicker to discover that she is loved, she also admits sooner that she is in love, though the admission be made only to herself. Thus, as we have seen, the Doctor's charm operated upon Agnes.

When Leon awoke that same morning, it was a sudden awakening from dreamless sleep. He recalled nothing of what had occurred during the previous night, nor had he even a suspicion that Agnes had been in his thoughts at all. Nevertheless he dressed himself with feverish haste, and, contrary to his usual custom, he left the house and went "for a walk," or so he explained his action to himself. Yet very soon he had reached the nearest station of the Suburban Elevated railroad, and was rapidly borne towards the city. During this trip he thought that he was going to town to obtain some chemicals which he needed in the laboratory, but, as there was no immediate necessity for them, he might have delayed their purchase for several days. The truth was he was answering a scarcely recognized inward restlessness, which demanded action of some sort. The cause of this change from his normal habit was that "something was the matter" with him, as he afterwards expressed it. But at the time he did not seek an explanation of his mood. He did procure the chemicals, but having done so, instead of returning home, he walked aimlessly for several blocks, until he stopped, seemingly without purpose, before a florist's shop. In an instant he had formulated a design, "on the spur of the moment" he told himself, though it was but the outcome of the secret agency which controlled his whole conduct that day. He went in and purchased some rose-buds, selecting red ones, and he wrote the card which Agnes found upon them. When he reached the signature he quickly scribbled "Leon," and then he paused. The thought within his mind was, "I have no other name." Therefore he did not continue. Thus it is evident that the single signature was not a familiarity, either intended or implied, but a response to that feeling, ever within his consciousness, that he had no right to call himself "Grath"! Upon this point he was ever sensitive. He hastened to the Judge's house and left the bouquet at the door. Then he returned to Villa Medjora with a lighter heart, and, man-like, he wrongly attributed this to the ozone with which the morning air was laden. As yet he did not suspect that he had fallen in love. I wonder why we use the term "fallen" in this connection, as though the acquirement of this chief passion of the human heart were a descent, rather than an elevation of the soul, as it surely is. For one must be on a higher plane, from that moment when he abandons himself as the first consideration of his thoughts, and begins to sacrifice his own desires, that he may add to the pleasures of another.

The first meeting between Agnes and Leon was one to which the former looked forward with anticipated embarrassment, while Leon scarcely thought of it at all, until the moment came. But when they did meet, all was reversed. The girl was self-possession personified, while Leon never before found words so tardily arriving to meet the demands of conversation. He went to his own room that night, and wondered what had come to him, that he should have been so disturbed in the presence of one for whom hitherto he had had rather a tolerance, because of her intellectuality, than any feeling of personal inferiority such as now occupied his thoughts. How could he be less than she? Was he not a man, while she–she was only a woman? Only a woman! Ah! Therein lies the mysterious secret of man's undoing; of his lifelong slavery, that the wants of woman shall be supplied. Yet women prate of women's rights, deploring the fact that they are less than those, who, analysis would show, are but their slaves.

From this time on, the bud of love in the hearts of these two young people advanced steadily towards maturity, and, before very long, Agnes was living in a secret elysium of her own creation. She no longer questioned her own feelings. She freely admitted to herself that all her future happiness depended upon obtaining and enjoying Leon's love. But she had come to be very sure of the fulfilment of her heart's desire, since Leon's visits became more and more frequent, and his books and science apparently lost their power to allure him away from her side. The situation was very entertaining to her, who was so fond of analyzing and studying the intricate problems of life; and, to such as she, what could be happier occupation than probing the heart of him to whom she had intrusted her own? She thought she saw so plainly that he loved her, that it puzzled her to tell why it was that as yet he himself was not aware of this fact. But at last the awakening came.

One pleasant afternoon in early summer, they were walking down Fifth Avenue, deeply engrossed in a discussion of another of Correlli's novels. Leon read novels in these days. He said he did so because it was so pleasant to discuss them with Agnes. Besides, he found that even in novels there might be something to learn. They were speaking of that excellent work, *Thelma*.

"I think that it is Correlli's most finished work," Agnes was saying; "but I am surprised at the similarity between it and Black's novel, *The Princess of Thule*."

"I have not yet read that. Wherein lies the resemblance?"

"In both books we find the story divided into three parts. First, the young Englishman seeking surcease from the *ennui* of fashionable society by a trip into the wild north country. Black sends his hero to Ireland, and Correlli allows hers to visit Norway. Each discovers the daughter of a descendant of old time kings; the *Princess of Thule* in one, and *Thelma*, the daughter of the Viking, in the other. The marriage ends the first part in each instance. In the second, we find the wedded couples in fashionable London society, and in each the girl finds that she is incongruous with her surroundings, and after bearing with it awhile, abandons the husband and returns to her old home, alone. The finale is the same in each, the husband seeking his runaway wife, and once more bringing her to his arms."

"Still, Miss Agnes,"–the formal "Miss Dudley" of the earlier days had been unconsciously abandoned–"what you have told is only a theme. Two artists may select the same landscape, and yet make totally different pictures."

"So they have in this instance, and I think that Correlli's management of the subject is far in advance of Black's, as beautiful and as touching as that master's story is. The death of the old Viking transcends anything in *The Princess of Thule*. I do not at all disparage Correlli's work, only–well–it is hard to explain myself–but I would be better pleased had there been no likeness between the two."

"Yet I have no doubt that it is accidental, or, if there was any imitation, that it was made unconsciously. I believe that a writer may recall what he has read long before, and clothing the idea in his own words, may easily believe that it is entirely original with himself. There is one speech which Thelma makes, which I think most beautiful. You remember where the busy-body tries to make mischief by telling Thelma that her husband has transferred his love to another? Thelma replies, in substance, that if her husband has ceased to love her, it must be her own fault, and to illustrate her meaning she says that one plucks a rose, attracted by its fragrance, but when at last it is unconsciously thrown away, it is not because of fickleness, but rather because the rose having faded, has lost its power to charm, and so is cast aside. I think it was very touching for Thelma to make such a comparison, charging herself with the fault of losing the love of her husband."

"Yes! It is very pretty and poetical, but like poetry in general, it is not very sensible. I think that if a man has enjoyed the attractions of his wife in her youthful days he should cherish her the more when her charms have begun to fade. There is quite a difference between a rose, which in losing its outward beauty loses all, and a woman who, however homely in feature, may still possess a soul as beautiful as ever."

"Indeed, Miss Agnes, I indorse your sentiments. Such a man would be a brute. But Thelma's husband was not of that mould. He was true to her."

"Yes," said Agnes, smiling; "but Thelma's charms had not faded, nor even begun to decline. Her simile was inapt as applied to herself."

"Exactly! It was her heart, and not her head that gave birth to the beautiful sentiment. But I am sure that her husband would have loved her, however ugly she might have grown. I am sure that, in his place, I would have done so."

"You? Why, Mr. Grath, I thought that you told me you would never love any one?" She spoke the words with mischievous intent, and glanced at him archly, as she watched the effect of the speech.

Leon blushed and became confused. He was at a loss for words, but was relieved from the necessity of formulating an answer, by an occurrence which threatened to end in a tragedy. They were crossing a street at the moment, and so intent had they become upon their discourse, that they scarcely heard the warning cries of the excited people. A maddened horse was running away, and as at length Leon was aroused to the imminence of some danger, intuitively, rather than by any well-defined recognition of what threatened, he gave one hasty glance in the direction from which the animal was approaching, and with a rapid movement he encircled Agnes's waist with his arm, and drew her back, barely in time to escape from the horse and cab which rattled by.

It was in this instant that Leon's awakening came to him. In presence of a danger which threatened to deprive him forever of the girl beside him, he became suddenly aware of the fact that she was essential to his future happiness. At last he knew that he loved Agnes, and from his silence as he took her home, and the tenderness of his tones at parting, Agnes instantly knew that he had been aroused. She already began to look forward to their next meeting, and to wonder whether he would at once unbosom himself. She meant to help him as much as possible. Poor fellow! He would be very much abashed, she had no doubt. She would not be coy and tantalizing as so many girls are. She thought that such affectation would be beneath her. Her sense of justice forbade it. No! She would be very nice to him. She would show no signs of uneasiness as he floundered about seeking words. She would wait patiently for what he would say, and then, when he had said the words, why, then—well, then it would be time enough at that sweet moment to decide what to do. She would make him happy, at any rate. Of that she was determined. There should be no ambiguity about her reply. And in this mood the girl awaited the wooing.

Leon did not sleep at all that night, or if he slumbered, it was only to dream of Agnes. A hundred times he saw her mangled beneath the hoofs of that runaway horse, and suffered agonies in consequence; each time awakening with a start, to find beads of perspiration upon his brow. Again his vision was more pleasing, and in dream-land he imagined himself united to Agnes, and living happily ever afterward, as all proper books tell us that married lovers do. At last the day dawned, and with impatience he awaited that hour when with propriety he could call upon his sweetheart. He had a very good excuse, for by accident, (*sic?*) he had left his umbrella at the house the day before, and already it was growing cloudy. He might need it, and therefore of course he should go for it before it should actually begin to rain.

It was scarcely noon when Leon was announced to Agnes, who was in her morning room, sipping a cup of chocolate, and wondering when he would come. And now he was here. She expected to find him *distrait*, and lacking in manner and speech, as she had seen him in the dawning of his passion. She was therefore wholly unprepared for what followed. If Leon had been bashful in her presence when he did not comprehend the cause of his disconcertion, having discovered that he loved Agnes, hesitation vanished. There was no circumlocution about his method at all. He was impulsive by nature, and, when a purpose was once well defined in his breast, he was impatient until he had put it into operation. Thus, without even alluding to the umbrella which he had ostensibly made the object of his visit, in accounting for it to himself, he addressed Agnes as follows:

"Miss Agnes, I have scarcely slept all night because of what might have happened through my carelessness yesterday."

"I do not understand you," said Agnes, and indeed she did not. She saw, however, that he intended to speak very directly, and was herself disconcerted.

"I mean the narrow escape which you had from being run over. I should have had my wits about me, and have prevented you from being in such danger."

"You saved my life!" she spoke softly, and drooped her head.

"I do not know. But for me it would not have been in need of saving. But if I did save your life, I know that I preserved what is dearest in all the world to myself. No! Let me speak, please! I have awakened from a dream. I have lived in dream-land for many weeks, and I have not understood. I have been near you, and I have been happy, but in my stupidity I did not see that it was because of your companionship that I was happy. In the moment when I was in danger of losing you, I realized how great the loss would be. Had you died, I must have died too. Because–because, Agnes, I, I, to whom the idea of love has always been repellent, I tell you that I love you. I love you with a species of worship which is enthralling. My whole being, my life, my soul is all yours. If you do not accept my love, then I have no further wish to live. Speak! Speak to me! I cannot wait longer. Tell me that you love me, or–or merely nod your head, and I will go!"

To such wooing as this how could woman answer? She had promised herself that she would not be ambiguous in speech, but now she learned that directness was demanded, and though her whole heart yearned for him, and she pitied the anguish which was born of his anxiety, she found it hard to say the words, which could not in honor be retracted. So, for a moment, she was silent, and he misunderstood. He thought that her hesitation was born of sympathy for him, and that she did not speak because she feared to cause him pain by refusing him. He felt a piercing throb of agony cross his heart, and his cheek paled. He reeled and would have fallen, for he had not seated himself, but he clutched the mantel for support. In a moment he mastered himself sufficiently to say hoarsely:

"I do not blame you! I am a nameless vagabond, and have been presumptuous! Good-bye!"

He turned away and was leaving the apartment swiftly, when his steps were arrested by a cry that thrilled him through with joy that was as painful as his sorrow had been.

"Leon! Leon! I love you!" Agnes cried, arresting his departure, and, as he turned and came again towards her, she was standing upright, and herself made the movement which gave him the privilege of embracing her.

By a singular chance, while they were thus enfolded in love's first rapturous clasp, and therefore oblivious of all the world except themselves, Judge Dudley, who had not yet left the house, entered the room. He saw them, but they did not observe him. Instantly he realized that the Doctor's scheme had borne fruition. He hesitated but for a moment, and then, stepping lightly, he went out of the room, and departed from the house.

How often do our joys and sorrows approach us hand in hand? There comes a moment fraught with bliss; the draught is at our lips, and we take one lingering sip of ecstasy, when on a sudden the brimming glass is dashed aside, and a cloud of misery enshrouds us round about! Thus it happened to Leon.

After an hour of joyous converse with Agnes, now "his Agnes," he started for home. Arriving there, he ran lightly up the steps, as if treading on air. He was whistling a merry tune, as he opened the door of his room, and closed it again having entered. His mind was filled with ecstatic anticipation of what the future had in store for him. It did not seem possible that anything could happen to disturb the sweet current of his thoughts. Yet a moment later he was arrested by the sound of a moan, an agonizing groan that filled his heart with dread. Again it was repeated, and immediately he knew that it was Lossy, who was suffering. He stooped and looked under the bed. There, indeed, was his fond animal friend, but around his mouth there was an ominous mass of foam. Had the poor beast gone mad? With a pang of anxiety, Leon drew the bedstead away from the wall, and went behind it to where Lossy had dragged himself. One glance into the dog's eyes turned up to meet his with all the loving intelligence of his customary greeting, and Leon dismissed the idea of rabies. Tenderly he lifted the dog and carried him to a table near the window, upon which he made a bed with pillows. He wiped the foam from his lips, and as he did so Lossy gently protruded his tongue and licked his master's hand. He also feebly wagged his tail, and endeavored to rise, but his exhausted condition prevented, and with a groan he dropped back and lay there crying piteously as a child might do. Leon could not comprehend the trouble. "What is the matter with him?" he asked himself. "He certainly was well this morning." As he looked, the foam began to gather again, as Lossy worked his lips in such a way as to eject the saliva from his mouth. Suddenly the explanation came to Leon. "Aconite!" he cried aloud. "Lossy has been poisoned! By whom? Perhaps he got into the laboratory. But how? How did he get at the poison? Oh! If I had only remained at home this morning!"

But regrets for the past are ever impotent, and Leon did not waste much time deploring what had gone before. He quickly procured some charcoal, and mixing it with milk administered it to his dog. The foaming ceased, and the beast seemed more comfortable, but it was questionable whether any permanent benefit would result from the use of the antidote.

While Leon sat watching his pet, with a growing pain gnawing at his heart as the conviction thrust itself upon him that the dog would die, his door opened and Madame Medjora appeared. Coming forward she looked at Lossy a moment, and then said:

"Do you think that the brute will die?"

"I am afraid that he will," mournfully answered Leon.

"Then why doesn't he die right off," she said. "It is several hours since I gave him the poison."

"You gave him the poison?" exclaimed Leon, springing up in wrath. "You poisoned Lossy, and you dare to tell me of it?"

"I dare to tell you? Yes! I dare do anything that woman can do. I am a descendant of soldiers. The brute ate one of my lace handkerchiefs, and I was glad of the excuse to be rid of him. There! You know the truth now, what will you do about it?"

As she uttered the words, Madame drew herself up to the full height of her commanding figure, and it would have been a daring man who would have attacked her. But when even feeble men are urged on by rage, they do deeds which braver men would hesitate to attempt. Utterly bereft of the restraining faculty of reason, by the information that his pet had been intentionally destroyed, Leon sprang forward, and would have seized the proud neck of Madame between his powerful hands, in an endeavor to carry out the desire to throttle her, which had forced itself upon his brain, but at that very instant Dr. Medjora came in, and, with a single glance, appreciating that the lad was beside himself, he rushed forward and held him firmly.

"What does this mean, Leon?" the Doctor demanded.

"She has poisoned Lossy! Let me go! I will kill her!"

Leon struggled fiercely to be free, but he found himself restrained by muscles which were like steel. The Doctor, however, was himself tremendously moved by what he heard. Addressing his wife he asked:

"Did you do that? Does he speak the truth?"

"I gave the beast poison. Yes! What of it?"

"Then you are a wicked fiend, Madame. Leave the room!"

"I will not!" replied Madame, with energy.

"Leave the room, or else I will release the boy. Go! go quickly whilst you may!" The Doctor's tones were imperative, and as the woman looked into the faces of the two men, her courage left her, and with a muttered imprecation she hurried from the room. As the door closed after her, the Doctor released Leon, but by a swift movement intercepted him as he endeavored to escape from the apartment, and turning the key in the lock he took it out, and thus prevented Leon from following his wife.

"Leon, my dear boy," said the Doctor, in tones expressive of the deepest sympathy, "let us see what we can do for Lossy. Perhaps it is not too late to save him, and it is better to do that, than to vent your anger upon a woman."

"A woman! Do not call her by that name. She is a contamination to her sex. Pardon my speaking so of your wife, Doctor, but—but—she has murdered Lossy. Murdered my dog, just as I called such a deed murder, in the little story which I showed to you that day in the woods. Do you remember?"

"Perfectly, but there can be no murder unless he dies. Let me see!"

"Yes! Yes! Save him! Use your wonderful knowledge to save this dumb brute, as I have seen you pluck infants from the brink of the grave. Save my pet, my kind friend! Save him and I will do anything for you! Only save my Lossy!"

Poor Leon! This was the one love which had been his for so many years. How long he had taken comfort and pleasure in lavishing his affection upon his dog, who had learned to understand and obey his slightest nod.

Dr. Medjora examined Lossy carefully, and looked very grave. Presently he looked up, and placing one hand tenderly on Leon's head, he spoke softly:

"Be brave, my lad. Many such bitter moments as this must be borne through life. You must meet them like a courageous man."

"There is no hope?" sobbed Leon.

"None! He is dying now! See how faint his respirations are?"

With a cry of anguish Leon fell to his knees and gazed into his dog's eyes. He patted the head lying so limp and listless, and in response poor Lossy made one feeble effort. He gazed back into his master's face, and Leon ever afterward claimed that, in that last lingering look, he detected the living soul which was about to depart from his dying dog. Lossy painfully opened his mouth and protruded his tongue so that it barely touched Leon's hand in the old-time affectionate salutation, and the soul of the dog departed for that realm beyond the veil.

Leon leaned forward a moment, with his ear to the dog's heart, listening for an answering vibration, which would indicate that life yet lingered, but, receiving none, with a cry he fell forward to the floor and burst into uncontrollable sobs.

Doctor Medjora, wise physician that he was, made no futile effort to restrain these tears, knowing them to be the best outlet for natural grief. With a glance filled with tender love for his *protégé*, he unlocked the door and passed out unobserved, leaving Leon with all that remained of the Marquis of Lossy.

CHAPTER XIII
THE DISCOVERY

Early in the morning of the same day upon which Leon had offered himself to Agnes, Madame Medjora, reading her *Herald*, had at last found the long-awaited personal, "Come," the signal which she had arranged with the detective. Immediately after breakfast, therefore, she had started forth to learn what had been discovered.

Arrived at the agency, she was at once ushered into the presence of Mr. Barnes.

"Well," said she, scarcely waiting to be seated, "what have you found out?"

"I have learned everything," said Mr. Barnes, without any show of feeling.

"You have? Well, go on. Why don't you tell me?" Madame was very impatient, but the detective was in no hurry.

"I have known what I have learned for over a week, Madame Medjora," said he slowly, "and during that time I have hesitated to send for you. Even now, when you are here, I am not sure that I shall be doing the right thing to give you any information upon this subject, without first communicating with your husband."

"Ah! I see," said Madame, with a sneer, "you think he would pay you better than I. You are mistaken. I have plenty of money. My own money. What is your price?"

Mr. Barnes arose from his seat, in anger, but perfectly calm outwardly. As deferentially as though he were addressing a queen, he bowed and said:

"Madame, pardon me, but be kind enough to consider our interview at an end."

"What do you mean? You wish me to go?"

"Precisely, Madame. That is my wish."

"But you have not yet told me—ah! I see! I have made a mistake. But you will pardon me, Mr. Barnes. I did not know. How could I? I judged you by what I have heard of detectives. But you are different. I see that now, and I ask your forgiveness. You will forget my stupid words, will you?" She extended her hand cordially, and appeared truly regretful. Mr. Barnes yielded to her persuasive influence, and sat down again.

"Madame Medjora, I do not fully comprehend your motives in this matter. That is why I hesitate to speak." Mr. Barnes paused a moment. "Suppose you answer one or two questions. Will you?"

"Certainly! Ask me what you please."

"Very well, Madame! You married Dr. Medjora after his trial for murder. At that time he had little money. Am I right, then, in concluding that you married him because you loved him?"

"I loved him with my whole soul!"

"And now, do you love him as well now?" Mr. Barnes scrutinized her closely, lest her words should belie her real feeling. But her answer was sincere.

"I love him more now than I ever did. He is all the world to me!"

"Ah! I see!" Mr. Barnes communed with himself for a brief moment, then suddenly asked: "You have had no children, I believe?" Madame grew slightly paler, and answered in a low tone:

"None!"

"Just so! Now then, Madame, you of course recall the trial. It was more than hinted at that time that the Doctor had a child by his first wife. Did he ever tell you the truth about that?"

"Never!"

"Suppose that he had done so, and had confided to you the fact that rumor was right, and that there was a child. Understand I am only supposing a case! But if so, what would you have done?"

"I would have taken the little one, my husband's child, and I would have cherished it for its father's sake!"

This was a deliberate lie, but Madame uttered the words in tones of great sincerity. She was a very shrewd woman, and half-suspecting the object of the detective's questioning, did not hesitate to tell this falsehood in order to gain her own end. She succeeded, too, for after a few moments more, Mr. Barnes said:

"After all, Madame Medjora, I am merely a detective, and it is my business to take commissions such as you have intrusted to me, and work them out. I will make my report to you. With the letter which you gave me it was easy enough to make a start. I found the writer, Matilda Grath, and a particularly unprepossessing old hag she is. As is readily seen by her letter, she is ignorant of even common-school knowledge. She is simply a rough product of her surroundings, and is as untutored as when she was born. But she had a younger sister, Margaret, who was very different. This Margaret was a very attractive girl, and having some ambition, attended school until she was fairly well educated. This her elder sisters called "putting on airs" and "flyin' in the face of the Lord, tryin' to know more 'n her elders." Margaret also had numerous beaux, and this was another source of irritation to her sisters. Finally there came a young man to the neighborhood, and in the language of the people thereabout, Margaret "set her cap" for him. However, he did not marry her, but after he had left the vicinity, Margaret went to Boston, where she remained several months. When she returned she brought a baby back with her. That baby was Leon."

"Then he was her child?"

"The gossips said so, but there is no doubt in my mind that he was not. He was the child of the man to whom she had given her heart, but the mother was his lawful wife."

"Then why was the baby given to Margaret Grath?"

"Because the mother died, and the father was tried for murdering her!"

"My God! You mean that—"

"I mean that Leon's father is your husband, Dr. Medjora!"

"Impossible!" Madame wished to disbelieve exactly what she had always suspected to be the truth.

"What I tell you is fact. I never do anything by halves. In the first place I had a hint of the truth from your own suspicions. You of course had little to go on, but you loved your husband, and when a jealous eye watches the relation between the beloved one and another, it will see much. I had no doubt that you had taken your idea from your observation of the love which the Doctor bestowed upon his *protégé*. Next I noted the coincidence of the dates. Margaret Grath appeared with the child a very few months prior to the death of Mabel Sloane. But I obtained substantial proofs."

"What are they?"

"Matilda Grath is an avaricious old woman. Her letter was in the nature of blackmail. She did not actually know that the

Doctor is the boy's father, but she adopted that idea merely from the fact that he appeared upon the scene as soon as the guardian died. Then at the auction, it appears that there was a squabble over the possession of a collie dog, and the Doctor settled the dispute by purchasing the animal, and presenting it to Leon."

"Oh! He did that?" Madame was inwardly incensed, but she quickly suppressed any expression of her emotion.

"Yes! Old Miss Grath thought this was 'queer.' Then when she subsequently learned, what she did not at first know, that Leon had been taken into the Doctor's home, her doubts vanished. This accounts for her allusion to the Doctor in the letter, and the reason why she did not write again, was that she had no proof with which to substantiate her suspicions. I instituted a search, however, and unearthed a package of old letters in a worm eaten writing-desk, upon which no bid had been offered at the auction, so that it had been thrown into the waste bin in the barn. Among these I found two, which were from the Doctor, alluding to the boy, and also a photograph of himself sent at the earnest solicitation of Margaret Grath, as one letter explains. I suppose he thought that this was the least repayment he could make for a lifelong sacrifice."

"You have those letters?" asked Madame, with some anxiety.

"I have them here," answered the detective. "Do you wish them?"

"I do!"

"I will give them to you upon one condition,—that you give them to your husband. They are perhaps more valuable to Leon, as the only evidence which would prove that he is the Doctor's son. But as the Doctor has taken him into his house, it is evident that he means to provide for him."

"I will accept your terms. My husband shall know what you have told me, and I will give him the letters to-night."

"With that understanding, I give them into your custody."

He handed a packet to Madame, who quickly placed it in her hand-satchel. Then she arose to depart. Handing him a check already signed she said:

"Please fill in the amount of my indebtedness to you."

Mr. Barnes took the check, wrote "five hundred dollars" on the proper line, and handed it back to Madame Medjora.

"Will that be satisfactory?" he asked.

"Quite!" she answered shortly, and left the office. Having accomplished her purpose she had no further need to assume a friendliness which she did not feel.

All the way home this woman's heart grew more and more bitter because of the jealous thoughts that rankled in her breast. Her love for her husband was of that selfish sort, that exacted all for herself. She wished not only to be first in his affections, but she desired to be second, third, and last. He must not love any other than herself, unless indeed it might have been a child of hers. Having been denied that boon, she could not bear to think that he had been the father of a child not hers. She hated that dead mother, and lacking opportunity to vent her spite in that direction, she transferred her venom to her offspring. She had never liked Leon, but now she despised him utterly. She thought of Lossy, the dog which her husband had bought and presented to Leon. That the Doctor should have been so solicitous for the lad, galled her. The dog had always been an object upon which she would vent her spite when it could not be known, but now she would give some open evidence of her displeasure.

As she entered the hallway at home, imagine her delight to see Lossy, poor dog, sitting down idly tearing a fine lace hand-kerchief with his teeth. It seemed to her that Providence offered her an excuse for what she contemplated. She called the dog to her, and the faithful, unsuspecting creature followed her up the stairs to his doom. She went into the laboratory, knowing that both the Doctor and Leon were out, and readily found a bottle marked "Aconite."

She sat upon a low bench and called Lossy. The confiding beast went to her, and, raising himself, planted his forepaws in her lap. He would have kissed her face, but she prevented him. Grasping his jaws in her powerful hands she forced them open, and poured the entire contents of the bottle into his mouth, holding his jaws apart until he was forced to swallow the liquid. Then she released him, and he ran to that asylum of refuge and safety, his master's room. Alas, that master was away, courting! Thus Lossy's fate was sealed!

Madame awaited for Leon's return, anxious to gloat over his grief at the death of his pet, and it was for this, and to carry out another design, that she went to his room while he was ministering to his dog. Before she could fulfil her other project her husband, having returned home, interrupted them, having been attracted by the noise from Leon's room.

When she left them Madame went to her own apartment, and after the death of the dog, Dr. Medjora followed her there, determined to discover the whole truth. As he entered she arose to meet him, facing him with an undaunted air.

"Cora," demanded the Doctor, "how dared you commit such a hideous crime? Why did you poison that dog?"

"Because it was my pleasure to do so!"

"Your pleasure to deprive a poor dumb brute of life? You should be ashamed to make such a confession!"

"I am not the only one who might make confessions!"

"What do you mean?" The Doctor instantly realized that a covert threat lay hidden in her words.

"You have deceived me," cried his wife, at last giving full play to her anger. "For years you have lied to me. But at last I know everything. I know who Leon is!"

"Do you?" The man was exasperatingly calm. He folded his arms and, gazing coldly upon the wrathful woman, added, "What is it that you think you know?"

"I do not think! I tell you I know! You brought him here, calling him a poor boy whom you wished to befriend. That was a lie! He is your own child!"

"How do you know that?"

"I hired a detective. He found out the whole hideous truth. I have your letters for proof, so you need not attempt denial."

"So you have found letters? Are they genuine? Let me see them?"

"I am not such a fool as that. I have hidden them where you cannot find them. I have a better use for them than to give them to you!"

"Indeed, and may I ask what use you intend to make of them?"

"I mean to take them to Judge Dudley, and to his daughter Agnes! Ha! That idea does not please you, does it?"

"With what purpose would you show them the letters?"

"I know what you are aiming at! I am not the fool that you think! I have studied you, and watched you all these years, and

I understand you very well. You wish Leon and Agnes to be married?"

"I do! What of it?"

"What of it? It shall never be! That shall be my vengeance for your long deception. I will prevent that marriage if it cost me my life!"

"If you dare to interfere with my plans it may cost you your life!" The words were said in threatening tones, which at any other time would have cowed Madame, but now she had thrown aside her mask, and could not be stayed from her purpose. She answered haughtily, and with a tantalizing sneer:

"No! No! My fine Doctor! You cannot rid yourself of me, as you did of Mabel Sloane! I will not drink your poison!"

"Woman! Beware!" He grasped her wrists, but with a wrench she freed herself, and stepping back spoke wildly on:

"Yes! You can strangle me perhaps! You are strong, and I am only a woman. But, before I die, I will frustrate your grand scheme to marry this miserable son of yours to an aristocrat. When I tell Judge Dudley that the boy is yours, he will hesitate to admit the son of a murderer into his family. For though he obtained your acquittal, and though he has been your friend for so many years, mark me, he will decline an alliance with one who was so near the gallows!"

She paused to note the effect of her words, a slight fear entering her heart, as she thought that perhaps she had said too much. To her amazement, her husband, without answering a single word, turned and left the room.

Leon lay beside his dog so long, that at last the twilight closed in, and slowly the light of day faded until darkness surrounded him.

He heard the strokes upon the Japanese bronze which summoned him to dinner, but he did not heed. It seemed to him that he would never care to eat again. Through the weary hours of the night Leon was struggling against suggestion. It will be remembered that, in his little story, he likened the killing of a dog to murder. Therefore in his opinion the killing of Lossy, was a murderous act; and thus the thought of murder occupied his mind. He considered Madame a self-confessed criminal, and, as such, justice demanded that she should be punished. But the justice of man did not include her act within the statutes of the criminal code. She had killed Lossy, but, were he to demand her punishment at the hands of the law, the law's representatives would laugh at him. But punished she should be, of that he was already determined.

If it seem to you that Leon over-estimated the wrong which had been done to him, then one of two things is true. Either you have never loved and been loved by a dog, or else you forget that the love lavished upon him by Lossy was all the affection which Leon had enjoyed for years. To the lad, his collie was his dearest friend. In the grief for his death he had even forgotten for the time his human love, Agnes. Thus it was that the idea of meting out justice against Madame himself, having once entered his mind, took a firm hold upon him.

How should he accomplish it? What should her punishment be? What is the usual punishment of murder? Death! A chill passed over him at the thought. Yet was not Lossy's life as dear to him, as Madame Medjora's was to her? Then why should not she lose her life in payment for the crime which she had committed, her victim being a defenceless and confiding dog? Leon pictured to himself how she had accomplished the deed. He saw, in his mind, the poor creature going to her, and thus placing himself within her power. The thought maddened him, and setting his teeth together he muttered audibly:

"She shall die!"

Then his brain sought some way to compass such an end with safety to himself, and before long he had concocted a scheme of devilish ingenuity. His knowledge of chemistry warned him that poisons could be traced in the tissues of the body after death, and that such means would be suicidal.

"But suppose she were to die a natural death? Then, not even suspicion would be aroused."

That was the idea. He must convey to her the germs of some deadly disease from which she would be apt to die. Then the *post-mortem* would show nothing out of the common. There would be no way to detect how the disease had been contracted. The attending physician would certify that the death was due to a known disease, and an autopsy, if held, would substantiate his statements.

What disease should he choose? Asiatic cholera? He had some pure cultures in a tube in the laboratory. But no! That would not serve his purpose. Cholera is such an uncommon and dangerous malady, that the Board of Health would strictly investigate a sporadic case. It might not be difficult to trace the fact that he had obtained the germs from the European laboratory whence they had been sent to Dr. Medjora for experimental purposes. It would be safer to select some disease of frequent occurrence. He had the germs of diphtheria also, in the form of a pure culture. Should he use them? It would not be sure that the woman would die, but at any rate she might, and surely she would suffer. Yes! He would cause her to contract diphtheria. But how to proceed? Ah! He would use chloroform upon her in her natural sleep, and thus obtain the opportunity for his inoculation.

And so the idea grew, and his plans were arranged and perfected hour after hour, until at last midnight had arrived. Stealthily he left his room and went towards the Doctor's study. Arrived there, he was about to cross and enter the laboratory, when his attention was attracted by a line of light under the door. Some one was evidently in the laboratory. Leon slipped behind a curtain and waited. The minutes passed tediously, but at last the door opened, and there appeared Dr. Medjora, only partly dressed, his feet slippered. In one hand he carried a night lamp, and in the other he held a bottle and a test tube. Of this Leon was certain. Closing the door of the laboratory, the Doctor crossed the study and went out into the hall. Leon stole after him, and saw him start up the stairs. He watched until, as the Doctor ascended, the light gradually disappeared. Then he heard footsteps overhead, and knew that the Doctor had gone to his own room. Madame slept at the other end of the dwelling.

"Some experiment which he is studying out," muttered Leon, and proceeded with his own grim purpose. He went into the laboratory, and lighted a lamp which was on the bench. He searched the closet where the drugs were kept, but the chloroform bottle was missing. He turned to the rack where he had left the tube in which the diphtheria bacillus had been cultivated, but that also could not be found.

In a moment, realizing that the means of committing the contemplated crime had in some mysterious way been taken from him, he awoke from the delirium of his thoughts, which had been brought on by his grief at the death of his dog, and he fervently thanked the fortune which had saved him from committing murder. Like a culprit, he returned stealthily to his room, head down, and there he sat at the window, looking out at the stars, grateful that he could do so, free from that dread secret which might have been his. He was saved!

On the next morning, however, Leon was horrified to hear that Madame had been suddenly taken ill, and that the malady was diphtheria, in its most virulent form. He could not understand it, but he was more than glad that his own conscience was free from stain.

Two days later, Madame Medjora succumbed to the disease, which is often fatal when it attacks one of her age; and so she went to her long account, with her sins upon her head.

CHAPTER XIV
SANATOXINE

Mr. Barnes was sitting in his office, looking listlessly over his morning paper, when his eye suddenly met a headline announcing the death of Madame Medjora. Instantly his interest was aroused, and he read the account with avidity until he reached the statement that the disease of which Madame had died was diphtheria. Then he put his paper down upon his desk, slapped his hand upon it by way of emphasis, and ejaculated:

"Foul play, or my name is not Barnes!"

He remained still for a few moments, thinking deeply. Then he resumed his reading. When he had reached the end, he started up, gave a few hurried instructions to his assistant, and went out. He visited the Academy of Medicine and obtained permission to enter the library, where he occupied himself for a full hour, making a few memoranda from various books. Next he proceeded in the direction of Villa Medjora, and arriving there he asked to see Leon Grath.

Leon entered the reception-room in some surprise, and seeing Mr. Barnes he asked:

"Is your errand of importance? We have death in the house."

"It is in connection with the death of Madame Medjora that I have called to see you, Mr. Grath. I am a detective!"

The effect of this announcement was electrical. Leon turned deathly pale, and dropped into a seat, staring speechless at his visitor. Mr. Barnes also chose to remain silent, until at last Leon stammered forth:

"Why do you wish to see me?"

"Because I believe that you can throw some light upon this mysterious subject."

"Mysterious subject? Where is the mystery? The cause of Madame's death is clearly known!"

"You mean that she died of diphtheria. Yes, that is a fact. But how did she contract that disease? Is that clearly known? Can you throw any light upon that phase of the question?"

Leon controlled his agitation with great difficulty. He had thought, when urged on by that terrible temptation which he had resisted, that a death such as this would arouse no suspicion. Yet here, while the corpse was yet in the house, a detective was asking most horribly suggestive questions. Questions which had haunted him by day and by night, ever since that visit to the laboratory.

"I am not a physician," at length he murmured. "I am merely a student."

"Exactly! You are a student in the laboratory of Dr. Medjora. You can supply the information which I seek. Do you know whether, three days ago, there was a culture of the bacillus of diphtheria in the Doctor's laboratory?"

"Why do you ask? What do you suspect?"

Leon was utterly unnerved, and stammered in his utterance. He made a tremendous effort, in his endeavor to prevent his teeth from chattering, and barely succeeded. Indeed, his manner was so perturbed that for an instant Mr. Barnes suspected that he was guilty of some connection with Madame's death. A second later he guessed the truth, that Leon's suspicion's were identical with his own.

"What I think," said Mr. Barnes, "is not to the point. My question is a simple one. Will you reply to it?"

"Well, yes! We did have such a culture tube in the laboratory."

"Did have," said the shrewd detective, quickly. "Then it is not there now. Where is it?"

"I do not know. I think the Doctor took it away. Of course he used it in some harmless experiment, or–or–or–or for making slides for the microscope."

"You mean that you surmise this. All you know is that Doctor Medjora took the tube out of the laboratory. Am I not right? Now when did that occur? You saw him take it, did you not?"

Leon stared helplessly at his tormentor for a moment, great beads of perspiration standing on his brow. Then starting to his feet he exclaimed:

"I will not answer your questions! I have said too much! You shall not make me talk any more," and with a mad rush he darted from the room, and disappeared upstairs.

Mr. Barnes made no effort to arrest his flight. Indeed he sympathized with the lad, well comprehending the mental torture from which he suffered. He pondered over the situation awhile, and finally appeared to have decided upon a plan of action. He took a card from his case, and wrote upon it these words:

"Mr. Barnes, detective, would like to see Dr. Medjora, concerning the coincidence of the death of his two wives. This matter is pressing, and delay useless."

This he placed in an envelope which he took from a desk that stood open, and then he touched a gong, which summoned a servant.

"Hand this to Dr. Medjora, immediately. I will await a reply here."

Ten minutes elapsed, and then the servant returned, and bidding Mr. Barnes follow him, led the way to the laboratory. Here Dr. Medjora received the detective, as though he were a most welcome visitor.

"So, Mr. Barnes," said the Doctor, opening the conversation, "you have attained your ambition, and are now a full-fledged detective. I have read something of your achievements, and have watched your progress with some interest. I congratulate you upon your success."

"Dr. Medjora," said the detective, with much dignity, "the object of my visit is so serious that I cannot accept flattery. We will proceed to business, if you please."

"As you choose! Let me see! From your card, I judge that you fancy that there is some suspicious circumstance about my late wife's death. You speak of a coincidence which connects hers with that of my first wife. What is it?"

"Both died of diphtheria," said Mr. Barnes, impressively.

"You are entirely mistaken, sir," said the Doctor, with a touch of anger. "My first wife, Mabel, died of morphine, self-administered, and fatal because of other organic disease from which she suffered. She did not die of diphtheria."

"A physician so testified, and signed a death certificate to that effect."

"He did, but he was mistaken. Physicians are mortal as other men are, and as liable to errors of judgment. I repeat, Mabel died of poison."

"Well, we will pass that for a moment. Your last wife died of diphtheria, and she did not contract that disease legitimately."

"No? You interest me. Pray then how did she contract it?"

"By inoculation with the bacillus of diphtheria, Dr. Medjora, and you administered this new form of poison, which an autopsy does not disclose."

"Quite an ingenious theory, Mr. Barnes, and I admire your skill in evolving it. It shows what an enterprising detective you are. You think that if you make a discovery of this nature, you will cover yourself with glory. Only you are wrong. I did not do what you charge. Why should I wish to kill my wife?"

"Because she had discovered your secret!"

"What secret?"

"That Leon is the child of Mabel Sloane and yourself!"

"Mabel Medjora, you mean," said the Doctor, sternly. "When a woman marries, she assumes her husband's name."

The Doctor was apparently very jealous of the good name of his first wife. Mr. Barnes was amazed at this exhibition of feeling. The Doctor continued, as though soliloquizing:

"So you are the detective that my wife engaged? Strange fatality! Very strange!" He walked up and down the room a few times, and then confronted the detective.

"Mr. Barnes," said he, "it is evident that you and I must have a serious and uninterrupted conversation. Leon may come in here at any moment. Will you accompany me to a room below, where we will be safe from intrusion?"

"Certainly!"

Dr. Medjora raised the trap-door, which revealed the secret stairway, and started down. Mr. Barnes arose to follow him, saying:

"You are taking me to some secret apartment, Doctor. I will go with you, but this trap must be left open, and I warn you that I am armed."

"You need no weapons, Mr. Barnes. No danger will threaten you. My purpose in taking you below is entirely different from what you have in your mind."

At the foot of the stairway he turned aside from the crypt of Æsculapius, and led the way into the secret chamber in which the hypnotic suggestion of love had been put into operation. At this time it appeared simply as an ordinary room, the staging and curtains having been removed.

"Be seated, Mr. Barnes," said the Doctor, "and listen to me. You are laboring under a misapprehension, or else you have not told me all that you know. A most curious suspicion has been aroused in your mind. Upon what facts is it based?"

"Perhaps it will be best for me to explain. I must again refer to the fact that your first wife was supposed to have died of diphtheria. Your second wife falls a victim to the same malady. It is uncommon in adults. This of itself might be but a coincidence. But when I know that, on a given day, I revealed to your wife the truth about Leon, which you had carefully hidden from her for so many years, and when I subsequently discover that Madame was attacked by this disease on the very night following her visit to my office, suspicion was inevitable."

"As you insist upon going back to that old case, let me ask you how you can suppose that I induced the disease at that time?"

"Just as you have done now. By using the diphtheria bacillus."

"You forget, or you do not know, that the bacillus of diphtheria was not discovered until Klebs found it in 1883, and the fact was not known until Löffler published it in 1884. Now my wife died in 1873."

"True, these scientists made their discoveries at the time which you name, but I feel certain that you had anticipated them. You are counted the most skilful man of the day, and I believe that you know more than has been learned by others."

"Your compliment is a doubtful one. But I will not dispute with you. I will grant, for the sake of argument, that your suspicion is natural. You cannot proceed against me merely upon suspicion. At least you should not do so."

"My suspicion is shared by another, whose mind it has entered by a different channel."

"Who is this other?"

"Your son!"

"What do you say? Leon suspects that I have committed a crime? This is terrible! But why? Why, in the name of heaven, should he harbor such a thought against me?" The Doctor was unusually excited.

"He saw you take the culture tube, containing the bacillus, out of the laboratory."

"You say Leon saw me take a culture tube from the laboratory?" The Doctor spoke the words separately, with a pause between each, as though stung by the thought which they conveyed. Mr. Barnes merely nodded assent.

"Then the end is at hand!" muttered the Doctor, softly. "All is ready for the final experiment!" Mr. Barnes did not comprehend the meaning of what he heard, but, as the Doctor walked about the room, back and forth, like a caged animal, seemingly oblivious of the fact that he was not alone, the detective thought it wise to observe him closely lest he might attack him unawares.

Presently the Doctor stopped before the detective, and thus addressed him, in calm tones:

"Mr. Barnes, you are shrewd and you are clever. You have guessed a part of the truth, and I have decided to tell you everything."

"I warn you," said Mr. Barnes, quickly, "that what you say will be used against you."

"I will take that risk!" The Doctor smiled, and an expression akin to weariness passed over his countenance. "You have said that, in your belief, as early as 1873, I knew of the bacillus of diphtheria, and that I inoculated my wife with it. You are right, but, nevertheless, you are mistaken when you say that she died from that malady. I must go further back, and tell you that the main source of my knowledge has been some very ancient hieroglyphical writings, which recorded what was known upon the subject by the priests of centuries ago. Much that is novel to-day, was very well understood in those times. The germ theory of disease was thoroughly worked out to a point far in advance of what has yet been accomplished in this era. The study required to translate and comprehend the cabalistic and hieroglyphical records has been very great, and it was essential that I should test each step experimentally. About the time of Mabel's death I had discovered the germ of diphtheria, but I found that my experiments with the lower animals were very unsatisfactory, owing to the fact that it does not affect them and human beings in a precisely similar manner. I therefore risked inoculating my wife."

"That was a hideous thing to do," ventured Mr. Barnes.

"From your standpoint, perhaps you are right. But I am a unique man, occupying a unique position in the world. To me alone was it given to resurrect the buried wisdom of the past. Even if I had known that the experiment might be attended by the death of my wife, whom I loved dearer than myself, I still would not have been deterred. Science transcended everything in my mind. Death must come to us all, and a few years difference in the time of its arrival is surely immaterial, and not to be weighed against the progress of scientific research. But I was confident that the disease, thus transmitted, would not prove fatal. That is, I was sure that I could effect a cure."

"But it seems that you did not do so. The woman died."

"She died from poison. I carefully attended her during her attack of diphtheria, until an unlooked-for accident occurred. I became ill myself. It was not an ailment of any consequence, but I felt that it would be safer to call in assistance, and I placed the case in the hands of Dr. Fisher. He afterwards stupidly called in Dr. Meredith. However, despite their old fogy methods, she made a good rally and was on the safe side of the crisis, when that hypodermic case was left temptingly within her reach. I think now that she shammed sleep, in order to distract my attention from her. Morphine *habitués* are very cunning in obtaining their coveted drug. However that may be, I was suddenly aroused to the fact that there was a movement in the bed, and turning my head, I saw her pushing the needle of the syringe under her flesh. I sprang up and hastened to her, but she had made the injection, and dropped back to the pillows, when I reached her. She had not withdrawn the needle, and I was in the act of doing that, when the nurse entered."

"Then you adhere to the story which you told upon the stand?"

"Certainly! It is the truth!"

"But, Doctor," said Mr. Barnes, "you have not, even yet, proven that she did not die of diphtheria."

"She did not! I tell you it was the morphine that deprived her of life. I know it! She died of poison! There is no question about that!"

Thus the Doctor, though admitting that he had produced the diphtheria, persistently asseverated that Mabel had not succumbed to its influence. Thus is explained his not advancing the theory of diphtheria as a cause of death, when arranging his defence, at the trial. To have escaped the gallows in that manner, would have been to burden his conscience with the murder of the woman whom he loved, for if she died of diphtheria, while he must have escaped conviction by the jury, he would know within his own heart that it was his hand that deprived her of life. Mr. Barnes replied:

"But there is a question in this last case. Madame died of diphtheria, and since you admit that you can produce it by inoculation, what am I to believe?"

"I care not what you believe," said the Doctor, sharply, "so long as you can prove nothing."

"Well, then, since you do not care," said the detective, nettled, "let me tell you that I believe you deliberately planned to kill your last wife. What is more, I do not doubt that a jury would adopt my views."

"In that you are utterly mistaken. Were I considering myself alone, I would permit you to accuse me, feeling perfectly confident that I would be in no danger."

"You are a bold man!"

"Not at all! Where there is no danger, there can be no special bravery. Why, my dear Mr. Barnes, you have no case at all against me. In your own mind you think that there is ample proof, but much of what you know could not be offered to a jury. You are aware of the fact that the diphtheria bacillus was known to me prior to my first wife's death, and so you trace a connection between the two cases. But my lawyer would merely show that the discovery was made ten years after Mabel died, and any further allusion to my first trial would be ruled out. I know enough about law, to know that previous crimes, or accusations of crime, cannot be cited unless they form a part of a system, and as your idea of induced diphtheria could not be substantiated, all of that part of your evidence would be irrelevant."

"That would be a question for the presiding judge to decide."

"If he decide other than as I have stated, we would get a new trial on appeal. The law is specific, and the point is covered by endless precedents. Now then, obliged to confine yourself to positive evidence in the present case, what could you do? You think you could show a motive, but a motive may exist and not be followed by a crime, and your motive is weak besides. Next, you declare that I had the knowledge and the opportunity. I might have both, and still refrain from a murder. But you say that the tube containing the bacillus was missing from my laboratory on that very night, and that my son, Leon, saw me take it. I think that you have formed a rash conclusion on this point, because I doubt that Leon has told you any such thing. However, granting that it is true, and even that the boy would so testify, I am sure that he would admit under cross-examination that it is a common habit for me to take such tubes to my room to make slides for the microscope." The detective recalled that Leon had made this same explanation, and he realized that the Doctor had made a valuable point in his own defence. Dr. Medjora continued: "We would produce the slides which I did actually make, and, being warned by you so early, it would be easy for me to remain in your company until I could send for an expert to examine the slides, so that at the trial he would be able to testify, that from the condition of the balsam he could swear that they had been very recently made. Thus, by admitting all of the damaging parts of your evidence, and then explaining them so that they become consistent with the hypothesis of innocence, we would feel safe. You would still be at the very beginning of your case. It would devolve upon you to show that I not only made the slides, but that I likewise used a part of the contents of that tube to inoculate my wife. You would need to show how such an act were possible. You have no witness who saw me commit the deed which you charge, have you?"

"No," said Mr. Barnes, reluctantly. "But I still think that the circumstantial evidence is sufficient." Mr. Barnes felt sure that this man was guilty, and however skilfully his defence was planned he was reluctant to yield.

"It is sufficient!" said Dr. Medjora, "Not to convict me at a trial by jury, but to raise a doubt of my innocence in the minds of those, whose good will I am determined not to forfeit. Therefore I will not submit to a trial."

"How will you escape? I intend to arrest you!"

"You intend to arrest me, but your intention will not be carried into effect. I mean to place myself beyond the reach of the law."

"You do not contemplate suicide?" asked Mr. Barnes, alarmed.

"Not at all! There is no object in such an act, and good reason why I should not resort to it. You do not comprehend my position, and I must explain it to you, because I must depend upon you for assistance."

"You expect assistance from me?" Mr. Barnes was puzzled.

"Certainly, and you will grant it. I must tell you that for many years I have planned a scheme which is now on the verge of accomplishment. I wish my son Leon to marry Agnes Dudley. I had some difficulty to obtain my friend's consent, but since he has discovered that the young people love one another, he has acquiesced. Only to-day he told me this. But if he was reluctant, when Leon's parentage was unknown, he would be more so, were he to learn that I am his father."

"But I thought that Judge Dudley was your warm friend?"

"He is! But even strong friendships have a limitation, beyond which they must not be tried. Judge Dudley would strenuously argue that I am innocent of the old charge. His friendship for me, and his pride at winning his first great case, would prompt him thus. But were he to hear your suspicions, like you, he would believe that both women died similarly, and he would not only be apt to accept your theory of Madame's death, but he might also come to think that I had murdered Mabel also."

"So! You admit there is some potency in my charge, after all."

"You would fail with a jury, but you would convince Judge Dudley, and that would forever prevent him from consenting to this marriage. He would move heaven and earth to stop his daughter from marrying the son of one whom he believed to be a murderer. Thus you see the disaster that threatens, if you pursue your course. You would blast the lives of two people, who love one another."

"Duty cannot consider sentiment!" said Mr. Barnes, though in his heart he was already sorry that he suspected, and that he had followed up his suspicion.

"Leon now troubles himself because he does not known who his father is," continued the Doctor, without noticing what Mr. Barnes had said. "It would be far worse for him to know his father, and then believe him to be a murderer, and even that he had himself supplied a clue against him. It would be too horrible! Agnes too would suffer. She might abandon her love, from a sense of duty to her father, but her heart would be broken, and all the bright promises of her youth crushed. No! No! It must not, it shall not be!" The Doctor became excited towards the end, and Mr. Barnes was startled at his manner.

"What will you do?" he asked, feeling constrained to say something.

"Place myself beyond the reach of the law, as I said before. But not by suicide, as you suggested. Do you not see that my only reason for avoiding the trial which would follow your accusation is, that I do not wish the knowledge to reach those three persons, in whose welfare my whole heart is centred? Suicide would be a confession of guilt. It is the hackneyed refuge of the detected criminal who lacks brains, and of the story writer, who, having made his villain an interesting character, spares the feelings of his readers by not sending him to prison, or to the gallows. Nor do I contemplate flight, because the effect would be the same."

"Then how do you purpose evading the law?" Mr. Barnes was intensely interested, and curious to know the plans of this singularly resourceful man.

"The law cannot reach the insane, I believe," said the Doctor, calmly.

"You surely do not suppose that you can deceive the experts by shamming madness?" asked Mr. Barnes, contemptuously. "We are too advanced in science, in these days, to be baffled long by malingerers."

"Observe me, and you will learn my purpose!"

Dr. Medjora went to a closet and returned with a hammer, a large staple, and a long chain. Mr. Barnes watched him closely, with no suspicion of what was to follow. The Doctor stopped at a point immediately opposite to the door, and stooping, firmly fastened the chain to the floor by nailing it down with the large staple, which was long enough to reach the beam under the boarding. He then stood up again. Taking a hypodermic syringe from his pocket, and also a small phial, he carefully filled the barrel, and was about to inject the fluid into his arm, when Mr. Barnes ejaculated:

"I thought that you said you would not commit suicide?"

"I have no such intention. In one moment I will explain my purpose to you. Meanwhile watch me!"

With dexterous skill he plunged the point into one of the larger veins, and discharged the fluid carefully, holding a finger over the wound as he withdrew the needle to prevent any escape. If Mr. Barnes was astonished by this, he was more surprised at what followed. The Doctor stooped and picked up the ends of the chain, which the detective now observed terminated in handcuffs. These the Doctor slipped over his wrists, and snapping together the spring locks, thus virtually imprisoned himself.

"What does this mean?" said Mr. Barnes. "I do not understand."

"Of course not," said the Doctor. "You are accustomed to deal with brainless criminals. Despite your boast, science is beyond you. I will explain: My object in thus chaining myself to the floor, is to insure your safety."

"My safety?"

"Yes! In less than half an hour I will be a raving maniac. If not restrained, I might do you an injury."

"Impossible!" cried the detective, incredulous.

"You will see! I ask in exchange for my thoughtfulness in preventing myself from harming you, that when I shall have become irresponsible, you will suggest the idea that I felt this attack of insanity coming on, and took these precautions for the sake of others. Will you do this?"

"Certainly! If—" Mr. Barnes stopped, confused by his thoughts.

"There is no if about this. I do not deal in chances. I have never yet made an error, and you will see that my prediction will be fulfilled. But time, precious time, is passing, and I have much to say before I lose my reason. You have heard of hydrophobia, have you not? And of Pasteur's experiments?"

"Yes! I have read what the newspapers have said."

"The investigators in this field have discovered that the virus of this disease is located in the brain, spinal marrow, and nerves of infected animals. They have also extracted the virus, and by inoculation produced hydrophobia in other animals. Along similar lines I have extensively experimented in connection with insanity. In the first place, I argued that insanity is due to a specific poison, a toxalbumen, and that this poison is a result of parasitical action. If I could isolate that poison, and the germ which causes it, I would understand the etiology of insanity. The discovery of an antidote would then be an almost assured consequence. To be able to cure insanity, would be a proud distinction for the discoverer of the method. I am convinced that I have the secret almost within my grasp. The preparation which I have injected into my veins is a formula of my own. I have named it 'Sanatoxine'!"

"Sanatoxine?"

"Yes! The word means 'poison to sanity,' and my Sanatoxine will produce insanity, unless I have made some mistake, which is unlikely. Hereafter, when the proper antitoxine shall have been discovered, it will be a simple matter to cure insanity. The patient will be given a proper dose of Sanatoxine, to convert his malady into a curable form of the disease, and then the antitoxine will counteract the poison which has deprived him of the use of his reasoning faculties."

"If you have made such a wonderful discovery," said the detective, "then you should not destroy your own reason, thereby depriving the world of the benefits of your knowledge. In this you commit a greater crime than that with which you stand charged!"

"Do I? Suicide is a crime within the definitions of the Penal Code, but there has been no enactment against self-inflicted insanity. But I must tell you how Sanatoxine is produced, and then explain how posterity may yet benefit by my discovery. One of the curable forms of insanity is delirium tremens. The worst of these cases are truly maniacal neuroses. I have seen a man die of such an attack, and a few minutes later I removed his brain and spinal marrow. These I macerated, and from them I extracted the virus which is the cause of the malady. I have inoculated the lower animals with it, and I have seen results which satisfy me that my deductions are correct. This cannot be absolutely known, however, until my Sanatoxine is tried on human beings. That important step in the advancement of science has just been made. If I become insane, my theory will have ample proof. For the future, Leon must complete my work. Among my papers he will find my views and formulas. It is inevitable that he will solve the riddle."

"But you sacrifice yourself, merely to test an experiment? You introduce into your own system a preparation abstracted from such a horrible source! It is fearful to think about!"

"Let me see," said the Doctor, consulting his watch. "Ten minutes have passed, and there is scarcely a rise of temperature. Singular!" He mused over the problem for a moment, and a shade of anxiety passed across his features, as he murmured, "What if I have made a mistake? No! No! It is impossible! Utterly impossible!" Reassured he turned again to Mr. Barnes:

"I mentioned awhile ago that I should need your assistance. You have said that I make a sacrifice. From the ordinary stand-point that is true, though not from my own. Suicide would have brought me death, an experience for which I yearn, with a long-ing based upon scientific curiosity, which perhaps you cannot comprehend. But I am equally desirous of knowing by personal experience what it means to be insane. Death will come to me in time, therefore I need not interfere, but insanity might never have been my lot, had I not pursued the course which I have followed. To-morrow you will be obliged to explain what you have witnessed, and the favor I ask is this. Do not render my self-sacrifice useless, by relating to others those horrible suspi-cions, the consequences of which I am so desirous of escaping. Be as merciful as the law, and keep silent that the innocent may not suffer. May I count upon you to do this?"

"Dr. Medjora, I cannot yet believe that you will succeed in this horrible experiment; but if you do, of course I would not harm others by arousing useless suspicions. If you escape from the law, you need have no fear of what I should do."

"I thank you from the bottom of my heart." Again he consulted his watch. "Twenty minutes gone, and still no alteration. What if I should fail? No! No! Failure is impossible! Mr. Barnes, another matter. My son is my natural heir, but I do not wish him to know it. Even without your story, Judge Dudley might hesitate to let Leon marry his daughter, if he knows him to be son of mine. There may be a doubt against me lurking in some corner of his brain, which would be vivified if he learned my secret. You will not reveal it?"

"No!"

"I thank you. The boy will not suffer. I have left a will in his favor, and there is another paper making him the guardian of my estates should I lose my reason. You see I have contemplated my experiment for a long time, and all my preparations are complete. The Judge has arranged to give Leon my name legally. So all will be well! All will be well! All my plans successful! I lose my reason without complaint! But, time is passing, and my reason remains! A horrible thought comes over me! I have made a mistake! By all the eternal torments, I have made a mistake, and here I am chained up so that it is impossible for me to rectify the error! They say I am an egotist, yet I have so little remembered my own mental superiority, that I actually have thought that a dose of Sanatoxine which would unseat the reason of an ordinary man, would effect me. Fool! Fool! Fool! How could I forget that I, Emanuel Medjora, the Wizard, am not as other men? How can my reason be destroyed by so small a dose as that which I have taken? But stop! There may be yet one chance! There may be more in the phial! Where is it?"

His excitement increased as he gave vent to his thoughts aloud, as though Mr. Barnes were not present. Now he looked eagerly about, and at last saw the bottle at some distance from him on the floor. Mr. Barnes also saw it, and stepped forward to pick it up. Instantly the Doctor sprang towards him, grasping the hammer which had lain within his reach.

"Touch that phial at your peril!" he screamed. "I will brain you as mercilessly as I would a rat! That phial is mine! Its contents are mine! Valuable only to me and to science! My experiment must succeed! It must! It must! It shall!"

Glaring at Mr. Barnes, who stood back awed by his threatening attitude, the Doctor moved towards the bottle, but, as he stooped to reach for it, the chains tightened and impeded his progress.

"The chains! I had forgotten the chains! Ha! I have never forgotten before! Perhaps my reason is yielding already! No! No! I feel that I have full sway over all my faculties! I must have that phial!"

He stooped to his knees, and stretched and writhed and twisted, in his efforts to reach the bottle. But ever it was just beyond his grasp.

"I will have it! I will! I will!" he muttered, gritting his teeth with such force that one of them was broken. But he took no heed of the accident. Down on his back he turned, and, by a wriggling motion, soon lay extended at full length, his feet reaching as far as the chains about the wrists permitted, his arms being stretched backward beyond his shoulders. He could now reach the bottle with his feet, but it was impossible for him to see it, the position of his arms rendering it very difficult for him to hold his head and shoulders high enough from the floor, so that his own body would not impede his vision. However, he did accomplish his purpose, and Mr. Barnes was amazed to see him at last clutch the phial with his two feet. Then began a series of contortions which were painful to see. With the utmost care the Doctor drew his feet slowly up, dragging the phial nearer and nearer, meanwhile crying out in a sort of hysteria:

"It is mine! I will have it! I will succeed! The Wizard never failed! Never! Never! No! No! Never! Never!"

Once, as he moved his feet, the phial slipped from them and rolled away again.

"Come back!" he shrieked. "Come back! Stop! Stop!" he cried, as though addressing a living thing. It ceased to roll, and with a cry of joy he found that he could still reach it. Again he slowly worked it towards him. Inch by inch he managed the coveted phial, until at last he assumed another position. Springing up from the floor he reached backward with one foot and touched it.

"Now it is mine! Mine! Mine!" His voice was shrill, and there was a passionate tone of exultation that smote Mr. Barnes to the heart. It was terrible to stand by and see the desperate effort which this man made to accomplish that from which all men shrink in horror. Slowly the Doctor proceeded with his task, until at last he was able to reach the phial with his hands. Swiftly stooping, as a hawk descends upon its prey, he grasped the little bottle.

"Ha! Ha! Ha! I have it! It is mine! The Wizard never fails!"

His laugh of joy had scarcely died away, before he uttered a most terrific shriek, and threw the phial from him, crying:

"Empty! Great God! It is empty!"

He stood silent and motionless for a moment. Then his eyes turned in the direction of Mr. Barnes, and he glared at him in such a way that the detective felt uncomfortable. Suddenly he burst forth with a tirade of abusive language.

"You! You are the cause of all this! You are the prying miscreant that has made all my trouble! I will have your life! I will drag you into the crypt of my great ancestor, and tear out your heart on the stone of sacrifice that still exists in there!"

He dashed forward with such force that the chains, reaching their limit suddenly, jerked him back so violently that he fell. As he did so his hand chanced to touch the hammer, which he had laid aside while trying to secure the bottle. With a shriek of joy that made Mr. Barnes shiver, he sprang up, holding the hammer aloft.

"I am chained! Chained! But you shall not escape! Take that!"

Swiftly he hurled the hammer, but Mr. Barnes, suspecting his purpose, dropped to his knees, and the missile went harmlessly over his head.

"Balked! Balked! I have failed! But I am the Wizard and I will succeed! Ha! Ha! Ha!" His laugh now filled the room. "You wonder how! I am chained and you think that you are safe! Ha! Ha! Ha! You are a fool! You do not know me! I am Emanuel Medjora! I am powerful. I will rend these chains, and then your life shall pay!"

He turned, and wrapping the chains around his two arms, he braced his feet against the floor, and tugged with all his might.

He pulled, and swayed from side to side. He savagely jerked the chains, and then again he grasped one with both hands, but his efforts appeared to be in vain. But so much power did he display, that, as his back was turned, Mr. Barnes decided that it would be safer to prepare for flight. He therefore cautiously advanced towards the door, and there paused, ready, however, to dart out on the instant should it be necessary.

Still the Doctor tugged and jerked and rattled the chains, shrieking and laughing demoniacally at intervals. Presently, with a shout of triumph, he did burst one of the chains. Turning towards Mr. Barnes, he shouted:

"You see! I am the Wizard! I do what I please! You did not think that I could break it! Ha! Ha! Ha! You do not know Emanuel Medjora! He accomplishes what he wills! The will controls the muscles, and the mind controls the will! But now through my brain a liquid fire courses that makes my mind doubly powerful! I feel that I am getting stronger every moment! In another second I will snap this last chain as easily as you would break a cord! Then, then,–Ha! Ha! Ha! I'll have your heart out! Ha! Ha! Ha! I have an idea! I'll kill you now!"

He rushed forward as far as the remaining chain would permit, and extending the other arm, to which dangled the end of the chain which he had broken, he drew it back and then switched the dangling links viciously towards Mr. Barnes, narrowly missing him. As he saw that even now he could not reach the detective, he uttered a cry of rage, and again and again endeavored to strike him with the dangling chain. But it was useless. Mr. Barnes was beyond his reach. Finally, with a cry of despair, the Doctor threw himself in a heap upon the floor, now weeping, now laughing, and shrieking madly:

"They say I am a Wizard! Ha! Ha! Ha! A Wizard! I a Wizard, and I cannot kill a man! Such a simple thing, and yet I cannot do it! A Wizard! I a Wizard! Ha! Ha! Ha! Ha! Ha! Ha!"

His Sanatoxine experiment had proven successful. Dr. Emanuel Medjora was a maniac!

Rodrigues Ottolengui

A Conflict of Evidence

CHAPTER I
THE CRIME

"It's my opinion they won't catch him. Marvel's no fool, if he is hot headed, and he knows enough to keep under cover now that they are after him."

"That's all right, Everly, and, as you say, I guess Marvel can hide away well enough. But what I want to know is, what's he got to hide for? He an't done nothin' as I can see, 'cept to fire off his pistol when he was mad as thunder."

"And right he was, too," said another lounger in the saloon where this conversation occurred. "I say any man of grit would have done the same. Why, didn't the old man try to disgrace him right before his sweetheart and a lot of girls?"

"Well, anyway," said the store-keeper, removing his pipe to speak, "smart or fool, I guess they'll get him. I hear as how the Squire is terrible cut up about this thing, and he's sent down to Boston for a regular detective."

"The Squire's sent to Boston for a detective?" said Everly. "I wouldn't have believed that the Squire would do such a thing. To set a spy on the track of one of his neighbors! Why, it's disgraceful!"

Over in the corner, on chairs drawn up close to the stove, sat two strangers. They had arrived in Lee, that morning, and after taking drinks at this the only tavern in the town, had apparently set about getting warm. The elder of the two here ventured a remark.

"Gentlemen," said he, "if you'll pardon the curiosity of a stranger, I'd like to ask you what crime this young man has committed?"

A pause followed, whilst the strangers became the object of a close scrutiny by all present. Finally, Will Everly stepped forward, and looking his interrogator steadily in the face, said:

"I am Will Everly—Walter Marvel's friend. Before I answer any of your questions I must know who you are, and why you wish to know this story."

"Your talk aroused my curiosity," said the stranger.

"Will you deny that you are a detective?" Everly eyed his man closely, but not a sign indicated that the question had caused surprise. He was disappointed, for he had expected him to be disconcerted. The reply was simple.

"I shall not deny it, for I never lie." He handed Everly a card upon which was neatly engraved:

"*John Barnes. Detective. Boston.*"

After reading it, conciliated by the detective's honesty, Everly said:

"I thank you for your candor. I suspected you, for we seldom have strangers in Lee. As I am Marvel's friend, and as you have come here to make trouble for him, you will pardon me if I give you no information which will be of use to you."

"No need, young man; we'll get along well enough without you!" Everly recognized the voice of Squire Olney, who had just entered, and he turned away. The Squire shook Mr. Barnes cordially by the hand, saying:

"You are Mr. Barnes, the man sent down by the Pilkingtons, I presume? I am glad you are so punctual. I expected to find you here, as I received a dispatch from your chief last night. As soon as you are ready, I shall take you up to Mr. Lewis's house, for it is in connection with his affair that I sent for you."

"I am ready to go with you at once," said Mr. Barnes in an undertone; "but first, let me introduce to you my friend Mr. Burrows. He is a young man in whom the chief is interested, and he works with the older men that he may acquire experience. He is a beginner, but he is shrewd, and promises to become a first-class detective."

Burrows arose, and the Squire shook hands with him, whereupon the three men exchanged a few words in an undertone. Meanwhile, another stranger appeared upon the scene. This was a man dressed in the garb of a sailor. He ordered a hot drink, for which he paid in advance. Then he asked one or two questions, whereupon the store-keeper called out:

"I say, Squire! Here's a man you may as well see."

Thus summoned, the Squire left the detectives and approached the new-comer.

"Well, my man," he asked, "what can I do for you?"

"My name is John Lewis," was the reply. "I have been at sea for several years, but have at last reached home again; or rather I should say my father's home, for this is my first visit to Lee. I was asking to be directed to my father's house, when this gentleman told me that you are about to go there, and might be willing to take me with you."

"I shall be delighted to do so," said the Squire, offering his hand to Lewis in cordial recognition. "I have often heard your father speak of you, and as I know that he loves you and longs for your return, it will be a pleasure to me to restore his son to him."

"You can't think how your words gladden me," said Lewis, apparently overcome by emotion. "I ran away from home when I was a youngster; and now that I have come back it is good news to hear that a welcome awaits me."

"Welcome? Yes, indeed! Your father has often said to me that he would cheerfully forgive your foolish escapade, if you would but return. But come, we must start at once. I have business of importance, with your father, this morning, and I am taking a detective with me to his house."

"A detective?" exclaimed Lewis. He seemed startled, and Tom Burrows who was watching him, noted that he glanced hurriedly around the room, his eyes resting finally upon Mr. Barnes and himself.

"Oh, you need not to be alarmed," said the Squire, observing his agitation, "it is in your father's interest that I have brought a detective from Boston. I will explain as we go along."

"You must excuse my being startled," said Lewis, "but it rather astounded me to hear that you were taking a detective to my father's house. At the instant, the absurd, but horrible idea, entered my brain that you meant to arrest him."

Tom Burrows thought it a significant fact that at the mention of the word detective, Lewis's eye should have sought the very men who were detectives. When he imparted this suspicion to Mr. Barnes, the latter suggested that possibly Lewis had seen them before, and that their faces attracted him, because he partly recognized them. Subsequently he learned that Lewis had seen them that same morning, on the train, but had reached Lee after them, because he had walked from Newmarket, whilst they had taken the stage.

Without further conversation the four men started on their way towards the home of John Lewis. As they walked, the Squire enlightened them upon the affair which had necessitated the presence of a detective.

"This business," he began, "is particularly unpleasant, because the best people in the town are mixed up in it. John Lewis came to Lee, fifteen years ago, bringing with him a little girl, then about six years of age. Virginia, she is named, though her intimates call her Virgie. We knew nothing of Lewis, but he appeared to have money, for he bought Riverside farm, on which he has lived ever since. He made friends rapidly as the town's-people came to know him, and he was reckoned an acquisition. The girl was not his own child, he explained, but an adopted one, the daughter of his sister, who had died. He mentioned having a son," the Squire here addressed Lewis, "but we never saw you. How was that?"

"When my father came to Lee," replied Lewis, "he left me at a military academy in New York; but I chafed under the restraint, and one day, very foolishly, ran away, and shipped for a voyage to China."

"Ah! That explains matters. About five years after Lewis settled here, the Marvels came. At first it was only for the summer months, but finally they bought a place, and since then have been permanent residents. Naturally young Walter Marvel—an only son—met Virgie, and, from boyhood, he has been attached to her. But whilst she has not rejected his attentions, she has never acted so that anyone, even her-most intimate friends, could be sure that she loved him. There are two others connected with what I am about to tell you. Alice Marvel, Walter's sister, and Harry Lucas, Walter's friend, currently supposed to be in love with Alice, though there are some who claim that, were it not for the friendship between him and Walter, Lucas would court Miss Lewis himself. That is probably only gossip. However, these four young people are fast friends.

"They are constantly together, and are partners in many enterprises of a social or charitable nature. Another fact which has a not unimportant bearing upon the subsequent events, is that all four of these young people are expert shots with a pistol. Some two or three years ago, a circus appeared in this neighborhood, the star attraction of which was a young girl who was wonderfully clever with a pistol. Virgie declared that she too could learn to shoot, and the result was that pistols were bought, and, I may say, a sort of shooting-club was formed, though only these four were members.

"Recently, Virgie attained her majority and arranged to celebrate it with a festival for all of her friends. As it was during the nutting season, the guests were invited to come for the day, the many nut trees near the river banks promising occupation to those who cared for that sort of amusement, whilst tennis-nets, and croquet were set upon the lawn. In addition, it was announced that there would be a shooting-match in which all could take part.

"All went merrily during the morning, and a sumptuous dinner, served upon tables in the open air, had been enjoyed by all, after which the party dispersed about the farm in small groups. I was sitting on a bench chatting with Lewis, when Virgie and Walter Marvel approached. The latter asked permission to speak to Lewis privately, and I therefore walked a little way from them with Virgie. At the time, I had no idea of Marvel's object in seeking the interview with Lewis, and was startled a few moments later to hear them talking in angry tones; but that you may better understand the affair I will relate just what occurred, as it was told to me afterwards, by Lewis himself.

"It appears that the shooting-match that day had a greater prize at stake than the trophy which had been offered. Marvel had asked Virgie to be his wife, and begged permission to speak to her adopted father. With a smile, and womanlike, desiring to keep him in suspense as long as possible, her reply had been: 'Beat me at the target and you may speak to father.' This he had accomplished, though by only a single point, and it was to ask for the hand of Virgie that he had impatiently sought the private conversation with Lewis. Lewis confessed to me that he had not suspected that there was any attachment between them, and he was therefore surprised by Marvel's request. He asked whether Virgie had given her consent, and receiving the affirmative reply, after a moment's hesitation, he informed Marvel that he would not sanction his suit. Marvel of course urged his cause, and Lewis made some angry remarks which at last were loud enough to attract my attention. Virgie and I then went quickly towards the two men, and others did the same, so that when the *finale* came there was quite a crowd of people about us. As we approached, Marvel said hotly:

"'Virgie, Mr. Lewis refuses his consent, and will not give his reasons!'

"'Why do you object—uncle?' asked Virgie. She strongly emphasized the word 'uncle,' a title by which she had never addressed him before. This incident will give you an insight into that girl's character; cool, self-possessed, and withal wilful and determined; though by wilful I do not mean that she is unrestrained by reason, but rather that once having formed a project she will carry it into effect at any cost. For a moment Lewis seemed staggered by her words, but he quickly recovered himself and replied:

"'Because I will not allow my daughter to marry into a family of jail-birds!'

"'What do you mean by that?' fairly screamed Walter, trembling with barely suppressed anger.

"'What do I mean?' retorted Lewis, speaking rapidly, and as though actuated by intense hatred, 'I mean that your uncle, the man whose vile name you bear, is a convict, and that he caused the death of an innocent girl!'

"With a wild cry of rage Marvel drew his pistol, which he had reloaded after the shooting-match, and fired at Lewis. The sequence of events had been so startling and so rapid, that none of us made a move to save Lewis, except Virgie, who exhibited her usual presence of mind. With a quick upward motion of her hand, she diverted her lover's aim, so that the ball went into the air. Having thus saved the life of her adopted father, she turned to Marvel and said the single word 'Go!' Walter looked at her a moment with despair upon his face, then, as she made no answer to his mute appeal, he threw his weapon from him, and rushed from the place, threatening Lewis with his vengeance.

"He had scarcely departed when Lucas pushed through the surrounding circle and upbraided Lewis for what had occurred. Lewis, by this time beside himself with rage, ordered Lucas to leave the premises, and threatened to set his dog upon him if he would not do so, or if he ever should return. Lucas muttered some threatening words, but prepared to leave, whereupon Alice Marvel pressed forward and said:

"'You are a coward to have insulted two gentlemen whilst they were your guests! I almost feel that I could kill you myself.'

"Alice is usually a quiet girl, but she is somewhat hysterical, and, as the two men were, the one her brother and the other her sweetheart, she was much overwrought. She and Lucas left simultaneously. Then Virgie, still maintaining her dignity, said:

"'Since my uncle has acted so churlishly to three of my guests, I advise the rest of my friends to retire, lest he should humiliate us further.'

"That she spoke of him as 'uncle' maddened Lewis, and he retorted angrily.

"'Go! All of you, but,' picking up Marvel's pistol, 'I call you all to witness that this is Walter Marvel's weapon, and that with it, he attempted to take my life!'"

The Squire paused a moment, and then resumed:

"I was an eye-witness of this scene, and I assure you that I have not exaggerated it in the least. On the following day Lewis applied to me to procure a warrant for him. As I was once a justice of the peace, he knew that I understand such matters. I tried to dissuade him from his purpose, but he was determined to have Marvel arrested for assault with intent to kill. He procured the warrant, but thus far Marvel has kept out of the way. After several more unsuccessful attempts to persuade Lewis to abandon his object, I was obliged to give up the task. Then the continued absence of young Marvel began to worry me, and I feared that he might return and kill Lewis. Therefore, I have decided that it will be best to find him before any such calamity can occur. This, as much for his sake as for the safety of Lewis. So I have sent for you, Mr. Barnes, taking a step of which Lewis is ignorant. And now, may I ask you what in your judgment will be the chance of apprehending Marvel?"

"Oh," said Mr. Barnes, "there will be no difficulty in finding him. I do not think he is hiding from the law. If at all, it is from the disgrace which he fancies that Mr. Lewis has cast upon him. But, if he really loves Miss Lewis, the thing is simple. We have but to watch her. He is sure to seek an interview, sooner or later."

"There," said the Squire, admiringly, "see how quickly you get at it. I should never have thought of such a mode of proceeding. You are right, too, as to your first conjecture. Marvel is high spirited, and I should not be surprised if he surrenders, as soon as he learns that he is wanted. That is why I have been worried by his disappearance. But here we are at the farm."

The house was an elegant frame building of the Queen Anne style of architecture. The grounds were on the south side of the road, so that the dwelling faced the north. It was recessed about fifty feet from a picket fence, and the party entered through a neat, painted gate, a brick-paved walk leading them up to the main door. This was standing invitingly open. Squire Olney seemed entirely at home, for he led the way straight in, without the formality of using the great brass lion's claw, which served as a knocker. This bold entry was not destined to go unresented however, for a huge mastiff appeared, coming from an inner room, and growled ominously. At a word from the Squire the dog assumed a less hostile demeanor, and prowled about the party, sniffing at their persons as though to make their acquaintance. When he reached Lewis, who was the last to enter, he raised himself up on his hind legs, and, planting his forepaws on his breast, tried to lick him on the face. Lewis resented the animal's familiarity, and seemed much annoyed as he brusquely pushed him down with an exclamation of impatience.

"Why, Mr. Lewis," said the Squire, "the dog acts as though he knows you. Can it be possible that he remembers you? I know that your father brought him here when he first came, but that is years ago, and he was a mere puppy then."

"I remember him well enough now, but I doubt if his recollection spans the interval between now and the time when I gave him bread and milk in his puppy days. I receive that kind of attention from nearly all dogs. Some of the fiercest have favored me at sight. Once, at a bench show in London, I bet that I could pat the head of any dog there. I won the wager, though the animal selected was a ferocious-looking bull-dog, over whose kennel was conspicuously displayed the warning placard: 'Dangerous, do not handle!' They say that a dog knows a friend instinctively, and I am certainly a friend of the canine species, ranking dogs next to human beings. But let us seek my father. I am anxious to meet him."

"Well, come in here," said the Squire, leading the way into a room on the left of the hall. "This is the parlor. Remain here while I hunt up Lewis."

The Squire had barely passed the doorway, when he uttered a cry of alarm, and hurried across the room. His companions hastened after him, and beheld the prostrate form of a man lying upon the rug, in front of the fireplace. The Squire leaned over the body for a moment, and then jumped up with horror depicted on every feature.

"There has been a terrible accident," said he. "My friend Lewis is here, dead!"

The others pressed forward. They saw the motionless body of a man. He lay on his side with his head near the fireplace, in which were the remains of a log fire. This fire must have been a hot one, as the face of the dead man, which had been covered in life with a heavy beard, was now scarcely more than a mass of charred flesh, and therefore entirely unrecognizable. In spots, there remained the burnt stubs of the hair on the face, and more on the head; but in many places it was burnt entirely away, exposing the flesh, a blackened human charcoal.

Lewis gazed in a dazed and semi-conscious way at the awful sight, and, in a low hoarse whisper asked:

"Is this my father?"

The Squire started at the question, and at once realized all the horror of the situation. He did not reply, but beckoned to the two detectives to follow him, and quietly left the room. Accompanied by them, he led the way across the hall into the library, and then repeated what he had exclaimed at first sight of the body, that it was that of John Lewis, in whose interest they had come to the house.

"But," continued he, "I cannot understand how it is that we find him dead, and in such a position. It looks at first sight like heart disease, or apoplexy. How terrible that he should have fallen into the fire, and have been so dreadfully disfigured."

"Did you ever fancy that your friend had any physical ailment of the kind?" asked Mr. Barnes.

"Why, no; I always considered him the stoutest, heartiest man of my acquaintance."

"Is it not singular, then, that he should be taken away so suddenly as this?"

"Now that you suggest the idea, it does seem so. The whole thing has been so startling, and so unexpected, that I have not collected my thoughts sufficiently to analyze the situation. I find my friend dead, on the floor of his own house, after having seen him alive and well only last evening, and I suppose I have adopted the first theory which presented itself."

"You say you saw your friend last evening?" asked Mr. Barnes, in a quiet voice, keeping his eyes steadily fixed on the Squire.

Something in his tone, or in his manner of asking the question, attracted the Squire, and he turned and faced his interrogator as he replied:

"Yes."

"Where?"

"There in the very room where we now find his corpse. I came to talk about this business once more, and to try to dissuade him from pursuing it further."

"Can you tell at what time you left him? Is there any circumstance by which you can fix the time accurately? Think well! It may be important!"

"Important?" echoed the Squire. "Why, man, what are you getting at? Surely you cannot think that—merciful heaven, do you suppose that my friend has been murdered?"

"Squire Olney, I cannot say that I have really formed such an opinion. But a man in my profession sees such things only too often, and, therefore, when he finds a dead body under anything like peculiar circumstances—such as these for example, his suspicions are aroused more quickly perhaps than might be the case with other men. But if you think our young friend, the son, may now have sufficiently recovered from his shock, we will go into the room again. An examination of the body may remove any doubts on this subject."

Mr. Barnes then started towards the next room, and the Squire followed, hardly daring to think of what they might be about to discover.

Appreciating the fact that the business before them was very serious, the three men entered the parlor quite gravely. As they did so, Lewis, who was bending over the body, rose and said, in a low voice:

"Gentlemen, my father has been murdered!" The Squire sank into the nearest chair. His last hope was gone. Lewis continued: "I repeat he has been murdered! There is a bullet hole in his left side, where it is almost impossible for him to have shot himself; therefore suicide is out of the question."

At the words "bullet hole," Mr. Barnes became all attention. Here was something tangible. Here was real evidence. The position of the wound, too, that was quite important, and Lewis's conclusion seemed logical enough. But he had used the correct words when he said "almost impossible." Mr. Barnes was a careful man in forming opinions, and experience had taught him that the seemingly impossible often occurs. Still, in the line of thought suggested by Lewis's words, he turned to Squire Olney:

"Can you tell us whether your friend was left-handed?"

"Yes; I am sure he was not."

"Then it is probable that he was shot by some other party than himself. Squire, the affair is now serious. It becomes our duty to try to find the guilty party."

At the word "duty," the Squire recovered himself instantly, and was all attention. Mr. Barnes continued:

"The coroner should be notified at once."

"I am the coroner of the county," replied the Squire. "In this town we have not needed such an officer within the memory of man. However, in this instance the duty devolves upon me. Therefore I am in charge of the case. Mr. Barnes, as you came down to serve me in a matter now at rest, I suppose you can place yourself at my disposal, and assist in finding the murderer?"

"Certainly," replied Mr. Barnes; "I will simply notify the chief of the facts, and he will grant me more time than I should have asked for before. Do you object to my having Mr. Burrows as my assistant?"

"Of course not. I want to see you commence your work at once. No time is to be lost. I may have been anxious to hush up the other matter, but I am alive to the seriousness of this. Whoever he may be, and at whatever cost, the murderer must be found and brought to justice."

"Very well, sir; from this moment we act under your orders. As you say, no time must be lost. The murderer has several hours start of us now, and we must catch up our end of the trail as quickly as possible. The first thing to be done is to examine the room and premises minutely for clues. I therefore suggest that you and Mr. Lewis leave us to work alone, while you summon men to form your jury."

"A very good suggestion. I will act on it at once. Come, Mr. Lewis; a walk in the open air will help you after the shock, which you have sustained." Taking Lewis by the arm, the two left the room.

CHAPTER II
SEEKING FOR CLUES

Left to themselves, the two detectives remained silent until they heard the front door shut by the Squire, as he and Lewis went out. Then Mr. Barnes said:

"Well, Tom, you are in luck. A mysterious murder, which will, in my judgment, require much skill to discover the truth. Come, now, tell me where you would begin?"

"I have found a clue already," quietly remarked Burrows.

"Good," said Mr. Barnes, well pleased at his pupil's shrewdness; "that is better than I expected. What is it?"

"I think that the murderer fired from the outside, through this window." Burrows indicated a window opening on the lawn to the east. "You see that there is a hole through the centre pane. That it is of recent origin is evidenced by the broken glass on the carpet, which also shows that the bullet came from without, since the pieces have fallen inward."

"Very well reasoned, Tom, as far as the time and origin of the shot goes, but you have jumped to one conclusion not as yet warranted." Mr. Barnes went to the window and examined it closely. "You started by saying just now that the 'murderer' fired from outside. That is where you have gone beyond your evidence. This pane of glass with that hole, and the fragments on the floor, probably attest the passage of a bullet, but there is nothing as yet to show that said bullet was fired by the 'murderer.'"

"Why, who else could have fired it?"

"I have heard that physicians make a diagnosis sometimes by exclusion, but it is a dangerous plan for a detective. Look again, and you will note that it is the lower sash which has the broken pane. Being raised as it is, the upper sash is between it and the point from which you argue that your pistol was fired. This proves conclusively—"

"That the lower sash has been raised since the shot was fired," interrupted Burrows. "You see I have thought of that. I argue this way. Mr. Lewis was standing in the room when he was struck by the ball; he turned and threw up the sash, endeavoring to discover the identity of his assailant.. Then he staggered from the window, and fell a few feet away; as we find him, with his head in the fireplace."

"It is of course possible. But, as he is in his night-dress, it is curious that he should have been in this room where an assassin, whose presence he did not suspect, could fire upon him. There is another chance, which is that someone has opened that window this morning. Now, looking out, what do we see?"

"A summer-house directly opposite," said Burrows. "A most convenient place for a man to hide in, and shoot his victim as he passed in front of a light in a room, at night."

"I see," said Mr. Barnes, "what we may be most grateful for, and that is fresh snow. We must extend our investigation presently, in the direction of the summer-house, and search for footprints."

He then turned towards the body. It was lying on the right side, thus plainly exposing a mass of blood which surrounded the wound. The burned condition of the head, owing to its proximity to the fire, has been mentioned. There was upon one finger a massive gold ring set with diamonds, which ring, Mr. Barnes thought, would necessarily be known to the dead man's family, and, besides, he found the name "John Lewis "embroidered upon the night-dress.

"Evidently not the work of a burglar," he remarked, pointing to the diamond ring.

"No," replied Burrows, "for here on the mantel is a handsome gold watch and chain."

"Notice, Tom, that he is in his night-dress. In connection with later discoveries that may prove a very significant fact. At present it puzzles me, for I cannot see why a man should be so dressed, in his parlor, and murdered without a sign of any struggle. The latter fact seems to strengthen your theory."

"There is a door," said Burrows, "let us see if it leads into his bedroom. In that event, he may have come here for any trivial purpose, and so have afforded the murderer the opportunity for which he was awaiting."

The younger man led the way, followed by Mr. Barnes. He opened the door and both entered, when they at once started back surprised. A young woman was sitting at a writing desk, a small upright cabinet, with one of the drawers open. This she hastily closed as the two men appeared. There was also a letter, sealed and addressed, lying on the desk, which she nervously concealed in the bosom of her dress, as she hurriedly rose and turned towards the intruders. This last motion caused a small object to drop from her lap, and roll half-way across the room, where it rested. The eyes of all three were attracted towards it. The woman moved forward to recover it, but Mr. Barnes, thinking it a thimble, with a quick "Allow me," stooped and picked it up. He was about to return it when, suddenly realizing what it was, he looked the woman straight in the eyes, still holding the object between his thumb and forefinger, and said:

"Madam, pardon me. You are, I presume, Miss Virginia Lewis?"

"That is my name. But who are you, and why do you enter my apartment, unannounced?"

"I assure you that when we entered, we had no thought of disturbing anyone, least of all a lady. We came to the house with Squire Olney, on business with your uncle. In the parlor we discovered—"

"My uncle's dead body!"

"Then you know "

"I found him, two hours ago, as you have seen him. I was naturally shocked and unnerved, and have been in here, ever since, trying to collect my thoughts."

"Miss Lewis, we are detectives," said Mr. Barnes, and making a brief pause, in order to watch the effect of his words, he noticed a slight tremor pass over her form; but it was barely perceptible, and he concluded that she was a woman of great self-control. Nevertheless, he detected an involuntary, instantaneous glance in the direction of the writing cabinet. Having gained this point, he continued:

"We came here with the Squire, at the request of your uncle, to discover if possible the whereabouts of his assailant, young Marvel." This time she showed no emotion. "As your uncle is dead, the Squire has asked us to investigate. It was whilst making an examination of the premises that we came in here, and I again ask your pardon for our intrusion."

Virginia bowed, and silently awaited his next words. Mr. Barnes felt that he must retire, but was determined to venture once more an attempt to learn something from her. He would have liked nothing better than to hold her in conversation, that he might study her manner as much as her words, but he saw clearly that he could not force her to talk long.

"Miss Lewis, I am aware that this interview must be painful to you, and, if you will allow me to ask one or two simple questions, we will withdraw." Receiving a sign that he might continue, he asked: "Can you tell me whether your uncle owned a weapon, or whether he had any cause to commit suicide? Some disease, for example, which he may have thought incurable?"

"My uncle did not own a weapon, to my knowledge, nor do I know of anything that would have induced him to take his own life."

"Did you hear a pistol-shot, during the night?"

"I did not."

Mr. Barnes left the room, followed by Burrows. Once more in the parlor, where lay the corpse, he said:

"Tom, did we discover anything in there?"

"Yes, I think so."

"Well, as you are the younger at this business, I am anxious to give you the chance to think for yourself. I suggest that you give me your views and deductions, from the different points that turn up, before you hear mine."

"Very well. Let me specify what I think we gained by going into the next room. We learned that we were not the first to find the body. Miss Lewis admits having been in this room. So she may have raised the window, which is especially probable since, as no other window is open, the room would have been full of the odor of the burned body when she entered."

Mr. Barnes nodded acquiescence.

"She hid a letter when we went in. I think she wishes the name of her correspondent kept secret. By the way, she must be a woman of singular temperament, to find the dead body of her uncle, and then go into the next room and write a letter."

"Exactly, and it may be of the utmost importance for us to learn the address of that letter and its contents, if possible. Anything more, Tom?"

"Yes, but first tell me what it was that you picked up from the floor. She dropped it from her lap as she stood up. Why did you keep it?"

"I thought it was a thimble, till I held it in my hand, and then I found it to be—the empty shell of a cartridge!"

"No wonder that you kept it. Now see this." He handed Mr. Barnes a small round brush, attached to a twisted wire handle. "I took it from the washstand."

"This fits my theory, exactly," said Mr. Barnes. "This brush is still damp, and slightly blackened. It has recently been used to clean the pistol from which this empty shell was taken. That pistol is in her cabinet. I am satisfied of that, by her glancing in that direction when she heard me declare that we are detectives. Follow out the train of action, and you will see why, with all her self-possession— and she has so much that I fear we shall not again surprise her into betraying herself—she could not resist a hasty glance at the drawer which she had just quickly closed, on seeing us. By her own admission she knew of this murder before anyone—as far as we now know—except the murderer. She retires to her own room, and at once proceeds to destroy an important clue—a recently discharged weapon. Remember that this man was more than her uncle, in the ordinary sense of that relationship — she was his adopted child. She must have had a powerful motive for carrying out such an act. What wonder then, when she has just effected her purpose that, being suddenly confronted by the announcement that detectives are already on the scent—what wonder, I say, that her eye should instinctively seek the place where she had hidden the pistol? Especially when she knew that I had the empty shell between my fingers? But, as I said before, she is on her guard now, and whatever she wishes to conceal from us, we shall need all our skill to discover. She will determine on a plan of action and adhere to it."

"Would we not have the key to the mystery, if we could learn her reasons for acting as she has?"

"Not necessarily, though of course it might be so. For example, suppose she has committed the crime herself?"

"Why, do you suspect her already?"

"No; I should not make so serious a charge against a woman, even to myself, on so little evidence. Nevertheless, in a case like this, we must consider all things as possible. By her anxiety to destroy a clue, she proves that she does not wish the murderer to be known. This may be accounted for in two ways. First, that she would hide her own guilt; and second, that she might be shielding someone else."

"That someone else must be one in whom she is deeply interested," said Burrows, thinking over Mr. Barnes's proposition. Then suddenly, as the idea came to him, "What if it be her lover— young Marvel? He would have a motive for killing Lewis."

Mr. Barnes smiled approvingly at his companion's quick perception of what he himself was thinking; but he replied:

"Not so fast! We have nothing against him yet, except the 'motive.' Many a man may have good and strong reasons for wishing another dead, and yet not stain his hands with blood. Besides, remember that the same motives which you attribute to Marvel, might equally well actuate the woman who loves him. However, at present, I do not think that Miss Lewis committed the crime."

"If not she and not Marvel, whom then do you suspect?"

"I must have more evidence before I suspect anyone. It is a different thing, however, to think one 'not guilty,' and, at present, I believe Miss Lewis is innocent. Later I may find in her the criminal. But I cannot think so yet."

"Surely, you are not influenced by her sex—you are not going to be sentimental—you, a detective?"

Mr. Barnes smiled faintly. He was amused and yet a little troubled, at his companion's ardor. Why should not a detective have sentiment? Because it is his business to seek out and punish the criminal, must he necessarily be without a heart? He could not accept such a theory, although he knew it to be one esteemed by the members of his craft. The majority of these men hunt down a criminal as a matter of business. A crime committed gives them work to do; a man found to fit the circumstances of that crime, and the detectives' work is completed.

It was not so with Mr. Barnes. He had a heart, and this very fact, though unrecognized by his superiors, made him the keenest man in the employ of the Pilkingtons. He did not work simply to fit a crime on someone 's, anyone's, shoulders; but rather that it should not be fitted to an innocent man. He sought diligently for the right man, that the wrong man might not be made to suffer, through the accident of implicating circumstances.

Replying to Burrows, he said:

"No, I would not think of her sex. A true detective should consider the evidence only. There is always danger, however, of our mistaking it, or rather to what it points. The evidence itself is always dumb witness of the truth. Unfortunately, our ability or skill too often fails to connect it. Now I will tell you why I think Miss Lewis innocent.

"It is plain, from the charred condition of the body, coupled with the fact that the fire has entirely burned out, that the man has been dead some hours. If Miss Lewis had done the shooting, herself, the probability is that she would have cleaned her pistol earlier. Still, she might have been disturbed, and, dropping her weapon in a hurried flight from the scene of the crime, she might have returned, later, to recover it. But, whilst I consider her a person of great will-power—from a physical standpoint quite capable of conceiving and executing a murder—yet, having done the deed, and accidently having left her weapon, I doubt her having the nerve power to return for it after several hours had passed. She might, within a short period of time, but in that case, the cleaning would have occurred then, and not have been left for the morning; for, had she premeditated the killing, she would also have premeditated removing this evidence. But remember, this is reasoning, not proof. The most specious reasoning may be, nay, often is, disproved by the facts."

"But you must think she has some knowledge of the crime?" said Burrows.

"My theory is this," replied Mr. Barnes. "Miss Lewis entered this room this morning, perhaps opened the window, and then discovered the dead body—the weapon—and perchance more; at any rate enough to make her suspect young Marvel. Here let me point out that the fact that she does so, is not sufficient reason for our suspecting him. It was not necessary for her to know him guilty for her to attempt to shield him. It was enough for her to entertain suspicion. Convinced of even the possibility of his guilt, she might try to save him from the consequences of the act."

Burrows had listened quite attentively to all this, and was much impressed by the reasoning. After thinking a few moments in silence, he asked:

"Do you think that the letter which she wrote is to her lover?"

Again Mr. Barnes was pleased to note that Burrows followed his line of argument. He replied:

"Yes, I think the letter is to Marvel; but her writing to him might be a sequence in either case. Whether she committed the deed herself, or thinks him guilty, she would probably write to him."

"It would be well then for us to get that letter?"

"Well, indeed! It would at least show us his whereabouts. But how to become possessed of it? That is the question. We need not expect to obtain it till it has left her custody, and be sure she will be very careful how she forwards it."

"If we could get the pistol, might we not be able to find out who is the owner of it? That would be something, perhaps."

"Assuredly! Besides, it is probable that though cleaned, one chamber may still be empty. We have the shell, and evidence of the recent cleaning. As soon as Miss Lewis leaves the house, as she will do to start her letter on its way, I will get the pistol from her cabinet."

"Is there anything more that we can discover in this room?"

"Let us look."

To approach the body they walked around a small table, which stood in front of the fireplace. On this was scattered loosely some papers. A drawer stood partly open, and a large cut-glass ink-well uncovered. Mr. Barnes glanced at these things as he passed, and his eye was attracted by a half sheet of paper, with a bit of writing, which protruded from under the other clean sheets. He picked it up, more from curiosity than interest, but after he had read it his manner showed at once that he thought it important. Burrows looked at him inquiringly, but for a moment Mr. Barnes did not heed him. He was looking at the table before him, and seemed studying the situation. At length he spoke:

"Miss Lewis has destroyed, or removed, another clue! See this!" He handed the piece of paper to Burrows, who took it and read as follows:

If I am dead in the morning my murderer is

The word "*is*" was followed by a huge blot, as though the pen had spluttered at that point. Burrows looked at Mr. Barnes in silence, and the latter continued:

"Mr. Lewis was not killed outright. He even saw and recognized his murderer. He attempted to warn his friends and insure justice. Fearing death before aid would reach him, he wrote that. Evidently excited, perhaps already growing weak, as he reached the name of his assailant his hand trembled, his pen spluttered and he threw it from him. Here it is, lying on a piece of paper, which it has blotted where it fell. However, he essayed again, and this time he succeeded, for see, he has placed the second pen carefully, the point on the edge of the ink-well, proving that he finished his note of warning. Miss Lewis undoubtedly found it. She read the name.

Whose was it? Her own?—or Marvel's? If any other, why should she remove it?"

"What would Miss Lewis do if you showed her this paper, and demanded the other?"

"I cannot tell. She might deny having it. She might admit taking it and refuse to yield possession of it. She might treat me with scorn and deny my right to question her on the subject at all. However, I may conclude to test her. I may ask her the question."

Burrows stood thinking and looking down, when suddenly he noticed something on the floor which attracted his attention. He stopped to examine it, and then called Mr. Barnes, who was still absorbed in the table and its contents. Mr. Barnes joined him, and looked at what Burrows picked up—some bits of plastering. Both simultaneously looked upwards, and saw just over their heads, a small hole in the ceiling.

"The mark of a bullet," said Mr. Barnes. He walked over to the window where he stood for a minute, alternately looking out, and at the bullet hole in the plastering. "That shot came from without, passed through this window, and struck as we see overhead. The summer-house there is just in the line. Evidently there was more than one shot fired, for that ball could not have passed entirely through the body and then have continued upward."

"Shall we examine the grounds now?" said Burrows.

"Yes; I think we have learned all we can, at present, in here."

Followed by his companion, Mr. Barnes then led the way out of the house.

CHAPTER III
FOOTPRINTS IN THE SNOW

The town of Lee, New Hampshire, though covering a large territory, is so sparsely settled that one might almost ride through it without meeting a half dozen persons. Indeed, it covers so much ground, that the various sections where there are clustered together any considerable number of houses all bear different names; as "Lee Hill"—"Lee Hook"— "Lee," or "Lee Depot "as it is more commonly known, because of the railroad station—and lastly "Wadley's Falls."

Wadley's Falls is the southernmost and most populous section of the town. It is in the immediate vicinity of the low falls in the Lamprey River, which runs through the place. This river, though at times so shallow that one might wade across in many places, yet turns numerous mills in its course. Both river and falls play an important part in this history.

A good road leads from the depot at Lee, and with a few easy turns winds its way up hill, passing the farm and homestead of the Lewises, and on a mile further, where the river is crossed by a bridge. Beyond one finds the Wadley's Falls post-office and the saloon. The bridge being of some interest to us, must receive a moment's description. To-day there is a neat iron structure at this point, but, at the time of which I write, a wooden ramshackle affair did duty for man and horse. It was situated about fifty feet to the south of the falls, and where the river winds under it, many a huge boulder projects, making the rushing stream the more noisy. Here, also, to the north, is a dam, and over on the east bank stands an old ruin which is still in use as a saw-mill.

The Lewis farm is bounded on the east by the Lamprey, and on the north by the road, which at this point runs eastward. After crossing the bridge it turns to the south, following a somewhat parallel course with the river, so that did one choose, he could leave the road on the south side of the bridge, and by crossing a narrow strip of land and the river, be upon the Lewis farm, which covers over two hundred acres.

That you may well understand the deductions which the detectives reached, from the study of the grounds, it will be best for you to follow closely a description of the place with the assistance of the accompanying map.

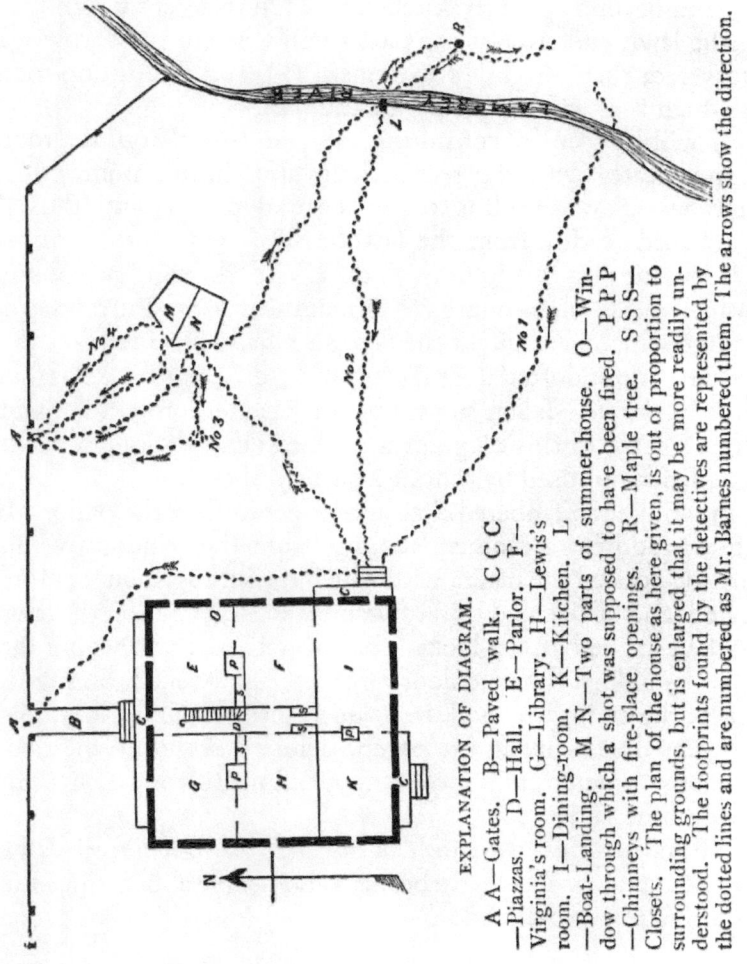

EXPLANATION OF DIAGRAM.

A A—Gates. B—Paved walk. C C C—Piazzas. D—Hall. E—Parlor. F—Virginia's room. G—Library. H—Lewis's room. I—Dining-room. K—Kitchen. L—Boat-Landing. M N—Two parts of summer-house. O—Window through which a shot was supposed to have been fired. P P P—Chimneys with fire-place openings. R—Maple tree. S S S—Closets. The plan of the house as here given, is out of proportion to surrounding grounds, but is enlarged that it may be more readily understood. The footprints found by the detectives are represented by the dotted lines and are numbered as Mr. Barnes numbered them. The arrows show the direction.

A beautiful grassy lawn is separated from the road by a neat paling fence, in which there are two gates, one opposite the main entrance to the dwelling, and the other opening into the grounds, about a couple of rods to the east (A A). Passing through the first of these a brick path (B) leads the visitor to a piazza (C) three steps above the ground, and extending the full width of the building. Entering, one finds himself in a spacious hall (D), which on the first floor divides the house in the centre, doors leading into the rooms on either side, and into one at the further end.

To the west is the library (G); back of that Lewis's bedroom (H), and beyond again the kitchen (K). On the east side, and facing the lawn and river, is the parlor (E), wherein the corpse was discovered; then Virginia's apartment (F), and the dining-room (I), which is as wide as the parlor and hall.

It will be seen by consulting the plan, that Virginia's room communicates with the parlor, hall, and dining-room, which latter has a door leading on to a small piazza, and thus, is approached readily from the lawn. "PPP" represent chimneys, each serving for two rooms, and "O" is the window looking towards the summer-house (M N), alluded to by Burrows, and through which he thought the fatal shot had been fired.

The various dotted lines represent the different tracks or footprints in the new-fallen snow, but further allusion will be made to these, later, as this diagram is a facsimile of the one made by Mr. Barnes and used by him in his study of the case.

It will be remembered that just before leaving the parlor Mr. Barnes stood for a moment looking from the window. Whilst there, he noticed the piazza with which the dining-room communicated, and he deemed this a suitable way to get out on the lawn. So when in the hall, he looked for a way to reach the room into which he judged that the door on the piazza opened. Seeing the door at the end of the hall, he at once entered the dining-room, and went thence out to the porch. Before descending the steps, he stood a moment and looked about him, Burrows at his side. At length he said:

"Tom, I think we are in luck, for here we have a fresh fall of snow, and plainly there have been several people about, since I see footprints in every direction."

"How can they help us? They may have been made by the servants, or—"

"Exactly! They may have been, but were they? That is the question, the solving of which may throw considerable light on this mysterious affair. I intend to follow, as far as I can, the different tracks before us, from the beginning to end. That will at least show me the ground travelled over by those who have been here, even though it tell but little of the object or personalities of the visitors."

"Well, since you say you will trace these footprints from beginning to end, we can commence here, for this seems to have been the point of departure for two people. See!" Burrows pointed to the ground before them. Mr. Barnes stepped down from the piazza, being careful not to destroy any of the impressions already in the snow. He examined the footprints closely a minute and then said: "As you say, here are two tracks. Which would you trace first?"

"The smaller," answered Burrows, after a little consideration.

"Why?"

"Mainly because it leads to the summer-house, which is what we intended to examine when we started out. Then, again, I notice that these two sets of foot-marks are very different. One is so large it must be that of a man, and equally, the other is so tiny, none but a woman's foot could have made it."

"And you would follow the woman's footsteps first, eh? What did you say awhile ago about not considering sex? But shall I tell you what you are thinking?"

Burrows looked up inquiringly, and Mr. Barnes proceeded impressively:

"Tom, you are making a great mistake; one which I cannot too much warn you to avoid, now and all through life. You have already formed your opinion of this case, and, unconsciously, perhaps, you are ready to fit to your theory any evidence that turns up." Burrows attempted to disclaim any such intention. But Mr. Barnes continued:

"I don't blame you exactly. You have youth and ambition as your excuse, and I am sorry to say I have known older and more experienced men drop into the same error. They are so anxious to discover a criminal—*a* criminal—mark the words!"

"But, really, you are mistaken—you misjudge me—I—"

"I am afraid not. I don't wish to stay your zeal either, but in cases like this it is wisest to make haste slowly, as the proverb has it. Now let me show you what you have done in your own mind. First, you find a hole in a pane of glass, and because you can weave enough evidence to show that it is of recent origin, you conclude that the fatal shot passed in that way. The fact is, all that evidence proves, is that a bullet passed through the glass, last night. Anything further is merely a matter of circumstantial possibility, or perhaps, in this case, I might go so far as to say probability. Second, you find a woman who is certainly acting suspiciously. I don't say you actually accuse her, but you incline to such a judgment. Thirdly, these footprints. Having in your theory settled that the shot came from without, and deeming it possible that a certain woman committed the crime, you would examine the woman's footsteps first, and if possible prove thereby, that the woman whom you would implicate was in the position to fire through the window. Thus you would strengthen your theory."

Burrows seemed confused, as though detected in a mean act. In truth he was to himself considering the chance of discovering the murderer by his own individual efforts, thus, if possible, forestalling the man with whom he was working. He was therefore not a little astonished at the accuracy with which his companion had read his thoughts.

"I am afraid you hit the nail on the head," said he, "and I am ashamed to be forced to confess it. But tell me, which of these trails do you decide on tracing first?"

"The same as you selected, but for this reason. Notice that here the direction is towards the summer-house, as you just now said; whilst on this side, the point of the toe shows that the owner of the foot returned to her starting-point. Unless we find another trail, leading from the house, we have here proof conclusive that this party has remained within doors."

"How so? I don't see that."

"Yet it is simple. Notice that the steps away from the house are very indistinct, whilst those coming towards us are, on the contrary, clear, and sharply defined. The woman left this spot whilst it was yet snowing; so the snow filled up the tracks somewhat. Wherever she went, and that we shall find out perhaps by following the trail, she did not start for home, or to be accurate, she did not reach here, till the snow had ceased falling, as the clear marks testify."

"Mr. Barnes, you are a genius. Why, all we have to do is to find out when the snow ceased, to have the time of this young woman's promenade."

"Why do you say young woman? You are smarter than I, if you can tell her age by these," pointing at the ground.

Burrows seemed a little abashed as he replied:

"Surely, since you proved that the woman is still within the house, who else can it be but Miss Lewis?"

"Her maid, perhaps," said Mr. Barnes, with some curtness. Of all things, he abjured conclusions which were too hastily, and therefore illogically drawn.

"Come," he continued, "we will follow this trail as far as the summer-house."

He started, his head bent and his eyes fixed scrutinizingly on the snow. Burrows followed in silence, feeling rebuked, and just a little resentful. The tracks led in almost a direct line to the summerhouse, which they discovered to be divided into two parts. It seemed that the unknown person, whose movements they were tracing, had entered the southern half.

"This was a place of meeting," said Mr. Barnes, "for notice that still another set of steps lead here, evidently a man's, judging from their size."

"Then you think the woman came here to meet some man?"

"Yes, and furthermore, the man arrived first, for his footprints, or at least those leading in, are more obliterated by the falling snow than are hers; similarly, arguing from the impressions which they have left for our examination, it is evident that they separated here, for the woman plainly walked off toward the river, whereas the man returned, as he had entered, through the little gate yonder."

"Mr. Barnes, as there seem to be so many sets of impressions, would it not be well to make a drawing of the grounds and the general direction of the tracks, for convenience, as well as reference?"

"A good suggestion. We will act upon it at once. But wait here a moment. There is a man going along the road. I will question him about last night's snow." Mr. Barnes hurried over to the fence, where he found the man awaiting him, having been attracted by a call from Burrows.

"Good morning, friend; do you live about here?"

"Yes, jest over the bridge."

"Then, perhaps you can tell me about what hour it stopped snowing last evening. It may seem a trifle to stop you about, but I have a good reason for inquiring, and hope you won't mind my troubling you?"

"No trouble 't all. Not the least in the world. Le' me see, I don't know as I kin tell you for sartin, 'cause I went ter bed 'airly last night. But stop a minute, come ter think I kin find out purty nigh, an' kin give you some notion myself."

"I shall be much indebted, and hope you can fix the time as near as possible."

"Well, as I said before, I went ter bed 'airly, seven o'clock in fact; 't was snowin' hard then, an' I 'lowed 't would keep up all night; I slept purty sound but was waked up by the noise my girls made comin' in from a visit ter a neighbor's. You know how 't is when a man's woke up? He's kinder crusty, an' more 'an all, can't tell whether he's slept ten hours or ten minutes. So as the girls went by my door, I growled out: 'An't you purty late gittin' home?' 'No, Pop, it's just nine o'clock,' come the answer. Seein' as how I had a good night's rest before me, I felt a leettle mite pleasanter an' in a' easier tone I said: 'I s'pose the snow's purty deep, an't it?' 'Not very,' says one on 'em, 'it stopped awhile ago, an' the moon's out now!' That's all was said. But you see that shows it didn't snow after nine, tho' ef you want it nearer, mebbe I kin find out from the girls."

"I should thank you to ask them. Will you please give me your name?"

"Jef Harrison's my name, an' anyone'll show you my house, ef you care ter come up an' speak to the girls yourself?"

"I am much obliged, Mr. Harrison, and perhaps I'll accept your invitation to call."

"I'll be glad ter see you. But, say, ther' an't nothin' wrong, is ther'? Nothin' speshul, hay?"

"No!" replied Mr. Barnes, not deeming it wise to tell of the death of Mr. Lewis, lest he be kept from his investigation by further talk.

"You an't got track of young Marvel yet, is ye?"

"Not yet."

"Well, good day ter you. Hope ter see you up ter the house by an' by."

Jef Harrison walked off slowly, evidently reluctant to leave. As he passed on he muttered to himself, "Guess he's the detective they told about down to Lee Depot. Guess he's a cute one. An't much of a hand at answerin' questions. A dog-goned sight better at askin' 'em. Wonder why he wants ter know when the snow stopped! Them fellers kin make a mighty sight out of durned little, that's what I think," and so he trudged on, still wondering at the presence of the detectives and what it all portended.

Mr. Barnes rejoined Burrows, and they followed each set of footprints thoroughly, the elder choosing his, and assigning the others to his companion. Then the two men returned to the parlor, where Mr. Barnes tore off half a sheet of paper from some which lay on the centre table, and upon it made a careful drawing, of which that upon page 297 is a facsimile. This completed, they discussed the situation.

"Well," began Burrows, "now that you have finished your map of the movements of the several parties who were about these premises last night, what do you learn from it?"

"We found four sets of tracks," said Mr. Barnes, "besides the dog's, which latter may prove of value. Two of these we think were made by women, and two by men. For convenience, I have numbered them 1, 2, 3, and 4. I will consider number 4, first."

"Why not take them in the regular order?"

"That is what I mean to do. But whereas I have numbered them in rotation as I discovered them, I will trace them in the order in which they were made."

"You don't pretend that you can do that?" said Burrows, incredulously.

"I think so, and commence with number 4. This was made by a woman. Unfortunately I can find no distinct continuation of any of the tracks outside the gates, for passing teams have obliterated them. We find the first of number 4, at the little gate. The woman went directly to the summer-house, and into the northern side (M). That she was the earliest on the scene is evident, because the tracks which she made going in are almost entirely destroyed by the snow which fell since. I even go so far as to venture the opinion that this woman suspected a meeting and came to this spot as an eavesdropper."

"Now you are going rather fast, are you not?" asked Burrows, sarcastically.

"I will give you reasons for all my deductions. The summer-house faces the west, and the northwest wind last night drifted considerable snow in through the doors; enough, at any rate, to show me that this woman sat quite still in a corner all the time while she was inside, for the mark of her foot shows it. Had she moved about more, the snow would have been more trampled. I even think she sat on one foot, as many women do, for there is but one imprint near the bench where she must have sat, and that is exaggerated out of all shape, as though in her impatience at the slow flight of time, she had nervously kicked this one foot about, and into the drifted snow."

"How much you make out of little things," said Burrows, admiringly.

"She came probably to hear what passed between the man and woman in the next compartment. Certainly she sat as close to the partition as possible. She stayed until after they had left. This she would naturally have done, to avoid detection, but I have stronger proof, in the fact that near the gate, I find an imprint from the foot of the man, and across it, is one of the woman. The latter is plainer than the first and was consequently made last. By plainer, I mean that the outline of the sole is easily traced across the larger footprint, which it obliterates where the two cross. There is another thing worth noting. Observe that this woman went almost in a straight line from the gate into the summer-house. In departing she came out in a straight line towards the house, and then turned and went to the gate. Just where this turn occurred she stopped for a moment."

"Why, you seem to discern a great deal. How do you deduce that?"

"Very easily, and almost certainly. If one walks, or runs, the footprints must be single, and about equi-distant. At the point where I say that she stopped, I find two imprints nearly side by side. So she stopped; but why?"

"Can you also tell that?"

"I think that I could make a very shrewd guess. But we will leave her, for the present, and take up the next set, number 3, a man's. He evidently had an appointment, for he too entered by the small gate and went directly to the summer-house. He returned as he came, which strengthens the theory that his sole object in coming was to meet someone at this place. That it was not to meet the woman whose movements I have followed, is shown by the fact that his steps pass the compartment, M, and go to the other, N. There is another point of great interest. He was attacked by a dog!"

"What? You don't mean to say that the footprints tell you that?"

"As clearly as though they spoke. I cannot trace the dog's movements, for his marks are all over the lawn, but at one point on my diagram you will observe that number 3's feet show a great many imprints in one place. Here he was stopped by the dog whose footmarks are numerous at the point indicated. Their exaggerated shape, too, shows clearly that the dog jumped upon the man, and that in falling back upon his haunches, the mark of his whole leg was made. Again from this point towards the gate, I note that the stride of the man increased. This means that he ran away. You followed the other two. What did you discover?"

"I gave you my drawings, and you have them shown quite accurately. Number 2, made by a woman, commences as you know, at the steps of the dining-room piazza and leads to the summer-house. From there I traced it over to the river, where I found a boat-landing. Thence, she returned to the steps again. Number 1, a man's, commences at the river bank about two hundred feet south of the landing, and leads directly to the steps. Thence it follows around the house and out through the main gate. Outside, unfortunately, our party this morning made so many footprints that I could not follow number 1."

"Did you cross the river, Tom?"

"No, but there is a boat there, and I meant to suggest that we go over together. I think we will find evidence on the other side that my lady crossed last night. Why else should she have gone to the boat?"

"Certainly, we will go at once; but first I have something more to communicate. Your theory was that the shot was fired from without, and by a woman, and you inclined to the belief that you knew the identity of that woman. What then do you think of this?" He handed Burrows a beautiful silver-mounted revolver, in the chambers of which were four loaded and one empty cartridge. The weapon had apparently been recently fired. Burrows looked at it a moment in amazement, and then asked:

"Where did you find this?"

"Outside of the summer-house, lying in the snow, just where I claim that the woman stopped. Now you see what I meant when I said I could guess why she did so. But you have not seen all yet, there is a name on it—read."

Burrows examined the butt more attentively, and there saw a piece of plate let into the stock, and neatly engraved thereon the name:

"*Alice Marvel.*"

"Mr. Barnes, what do you make of that?"

"I think that someone had that pistol last night and fired it. From other evidence that I have, I should say it is a circumstantial probability that Miss Marvel herself was here last night and fired her pistol."

"This is the second time you have used that phrase, 'circumstantial probability,'—won't you explain it?"

"Certainly. We are considering a case purely on circumstantial evidence. I have all my life made a specialty of such, and I divide it into three grades, according to the logical deduction which it indicates. The first of these I call a 'circumstantial possibility.' For example, had the wound in this case been differently located, it might have been a 'circumstantial possibility' that it was a suicide. Second, we have a 'circumstantial probability,' such as I have here, and will explain. Third, the 'circumstantial proof,' where the attendant facts leave absolutely no room for doubt; in my experience a rare thing."

"I understand. Now will you tell me why you think it a circumstantial probability that Miss Marvel was here and fired the pistol?"

"From the facts which I have already given you, I should say it was a question whether she was here, or whether someone else had her pistol. But I found another pistol."

"The deuce you did!"

"And this one," producing a duplicate of the one already shown, "also has a name—Harry Lucas. Now follow my argument. Squire Olney told us that these two young people are sweethearts. The tracks indicate that a woman played the spy on a man who came to meet another woman. The weapons bear the names of a man and his sweetheart. Is it not plain? Miss Marvel came to hear what the other girl had to say to her lover, and he to her?"

"You are right," said Burrows, excitedly; "and is it not equally evident that the second woman is Miss Lewis? Remember, the meeting was in her own grounds."

"I am more inclined to think so, than at first, though I do not commit myself, yet. But there is another matter worth considering. I found Lucas's weapon in the snow at the point where I claim he was attacked by the dog. There is also a little blood-stain—"

"Ah! I see, you argue that he drew his pistol and fired at the dog, and so account for the empty shell there?"

"Yes. But the blood-stain is important. I think that came from a wound made by the dog's teeth. As the discoloration is visible, although somewhat covered, I believe the snow stopped shortly after. Thus I reckon that he left about nine o'clock. The woman left after the snow had ceased."

"You think Lucas shot at the dog and dropped his pistol in the scrimmage. Do you think Miss Marvel shot at the dog also?"

"That we must find out. I have shown you the probability of the case, ending with the idea that both of these pistols were fired at the dog. But there is another aspect which you must not neglect, and that is the 'circumstantial possibility!' Remember that both Lucas and this girl, according to the Squire's story, had threatened the dead man. They both came here armed, an unusual thing for a woman at all events. Suppose that Lucas saw Lewis through the window, and shot at him. The noise may have attracted the dog, and thus that contest may have occurred after the discharge of the weapon, instead of before. Further, suppose that, seeing that her lover had left, the girl had also taken aim at the same target. One shot may have made the hole in the ceiling, and the other may have reached the mark."

"Why this becomes more complicated every minute—what about the pistol in Miss Lewis's room?"

"Ah! That is the problem—but come, we will go across the river."

Thereupon they proceeded to the boat-landing, marked "L "in the diagram, and crossed in a light row-boat, which they found fastened at that place. On the other bank they found a continuation of the footprints marked number 2. These led to the base of a gigantic maple around which a seat of boards had been arranged. Mr. Barnes examined the spot critically, and finally said:

"I guess it was Miss Lewis after all. See, this tree is covered with carved monograms of her initials and Marvel's. Evidently this has been a trysting place for that pair of lovers. Here is another evidence that the snow stopped shortly after the meeting at the summer-house, for whereas she came here directly, her footprints on this side of the river are quite distinct, showing that the snow ceased during her trip over to this place."

"She met a man here too; see his footprints! Could it have been the lover this time! I mean Marvel?"

"Possibly. But let us see if we can trace him to where he crossed the river, if, indeed, it was he who did."

They followed the tracks, but they entered the woods just back of the maple, and were lost. However, a diligent search along the river-bank discovered a track which emerged from the wood and approached the river. They got into the boat, rowed across to a point opposite, and found there the beginning of the track on that side, marked in the diagram, number 1.

"The directness of this trail from this point to the house," said Mr. Barnes, "is circumstantial proof that the man crossed the river with the intention of visiting that place. For what? Whether he was, or was not Lucas, he had already had an interview with Miss Lewis, and therefore his visit was scarcely to her."

"How could it be Lucas?"

"Supposing he intended to kill Lewis, after being interrupted by the dog, could he not have gone around by these woods, and returned later to complete his work? It is barely possible that the whole thing was planned; that the interview at the summer-house was a preliminary, and that Miss Lewis went to the maple where she was later joined by Lucas, who told her the result of his first attempt and arranged the second."

"How could he know that he had failed in his first shot?"

"I don't like to follow this line of thought much, as it is all guess-work; still it is one of the possibilities, and in case it turns out wrong, will teach you how easy it is to misconstrue circumstantial evidence. To continue it, suppose that at the meeting over the river Miss Lewis and Lucas determined to finish what they had begun. The object would be that by killing old Lewis the prosecution of Marvel would cease, the complainant being dead. Miss Lewis undertakes to furnish a weapon, because he had lost his. She owns one as the Squire has explained. Therefore Lucas enters the house through the side door, and from the dining-room has access to the girl's bedroom, where she gives him a pistol; thence he easily enters the parlor. Such an arrangement of events would readily account for her destroying the evidence that her weapon had been used. But don't lay too much stress on all this, for as I said, it is purely guess-work. There is a flaw in it too. Why did Miss Lewis leave her coadjutor on the wrong side of the river when they separated, and thus force him to wade a stream of water on a cold night?"

"That may be discovered later. But look—there she is leaving the house!"

"Now, Tom, I will give you a chance to do some work alone. That girl has gone to mail her letter. The nearest post-office is in the vicinity of the bridge, and in a private house. See, she is going in that direction. By the road it is more than a mile. By the river you can readily reach there first, as it is shorter. Row as hard as you can, and hide near the post-office. If she enters, wait till she comes out and then go in and learn the address on the letter. You will find it in a cupboard in the hall, where the mail is kept. That is the main thing which we want. I will wait for you at the house, unless something should turn up to make me change my plans."

Burrows was already in the boat, and started as soon as these last words were uttered. Mr. Barnes waited till the girl was out of sight, and then returned quickly to the house. He went straight to Virginia's room and over to the writing cabinet in which she had placed the pistol. To obtain this, he meant to break the lock if necessary. Greatly to his surprise he found the key in the lock. He opened the drawer, but did not find therein the object of his search. Looking around the room he was startled to find the pistol lying on the bed. He picked it up and noted that it was of the same pattern as the other two which he already had, and like them, bore a plate with its owner's name, in this instance, "Virginia Lewis."

"Is my last guess correct?" thought Mr. Barnes, "and did that young girl instigate and assist at a murder?—Why, what is this? This weapon has an empty cartridge in it." He examined it closely, and gently raised the hammer. "By heaven, she has replaced a shell for the one which she removed. I see it all. She wishes to get the best of me in some way. She knows that I picked up the shell which she had drawn, and there would no longer be anything gained by reloading the pistol. Why, she has even taken the precaution to so place the cartridge that the hammer rests in the little indentation made in the rim when fired. And there on the desk is a little box of empty shells. Evidently if I showed the one which I have, she would laugh and show a box full. However, I still have the brush with which she cleaned the barrel. But I am wasting time. This girl will outwit Burrows. I must go after her myself."

When passing through the dining-room he had noticed behind the door several hooks on which hung some clothing. Hastening there he found these to consist of two suits of overalls, such as farm hands use when at work, and evidently left there when the owners had last taken them off at meal-time. In New England the farmers and their help often eat together. Mr. Barnes quickly donned one suit of these, and taking some whiskers from his pocket, was soon sufficiently disguised. Having finished these arrangements, he left the house and hurried towards the Wadley's Falls post-office.

CHAPTER IV
THE LETTER

When Mr. Barnes reached the road, he started on a run, for he was anxious to overtake Virginia Lewis before she should discover that she was watched by Burrows. After what he had just learned, he very much doubted whether his young assistant would be able to circumvent this shrewd girl. It is not as easy to shadow a person along a lonely country road, as it might be in a city, where the crowded streets offer ready opportunities for hiding.

As Virginia had only a few minutes start of the detective, and walked at a moderate gait, Mr. Barnes caught sight of her just as she began to cross the bridge. As she passed over it, he noted that she was attracted by something, for she stopped, looked over the rail, and then around her in every direction. Mr. Barnes was glad that he had found a chance to assume some sort of disguise, as there was no way of avoiding her gaze. In a moment she went on, and when he reached the bridge he saw at once what had aroused her caution. It was the sight of her own boat, which Burrows had used to reach the place. As she knew that she had left it up the stream the night before, its presence at this landing must have been sufficient to indicate to her that she was being followed, for she had evidently chosen the time for her errand when she knew the detectives had gone off exploring near the river-bank. It was easy for her to guess that her departure from the farm had been observed, and that her own boat had brought a spy after her.

Mr. Barnes was disappointed that she should have thus been placed upon her guard. She would now almost certainly not post her letter at the office. She walked on about a hundred yards beyond the bridge, and, from the alert glances which she cast about her, it was plain that she was looking for the detective, of whose presence she felt assured. She passed the post office and going a little farther entered a house on the opposite side of the road. Mr. Barnes did not follow, because there was nothing to be gained. She was beyond his reach for the present, and having seen him behind her, may have entered a friend's house merely to observe him as he went by, being suspicious of strangers. He therefore went into the saloon where he had met the Squire that same morning. If Virginia was watching him it would perhaps disarm her suspicion of him, since it was a natural place whereat one dressed as he was, might stop. Furthermore, being near the post-office, he could watch that place and see if she mailed her letter herself, or by proxy, sending someone from where she was. He was scarcely within the doorway, before he became aware of the presence of Tom Burrows, who was seated near the window and evidently watching the post-office. Satisfied, therefore, that there was no immediate need for him to do so also, and noticing that the place was more than ordinarily crowded, and that the inmates were in deep conversation over some very absorbing topic, which he at once guessed must be the murder, Mr. Barnes moved to the back of the store and mingled with the loungers there.

Almost the first person whom he noticed was Will Everly, the young man with whom he had had the brief conversation in the earlier part of the day. He was still staunchly defending his friend Marvel.

"I tell you, Harrison," he was saying, "it is wrong in you to accuse Walter of this thing, when you know very well that he has not been in this neighborhood since the night of that party, when he and Lewis had the spat—"

"Spat? That's a mild way ter put it when he tried ter shoot the old man." The speaker was the man who had given the information about the snow. "But I say, Everly, I don't exactly accuse Marvel; I merely say it's a bad business for him, seein' as how he threatened ter do this very thing."

"Well, what if he did? A threat when a man is mad, is a very different thing from actually committing a murder. As to that, why, Lucas threatened him too."

"Why, of course I hope Marvel will come out all right. He's a fine fellow, and I like him. It's a lucky thing the Squire had them detectives right on the spot. They'll clear up matters mighty quick, I reckon."

"Whatever they do they won't find that Walter is in this ugly business. I can prove that he was not in town anyway."

"How kin you do that?" Mr. Barnes became interested at once.

"Why I have a letter from him this morning from Epping."

"Bosh! What does that amount ter? That's only five miles off."

Mr. Barnes noticed that Everly spoke louder than was absolutely necessary, and as he glanced towards Burrows occasionally, it seemed that his defence of his friend was, in a measure, meant for that detective's ears. At this point, a lad entered, and approaching Everly, said:

"Will, Miss Alice asks you if you can go as far as New Market for her."

"Tell her I'll be with her as soon as I can hitch up my horse." As Everly started to go, Mr. Barnes touched him on the arm, and said:

"Friend, if you are going to New Market I'll thank you to give me a lift, if you would be so kind. It will save me a long walk."

"Who are you?" Everly was suspicious of strangers.

"I live up on the Nottingham road, and am going to New Market to try for work on the new factory they are building. I am a carpenter by trade."

"All right," said Everly, after a little more hesitation, "look out for me as I come back, and I'll pick you up."

As soon as he had gone, Mr. Barnes took a notebook from his pocket, and, tearing out a page, wrote as follows:

"DEAR TOM:

"It is of no use. She saw the boat, and has taken the alarm. I think she means to send the letter to the post at New Market. If you see me remain in the wagon with Everly, you will know that this surmise on my part is correct. In that case I will take care of the letter. Tell no one where I have gone, even though I should not return for a day or two. Tell the Squire to empanel his jury, turn the body over to a doctor for a *post-mortem,* and then adjourn until I get back. Meanwhile keep your eyes open. Watch young Lewis! Remember he is a stranger and should prove his identity beyond a doubt, especially if a will turns up drawn in his favor. Pump him all you can without his suspecting that you have a motive.

"BARNES."

Having written this note, the next thing to do was to give it to Burrows without arousing suspicion of collusion. It must be borne in mind that every one present knew that the man by the window was a detective; and, further, that Burrows had failed to recognize Mr. Barnes in his disguise. The latter went to the door and stood there a few minutes, whistling a tune that was a great favorite with Burrows. He kept this up until at length he attracted his notice. As soon as this was accomplished, having his back to the others, he slightly lifted his false beard, thus revealing his identity, and then held up the note. Sure then that Burrows understood him, he dropped into a chair, picked up a copy of the *Boston Herald* which lay there, and pretended to read, until Everly at length appeared in the road. He then simply laid the paper down, having hidden the note therein, and joining Everly was taken into the wagon. Thus nothing was left to Burrows but to possess himself of the newspaper and note, which he easily did.

Reaching the house into which Virginia had gone, the horse was stopped, and Everly jumped out. He started to enter the gate leading to the dwelling, when the main door was opened and a young woman, emerging therefrom, came down the gravel walk to meet him. She greeted him familiarly and they stood conversing in low tones for a few moments. Mr. Barnes watched them closely in his endeavor to see whether she intrusted a letter to his care. He did not actually detect her doing so, but he saw by the motion of Everly's arm that he carefully placed something in the inner pocket of his coat. Satisfied that this was the letter, the superscription of which he was so anxious to see, he determined to keep his seat and accompany Everly to New Market. On the road thither, he attempted but little conversation, fearing to reveal his identity, and thus destroy all hopes of success. As his companion seemed little inclined to talk, the trip, which occupied about three quarters of an hour, was made in comparative silence.

Arrived at New Market, he deemed it best to alight as soon as they reached the hotel. Entering, he posted himself so as to watch whither Everly should drive, and the latter, entirely unconscious as to whom he had brought with him, went straight to the post-office, situated about a block farther. With considerable satisfaction Mr. Barnes saw him presently emerge again, and immediately turn his horse's head homeward, thus showing that his sole errand to the town had been to post the letter.

As soon as Everly was out of sight, Mr. Barnes removed his disguise, and making a bundle of the overalls, intrusted it to the care of the hotel clerk to be kept until he should call again. He then hurried over to the post-office, where he asked for the postmaster. To this official he declared himself to be a detective, and stating that in his belief a letter had just been mailed to an important witness in a case which he was investigating, received permission to examine the letters uncancelled. This he proceeded to do, and at length he found the object of his search. He held in his hand a letter, the contents of which he thought would throw considerable light on the mystery. He copied the address, which was as follows:

"Walter Marvel, Esq., Portsmouth, N. H."

"Keep till called for."

Leaving the office, Mr. Barnes hurried over to the railroad station, and purchasing a ticket for Portsmouth was soon on his way thither.

Arriving there that same evening, he lost no time in proceeding to call on the postmaster of the city, and, acquainting him with the nature of his business, easily arranged a plan whereby he hoped to discover Walter Marvel. As the man whom he was seeking was an entire stranger to him, it would be impossible to recognize him. Therefore he determined to station himself at the inquiry window, and arranged a signal whereby the clerk was to warn him when anyone should ask for a letter for Walter Marvel. As, however, he was informed that the mail just in would not be ready for delivery until the following morning, he went to a hotel and retired for the night.

The post-office opened at seven o'clock, and promptly at that hour Mr. Barnes commenced his vigil. He did not have his patience very sorely tried, for it was scarcely eight o'clock when he received the signal from the postal clerk, and saw the letter handed to a man at the window.

Not knowing whether this was Marvel himself or merely some messenger, Mr. Barnes determined, for the present, simply to follow him, more especially as he did not break the seal of the letter, but after glancing at the address consigned it to his pocket. Leaving the building, the man proceeded to a small hotel, at a considerable distance from the post-office, and in the vicinity of the docks. Mr. Barnes concluded that it was little more than a sailor's boarding-house, and it puzzled him to guess why Marvel had chosen this place. Entering the door which led in on a level with the street, the man seated himself on a chair, and then producing the letter, broke the seal and read.

The act satisfied Mr. Barnes that Walter Marvel was before him, but it suited him still to spy awhile upon his movements, hoping thereby to learn something. Of course Marvel could not guess that the man standing in the doorway was a detective, or that he was watched. Therefore he would act as his real intentions prompted him. He seemed wholly absorbed in the paper before him, which he read and re-read a number of times, ending by crumpling it up in his hand and starting up from his chair. He stood gazing from the window, awhile, and then paced nervously up and down. This lasted some minutes, when he suddenly resumed his seat, took the crumpled letter from his pocket where he had thrust it, and carefully smoothed out the creases on his knee. He again read its contents over and over. Suddenly, with a smothered ejaculation, he tore the letter into pieces and scattered them on the floor. Then he spoke a few words to the hotel clerk and hurried upstairs.

Mr. Barnes at once proceeded to collect the scattered fragments of the letter, and carefully placing them in an envelope, consigned that to his wallet until such time as he might be able to match the pieces together again. This done, he quietly seated himself and waited.

In about ten minutes Walter Marvel reappeared coming down the stairs, and hurried out to the street, Mr. Barnes following him.

He directed his course towards the wharves, and finally walked to the end of one where he went aboard a schooner lying there. By inquiring among the longshoremen the detective soon learned that this vessel, *The Eclipse,* was bound for the West Indies, and was to sail immediately. Mr. Barnes saw at once that it was now time to take active measures, or he would lose his man after all. Boarding the vessel he sought out the captain, and explained to him what he wished to do. The master seemed of a surly disposition and little inclined to render any assistance. He did not, indeed, refuse to let Mr. Barnes see Marvel, but he positively declined to take any part in the matter himself.

Descending to the cabin, almost the first individual whom he met was Marvel, and Mr. Barnes approaching him, addressed him as follows:

"Mr. Marvel, I believe?"

"That is my name; but you are a stranger to me!"

"Mr. Marvel, I have a very unpleasant duty to perform, and hope you will pardon me if I proceed at once to explain, as I fear that the captain may sail at any minute."

"You cannot explain too quickly to suit me," replied Marvel.

"Mr. Marvel, how long is it since you left Wadley's Falls?"

"Why do you ask?"

"Please answer me first, and I promise full explanations afterwards."

"That arrangement does not suit me. You are a stranger to me—I do not even know how it is that you are acquainted with my name—and I, therefore, deny that you have any right to question me."

"Mr. Marvel, I am a detective."

"Well?"

"A murder has been committed at Wadley's Falls, and—" Mr. Barnes paused to note the effect of his words, but Marvel seemed turned to stone, he was so impassive. "Will you venture to guess who the victim is?"

"John Lewis!" said Marvel, in a hoarse whisper. He dropped into a chair and buried his face in his hands. His trouble seemed so poignant, that for some minutes Mr. Barnes could not find it in his heart to disturb him. Finally, however, realizing that time was precious, he said:

"Mr. Marvel, will you return with me to Lee?"

"Why should I?" answered Marvel, looking up suddenly, aroused by the question.

"Because it may be necessary for you to prove your where-abouts on that night, in order to disarm suspicion, and—"

"Do you mean to accuse me of this crime?" said Marvel, vehemently.

"I never make an accusation till I have positive proof," returned Mr. Barnes, "and that I have not in this case,—at least not yet. I advise you to keep your temper, and be guarded in what you say, for your words may be used against you."

"You are insolent! How dare you speak to me in that way—"

"Come, Mr. Marvel, time presses. Will you accompany me peaceably?"

"Do you mean as your prisoner?"

"No! Let us say as a witness," but at that word Marvel recoiled and seemed alarmed. All the anger departed from his voice as he said:

"Have you a warrant for my arrest? Can you force me to go?"

Mr. Barnes shook his head negatively, and Marvel heaved a sigh of relief as he muttered, "Then I will not go—I cannot! I cannot!"

Mr. Barnes was nonplussed. He had counted on finding Marvel willing, nay, anxious to return as soon as he should know that there was any possibility of his being implicated in the crime. But what was he to do, now that he refused to go back? He could not compel him without a warrant, and that he not only did not have, but could not procure before the vessel would sail. He determined to try to induce the captain to delay starting, though with little hope of success, remembering how surly he had just shown himself. As he anticipated, the master declared that he would not change his plans.

Seeing that nothing was to be accomplished in this way, Mr. Barnes sought the cabin, hoping even yet to persuade Marvel that his best course was to accompany him, since if he were guilty he could not hope to escape extradition, which would be very simple, his destination being known; while if innocent, it was his duty to return and assist in clearing up the matter, thus removing all doubt.

He found Marvel sitting where he had left him, staring vacantly before him. He was so absorbed in thought, that the detective was obliged to touch him to attract attention, and then, before Mr. Barnes could say a word Marvel exclaimed:

"Is it you? I am glad. I will go back with you."

"You will go back with me?" Mr. Barnes was much surprised at this sudden change.

"Yes. I am sorry now that I refused at first. I see that it is the best course to pursue. Yet I had reasons, that seemed to me at the first moment of my surprise, to be unanswerable, and which led to my decision. I am now ready and anxious to accompany you."

Mr. Barnes scrutinized Marvel closely, to determine whether this were a genuine or an assumed manner. He was puzzled.

"I am glad," said he, "that you will go peaceably. You save me a great deal of trouble. I would have taken you back, even though it had been necessary to get a warrant and follow you to sea in a tug. Then you would have been under arrest. Now, since you offer no resistance, you shall receive every consideration. I will take you back as a witness."

"I will not go with you as a witness. I will submit to arrest though you have no warrant, but if I go with you it must be as your prisoner."

"As you please. It matters not, so long as you return."

Mr. Barnes and Marvel left Portsmouth on the first train available, and reached Wadley's Falls the next morning. Whilst on the train, Mr. Barnes found an opportunity to be alone in the smoking car long enough to piece together the fragments of the letter which he had picked up, when thrown away by Marvel. With mucilage which he had procured at Portsmouth, he pasted each piece to another sheet, so that finally the letter was once more legible. It read as follows:

"After the events of last night it is best that you leave the country. Do so without delay. It would be madness to think of marriage now. Farewell!

"VIRGIE."

After studying this, for a long time, Mr. Barnes was forced to admit that the whole affair was as great a mystery as ever.

CHAPTER V
THE TWO GIRLS

Virginia Lewis, though living in New England, would never be mistaken for a native of that section. She lacked the phlegmatic temperament of the people about her, notwithstanding the fact that she had been reared among them. Her environment had undoubtedly affected her character to the extent that, outwardly, she moved, spoke, and acted like her neighbors. But there was a certain suppressed emotion, always distinguishable, however well controlled, that bespoke a birthplace in a warmer clime. However mildly she might address her friends, and there were few of gentler speech, the slightest antagonism betrayed by anyone present would be met with an instantaneous answering flash of her lustrous dark eyes, which betokened danger if the subject were pursued. No one, not even those most dear to her, had the courage to take liberties of conversation or of act, with Virginia Lewis. Nevertheless, she was the best beloved and most popular young woman in the township. Half the young men the country round were her admirers, ready to become obedient servitors in exchange for a friendly nod. Rarer still, she had no enemies among the women folk.

She was not beautiful, yet by many called so. I think this was because of the marvel of her eyes, which, always brilliant, and ever restlessly moving as though to absorb all about her, attracted with a fascination, or magnetism, which none resisted. It was no wonder that the rays of genuine intelligence shed by those orbs should have been mistaken for beauty, for, after all, it is expressiveness, rather than symmetry of lineament, which men most admire in a woman.

When at rest, there were hard, set lines about the mouth, which to the physiognomist unmistakably proclaimed her possession of that excessive willpower and dogged persistence, which Squire Olney truly mentioned as characteristic traits. Mr. Barnes had said that he would not expect to surprise her again into a betrayal of herself, or her purposes, and in this he showed a keen perception.

She had been very much startled by the abrupt entrance of the two men, and their subsequent announcement that they were detectives. She noticed that Mr. Barnes had kept the empty cartridge shell which had dropped from her lap, but, in the moment of her surprise, she had not time to decide upon the best course consistent with whatever purpose she was bent upon accomplishing. When they left her she sat down and meditated for some time. Presently she arose, and it was evident that her plan had been formulated. She took the pistol from the cabinet, where Mr. Barnes had shrewdly guessed that it was.

Whatever had been her reason for removing the shell which Mr. Barnes had taken, it was plain that she now considered her purpose unattainable. Opening the drawer of her bureau, she took therefrom a small mahogany box, which she unlocked. In it were several pasteboard packages of ball cartridges. One, however, contained shells which had been exploded. She next withdrew a cartridge from the pistol, and in its stead inserted an empty shell, being careful to see that the hammer exactly rested upon the indentation in the rim. Thus, it is evident, that if she had removed from this pistol the empty shell which Mr. Barnes had picked up, she must have reloaded the weapon prior to his entrance. Now she was restoring it to its original condition. She threw the pistol on the bed, as though desirous that it should be readily found.

Next she opened a drawer of the cabinet, and took out two pieces of folded paper. One of these was a duplicate of that found by the detectives, bearing the words: "If I am dead in the morning, my murder is," except that, as Mr. Barnes had guessed, this one bore a name, the sentence being completed. Virginia scrutinized this for some moments, sighed deeply, and refolded it. The other was also a half sheet, and bore a few lines addressed to herself. She read this several times, and then folded it also, placing both papers in her dress.

Approaching the door which communicated with the parlor, she listened attentively for a few moments, and then entered that apartment, which was empty, the detectives, by this time, having gone out upon the' lawn. Peeping from the window, careful that she herself should be hidden from sight by the curtains, she saw Mr. Barnes and Burrows near the summer-house. She watched them until they were again approaching the house, whereupon she returned to her own room. Here she remained till the detectives had made the map of the grounds, and again sallied forth towards the river. This time she watched them from the window of her own room, and realized, from their actions, that they were studying the footprints between the house and the river. She also saw them get in the boat and cross the river.

Once more she entered the parlor. One would think, from her repeated visits to the place where lay the dead body, that it had some fascination for her. As though, indeed, this were the case, she went straight to where it lay, and bending down, gazed at it intently. Especially did she look upon the disfigured face. Finally, she turned her attention to the hand, and examined a ring on one finger. This seemed to satisfy her. In rising, she stepped on the hem of her dress, and fell to her knees, striking against the corpse, which was thus slightly turned over. This action brought into view the other hand, which before had been under the body. She shuddered as she jumped up, and then, noticing that the fist was doubled up tight, her curiosity was aroused, and she determined to investigate further. She endeavored to open the fingers, and though they were tightly clenched, she at length succeeded in relaxing two. This enabled her, not only to see that there was something within the dead man's grasp, but also to withdraw it. This done, she evidently had enough of the company of the corpse, for she hurried to the next room, and hastily closed the door after her.

She then examined the article which she had just obtained, and found it to be a small, gold locket. Opening it she saw that it contained a miniature of herself, which had been made when she was yet a child.

She was evidently disturbed at the discovery, for she gazed at it long and earnestly. Perhaps her conscience troubled her, and the thought came to her, that, even at the moment when he was killed, her uncle had just been looking at this picture of herself, thinking of the time, when, a young and attractive child, she had been his idol—, and then of the past week, when, before all their friends, they had antagonized their wills. She threw herself on the bed, buried her face in her hands, and for some minutes she sobbed like one in dire distress. Presently, rising from her recumbent position, controlling her emotions by an effort of will, she first hid the locket in her dress, as she had done with the letters, and then bathed her face, and went to the window. She looked towards the summer-house, but saw nothing of the detectives. Turning, she hurriedly put on her hat, arranged her toilet, and started out from the house, in the direction of the post-office.

She thought that she had avoided the observation of the detectives, but in this, as she herself subsequently suspected, she was mistaken. Reaching the bridge, she noticed the boat, and as she had last seen the two men entering it, she concluded that they were now in the vicinity, though she did not yet guess that they had followed her. As she passed the saloon, however, she caught a glimpse of Burrows, and as he immediately withdrew, so as to hide himself from her view, she at once decided that he was there to watch her movements. Thus she was compelled to abandon her project of mailing the letter herself, which had been her object in coming out. She went on to the house of the Marvels.

Being on terms of closest intimacy with the inmates, she unceremoniously entered, without knocking, and went into the parlor. Here, seated in front of a rousing log fire, she found Mrs. Marvel, busily engaged with some knitting, and evidently ignorant of the fact, that, at that very time, grave suspicions were entertained against her son. The old lady politely rose and welcomed her visitor, but Virginia, without accepting her invitation to be seated, at once inquired for her daughter Alice.

"Alice is not out of bed yet," said the mother. "She sent me a message, at breakfast-time, that she had a headache, and preferred to sleep. But you can go up to her room, if you wish. I guess she is not seriously ill." She smiled, well knowing that her daughter was fond of her morning nap, and that "a headache," was often a convenient excuse.

Virginia at once went in search of her friend. Ascending one flight of stairs, she entered Alice Marvel's bedroom. Alice was in bed, but not asleep. On the contrary, she seemed very wide awake, although completely absorbed with her thoughts.

A moment's description of this young lady may not be amiss. Though, like Virginia, a brunette, she was nevertheless totally different in appearance. Her friends called her pretty, and the term was applicable; for though she possessed a charming face, she could be called neither handsome nor beautiful. Small, well-chiselled features, a rosy, pert little mouth, piercing black eyes, chestnut-brown hair, and a clear complexion with considerable color; these were the salient points in her favor. In stature she was *petite*. But it was her manner, more than her physical charms, that was her chief attraction. Vivacious, impetuous, with powerful emotions, loving and hating with a degree of intensity foreign to the American-born, it was easy to detect that Alice Marvel had French blood in her veins.

Her father had chosen his bride in Paris, and continued his residence in that city until Alice was fifteen. Then he returned to America with his family, which included Walter, who was two years older than his sister, and immediately thereafter settled in Lee. Thus Alice was now in her twenty-fifth year.

Startled from her meditations by the abrupt entrance of her friend, Alice stared at her a moment in silence, and then suddenly exclaimed:

"Is he dead?"

"Is who dead?" asked Virginia, amazed at the question.

"Your uncle, Mr. Lewis?" replied Alice; at which Virginia was so bewildered that she stood speechless. Knowing that the fact of her uncle's death had been so recently discovered, and also that Alice had not left her own room, Virginia was at a loss to understand how she had become aware of the true state of affairs. It occurred to her that perhaps, after all, the maid-servant had informed Alice, but in that case it should have been known also by Mrs. Marvel, whereas that lady had acted in a way which precluded the supposition that the news had reached her ears. Recovering somewhat from the first effects of her surprise, she asked:

"How did you know that he is dead?"

Alice started at this question, and then, as though awakening from a dream, replied:

"*I* don't know what I have been saying. I think I was dreaming when you came in and—and—and I must have continued aloud what was passing through my mind."

"Your dream, then, is wonderfully near the truth, for my uncle was found dead this morning, and he has undoubtedly been murdered."

"Murdered! My God, this is frightful!" With a convulsive tremor, which passed over her whole frame, Alice lay back and buried her face in her pillow. Virginia gazed at her, not knowing how to construe her agitation. A moment later Alice, with one bound, leaped from the bed, and, rushing up to Virginia, exclaimed excitedly:

"You say he was murdered! How do you know it? Who can prove it? Did anyone see it? Who did it? Who did it, I say? Tell me—"

"Hush! Do you know what you are saying? If anyone heard you it would be suspected—"

"What would be suspected—what is suspected— tell me! I must know, I will know—I—"

"Silence! Are you still in a dream? You must stop this wild language! Stop it! Stop it instantly!" Taking Alice by the shoulders, she shook her, and by her words and manner Virginia at length subdued somewhat the intensity of her friend's excitement. Then occurred the inevitable reaction. Alice threw herself on the bed, and abandoned herself to a wild paroxysm of tears. Virginia endeavored to calm and soothe her, but for a long time her attentions only aggravated the hysterical sobbing. After awhile, however, she became more quiet, and Virginia sought an explanation.

"Now, Alice," said she, "you must tell me how you knew that my uncle is dead."

"Hush! I cannot tell you! I cannot! I cannot!"

"But you must! Evidently you know something about this, and you must tell me!"

"It is impossible!"

"Can you not trust me? Come, Alice, you must be reasonable. We are wasting time that is most precious. Do you know who is, or will be, suspected of this crime?"

"Do you know? Then tell me?" said Alice, in feverish anxiety.

"Listen! There are two detectives—"

"What, already?" interrupted Alice, in a terrified voice, "and you say they suspect someone ?"

"Alice, you too suspect someone . Who is it? If you and the detectives suspect the same man, I will help to shield him. You know that!"

"Him? Whom do you mean?" Now it seemed that Alice was puzzled.

"Whom do I mean? Who was it that quarrelled with my uncle? Who was it that threatened to kill him?"

"My God, you mean my brother!" Alice sank in a chair, and sat staring like one in a trance. Finally, by a great effort she aroused herself, and seemed to regain her self-possession.

"Virginia, you must think me out of my mind to have acted as I have; but I have had a terrible night. In my dreams I have seen your uncle murdered in a thousand fantastic ways. Therefore it is not strange that when you startled me, I should have addressed you as I did. It was a tremendous shock to have you announce that all, which my imagination had pictured, was really true."

"Undoubtedly, Alice, but it is a strange coincidence that you should have had such dreams. What were you thinking of when you retired, that my uncle should have been so conspicuously in your thoughts?"

"I was thinking of him. But I will tell you the truth at once."

"Stop a moment! I will listen to your story after awhile. It is of vital importance that no more time should be lost in warning Walter of the danger which threatens him."

"Yes! But how will you do it? Do you know where he is?"

"He is in Portsmouth by this time, I hope. He will expect a letter from me to-morrow morning. I came out to post it, but I am certain that I am watched by the detectives. I did not dare to go to our office for fear that they would discover just what I do not want them to know. The only way left is to send the letter to New Market, and mail it there. How can we do that?"

Alice had entirely composed herself, and whilst her friend spoke, was rapidly dressing. She replied:

"I know the very one to trust, for, of course, it must be a tried friend, as the bearer of the letter will discover the address. Will Everly is the man for this emergency. Walter, you remember, saved him once, when he was nearly drowned, and since then I believe he has been ready to sacrifice his life for my brother at any moment."

"Will is the man that I had in my mind. Can you send one of the boys to his house for him?"

"Wait here till I return, and I will fix it." With these words Alice quitted the room. Left to herself, Virginia was at once thoughtful. She could not believe that all the agitation which she had witnessed in her friend, was solely due to the coincidence of a nightmare. Yet how could Alice have really known anything of the crime, since she had not been out of her own room, unless indeed she had been present the night before? Alice returned, and as she entered, said:

"I have sent Frank, one of the stable boys, for Will. Now, shall I tell you what I did last night?"

Virginia signified her assent, and her companion proceeded.

"Harry Lucas had promised to take me to drive, in the evening, but, during the afternoon, he called and told me that it would be impossible to do so, as he had received a note, which would make it necessary for him to leave town. I did not doubt his statement, and after a little conversation he left the house. After his departure, I found on the floor a note, which he must have dropped in taking his handkerchief from his pocket. Of course I had no right to read it, and I did not think of doing so until I recognized that the address was in your writing."

Alice paused, but Virginia said nothing, though the color deepened on her cheek. Alice continued:

"I suppose that, knowing you had accepted my brother's love, it was a contemptible thing for me to feel jealous. Nevertheless, I confess with shame and regret that such was the case. Therefore I opened the note. As you know the contents, you can readily imagine that what I read was scarcely calculated to dissipate my anger. You invited him to a secret meeting. The hour named was for last evening. Thus Harry had broken his promise to me, giving me a false excuse, in order to meet you. Impetuous, as you know I am, I at once determined to be present. You had specified that he should wait for you in the south side of the summer-house on your lawn. I had only to go early, and conceal myself in the northern division. As I drew on my cloak, preparatory to starting, my eye fell on my pistol, which lay on my dressing-case, and, though I did not think of needing it, or of using it, in my excitement I took it up and slipped it into my pocket. I reached the place first, as was my intention, and patiently awaited your arrival. Harry came, and you joined him promptly. I need not tell you what occurred between you. I overheard every word, and you can imagine how much ashamed I was of my doubt of Harry, and of yourself, when I learned the real object of the meeting. I felt like revealing my presence, and begging your pardon, but my pride prevented me. So I remained in my place of concealment until both of you had left. Then I hurried home."

"But this would scarcely account for the dreams," said Virginia, without commenting on the rest of the story.

"I have not finished. I said that I had taken my pistol with me when I went out. On my return, I was alarmed at not finding it, for, as you know, my name is engraved on the stock. My imaginative mind at once commenced to picture all kinds of trouble. What if someone should find the weapon, and commit a crime with it? Might not the finger of suspicion point at me? I felt inclined to return and look for it, but the distance is a long one, and besides, I could not be sure of recovering it. Therefore, trying to persuade myself that my fears were silly, I endeavored to go to sleep. But, oh! Virgie, what a night I have passed!" She shuddered at the recollection.

"I can readily understand, and am now not surprised at what you said when I came in. Shall we go down and see if the boy has returned?" The two girls left the room, and descended to the floor below. Here they found their messenger, and were informed that Will Everly would be ready to go on their errand as soon as he could get his horse out. A quarter of an hour later, Everly drove up, and Alice carried the letter out to him.

As soon as the horse and wagon were out of sight, on the road to New Market, Virginia prepared to return home, whereupon Alice expressed her intention to accompany her, hoping to recover her pistol, and together they started to walk to Riverside.

CHAPTER VI
MYSTERIOUS NOISES

In pursuance of the directions left by Mr. Barnes, and communicated to him by Burrows, Squire Olney impanelled a jury, taking them to the Lewis farm and allowing them to examine the corpse, where it lay in the position as when discovered. He then adjourned the inquest until the return of the absent detective. Meanwhile he ordered Dr. Snow, a competent surgeon, to make an autopsy, placing the corpse in an upper room, and in charge of the physician.

The jurymen and assembled neighbors dispersed slowly, as though loath to leave the vicinity. Burrows mixed with them, hoping to extract some clue, by conversation, which might prove of value to him. In this he failed entirely. The greater number apparently suspected that Walter Marvel was implicated, and as he was a general favorite, they feared to speak with the detective, lest they should compromise their friend.

One man, however, voluntarily approached him, and said:

"They tell me as how you're the detective?"

"You are quite right," said Burrows, hopefully.

"My name's Skene," said the other. "Josiah Skene, station agent down to Lee Deepo'. I hearn 'bout this here inquest, an' tho't I'd run up an' see how ye're gittin' on. Anybody 'rested?"

"Well, hardly," answered Burrows, with a smile. "We have only been at work a few hours, you know."

"Well, that only goes to show. I always tho't as how them stories in the Borston papers wuz kinder farfetched. They make out's though you detective fellers wuz quicker 'n greased lightnin'. I guess you an't no smarter than other folks. I guess I could put you up to snuff in this case anyway." Mr. Skene took his long chin whisker in his left hand, stroked it once, and then turned it up so that he readily bit the end, the while looking at Burrows through the corner of his eyes, his head turned partly away, as though he were contemplating something on the distant horizon.

"Do you know anything?" Burrows spoke with a little anxiety. He recognized that the man was an eccentric, and feared to do, or say something, that would antagonize him. After a long pause, came the reply:

"Mebbe!" Only this one word, muttered without removal of the whisker from, his mouth. Burrows waited for more, but was forced to continue the conversation himself.

"Mr. Skene, this is a dreadful business, and if you can help us to unravel it, I am sure you will do so."

"An't that what I 'm up here for? D' you s'pose I tramped up here for exercise? Not much! But the joke is that you should need me to tell you anything. You're a detective from Borston. I tho't as how you fellers wuz so cute like, that you jest looked at the dead man, and 'rested the murderer straight off. Saw his likeness in the corpse's eyes, or suthin'. I've read that in books, but I guess you reel detectives an't so darned smart as all that, hay?"

"No, I am afraid not. We are no smarter than other folks, only we make a business of putting two and two together, that's all. You could tell that it would make four, as easily as I could. But you have your railroad business, Mr. Skene, and I have to look for criminals. That is the only difference." Burrows tried a little conciliatory flattery, and it operated to make Mr. Skene more communicative.

"By Jehosaphat! You hit it square that time. I kin smell a rat, but it an't my place to hunt him down. So I guess I'll tell you who killed Lewis, an' let you ketch him. Only seems to me you oughtn't to git all the glory, hay?"

"You give me the clue, Mr. Skene, and when I arrest the man you shall have full credit for giving me the clue."

"Oh! I'm only jokin'. You ketch the feller, an' I'll be satisfied. I an't lookin' for no notoriety." Nevertheless he wore a pleased expression, as when a shrewd New Englander has just arranged one of those typical Yankee "bargains," in which each man swaps what he does not want for what he does want, and chuckles because he has cheated the other man. Mr. Skene thought a moment, as though deciding where to begin. Then he resumed: "You noticed that I said I could tell you who killed Lewis?"

"I did," said Burrows, "and I wondered whether you had seen the crime committed."

"Seen it?" cried Mr. Skene. "Why, man alive, d' you s'pose I 'd have let the murderer escape? No, I didn't 'spect him last night, but I seen him, I seen him twice."

"Whom did you see twice?"

"Why, an't I tellin' you? The murderer! I seen the murderer twice. The fust time wuz when the up train come along. When she stopped, he got off. I didn't pay no speshal 'tention to him till the train wuz gone, when he came up an' spoke to me. He asked me how to git to the Lewis farm."

"This is important. You say a man came up on a train last night and asked to be directed to the Lewis farm?"

"That's jest what I said. I tol' him, an' then he asked for a time-table an' wanted to know ef he could go back las' night. I give him a time-slip, an' off he went. I never tho't no more of him till I seen him again, pacin' up an' down jest before the down train come in. I nagged the train to stop, an' he boarded her."

"Did you recognize him? That is, had you ever seen him before?"

"As fur's I know, I never sot eyes on him till las' night, tho' once I tho't as how his voice wuz kinder familiar. But don't lay no stress on that, 'cause I an't no good rememberin' sounds. An't got no eer for music. All I can tell you is, he wuz a medium-size man with a full beard."

"Did he have any baggage?"

"I wuz jest comin' to that, 'cause it is kinder queer. He didn't have none when he come, 'less it wuz on the platform an' I didn't see it, which an't likely. But, when he come back from Lewis's, he had a satchel."

"Where did he go from here? That is, for what point did he buy a ticket?"

"He didn't buy none from me. That wuz one thing made me sort of 'spicious. Then when I hearn of the murder, why it all come to me as plain as a pikestaff. That mysterious visitor come up expressly to kill Lewis. That's why he wuz so darned anxious to git outer town agin las' night. Under them circumstances, it an't likely as how he 'd buy a ticket from me."

"At what time did he arrive, and at what time did he leave?"

"He come in at 9.07, an' he ketched the 10.39 down."

"Which way do you mean by down?"

"Why, man alive, don't you know that much? Down is down. Down to'ards Nashuway, Wooster, an' that 'ere way."

"You must excuse my ignorance," said Burrows, humbly. "I don't pretend to know everything, you see. Now, one thing more.

I must tell you, though I presume you know it already, that it is of the utmost importance, when a detective is trying to catch a criminal, that he should keep a close mouth. As you and I are working together, as it were, I must ask you to speak to no one but myself."

This speech was adroitly worded. Burrows was anxious that Mr. Barnes should not hear of this new clue, intending if possible to work it out alone. In order, therefore, to close the mouth of this egotistical countryman, he ingeniously included him in his work, having discerned that the fellow was anxious to have a tale to tell to the frequenters of the saloon, of how, "Me and the detective from Borston worked up the case." Mr. Skene, however, made one feeble protest.

"Well, as to that," said he, "I tho't as how I 'd have to go on the stand at the inquest, an' tell what I know?" He evidently counted upon the notoriety to be gained by such a procedure.

"Oh, of course!" said Burrows, hastily endeavoring to satisfy him upon this point. "I will tell the Squire, and he will call you, unless he should be afraid to let your story be known too soon. I think, though, that you will be called. What I meant was, that you must not speak until you are."

"Oh, that's diff rent," said Mr. Skene, quite satisfied, now that the prospect of being a real witness, in a genuine murder case, was still in prospect. "I guess I kin keep my mouth shet. I guess Josiah Skene knows enough, to know when to talk, an' when to keep still. You kin count on me. Well good day. Let me know how you git on."

As he sauntered off, down the road towards the station, Burrows wondered whether he would really keep the story to himself. He doubted it, but as much as he should have liked to start in pursuit of this strange visitor of the night previous, he scarcely cared to leave before the return of his superior.

He had been standing in the road, near the main gate, during his conversation with the station agent, and now turning towards the house, he saw a young woman coming out. He recognized her as one who he had supposed was a servant, from the fact that he had seen her cooking in the kitchen whilst the inquest was started. He decided to question her, and as she came out, and was passing him, he said:

"Pardon me, but I wish to say a few words to you."

The woman faced him in silence and waited for him to speak.

"Will you tell me your name?"

"Sarah."

"Your last name also, if you please."

"Carpenter."

"Now will you tell me what you know about what occurred last night, and whether you heard any pistol-shot?"

"No I won't, and that's flat."

Before he recovered from his surprise at the asperity of her reply, she abruptly turned from him and proceeded along the road. He looked after her wonderingly. Was it possible that this woman held the key to the situation? If so, it became most puzzling, from the fact that it did not seem to fit any theory as yet advanced. Yet her manner was not that of one who was entirely ignorant. He decided to speak to Mr. Barnes about this, and to leave it to him to obtain her secret, if she had one. He went into the house in search of Squire Olney, and found him in the parlor conversing with Lewis. As he entered he heard the Squire say:

"I suppose, Mr. Lewis, that you will sleep here to-night, as this house is now yours?"

It occurred to Burrows at once, that this was his opportunity to continue the line of inquiry suggested by Mr. Barnes in his note. Therefore, without waiting for Lewis to reply, he said:

"Squire, you say this house is now the property of this young man. I hope both of you will pardon my asking whether a will has been found."

"I am not at all offended," said Lewis, promptly. "That is a very proper question. Squire, do you know anything about this?"

"Why, yes! I should have spoken to you before. I have the will in my pocket now. It was given into my keeping by your father, some time ago. I do not, however, know its contents, except that I am named as one of the executors, for he had the document drawn in Boston and gave it into my hands in a sealed envelope. Here it is, as I received it." He drew forth a legal-looking envelope of large proportions. "Shall I open it?"

Lewis nodded, and Burrows was too curious to know its contents, to call attention to the fact that it might be as well not to read the will, until notice could be given to other possible beneficiaries under its provisions. The Squire forthwith opened and read the paper. In substance it was to the effect that the house, and all available funds, should become the unconditional property of Virginia Lewis. There was a clause in which an allusion was made to the son, but, far from making him a legatee, it was plainly explained that Lewis *pere* considered that his son had forfeited all claim upon his bounty, and therefore no direct provision was made for his receiving any part of the estate. But there was a request that in case the young man should return home, Virginia should do for him whatever his circumstances seemed to require.

Burrows listened with close attention, and noted this clause with much interest. Here was evidence that the young man, then present, could not have committed the crime with the certainty of inheriting. Lewis then said:

"Well, gentlemen, it seems that I am not the owner of this house after all, and therefore I cannot sleep here without the permission of my cousin. But I suppose you can arrange that much for me, at least?" He appealed to the Squire, who replied:

"I am sure of it. Virgie would not turn a stranger from her roof, and I am confident that when she understands that you are so near a relative, she will offer you the hospitality which is due to you. In fact, if I know her character, I doubt if she will accept the property at all, now that you have returned."

"Once more," said Burrows, "I hope you will see that I am speaking conscientiously when I remind you, Mr. Lewis, that you have given us no proof of your identity. Of course, your word alone was sufficient this morning, when we were coming here. We expected to find Mr. Lewis alive, and it would have been his privilege to satisfy any doubt. But now—under the peculiar circumstances—I hope you don't misconstrue my motives "

"Not in the least," replied Lewis. "You are investigating a murder, and are right to demand a thorough explanation of my movements and proof of my identity. I am a stranger to you, and you have but my unsupported word. I am more glad than sorry that I am disinherited by my father's will. I did not deserve any consideration at his hands anyway, and under the distressing circumstances, and considering my appearance just after his violent death, were I his heir it might seem—you understand? I might be implicated!"

"Nonsense! Nonsense!" exclaimed the Squire. "No one would think such a thing." The Squire's positive assertion made Burrows feel a little uncomfortable, for he was inwardly conscious that he was entertaining the very idea at that moment. Lewis continued:

"As to my identity, fortunately, I foresaw that the time might someday come when I should wish to prove to my father that I am indeed his son. Therefore I have carefully preserved the last three letters which I received from him, determined, should it ever be necessary, to produce them as proof of my identity, in the event of his failing to recall my changed face. Now he is dead, but the evidence thus attainable assumes, it seems, an increased value. I have preserved the letters in my pocket-book through all these years, and from frequent reading they are not in a very perfect condition, though I hope sufficiently decipherable for you at least, Squire, to recognize their genuineness." So saying, he produced a dilapidated wallet, and took from it three letters, apparently quite old. They were in envelopes that scarcely held together, and the edges of the folds of the letters were almost worn through in places. Nevertheless the writing was sufficiently distinct to be legible. The Squire and Burrows looked through them, and the former unhesitatingly declared that he recognized the handwriting as that of John Lewis. The contents were not especially interesting, being simply such as a father would send to a son absent at school. A detective is naturally suspicious. He is apt to doubt and question to the last, and though Burrows was comparatively new, he nevertheless possessed this trait to a strong degree. He therefore examined the date of the post-mark, which was 1872. Although he could not but accept this as unimpeachable evidence that the young man's story was correct, still, without knowing exactly why he did so, he copied down the address on the envelopes, which was:

"John Lewis, Jr. Care T. Jamison, Esq., Washington Heights, New York City, N. Y.

"Mr. Lewis," said the Squire, "I am satisfied that you are my friend's son, and I am sorry that this will leaves you nothing, by its provisions. I am sure, as I told you just now, that Virgie will do what is right. I will see her at once."

He tapped gently on the door of Virginia's room, and was admitted. Whilst he was absent Burrows took the opportunity to ask Lewis a few more questions.

"Mr. Lewis," said he, "how long is it since you were at sea, and why did you give up the life? Though perhaps you mean to return to it?"

"Oh, no! I have had enough of it. The beautiful ease and comfort of the mess-room, described in the books of adventure written for boys, is very much overdrawn, I assure you. It was this kind of literature which first made me long for the sea. After I became a sailor in earnest, the charm of the romance dimmed considerably before the stern reality. I was sorry enough that I had left home."

"Why, then, did you not return sooner?"

"Ah! That is easier said than done. I shipped for a voyage to China. There I was forced to leave my ship, and find another homeward bound, which was not easy, or else to follow the fortunes of my messmates. I chose the latter, the consequence being that it was five years before we reached the States again, and then it was on the Pacific coast. As there was little chance of finding my father, anyway, since I knew he had contemplated a trip to Europe, I scarcely felt like crossing the whole breadth of the country on the errand. So I shipped again; and so it was from one ship to another, and the years rolled by."

"Still, you have come home at last, and found out where your father was located, too?"

"Yes. My ship touched at Portsmouth. As we were so near to where my father last was, and as I was pretty well sick of the sea, I concluded to give it up and come to Lee, with the faint hope that I could hear something of my father's whereabouts. The result you know."

"Yes, and I sympathize with you very much, I hope, you will pardon my having appeared to doubt your identity. I am trying to discover a murderer, and it is my duty to make every one account for himself."

"Let us say no more about it. I understood your motive exactly, and am really glad that you are so careful in your investigations. I hope you will be successful in finding the criminal. He must be discovered at all hazards. I may have been a bad son to my father whilst he was living. Now I must do all in my power to avenge him." Lewis spoke with so much feeling that Burrows did not for a moment doubt his sincerity, and determined to redouble his efforts to be the one to place the murderer in custody.

At this juncture the Squire returned, followed by Miss Marvel and Virginia, both of whom he introduced to Lewis and to Burrows. To the former, the young ladies bowed cordially, and it was evident that the Squire had left no doubt in Virginia's mind as to his identity, for she greeted him as a relative, though with no undue show of feeling.

Towards Burrows it was different. Though she offered him a room in the house during his connection with the case, it was done in a formal way, and with a certain *hauteur* of manner not easily misunderstood. However coldly offered, it suited Burrows to accept the invitation, and she showed him to a chamber on the next floor, just above the one which had been used as a sleeping-apartment by John Lewis. Virginia then descended to the parlor, and addressing Lewis, she said:

"If you do not mind, I will give you the same room that your father had?"

Lewis acquiesced, and followed her as she led the way.

The Squire thereupon started for his home, and escorted Miss Marvel to her residence.

Burrows retired early that night, intending to be as fresh as possible for the next day's work. He slept so soundly, that when he awoke with a sudden consciousness of having been disturbed by some extraneous sound, it was impossible for him to determine whether he had slept for hours or minutes. Indeed, he could not even understand thoroughly what it was that he had heard. It left the impression on his mind of an object, such as a chair perhaps, which had been overturned, but whether he had really heard anything, or only imagined it in connection with some vagary of dreamland, he could not be sure. However, though he had been sleeping soundly, he was now thoroughly aroused, and could not dismiss the idea that he had heard a distinct and loud sound. But whether in his own room, or in an adjoining apartment, or even downstairs, puzzled him. He lay quietly, straining to catch the least evidence of a repetition, but no sound reached his acutely attentive ear, save his own breathing and the ticking of his watch beneath his pillow. The latter, however, suggested that he might at least learn how long he had slept. Striking a match, he lighted the oil lamp, and found it to be but ten o'clock, whereas he had thought that it must be near day. Finding that there would be time enough to spare to an investigation, and still to obtain a good night's rest afterwards, he dressed and left the chamber. Crossing the hall, he entered the room on that side of the house, thinking that from that direction, had come the noise which had disturbed his slumbers. Looking about him, it seemed evident that nothing had been disturbed, or else it had been rearranged. He was about to prosecute his search further, when he fancied he heard footsteps. Listening attentively, he could almost have sworn that they came from the direction of his bedroom. Hurrying back thither, he found everything just as he had left it. What could this mean? The first sound might have been in a dream, but surely he was awake the second time? Nevertheless, though he had apparently heard someone walking in his chamber, when he reached it it was as vacant as when he had left it. There was the supernatural possibility that the ghost of the corpse in the adjoining room was promenading in the moonlight, but Burrows was above entertaining such an idea, and, as it occurred to him for a moment, he smiled as he thought "it is not midnight." However, if the footsteps had been in that room, whether of the living or of the dead, he could not discover, for the doctor had taken away the key. Was it possible that Lewis was up, and walking about downstairs? This seemed to promise an explanation, and Burrows at once went to the floor below. He entered the chamber which he knew had been assigned to Lewis. It was empty, and the bed bore no evidence of having been disturbed. Was this last surmise correct then, and was it Lewis whom he had heard? If so, what was he doing prowling about at such an hour? And where was he at the present moment? This last question he would endeavor to answer, for, if he had just heard him walking, he must be in the house. But Burrows went into every room, except, of course, Virginia's, only to find them all empty. Determined to solve the mystery, he replaced the lamp in his bedroom, and, again descending the stairs, seated himself on a chair in the hall, where it would be impossible for Lewis to pass him unnoticed. To a detective, long vigils of patient watching become almost a habit, but sleep will overpower a man, even though he be a detective. Burrows kept awake for four hours, occasionally striking a match to note the passage of time. Finally, when it was nearing the hour of three, he would start up every little while from a doze. Finding at length that he must sleep, with commendable perseverance he still resolved not to abandon his self-imposed task. In his dilemma he decided upon a bold plan, which was to lock the door of Lewis's room, and tip his chair back against it. Thus he might sleep, rather uncomfortably, but yet with the knowledge that Lewis must disturb him to pass him. When he awoke again, it was once more with the consciousness of a loud noise near him, but this time it continued after he had jumped up. It was now day, and quite light. As he stood rubbing his eyes, trying to collect his senses, upon recollecting what had occurred he was astonished to find that the noise, which still continued, was occasioned by someone within the room shaking the door which he had locked. In wonder, he turned the key, and was amazed to see John Lewis standing before him. They looked at each other a moment in silence, and then Lewis, said:

"Good-morning! What was the matter with the door? I could not open it." Burrows recovered himself at once, and replied:

"I don't know. I was just coming downstairs and heard you trying to get out. Seeing a key in the door, I turned it, but as I turned it more than once, I don't know whether you were locked in or not when I commenced.

"I hardly think that, for who would want to fasten me up? This is the only exit, as the other door leading into the library, is locked."

"I suppose it could not have been," stammered Burrows, a little confused. What could he think? How was it that Lewis had come out of this room, when he was sure that he had found it empty the night before, and had subsequently kept guard all through the lonely hours of the early morning? He left Lewis and went into the library. Going to the door which opened from that room into the apartment which Lewis had just quitted, he found that it was locked as he had stated. Moreover, the key was in the lock, on the library side. Burrows unlocked the door and entered, curious to determine whether Lewis had slept in the bed or not, and upon investigation, decided that he had. More than ever puzzled, he regretfully concluded to await until Mr. Barnes should arrive, and seek his assistance in solving this mystery. As it was yet early, he went to his room, and was soon sleeping soundly.

CHAPTER VII
THE AUTOPSY

After being released from his room by Burrows, Lewis crossed the hall and went into the parlor. Though New England farm people usually arise early, he judged from the stillness in the house that no one else was yet astir. He heard the detective go upstairs and close his door behind him. In the quiet of morning in the country, the least sound is heard afar off. He wondered how it was that Burrows had been in the hall so early, and why he had returned to his bed-room, but there was no way of having his thoughts answered. He stood near the fireplace for a long time with one elbow on the mantel, his head on his hand, gazing upon the spot where the corpse had been found, as though fascinated. There are some who avoid the presence of the dead, or places where the dead have been. These would strenuously deny the possibility that spirits of the departed return to earth, yet in their secret hearts they admit that it might be. They scoff at ghosts, yet avoid a chance of meeting one. There are others who would no more enjoy such an encounter, but who, having speculated little as to the possibilities, or probabilities, yet, in an undefinable half conscious way, wonder whether such things can be. These are attracted to the scenes of deaths, and especially of homicides. For, if any ghost shall have the desire to return, would it not be the grim spectre of one who has been forcibly ejected from his earthly shell? Might not his unfinished career contain some incompleted purpose, so strongly impressed upon the soul, that he would try to get back into communication with someone , whom he might inspire to do his bidding, so that he, poor ghost, might continue upon his long journey, lighter hearted? Or, in a case of murder, might it not be that the keen following of a scent by the quick mind of a shrewd detective, results from the whisperings of the spirit of the deceased which hovers about the scene, till justice be done? If this be a possibility, would it not be a probability that such would be the case, where suspicion had fallen upon some beloved one? For whether she, if a woman were suspected, were even truly guilty, might not a kindly, loving ghost, be willing to save her from vengeance even though some other, perhaps his enemy, would suffer in her place?

However this may be, the fact remains that though we may speculate, and speculate, we know nothing. And, knowing nothing, we speculate. Thus it was not strange, that in that room, and on that spot, Lewis should allow his thoughts to wander afar off, so far indeed that we need not follow him. But whilst he stood there blind and deaf, as the abstracted always are, though their eyes and ears may be in perfect order for the reception of impressions, there entered one whom he neither saw nor heard. I use this pronoun although I am alluding to the great mastiff, for it was the dog who stalked silently into the room. I believe that religionists, in their egotism, have selfishly appropriated all the souls in creation, and bestowed them upon the king of all animals, man. To my mind there is something inherently wrong about this dogma. I have met too many good dogs, and too many bad men, to easily believe that man alone is immortal. For surely if there be any immortality at all, the good in the world must share it. So I think the good in the dog is more worthy of perpetuity, than the evil that resides in man.

The mastiff, having entered the room, went close to where Lewis stood, and after sniffing at his legs a moment, gently licked the hand which hung down, reaching it without an effort, so tall was he.

Lewis must have indeed been lost in thought, for he heeded not the "good-morning" of the brute. His salutation unnoticed, the mastiff dropped upon his haunches, and so sat staring up into the face of the man as though to ask wherefore he was not observed. There is the picture! The man leaning against the mantel, present in the body, but absent in mind or spirit, and the dog sitting, patiently waiting for the return of consciousness in the man, so that he might be recognized. As he continued to stare up at Lewis, who will say, that, dog though he was, he would not be able to note the first expression on the face, which would show that the man's mind had returned from its pursuit of the unknowable? The position remained unchanged for many minutes, till at last the dog must have concluded that he deserved more than was accorded to him. He raised one of his huge paws and placed it upon the man's leg, repeating the action, as though intentionally touching him to attract his attention. Still failing, he reached a little higher, and let his paw rest on Lewis's hand.

This aroused Lewis and even before he fully recovered from his revery he closed his fingers upon the proffered paw, grasping it tightly. He looked down, but as he met the mastiff's eyes, they were turned away. What is there about a dog which causes him to do this? He will stare at you by the hour, but, look at him, and he turns away as though caught in an act of which he is ashamed. Is it a recognition of the superiority of man, and does he instinctively feel that it is a liberty for him so to stare, even though the proverb allows the cat to gaze upon majesty?

Lewis stooped and patted the huge head, and the dog turned his mouth up, so that he could lick the hand which caressed him.

"Poor dumb brute," said Lewis, aloud," I wonder if you know that I am in trouble, and are offering your sympathy?" He leaned farther forward, and the dog licked him in the face.

"You seem to be fond of dogs!"

Lewis looked up quickly, releasing the dog's paw, and saw that it was Virginia who had spoken.

"Yes," he replied, "I am devoted to the species. I feel quite complimented at the favors shown to me by this one. He does not look like a dog who would make friends with every one, and it is said that these intelligent brutes instinctively avoid the evil disposed."

"You are the first man of whom Savage ever made a friend at sight," replied Virginia. "I think that his name is a good exponent of his nature. There are few about this neighborhood who do not fear him. I wonder if what you say is true? I mean, that a dog can do what a man cannot—read character, and distinguish between the good and the bad?"

"I cannot be certain, of course, but I think so. It is all speculation, though there are stories in substantiation of that theory. However that may be, I am glad that Savage is friendly with me, since I am to be your guest. It would be very awkward otherwise. I should fear to leave my room at night."

"You must not call yourself my guest," said Virginia, in friendly tones. "Despite what the detectives, or others, may have told you of my recent unpleasantness with my uncle, I loved him dearly. As you are his son, I look upon you as his rightful heir, regardless of what the Squire tells me are the provisions of the will. You must consider yourself entirely at home."

"You are very kind to the prodigal." He paused a moment. "You said just now that you dearly loved my father." His voice trembled a little, and he stopped, to regain control of himself. "I am glad to have you say that. I am glad that someone loved him." Again he was obliged to pause. "You see I forsook him, and he must have been a very lonely man had you not given him your affections. Now that I have come back, in face of the dreadful calamity that has befallen us, your kind words lead me to hope that—that you will give me your good opinion and, your good will, now, and that later we may grow to be firm friends, and, perhaps, affectionate cousins. Am I—am I too bold?"

"I told you the truth when I said that I loved my father—for he was a father to me. How could I help loving him? He was so good to me." She was not answering his question directly, and as she said the last words she choked back a sob, and turned her head away to hide her emotion. For this reason she did not see an involuntary movement towards her which Lewis made. He stretched forth his arms, as though he would infold her with them by way of sympathy. Almost as quickly as he had been moved, he checked himself and seemed calm when she looked at him again. "Do you know," said she, "your voice is very like your father's? And you are like him, too." Then after a moment, offering him her hand impulsively. "Yes, I think I can promise that we shall be friends." Lewis took the proffered hand and held it without saying anything. Virginia immediately withdrew it, not resentfully, but yet firmly. Her emotions, aroused by the subject which they had discussed, had betrayed her into more demonstrativeness than was her custom. Now, she returned to her usual mood, and said a little more coldly, "Come, we will have breakfast. I came in to call you." Lewis sighed as he followed her. The mastiff had sprawled off on the rug, lying on his side, his long legs outstretched, and appeared to be asleep. But as soon as the two left the room he jumped up and went after them.

It was about noon when Dr. Snow arrived, and by this time Burrows had arisen. Meeting the doctor, he asked if he had come prepared to make the *postmortem* examination, to which he received a reply in the affirmative.

"Will you go up to the room at once? May I accompany you?"

"Yes," said the doctor, "I meant to come earlier, for I am anxious to make this examination as soon as possible, but I had to make a call on a very ill patient some miles away. As to your being present, it is what I wished. It is always best that more than one should witness such an investigation, in case anything of an unexpected nature should be discovered."

"Very well, let us go at once, for you cannot be more anxious than myself to begin. In fact, there is another reason why I would like to see the inside of the room."

"What is it?" asked the doctor, with some curiosity.

"Well, the fact is," said Burrows, "last night I thought I heard someone in the room, and also that a chair, or other piece of furniture, was overturned. I am curious to see if we find any corroboration of it in the appearance of the place."

"I doubt very much that we shall, for I have the key in my pocket, and so you see no one could have gained entrance."

The two men then proceeded to the apartment where lay the dead body. The doctor unlocked the door, allowing the detective to enter ahead of him. Burrows gazed eagerly around, but nothing seemed to indicate that anyone had been in the place since it had been closed, the day before.

"You see," said the doctor, "nothing has been disturbed. I am afraid your imagination played some trick upon you."

Opening a satchel which he had brought with him, Dr. Snow produced his instruments, and immediately began his. work. First he stripped the body, and found a considerable quantity of blood clotted about the parti.', which with a sponge he carefully cleansed. He had scarcely done so, when Burrows, who had been following his actions with eager interest, excitedly exclaimed:

"Look, doctor, there seem to be two wounds!"

"As you say, so it seems," said Dr. Snow, phlegmatically; "but before we make a positive assertion, let us examine further." With these words he took up his probe. Passing it into one wound he worked in silence for some time, Burrows endeavoring to command his impatience. Finally he removed the instrument and inserted it into the second opening. With a little manipulation it passed superficially through the flesh, and then emerged again about six inches from the entrance, and towards the back. At length the doctor spoke:

"I think," said he, "that you are correct in your surmise, and that two bullets have entered here. One I can feel with my probe, the other passed out, as you see this second track indicates. Both wounds are close together."

"Will you extract the bullet?" asked Burrows.

"Of course—it will give us a needed clue as to the bore of the weapon used." Thereupon he continued, determined to complete the task before him. Whilst he was thus busily engaged, Burrows stood looking from the window, and was deep in thought over this last point in the evidence.

In the talk between him and Mr. Barnes, both had thought that but one bullet had found its mark in the dead body. Now it was incontestably proven that there were two wounds. How to explain that, in connection with what they had already discovered, was the problem, and his astute mind quickly evolved a theory to fit the case. It will be remembered that the pistols found on the lawn had each one empty shell, and as but one shell, had been picked up in Virginia's room, he concluded that that weapon also had been fired only once. The tracks in the snow seemed to indicate that Virginia had met Harry Lucas (whose name was on one of the pistols), and then left him to go to the woods. Suppose, then, that Lucas had fired his weapon at Lewis, and that the ball had struck at the point where it made but a flesh wound, and then had passed out? From this point Burrows reasoned as follows: "Lewis, finding himself wounded, had taken the precaution to write the name of his supposed assailant on the paper which Mr. Barnes thought that Virginia had taken from the table. He had then retired to his bed, as was evident from his being in his night-dress. Then the man, whom Virginia had met across the river, and who had unquestionably visited the house afterward, as was easily shown by his tracks, had entered, and fired the shot which proved fatal." As he reached this point in the case which he was constructing to fit the facts, he started with a new idea. "As Virginia had been cleaning a pistol, suppose that it was her own weapon, and that it was she who, having planned the deed with Lucas, had finished it when she returned home and found her uncle still alive? This seems more probable, because Lewis might have left his own room to tell her of his wound, when she came in, whereas the man would have sought him in his bedroom, and have killed him there." Two points occurred to him in connection with his theory, and he approached the table where the doctor was at work, and asked:

"Can you tell from what distance these shots were fired?"

"I have just been looking into that point. Of one thing I am convinced, and that is, that one was fired at very close range, for the cloth of the gown is blackened with powder."

"Which wound was that?"

"That is the curious part of it. There is but one hole in the gown, and there are two wounds. I cannot be sure which bullet passed through the garment, because the wounds are so close together."

This satisfied Burrows, and he came to his second point. If he could find the suit of clothes which the murdered man had on when the first shot struck him, and if he found a bullet-hole in the garments, it would bear out his theory that Lewis had received one bullet from without, and then had undressed, the second and fatal shot coming after.

Burrows was now anxious to search for the suit of clothes necessary to his theory of the crime, but was obliged to wait until Dr. Snow had concluded his investigation. This occupied some time, for he very carefully made notes of all the results. However, at last the doctor signified his readiness to dismiss the case for the day. The two men left the room together, Dr. Snow carefully locking the door and placing the key in his pocket. They passed down the stairs, and meeting no one they parted at the gate, the physician jumping into his wagon, and turning his horse's head homeward.

Left to himself, Burrows hastened to commence his search. First he satisfied himself that he was alone in the house, the others apparently having gone out. Feeling thus safe from danger of interruption, he unhesitatingly proceeded to the room which had been occupied by John Lewis. Here he found clothing in the closet, and in the drawer of a bureau. He examined everything most thoroughly, but was chagrined and disappointed by not finding what he sought. At length, however, he was compelled to admit that there was no sign of such evidence as he sought, and he commenced replacing things as he had found them.

Whilst thus occupied, he heard the door open behind him, and turning, saw Virginia.

"What are you doing?" said she. "Those are my uncle's things. Why are you disturbing them?"

Burrows flushed, as though detected in some dishonorable act, and though he felt that he had done but his duty, he would have been glad if Virginia had delayed her entrance by half an hour. However, he determined to tell the truth, and it even occurred to him that he might discover something by closely watching Virginia's face, as he disclosed his suspicions to her.

"Miss Lewis," said he, "I confess it may seem strange that I should be thus engaged, but as a detective, endeavoring to find the murderer of your uncle, I suppose you will admit that I may use all means to compass that end?"

"I am not sufficiently versed in the methods of the thief-taker to be a judge," replied Virginia, coldly. Burrows colored at the evidently intended slur, and with some asperity he answered:

"If I am a thief-taker, it is only the criminal who has need to fear my methods. The innocent can be in no danger—"

"You are egotistical! Beware that you do not make the innocent suffer for the guilty in this case!"

"Ah! You know who the guilty is, do you not? Tell me what it is that you know, and what you are concealing?" At these words Virginia drew herself up to the extreme height of her commanding figure, and with withering scorn, she replied:

"Mr. Burrows, you forget yourself! How dare you speak so to me." Burrows was about to reply, but before he could sufficiently control himself, she continued: "Enough of this. I am not here to aid you in capturing the criminal, but I want to know what you are doing among my uncle's clothing?"

By this time Burrows was determined to deal with her with entire disregard of her sex, remembering only that she was possessed of guilty knowledge, if nothing more. He watched her narrowly as he asked:

"Where are the clothes which your uncle wore when he was shot?"

The girl's countenance did not change, save that a slight, a very slight smile crossed her lips.

"It appears that my uncle was in his night-dress when he was killed, therefore your question is unintelligible," she replied.

"Your uncle was in his full dress when shot, and I am seeking the garments which he wore."

"Have you found them?" asked Virginia, still with her countenance under perfect control.

"No, I have not," admitted Burrows, a little disconcerted. Before he could continue, he was surprised to hear her say:

"Will you come in to dinner? I came to call my cousin, but he does not appear to be here." Without waiting for his answer she left the room.

Burrows was disconcerted at the readiness with which she had dismissed the whole topic. Could it be, he thought, that after all, she knew nothing? He could not bring himself to admit this, remembering her evident interest in keeping some secret of which she was possessed. "The deeper I get, the more complicated the whole thing seems to be," he muttered, as he followed his hostess to the dining room. At that moment he sincerely wished for the return of Mr. Barnes.

Nothing of any consequence occurred during the remainder of the day, and Burrows retired early to sleep that night. Once in bed, he could not help wondering whether there would be a repetition of the mysterious noises of the night before. His slumbers were undisturbed, and he awoke much refreshed the next morning. Immediately after breakfast he left the farm, and went to the saloon, where he and Mr. Barnes had stopped on their first arrival. Here he found, as he expected, that their trunks had been sent from New Market, and he was thus enabled to make a change of clothing, of which he felt sorely in need. This done, he proceeded to the Squire's house, to ascertain if anything had been heard from his superior.

He was ushered into a most comfortable parlor, and was shortly joined by the Squire himself, who entered with a dispatch in his hand.

"Good morning, Mr. Burrows," said he, advancing; "I presume you are anxious to know about Mr. Barnes. I have just received a message from him, sent from Portsmouth. He promises to be with us to-day. Do you know what called him to that city?"

"Not exactly, Squire, though I fancy I might guess. He left me, to find out the address on a certain letter, which he thought it of importance to have. I suppose he must have followed the letter to its destination, in order to come up with the party to whom it was written."

"And who may that be?" asked the Squire, with considerable curiosity.

"I cannot say certainly," replied Burrows, "but as the letter was written by Miss Lewis, I fancy it may be her lover, Walter Marvel. If this should prove to be the case, you will see how well Mr. Barnes foretold how he should find this man, when he said that he would only need to keep a watch on the movements of the lady."

"But does he, that is, does Mr. Barnes think that Marvel is connected with this case?" The Squire's voice quivered slightly. Evidently he was sorry to have this young man implicated.

"You will find, when you know Mr. Barnes better, that he is very slow to express any decided opinions in cases of this kind. In fact, it is commonly said among the men on the force, that, 'When Mr. Barnes accuses a man, he always proves him guilty.' Therefore, you see, it is impossible for me as yet to say just what he does think."

Before the conversation could be carried any further, there was a loud rap on the knocker of the front door, and the Squire himself hastened to open it, ushering in Mr. Barnes and Walter Marvel. Squire Olney was as one struck dumb, when he saw and recognized the latter. How quickly this shrewd detective had accomplished what had baffled the efforts of so many others! In just twenty-four hours he had apprehended the man whom he had come to find. Marvel was the first to speak.

"Good morning, Squire! You seem surprised to see me!"

"I am," rejoined the Squire, briefly.

"Mr. Barnes here has told me what I did not know. You have offered a reward for my capture?"

The Squire hastened to disavow any personal responsibility for that action, and continued: "I hope, Walter, you know that I am your friend? I have only done my duty."

"I understand perfectly, Squire. However, under the circumstances, and because of later occurrences, I accepted the advice of Mr. Barnes, and returned at once."

"Oh! Then you are not under arrest?" asked the Squire, anxiously. Walter changed color slightly, and Mr. Barnes hastened to relieve his embarrassment by saying:

"No, Squire, he came with me voluntarily. But now, if you can offer us any refreshments, we should be grateful. We walked from New Market, and it has sharpened our appetites, has it not, Mr. Marvel?"

Walter nodded assent, and Burrows, who was watching the scene with interest, was surprised at the apparent good-will which seemed to exist between them. The Squire at once led the way to the dining-room, and his wife soon spread a bountiful repast before them.

CHAPTER VIII
THE INQUEST

It was decided that the inquest should be continued that same afternoon. The Squire had notified the district attorney at Dover, to be present and assist, and he arrived during the morning. All of the jurymen and witnesses were therefore notified to be present at the Squire's house at two o'clock. This was at the suggestion of Mr. Barnes, who had a special reason for not going back to the farm. He did not wish Virginia to know that Marvel had been captured until after she had testified. To further this end, Marvel was instructed to remain in one of the upper rooms, and though he was not actually under arrest, he felt constrained to obey.

Mr. Barnes learned from Burrows of the strange noises that he had heard on his first night at the farm, but told his young assistant that he had probably been dreaming. When informed of the singular behavior of Sarah Carpenter, he thought that of sufficient importance to have her name added to the list of witnesses. Burrows told nothing of the information imparted by Josiah Skene.

Mr. Barnes then sought the district attorney, and was closeted with him for an hour, during which they arranged their plans for conducting the examination.

The inquest was to be held in a large room on the ground floor. It was well adapted for the purpose, because of the fact that the Squire had allowed it to be used as a school-room whilst the selectmen were having the regular school-house enlarged and remodelled. Thus there was a raised platform at one end, upon which the Squire and the witnesses could sit, whilst the rows of benches readily afforded seats for the jurymen and the spectators.

News of any importance travels rapidly in a small town like Lee, and before the time set for the inquest, quite a motley crowd of people had congregated about the Squire's grounds. There were men and women, farmers, workmen, and idlers, all more or less interested in the proceedings which were about to commence. And each had some theory, all his own, as to the identity of the guilty one. One man remembered a farm-hand who had been discharged by Lewis, and who had left the town, breathing vengeance. Another had met a suspicious looking tramp prowling about Riverside on the very day of the crime. Being reminded by a neighbor that he had spent all of Saturday and Sunday over in Dover, he was forced to admit that it might have been on Friday when he had met the tramp, but, nothing disconcerted, he continued to urge his opinion that that individual would yet be proven, to have a guilty connection with the affair. This proposition was ridiculed by another, for the simple fact that nothing had been stolen, would tend to exonerate a tramp, who could not possibly have any other motive but theft, and then he drew attention to the suspiciously close arrival of the man who claimed to be the son, and who would now come in for a share in the property. But yet another had only that morning heard that the entire property would go to the daughter, and so settled that theory. An old lady at this juncture mysteriously announced that the whole truth of the matter had been revealed to her in a vision, but just what it was she declined to state "till the proper time comes." So they argued and talked over the situation, till at length Mr. Tupper, the district attorney, appeared, walking with Mr. Barnes. All then knew that the investigation would at once begin, and forthwith pushed their way into the room which was to be the scene of the inquiry.

The proceedings began promptly. The Squire entered, followed by Mr. Tupperand the two detectives, and took a seat in a leather-covered chair, which had been brought from his library and "placed upon the stand, a similar one awaiting the witnesses. Mr. Tupper and Mr. Barnes took chairs at a small wooden table in front of the Squire, and Burrows went to a seat amongst the crowd. The jurymen were called, and, as they responded to their names, were directed to places on benches, placed laterally beside the stand, by the end nearest to the witness chair. It is worthy of remark, that though this was in a small, isolated country town, the composition of this jury was far above the average to be met with in large cities. Here, all were men of families, and identified with the interests of the community in which they lived. Each, as he sat, was the embodiment of earnestness and sincerity. Rough garbed though they were, they possessed shrewd minds and good common-sense, and therefore would make admirable jurors.

The preliminaries over, the examination was begun. Mr. Barnes was asked to take the stand, and he testified to the discovery of the crime, and the position and condition of the corpse as first seen by himself, when he accompanied the Squire to the house on Monday morning, and to other facts which have been already told.

The next witness was Dr. Snow. The Squire interrogated him.

"Dr. Snow," he asked, "have you prepared a report of the autopsy, made by you yesterday, upon the body of the deceased?"

"I made a thorough examination, and have notes of all that I discovered, which could, in my opinion, be of the least assistance."

"Very well! What then do you find to have been the cause of death?"

"The man was shot. The ball is of large size. I am not expert enough to give the exact calibre, but think it is a No. 32."

"Did you succeed in finding the ball?"

"Yes, here it is!" He passed it to the Squire who, in turn, handed it to Mr. Tupper.

"Dr. Snow," said the latter, "can you tell how long the deceased lived after the shooting?"

"I found the bullet lodged in the heart. Therefore death must have been instantaneous."

"Did you find any other marks of violence?"

"In addition to the wound which proved fatal, I found another, which was only superficial."

"Did you find that ball also?"

"No, it only passed a short distance through the body, and emerged again."

"Can you describe the direction which it took?"

"From the front towards the back."

"How was the body dressed?"

"In a night-dress, and it is a noticeable fact, that, though there are two wounds, there is but one hole through the garment."

"Did the fatal bullet pass through that hole?"

"It would seem that it did, but as the nightdress is a loosely fitting garment, it is impossible to say, as the two wounds are so close together."

Mr. Barnes whispered to Mr. Tupper, who then continued:

"Was this last wound above, or below, the other? What I wish to know is, was it high enough for the bullet to have come from a pistol fired from the lawn, and through the window?"

"Yes. I thought of that point, and therefore measured the height of the window-sill from the ground, and from the floor inside. I found by these measurements that the sill is about five feet from the lawn outside, and only two feet above the floor within. The wound which we are now considering is above the fatal one, though only slightly so, and is so located that, if the deceased had been standing, it would have been about four feet above the floor, and so two feet higher than the window-sill."

"Then, in your opinion, that wound may have been made by someone on the lawn?"

"I am sure that it would have been possible. Of course, it might depend on how near Mr. Lewis stood to the window."

As the doctor was about to withdraw, Mr. Tupper stopped him by asking:

"Will you please tell us if you found any marks, scars you know, or birth-marks, by which the identity of the corpse might be established?'

"Nothing whatever. The face and head have been burned beyond all possibility of recognition."

"Were these burns of such a nature that they may have been the cause of death?"

"I should say not, but of course if a man were burned as badly as that, he might subsequently die, though not so quickly."

Mr. Tupper, addressing the Squire, said:

"I suppose there is no doubt as to the identity of the body, but in the face of the fact that the features are so much disfigured, it would perhaps be as well to seek some evidence in this direction."

"I have no doubt," said the Squire, "that Miss Lewis may be able to help us better than anyone, though I will say this much myself. When I first saw the body lying by the chimney, and leaned over it, I noticed that there was a name on the night-dress in large letters."

"I saw that also," said Dr. Snow. "It is in indelible ink, and done with a stencil-plate. As might be expected, the name is 'John Lewis.'"

"That in itself seems almost conclusive," observed the Squire, "but we can ask Miss Lewis about the matter when she is called."

Dr. Snow was then allowed to leave the stand.

"Now," said Mr. Tupper, "if we can, we must try to discover the time of the crime. I believe, Squire, you are the one who last saw Mr. Lewis alive? Can you tell at what hour that was, as near as possible?"

"I went to see Mr. Lewis on the night of the murder, and was in the parlor with him nearly an hour. I must have left about eight o'clock, for it was but half-past when I reached my own home."

"Then of course he was alive at that hour. The detective, Mr. Barnes, has described to us the tracks which he found in the snow, and also the discovery of the two pistols. These, he thinks, were fired at the time when, or immediately after the snow had ceased falling last night. Whether either of these shots caused the death of Mr. Lewis, at least it is possible that one of them made the flesh wound which Dr. Snow has described. It will be well, therefore, to fix the time when the snowstorm ceased."

Jef Harrison was then called, and swore to the facts which he had related to Mr. Barnes, and added that he had again questioned his daughters, and that they substantiated the opinion which he had given.

The next person called was Sarah Carpenter. She came in from an adjoining room, as did all the witnesses, it having been considered important that one should not hear the testimony of the others, prior to being examined. Miss Carpenter sat down rather stiffly, and it was evident that she was a reluctant witness.

"You are a servant at Riverside farm?" asked Mr. Tupper.

"I assist Miss Lewis in taking care of the house, but I do not call myself a servant," was the reply. The lawyer had evidently gained her ill-will at the outset, but he took no notice of the asperity of her manner.

"Are there any servants at all?"

"I suppose so."

"How many?"

"I don't call any of them servants. There are four men who work on the farm, and a boy to do the chores."

"Do any of these sleep in the house?"

"No, they all sleep in a separate out-building."

"How far is that building from the main dwelling?"

"It is on the other side of the road altogether. Mr. Lewis bought the farm opposite his own, about two years ago, and, ever since, he has had the men sleep there."

"And where do you sleep?"

"In my own house," answered the girl with an indignant toss of her head, but her temper affected Mr. Tupper as little as though he had been made of stone. With perfect composure he continued:

"At what time do you leave Riverside for your own home?"

"When I feel inclined."

"Come," said Mr. Tupper with just a little sternness, "answer my question."

"I did answer it."

"Answer it again! What time do you leave the farm?"

"When I get through my work," she answered, sullenly.

"Ah! That is better! Now then tell us about what time that is, usually?"

"I can't tell. I have not kept track of it."

"Well, then, at what time did you start for home on Sunday evening?"

"Look here, what right have you to ask me all these questions?" Then quickly turning to the coroner she continued: "Squire, have I got to answer everything this man asks of me?"

"You must tell all that you know," replied the Squire.

"And what if I won't?"

"You would be guilty of contempt."

"And what of that?"

"I could have you confined in jail, and kept there until you be willing to answer the questions."

She pondered over this awhile, and then turning to Mr. Tupper again, said sharply:

"Tell me at once what it is you are trying to get out of me?"

"I want to know at what time the shot was fired that killed Mr. Lewis?"

"How should I know?"

"You would have heard the report if you had been in the house."

"And how do you know I was in the house?"

"That is what you must tell us."

"Well, then I was not in the house."

"If not in the house, where were you when the shot was fired?" But she was too shrewd to be caught in this trap, and replied:

"I did not say I heard the shot."

"You said you were not in the house when the shooting took place. How could you be sure of that unless you heard it from some other point?"

"You said I would have heard it if I had been in the house," replied the girl triumphantly, but Mr. Tupper quickly went on:

"Ah! Then you mean to say that you did not hear the report?"

"I don't mean to say anything of the kind," she retorted with similar rapidity. This was a trick of Mr. Tupper's, to get his witness excited, and then by rapid questioning to surprise her into such an admission as she had just made. The words were scarcely uttered before she saw their import, and she continued savagely: "You are making me say what I don't mean. Why don't you ask for what you want to know, without so much beating round the bush?"

"Well, then, come to the point. Did you hear the pistol shot on Sunday night?"

But the girl kept silent awhile, and then jumped off the stand and, dropping into a seat, burst into tears. Mr. Tupper and Mr. Barnes talked in low tones for several minutes, and then the former whispered to the Squire, who called to the stand the workmen alluded to by the last witness. The Squire himself questioned them, whilst the lawyer and detective consulted.

The witnesses appeared separately, but their testimony shed no light on the matter, as the four older men had spent the evening at the saloon, whilst the younger had retired to the house across the road, and had gone to sleep at seven o'clock on the evening in question, and he declared that he had heard nothing during the night. By this time Sarah Carpenter had recovered from her emotion, and was sitting quietly on the front bench. Will Everly was then called, and took the stand. As he did so, Sarah seemed much agitated, and with difficulty kept her composure. Mr. Barnes, who was watching her, noticed her discomfort, and smiled to himself as one conscious of being correct in some surmise. Mr. Tupper proceeded.

"Mr. Everly," said he, "I believe you are a friend of Mr. Walter Marvel?"

"I hope so, sir."

"You are under some obligation to him, I believe?"

"Yes, indeed! He saved my life."

"How was that?" In reply Everly related the incident in detail. Mr. Tupper continued:

"You consider, then, that you owe your life to this young man?"

"I do, most emphatically. I should hesitate at nothing to do him a service."

"I have heard that you have repeatedly said that you would risk your life for him. Is that true?"

"It is! Did he not risk his life for me?"

All through the above, Burrows, who was watching Mr. Barnes, was surprised to notice that Mr. Barnes was keenly scrutinizing the girl Sarah Carpenter, who was in evident distress, and he at length suspected that this examination of Everly was really, in some way, aimed at the young woman. Mr. Tupper continued:

"Were you present when Marvel quarrelled with the deceased?"

"He did not quarrel with Mr. Lewis," answered Everly with some heat, "he simply did what any man would. He resented a gross insult!"

"I think he fired at Mr. Lewis, did he not?"

Everly was a little confused as he replied:

"He was very much excited and took out his pistol. I don't think he would really have fired it, but Miss Lewis struck his arm, and the weapon was discharged. I think it was an accident."

"But did he not utter threats against Mr. Lewis, as he went away?"

"He only said what was natural under the circumstances: that he would get even. But I know Walter, and I doubt if he remembered what he had said, as long as the next day."

"Mr. Everly," said the lawyer impressively, "it is very worthy of you to defend your friend, but be careful lest in doing so, you damage your own cause."

And Burrows saw Sarah Carpenter shrink closer into the corner, vainly endeavoring to appear unconcerned.

"Why, what do you mean?" asked Everly.

"I will be candid with you. You have just admitted that you would imperil your life to serve your friend. You knew, after the quarrel between these men, that John Lewis would ever be a barrier to keep Marvel from marrying the woman of his choice. Do you see your position now?"

"Not clearly! Go on!" said the witness hoarsely.

"Unless you can prove that you were not at Riverside that night, it might be thought, I say it might be, that you committed this crime."

Everly hung his head as he replied: "I was at the farm." This statement was followed by a suppressed cry from the corner where Sarah Carpenter was sitting. All those present looked grave, for the words, as Everly spoke them, sounded almost like a confession of guilt. Mr. Barnes alone seemed not to be surprised.

"What were you doing at the farm?" asked Mr. Tupper, resuming the examination.

"I went there to see Miss Carpenter." He blushed deeply.

"Are you in love with that lady?" The women present thought this a merciless question, but though the color deepened on his cheek, Everly straightened himself up as he replied:

"Miss Carpenter has promised to be my wife." This caused quite a sensation. It was tolerably well known that they were fond of each other's society, but every one had considered it a "boy and girl" affair, as the two had grown up together and had been schoolmates.

"How long were you at the farm, that night?" continued the lawyer.

"From six until half-past eight."

"You left at that hour?"

"Yes."

"Before you did so, did you meet Mr. Lewis?" Everly hesitated a moment, then replied:

"I think I would rather not answer that question."

"As you choose. You need not criminate yourself. When you left Riverside, where did you go?"

"I went straight to the saloon."

"Do you know at what time you reached there?"

"At a quarter to nine. I had an appointment with a friend at that hour, and just kept it."

"Was your friend punctual also?"

"He was waiting for me. That is how I fix the time so accurately. He claimed that I was late, and we compared watches."

"Could you prove this by your friend?"

"He lives near here. You can send for him, if you wish. It is Mr. Harrison's son, Joe."

Mr. Tupper requested the Squire to send for this man at once, and a messenger was despatched for him. Mr. Tupper continued:

"Do you own a pistol?"

"Yes, sir."

"Can you send for it?"

"I have it with me." Taking it from his pocket he handed it to the lawyer, who examined it closely and then said:

"I see that one barrel has been fired off. Did you discharge it?"

"I did."

"When?"

"I prefer not to say."

"What is the calibre of this weapon?"

"It carries a No. 32 cartridge."

"Did you ever see the weapon which Mr. Marvel had, on the night of the trouble at the farm?"

"Yes, sir."

"What kind of pistol is it?"

"It is of the same pattern as this. There are five, to my knowledge, in Lee."

"Can you tell us who the owners of these weapons are, and how it happens that they are all alike?"

"Besides mine, there are four, owned, respectively, by Walter, Harry Lucas, Miss Marvel, and Miss Lewis. Each has the owner's name engraved on the stock. About two years ago, the ladies expressed a desire to learn to shoot, and Harry Lucas bought the pistols. The four would frequently meet, and practise at targets. As to mine, I saw Walter's, took a fancy to it, and got one."

"I suppose you all are fairly good shots?"

"All are experts."

At this moment the young man, who had been sent for, arrived, and Everly was allowed to leave the stand. The newcomer took his place and Mr. Tupper questioned him.

"What is your name?"

"Joseph Harrison, commonly called Joe."

"Do you remember where you were last Sunday night?"

The witness hesitated and glanced towards Everly. To reassure him, the lawyer said:

"It is all right, you need not hesitate to speak. It was at Mr. Everly's request that you were called." At this he seemed much relieved.

"Oh! Very well! I met Everly by appointment at the saloon."

"At what time did he reach there?"

"At a quarter to nine by his watch, but ten minutes to nine by mine. We compared watches."

"Was there any special object in this meeting?"

Again did Harrison let his eyes wander towards Everly, but the latter held his head bowed on his breast, and gave no answering sign. The question was repeated and the witness answered:

"Yes, sir; he wanted me to take a letter for him."

"Did he have it already written when he entered the saloon?"

"No, sir; he wrote it after I met him."

"Where did you take this letter?"

"To Epping."

"Why could he not have sent it by mail?"

"Well, you see, I don't suppose as how it makes any difference, now that Mr. Lewis is dead. But at that time, they were tryin' to find Walter Marvel and Will was afraid, if he sent a letter by the post, he might be puttin' the authorities on the right track."

"This letter then was addressed to Walter Marvel?"

"Yes, sir."

"Did you deliver it to him that night?"

"No, not till next mornin'. I put up at the hotel, and then hunted him up in the mornin'."

"Where did you find him?"

"His mother owns an old house down there. It is out of repair and an't been used for years. But Walter keeps one room fixed up, so's when he goes huntin' he can stop over night, and it was there I found him."

"Did Mr. Marvel read the letter before you, and did he make any remark?"

"Yes, and he said: 'Will is a good friend and has done more for me than many would.'"

At this point Sarah Carpenter caused considerable excitement by jumping up and exclaiming:

"You are all going on the wrong track! Let me go on the stand again, and I will prove it." Mr. Barnes smiled quietly, and Burrows knew from the expression of his face, that this was just what he had been counting upon. Her request being granted, the girl did not wait for the formality of questions, but spoke rapidly:

"I am sorry now that I did not tell all I knew, awhile ago. I did hear the report of a pistol, yes, and more than one. I did not tell before, because I was afraid it was Will who had done the shooting. But now I know it was not. He left me at half-past eight o'clock to keep his appointment, and I went into the house to get my things on. We had been up at the barn. When I was ready to start for home, I found that I had lost my key. Thinking I must have dropped it in the barn, I went there to look for it. Whilst there, and fully half-an-hour after Will had left me, I suddenly heard the report of a pistol, and then another, and I think a third, though I can't be sure. I know though, that I ran to the door of the barn, and saw a man run across the lawn and down the road. I don't know why, but it struck me it was Will at the time, and that is why I have been so troubled ever since. But now I know differently, for, thank God, he has proved that he went straight to the saloon. You suggested to him that he might have committed this crime to serve his friend, but none of you see that though he is innocent of having risked his life in that way, he is ready to risk it now, by letting it seem that he is guilty, that no suspicion may attach to Walter Marvel. My God, are you all blind?"

CHAPTER IX
INTERESTING TESTIMONY

During the delivery of the statement made by Sarah Carpenter, there was the stillness of death. Her words caused a profound sensation, and even after she ceased, no one spoke, but eagerly waited to hear what those in charge of the investigation would have to say. The Squire at length addressed the witness:

"You say it was about half-an-hour after you had parted from Everly, when you heard the shots fired?"

"Yes, sir," said the girl, eagerly. "I am certain it was as long as that, for I went to the house to get my things, as I said, and when

I found that I did not have my key, I looked all about the room first, and it was some time before I concluded to search in the barn. When I did, I had to get a lantern, and it was quite a long time after I got to the barn before I heard the shooting."

"Then, provided your estimate of the time which elapsed is correct, it must have been about nine o'clock when this occurred?"

"I am sure of it. I left just after and went home, and it was a quarter past nine when I wound my watch, before going to bed."

"Miss Carpenter," said Mr. Tupper, "how is it that, if you suspected your friend Mr. Everly, you did not go to him and ask him about this matter?"

"I came over here yesterday for that purpose, but Will had gone to New Market."

"Was it snowing when you left the farm on Sunday night?"

"No, sir; it had stopped."

She was then allowed to retire, and Mr. Tupper called attention to the fact that her evidence had corroborated the detective's theory as to the time of the shooting.

The next witness called was Harry Lucas.

"Mr. Lucas," asked the Squire, "do you recall the day on which Miss Lewis celebrated her birthday at Riverside?"

"Certainly! I was there," answered Lucas.

"Do you recollect the trouble between Mr. Lewis and Marvel?"

"Yes, sir; perfectly."

"When Marvel was leaving, did he utter any threat against Mr. Lewis?"

"He said some angry words. I should not care to state positively what they were. I was too much excited myself at the time."

"Do you recall what you yourself said to Mr. Lewis?"

"Not exactly, sir."

"Did you not threaten him?"

"I don't recollect—I may have—I was very angry and quite excited."

"You have heard of the death of Mr. Lewis, I suppose?"

"I have, sir."

"Were you in Lee on the night of the murder?"

"I was."

"Did you tell anyone that you intended leaving town that night?"

Lucas remained silent.

"I have been told by several parties, that you were heard to say that important business would call you out of town. Was that true?"

"I did tell several people that, but it was not true."

"I am to understand then that you told a lie?"

Lucas colored deeply. "I did not look upon it in that way. I had good reasons for wishing people to think me out of town, and, under the circumstances, did not hesitate to speak as I did."

"Will you tell me what those circumstances were, which would make you think it excusable to resort to a falsehood?"

"I would rather not."

The Squire nodded to Mr. Tupper, who took the witness.

"Mr. Lucas," said he, "was it not because you intended to visit Riverside farm, that you spread the story of your absence?"

Lucas made no reply.

"Did you not go to Riverside that night to meet a lady?" Mr. Tupper spoke slowly, and Lucas started and looked confused, but still persisted in his silence. The lawyer continued:

"Did you not meet a lady in the summer-house, and was not that lady Miss Lewis?"

"How did you know that?" blurted out the witness, at last aroused to speech, and evidently amazed. Mr. Barnes smiled slightly.

"How I know is of small consequence," said Mr. Tupper, "but I will tell you. The detective has been all over the place, and as fortunately there was snow on the ground, the imprints of your feet left no room for doubt that there was a meeting between a man and a woman in that summer-house. All that was left was to discover their identity."

"And how have you done that, that is, if you have done so?"

"Do you deny that you and Miss Lewis met at that place, and on that night?"

"I neither deny, nor admit it."

"Perhaps you will later. You say you were in Lee. If not at the farm, where were you?"

"I was out for a time, and then went home."

"Mr. Lucas, did you hurt yourself that night?"

"I believe not. How do you mean hurt myself?"

"Did any accident happen to you?"

"I don't recall any."

Mr. Tupper stooped and picked up a small paper covered parcel, which he unrolled, and taking therefrom a man's white shirt, handed it to Lucas and asked:

"Do you recognize that as your property?"

"I can't be sure," faltered Lucas.

"It has your name on it," suggested the lawyer.

"Where did you get it?"

"Never mind that, just tell us if it is yours."

"It looks like one of mine."

"Exactly. Now, if you please, how did you get the blood on the wristband?"

Lucas examined the garment more closely, and seemed a little nervous as he saw the blood mark.

"I don't know how it got there," said he, and then with some anger, added: "I won't answer another question, till you tell me how you came in possession of this shirt."

"It was sent to your washer-woman on the day following the murder, and as she had heard of the crime she kept the blood-stained garment."

"Do you mean to say that you accuse me of killing Mr. Lewis?"

"I accuse no one, but I will remind you that it is the duty of every honest man to help, and not to hinder the machinery of justice. If you are an innocent man, you should not hesitate to reply to my questions. That we may have no more evasion, I will tell you at once that I know how the blood got on your shirt."

"How should you know, when I tell you I do not know myself?" asked Lucas, incredulously.

"The blood is your own. You were bitten by a dog!" continued the lawyer. Lucas started in surprise. "You went to Riverside and you were attacked by the mastiff."

"You seem well informed!"

"I only state what is a fact." Then suddenly producing the pistol, "do you recognize this weapon?"

At last the young man showed signs of distress, as he replied more humbly, "Yes, sir, it is mine."

"It was found at the farm near the summer-house. Will you admit now that you were there?" Lucas made one last effort:

"I may have dropped it there at any time—"

"In which case," interrupted Mr. Tupper, "it would have been covered by the snow." Lucas now seemed to recognize that further attempt at concealment would be useless, and Burrows even thought that he seemed relieved, as though, in fact, he had been previously playing a part which little pleased him.

"You have the best of me," he replied. "Go on! I will answer your questions."

"Very well. You admit, then, that you went to the farm to meet Miss Lewis, and that you did see her?"

"Yes, sir."

"At what hour was your appointment with the lady?"

"A quarter to nine."

"Miss Lewis left you at the summer-house, and went towards the river, did she not?"

"How do you know that?" Lucas was plainly very much surprised at the knowledge displayed by the district attorney, who of course had previously been posted by Mr. Barnes.

"Footprints," said Mr. Tupper, tersely.

"Oh, well! You are right."

"When did the dog attack you?"

"As soon as Miss Lewis left me I started for home, and the brute came for me."

"Did he bite you?"

"Yes, sir, on the arm"; drawing up his sleeve, he showed that his arm was bandaged.

"Ah! Then that accounts for the blood on the shirt, as I supposed. Now then, Mr. Lucas, there is another matter. This pistol of yours has an empty shell in it. How do you account for that?"

"I used the pistol to defend myself against the dog, but he was too quick for me, and before I could aim at him he had buried his teeth in my arm. The weapon was then discharged."

"You are sure," said Mr. Tupper, speaking with great deliberateness and looking Lucas straight in the eyes, "you are sure that you did not fire this pistol first, and that the noise did not attract the dog, and make him attack you?"

"What should I have fired at?" asked the witness.

"Mr. Lewis, perhaps," continued Mr. Tupper, in the same measured tones. Lucas seemed about to make an angry retort, but controlled himself and answered:

"The whole thing occurred as I have related it. As soon as the dog opened his jaws again I ran for my life, and, as I did so, I thought I heard two shots in quick succession."

As this seemed to corroborate the story told by Sarah Carpenter, Mr. Tupper paused in his inquiries, and the Squire asked:

"Did you see who fired these shots?"

"No, sir, I did not think of looking around. I was too intent on getting away."

"Can you say about what time this shooting occurred?"

"I met Miss Lewis at a quarter to nine, and we talked till about nine, I should say. It was a few minutes after, when I started to leave."

Mr. Tupper resumed the examination.

"Can you tell me who it was that Miss Lewis went to meet on the other side of the river?"

"Did she cross the river?"

"Her footprints were found over there, and also those of a man. Now, you must know who that man is?"

"I don't see how that follows."

"Why did Miss Lewis have you meet her at so late an hour?"

"I do not think that this is my secret. I would prefer to have you ask the lady herself."

"I think we may do that, Mr. Tupper," said the Squire.

"Yes, yes, Squire, that will do quite as well," replied Mr. Tupper, and, with a nod, the Squire dismissed the witness. He then called for Miss Marvel. The young lady appeared and plainly showed that she was very nervous over the prospect of testifying.

"Now, Miss Marvel," began Mr. Tupper, "we are sorry to trouble you in this matter, but it is so very serious, that we are compelled to examine every one who, by any possibility, may be able to throw any light on the terrible crime."

"How should I be able to do so?" asked Miss Marvel, already alarmed.

"We do not know that you can," replied Mr. Tupper, hastening to reassure her. It was plainly evident that if anything was to be learned from this witness it would be by dint of the greatest care. "But," continued he, "if you do know anything we feel certain that you would not hesitate to inform us at once."

"But I tell you I do not know anything about it, except what I have heard."

"Perhaps even that may prove valuable. But stop a minute," for she was about to interrupt him, "let me ask the questions, and you answer. That will be the quickest way of proceeding. To begin, then, when did you first know of the murder?"

"Monday morning. Virgie came and told me."

"You are sure you did not know of it sooner?"

"Virgie found me in bed, so how could I hear of it sooner?"

"I said 'know,' not 'hear.'"

"Well, know then, it is all the same."

"Were you at home on Sunday night?"

"Why—why—of course—where else should I be?" stammered the girl.

"You told my daughter that you were going to drive with Mr. Lucas," interrupted the Squire, in his kindliest tones.

"Mr. Lucas could not keep the appointment."

"Do you know why?" asked Mr. Tupper.

"I suppose he had some business. In fact he told me so."

"Did he say that it was out of town?" The girl started with surprise.

"Yes, sir; how did you know?"

"He told the same thing to others. Do you know why he should have told so many people that he was going out of town, and then not have gone?" Alice in great perturbation looked appealingly towards Lucas, but the latter avoided her glance. Very hesitatingly she answered:

"Mr. Lucas could tell you better than I." Her equivocal reply made Mr. Barnes conclude that she knew the reason, which, it will be remembered, Lucas had refused to give, and he gave the lawyer a sign to press the point.

"The question has been asked Mr. Lucas, but we want to hear what you know about the matter. Have you seen him since Sunday, when he told you that he meant to leave town?"

"That is the last time he called."

"But have you seen him?" Alice was evidently troubled by the question, and the lawyer determined to come to the main point at once. He continued:

"After he left you on Sunday, where did you go?"

"I did not go anywhere," stammered the poor girl.

"Come, you will best serve yourself and your friends by telling the truth."

"The truth! Why, what do you mean?" She seemed greatly agitated, if not positively alarmed.

"After he left you," continued Mr. Tupper, "you went to Riverside farm. You went there not to see your friend Miss Lewis, but—"

"How do you know I did not go to see Virgie?" interrupted Alice excitedly.

"You did not go to see her, because you had discovered that there was to be a meeting between her and Harry Lucas."

"It is false—how can you say such a thing!"

"You went into the summer-house and hid there, so that you might overhear what passed between the two."

"It's all a lie—a wicked lie!" cried the girl, hysterically sobbing between the words. "I did not go near the farm, and I did not go after Harry— and—it's all made up—and—" here she broke down utterly, sobbing so that it was necessary to delay the proceedings till she could recover from her agitation. Lucas, much disturbed, arose and addressed the coroner:

"Squire, is it necessary to continue the examination of Miss Marvel?"

"If it could have been avoided I should not have called her."

"But can you not let it drop now, since you see that she knows nothing?"

"She knows what passed between you and Miss Lewis in the summer-house," said the Squire, sharply. "If I cease questioning her, will you give us the information which we want?"

"It is impossible," said Lucas, despondently, "and I doubt that Miss Marvel knows anything about it."

"We will let her answer that question; she seems to be recovering her self-possession." Lucas reluctantly returned to his seat. As soon as Alice had sufficiently regained her composure, Mr. Tupper resumed:

"Now, Miss Marvel, you see that prevarication is useless. We are fully informed as to your movements on the night in question. What we want you to tell us is, what passed between Miss Lewis and Mr. Lucas?" A great weight seemed lifted from Alice's mind, and she replied quite readily:

"Oh! If that is all I'll tell you the whole thing." Lucas barely suppressed a groan. "Before I go any further I must tell how I came to be at the farm. Mr. Lucas came to me on Sunday, and told me that he could not go driving, as we had planned, because he had to go out of town. Of course I believed him and was satisfied. After he had gone, I found a note on the floor, and, picking it up, knew that Mr. Lucas must have dropped it from his pocket, for it was addressed to him. I should never have thought of reading it, but I recognized the writing and knew it came from Virgie, so I read it at once."

Lucas started in surprise but did not speak. Alice continued:

"When I saw by the contents of the note that Virgie invited Mr. Lucas to meet her at night in the summer-house, I determined to be there also. I did so because—" Here she seemed a little confused and her rich blood mantled her cheek. "Well, because Virgie is engaged to my brother, and for the minute I could not understand why she made an appointment with another man." Most of those present smiled at the girl's *naive* explanation. "I reached there first and hid in one side of the appointed place. Not long after, they came. I heard nearly all that passed."

"Tell us please as much as you can remember?"

"They talked quite a while, and then she left. What they said was all about my brother. It seems that he had written to Virgie, in the care of some friend, and asked her to meet him that night down by the river, and tell him whether she would marry him. He said that would be the only way he could come back, after what Mr. Lewis had done. Just at this point the dog commenced to bark, and they spoke lower, perhaps because they thought the dog had heard their voices, and they were afraid to attract attention. And in fact, after a minute, the brute did stop his noise, but it was hard for me to hear the rest of the talk. At any rate I made out that Virgie was afraid that Walter would be angry if she did not go away with him at once, and that, she said, was out of the question. She asked Mr. Lucas to meet my brother after she had seen him, so as to prevent him from doing anything desperate."

"What did you understand her to mean by 'desperate'?"

"I think she was afraid he might commit suicide."

"It did not occur to you that she might be afraid he would kill her uncle?"

"No! Of course not!" Once more she seemed excited. "You surely do not think—my God! What have I been saying?"

"Come, come, Miss Marvel, there is no need to be worried. No one accuses your brother. Let us come to another point. Whilst you were at the farm, did you hear any pistol shots?"

She looked at him and trembled violently, but uttered not a word. The lawyer then produced the weapon with her name on it.

"Is this yours?" he asked.

Alice covered her face with her hands and groaned.

"Miss Marvel," said Mr. Tupper, after a few moments' pause, "pray calm yourself. A great deal depends upon your testimony. A man is in danger of being accused of this great crime, unless you can throw some light on the subject, which will corroborate his statements." She seemed dazed, as she asked almost in a whisper:

"Who is he?"

"We found a pistol, with one chamber empty, lying near the summer-house." She shivered. "That pistol bears the name of Harry Lucas."

"Is he the man whom you accuse?"

"It will depend on your evidence, whether we do, or not. His pistol is empty, and he admits having fired it there that night—"

The girl made a superhuman effort and spoke rapidly:

"And you think that he killed Mr. Lewis? It is not true! I know to the contrary, for I saw Mr. Lewis alive when Harry was running from the place."

"Ah! Now, are you willing to tell us how that happened?"

She hesitated a moment, but she had gone too far to stop, and besides, her fear for her lover spurred her on.

"I was still in the summer-house when I heard the growl of the dog. I looked out, and saw the beast attack Mr. Lucas. I heard the pistol fired, and also the sound of breaking glass. I guessed that he had tried to kill the dog, and his bullet must have entered the house through the window. But it did not strike Mr. Lewis. Of that I am positive, for, as I stepped to the door to see what was going on, I distinctly saw Mr. Lewis push up the sash and look out. What is more, he raised a pistol and fired at Mr. Lucas, who was running away from the dog."

"Did you actually see Mr. Lucas fire his pistol?"

"No, I was then in the summer-house."

"Then, although you saw Mr. Lewis come to the window, it is possible that Mr. Lucas may have fired at the deceased instead of at the dog, which latter is only a guess on your part?"

"I tell you Harry is innocent! I know that he is!"

"How can you know it?"

"Because, when I saw the coward fire at a man who was already fighting with a dog, I shot him myself!"

Then, overcome by the strain upon her nerves, Alice swayed, and fell forward in a swoon.

CHAPTER X
VIRGINIA LEWIS TESTIFIES

When Alice made the statement that she had shot Mr. Lewis, all present, for a moment, sat dumb with amazement. When they saw that she had fainted, all were immediately possessed by the desire to minister to her wants; the result being, as is usual in such cases, that the prostrate form of the young woman was surrounded and she was deprived of all chance of fresh air. Fortunately, Dr. Snow was present, and calling upon Lucas to assist him, together they bore her from the room, permitting only a couple of women to follow them.

The Squire, utterly confounded at the unexpected turn of events, scarcely knew what to do next, and in order to gain time, declared a recess of ten minutes. The jurymen started to leave their seats, but the Squire requested that they would not do so, and that they would not converse about the case with the other persons present. The crowd fell to discussing the situation and a hum of voices filled the room.

Mr. Barnes and Mr. Tupper arose, and went on the stand with the Squire.

"Well, gentlemen," said the Squire, "this is a surprising affair. What shall we do now?"

"Mr. Barnes," said the lawyer, "you are more conversant with the case. What is your opinion of Miss Marvel's statement?"

"Gentlemen," said Mr. Barnes, "it is evident that Miss Marvel really believes that she killed Mr. Lewis. It is plain to my mind, however, that we should be most careful in accepting such a theory. In the first place, I would call attention to the evidence offered by Dr. Snow. He tells us that he found two wounds, one having passed through the night-dress, and the other not. This simple fact proves beyond doubt that the deceased changed his clothing, after receiving the first wound. Therefore, it is manifestly clear that the shot which Miss Marvel admits she fired at him could not have proven fatal, for, if so, we would be obliged to believe that the other wound was made by the bullet from the pistol of Lucas, in order to account for their being two wounds; but these shots followed in such close succession, that there was not time for him to have effected the change of clothing. There is, however, a bare possibility that he had already received the first wound, and was in bed, when, attracted by the dog, he arose and went to the window. In that case, he might have been killed by the ball from Miss Marvel's weapon. Thus far, however, we have no evidence that would substantiate a suspicion of this kind. Miss Carpenter and Mr. Everly would have heard the report, if a shot had been fired earlier. Miss Carpenter heard shots at nine o'clock, the time when Miss Marvel discharged her weapon. There is, however, more convincing evidence which I can adduce to corroborate me, in the stand which I take. I am in doubt whether the wound which did not prove fatal was made by Miss Marvel or not, or whether by Lucas, either accidentally, as he claims to have fired, or with design. But I am positive that neither of the shots fired at that hour was the one which destroyed the life of the deceased."

"You allude to the scrap of paper of which you told me, do you not?" asked Mr. Tupper.

"I do," replied Mr. Barnes. "But let me explain to the coroner so that he may be convinced of the necessity of continuing. I found upon the table in the parlor, a sheet of paper, upon which was written,

'If I am dead in the morning my murderer is,'

the sentence being unfinished. This seems to prove that Mr. Lewis recognized his first assailant at least, and that, fearing death, he meant to warn us as to the identity of the person. True, the name does not appear, but the words are sufficiently significant. I presume there is no doubt as to the writing?" Mr. Barnes handed the paper to the Squire, who examined it closely, and with great interest. After a moment he replied:

"I recognize this as the handwriting of Mr. Lewis. I am perfectly familiar with it, and there can be no doubt."

"The deduction then is self-evident," continued Mr. Barnes. "Dr. Snow has testified that death was instantaneous. Consequently this writing refers to the first assailant. Therefore, unless it can be shown that he received a wound prior to nine o'clock, Miss Marvel did not inflict the fatal wound, if her shot reached him at all. There is a break in the plastered ceiling of the parlor, showing the furrow of a bullet. That was probably made by Miss Marvel, or by Lucas. We cannot determine which."

"Mr. Barnes," said the Squire, "your reasoning convinces me, that whatever may have been the girl's intent when she fired, her bullet did not kill Mr. Lewis. The worst that can be claimed is, that she is responsible for the lesser wound, and, as you say, even that would be difficult to prove. If you take the same view, Mr. Tupper, we will continue?"

"I certainly agree with Mr. Barnes in all his deductions," said Mr. Tupper. "I am confident that we do not yet know who fired the last shot. It would help us if we could discover what name was meant to complete that sentence, and if you will now call Miss Lewis, acting upon a suggestion from Mr. Barnes, I hope to learn it."

The Squire then announced that the inquest would be continued, and immediately all resumed their seats, and ceased talking.

"Gentlemen," said the Squire, addressing the jury, "Mr. Barnes, the detective in this case, the district attorney, and myself are satisfied that a true verdict cannot be rendered without more evidence. Therefore, notwithstanding the words uttered by the last witness, we will proceed. I will merely call your attention to the fact that though Miss Marvel admits that she fired at Mr. Lewis, Dr. Snow testified that he found two wounds. Miss Marvel could not inflict two wounds by firing one shot, and cannot know herself whether or not she has committed a homicide. Call Virginia Lewis!"

Virginia entered and took the stand. Mr. Tupper conducted the examination.

"Miss Lewis," he began, "I believe you are the only one, save the deceased, who slept at the farm on the night when your uncle died?"

"I believe that is true."

"Did you hear any shot fired, whilst you were in the house?"

"I did not."

"Then you have no idea who killed your uncle?"

"Any idea' that I have would be no proof, and therefore is not worth consideration."

"Oh! You suspect someone, do you?"

"Any suspicions which I may have would not be evidence."

"Were you in the house all the evening?"

"No, sir."

"At what time did you go out, and when did you return?"

"I did not expect to be questioned, and so made no note of the hours."

"Will you tell us where you went?"

"I will not, as that is my private affair."

"No one's affairs are private when murder has occurred; however, since you refuse, I will tell you where you went. First, you met a man in the summer-house, and then you crossed the river to meet another man." The lawyer paused, waiting to note the effect of his words, but Virginia remained impassive.

"I will go further, and tell you that the first was Harry Lucas, and more, that you invited him to the meeting. Since I have shown you how much I know, you will doubtless see the folly of any attempt at concealment."

"Since you seem to be so well informed, I cannot see why you appeal to me at all!"

"We do not claim to know everything. Will you please tell us why you asked Mr. Lucas to meet you?"

"I had a private commission to give him."

"Do you refuse to give us any information as to the nature of this commission?"

"I do."

"Miss Lewis," said the lawyer, "I have intimated that we have discovered the identity of one of the men whom you met that night, and it is perhaps as well to tell you that we also know who the other was."

"You appear to have learned a great deal," replied Virginia, coldly.

"We have found out something, but not all that we wish to know. You met Mr. Lucas. Your conversation was overheard, and we therefore know that you sent for him to ask his aid. You expected to meet Mr. Marvel." Mr. Tupper spoke in his usual measured tones, and both he and Mr. Barnes watched Virginia closely, but, even at this name, she did not flinch. Mr. Barnes wondered how she would act when they would produce the man himself. Mr. Tupper continued:

"You had been notified that he would await you in the woods across the stream, that night, and you were to determine whether or not you would elope with him. This you concluded not to do. Therefore you feared that he would become desperate, and you decided to have his friend, Mr. Lucas, opportunely meet him, after you left him, to see that he did no harm. Now will you tell us what you feared he would do?"

"I see that you have managed to discover all that Miss Marvel knew. Will not that suffice?"

"We wish to know why you were so fearful of leaving this young man to his own society?"

"I believe such a thing as 'fear' is unknown to me, so you are far from the truth. No man is in an enviable frame of mind when a woman rejects him. Was it extraordinary, then, that I should have wished his friend to join him at such a time?" She spoke with considerable feeling.

"No, Miss Lewis, your action under the circumstances was very commendable. But did you not have a deeper motive? Did you not think that he might become desperate enough to take life?"

"I admit that I did."

"Whose? Your uncle's?"

"No! No! I thought he might commit suicide —he is passionate and impulsive. I thought that, in a moment of despair, he might raise his hand against himself. He would never take another's life."

"He attempted to do so once before, I believe?"

To this Virginia made no reply, but her face assumed an expression of the utmost contempt.

"Miss Lewis," continued the lawyer, "will you kindly tell us about how long you remained at the interview with Mr. Marvel? I don't expect any exact reply. An approximate one will do."

"I cannot tell very closely, though I know about when I reached the house again. But I will not answer unless you explain why you wish to know."

Mr. Tupper had recognized, at the outset, that Virginia was not to be frightened into anything, and he determined to deal with her openly.

"I will do so willingly," said he. "We have found that you left the summer-house at, or near, nine o'clock. Soon after, several shots were fired, one at least at the deceased. We are not sure, however, that either of these killed your uncle. Now, if you can give us the time when you returned, it may be the means of proving whether he was alive, or dead, at that hour. These matters of time often prove of inestimable value."

"Very well. It was half-past ten when I reached my room."

"Thank you." It was his cue to conciliate her as far as possible. "When you went in, did you pass through the parlor?"

"No, sir. I entered my apartment by the door opening into the dining-room."

Mr. Barnes believed that this was true, for he had traced her footprints from the steps of the piazza by the dining-room, and, returning, they reached the same place. Thus she must have entered the house at that point, and naturally passed through the dining room to her own chamber. Resuming the examination Mr. Tupper asked:

"During the night, did you hear your uncle moving about?"

"No, sir."

"Now let us come to the discovery of the crime. You will recall that when the detectives accidentally disturbed you in your room, the morning after, you admitted that you had already found out that your uncle had been murdered. Thus you were the first to do so. Is that a fact?"

"I believe so. At least it is true that I knew of the death of my uncle at that time."

"Exactly! You had gone into the parlor, and you had found the body, which you recognized as that of your uncle, or I may say step-father, before the Squire and the others arrived?"

"Yes, sir."

"Did you take anything from the room?"

"Yes, sir, I took a pistol."

"Where did you find this pistol?"

"On the floor."

"Why did you take it?"

"Because it is mine and has my name on the stock, and because, if found by anyone else, it might have been unpleasantly suggestive."

"I believe it showed evidence of having been fired off, did it not?"

"That was another reason why I was anxious to have it."

Virginia was causing profound astonishment by her admissions. Even Mr. Barnes himself was puzzled to understand why she should acknowledge that she had purloined the weapon to avoid suspicion, when that very confession would undoubtedly attract a closer investigation into her connection with the crime.

"Miss Lewis," said Mr. Tupper, "how came your pistol to be discharged?"

"I use it constantly, and therefore it is quite possible that I fired at something on Saturday."

"That is, the day before the murder?"

"Yes, sir."

"How did it happen to be out of your possession on Sunday night?"

"I had it when I started out, but changed my mind about taking it with me, and as I passed through the parlor I laid it on the mantel."

This answer suggested the possibility that this was the pistol used by Mr. Lewis when he fired at Lucas, as had been testified by Miss Marvel. The next question was:

"Now, if you please, will you explain why, if you were so anxious to avoid suspicion by hiding the pistol, you should now be so ready to tell the whole story?"

"I never intended to conceal the fact that the weapon was found by me where it was, but I thought that if I offered it in evidence myself, I would avoid the suspicion which might naturally enough have been aroused, had any other person made the discovery."

Mr. Barnes knew that this was not true, and that her first intention had been to destroy all trace of the use of the pistol, as was plainly proven by her having cleaned the barrel. He knew also that she was at present following out the plan which she had formed after she had seen him pick up the cartridge cap in her room, the first step in which had been to replace the empty shell with another. Her examination was continued.

"Did you remove anything else from the room where the corpse lay?"

"I did."

This reply was a complete surprise to Mr. Barnes. He knew that Mr. Tupper was alluding to the paper, upon which, they thought, was written the name of the murderer, and he was astonished to find that she appeared about to admit its possession. The next question was:

"Will you kindly state what that was, and why you took it?"

"It was a medallion locket. I took that also because it is mine."

Mr. Barnes now understood why she had admitted taking something, since it was not the paper. He was, nevertheless, curious about this new point.

"Where did you find this locket?" asked Mr. Tupper.

"I noticed that my uncle had his fist tightly closed, as though holding something, and, forcing it open, I removed the locket."

"Have you it with you?"

"Yes, sir!" Taking it from her bosom, she handed it to him. Mr. Tupper examined it closely, and opened it. Looking at the portrait which it contained he asked:

"Do you know whose likeness this is?"

"It is mine. It was taken when I was quite a child."

Mr. Tupper was about to pass the trinket to the Squire, when, as he closed it, something attracted his attention, and scrutinizing it more carefully, he dropped it into his pocket and asked:

"Miss Lewis, I think you said that this belongs to you?"

"Yes, sir, though I have not had it for some time."

"Ah! How was that?"

"I had concluded that it was lost, but now I see that my uncle must have had it."

"How can you be sure that this is yours? Has it your name, or any other mark by which you would know it?"

"No, there is no name on it, but I know that it is mine, for, as you see, it is of a peculiar pattern. I have been told that my mother had it made specially for my picture, and it has been in my possession, except lately, for as long as I can remember."

Mr. Tupper pondered a second, but said no more on this subject at that time. Nor did he pursue the point about the piece of paper directly, but determined to approach that by another method.

"Now then, Miss Lewis, we will go back to the meeting across the river, if you please. Did you meet Mr. Marvel—but stop, you have already admitted as much. Tell us whether you left him on the other side, or whether he crossed over with you?"

"We separated before I rowed back to the farm."

"Then you left him across the river?"

"Yes, sir."

"Did he say where he meant to go?"

"To Epping."

This seemed doubtful to Mr. Barnes in the face of the fact that he had found Marvel at Portsmouth; but then he remembered that Joseph Harrison had testified to meeting Marvel at Epping, on the morning after the murder. Mr. Tupper continued:

"Did he say where he would go after that?"

"He did not lay out a route, and furnish me with a complete plan of his movements for the future. He did, however, mention that he would return to Epping, from which place he had come that night."

"Do you think that he proceeded to that place immediately after leaving you?"

Virginia was very cautious, now that the subject involved information about her lover.

"How should I be able to reply definitely?", said she.

"Do you know, then, whether he crossed the river and visited the house, after parting with you?"

"I should say not, as I took the boat."

"Do you mean to say that you did not see him after you left him at the maple tree?"

"I mean to say that I have not seen him since then."

"Then why should he have crossed the river?"

"What makes you think that he did so?"

"I do not think! I know!"

"You cannot know unless you saw him, and that is impossible."

"Miss Lewis, there was snow on the ground, and not only do I know from his footprints that he visited the farm, but that he actually went to the very door by which you had re-entered. Of course, I cannot know that he went in, for, unfortunately, there is no snow within, as without."

Virginia was silent, and despite, her strong control of her features it was evident that she was troubled.

"Now then," said the lawyer, continuing, "the question arises, why did Mr. Marvel visit your house at that late hour! You say he did not see you. Could it be that he sought your uncle, hoping to effect a reconciliation? I understand that the only obstacle to your union was his opposition, was it not?"

"That Mr. Marvel should have sought my uncle at that hour is preposterous. You say that he did come to the house, which I doubt, but even though he did not succeed in seeing me, is it not more probable that it was his object to do so?"

"If so, how is it that he did not succeed?"

"I retired as soon as I reached home, and did not hear anyone enter after me. That is why I doubt your theory, for I am a light sleeper."

Mr. Tupper now executed a bold move. Taking the paper which Mr. Barnes had found in the parlor of the farm house, he folded it so that only the first half of the sentence could be read. Approaching Virginia, he suddenly held it up before her eyes and said:

"Did you ever see this before?"

This was so unexpected, that Virginia was thrown off her guard. At the first glance she smothered an exclamation, and hurriedly put her hand to her breast. Instantly, however, her agitation passed, and she replied quite calmly.

"No! Never!"

"I believe you, for had you done so, it would never have reached my hands. Now please take it and examine it closely."

She did so and then said: "It looks like my uncle's writing, and it would seem that he tried to communicate to us the name of his assailant."

"Precisely, and more, he made another attempt, and—succeeded. Miss Lewis, the second paper is in your possession!"

"You are mistaken," she replied, coldly.

"I am not. I say, not only did you take that paper, but you have it, secreted about your person, at this very minute."

Virginia answered by a half scornful smile. Mr. Barnes showed some little excitement. He was accustomed to deal with wary criminals, but had never met a woman so provokingly self-possessed as this one.

"Come, Miss Lewis," said Mr. Tupper, "it is useless to deny what I say. I set a trap for you deliberately, and you were caught, in spite of all your strength of will. When I showed you that paper, I well knew you had no idea that it existed, and therefore, my object was to see what you would do, believing that your first glance would make you think it was the other paper. As I expected, you at once feared that you had lost it, and instinctively felt for it in the bosom of your dress."

"Did I?" with a shrug of the shoulders.

Mr. Tupper looked at her a moment and then, with his eyes still intently upon her, he said: "Call Walter Marvel!"

CHAPTER XI
THE VERDICT

There are some individuals whose nerves are so well trained that they can be made to sustain almost any strain without giving evidence of the tension to which they have been exposed. Virginia Lewis was of this kind. There is, however, in all probability, no force in nature that has not a breaking point, beyond which it is impossible for integrity to endure; and so it was in the case of this most remarkably strong-willed girl. She had passed through a fiery ordeal bravely, and I might say successfully, until, at last, the unexpected had come to destroy all her powers of control.

Nevertheless, she was not one to give way, like her friend Alice Marvel, and though she certainly started very perceptibly when her lover's name was called, she looked like a frightened animal, who, though awaiting a death blow, was yet prepared to die hard. As she stood expectant and defiant, she won the admiration of all the men in the room, a thing of no small consequence when it is remembered that twelve of these composed the jury. There was a painful silence until the entrance of the next witness. At last he came, and when Virginia saw him, and knew that this was no trick, that was being played to frighten her into revealing that which she had determined to conceal, she could not repress a slight cry, as she stepped from the stand and dropped into the nearest seat. Then she assumed a stolid expression, which defied the scrutiny of Mr. Barnes, or any of the others.

Marvel cast one hasty glance in her direction, and with his lips a little firmly compressed, he took his place on the witness stand. Mr. Tupper at once began:

"Mr. Marvel, do you remember the day of the *fete* given by Miss Lewis, at Riverside?"

"Most distinctly."

"I believe you attempted to kill Mr. Lewis on that occasion?"

"I drew out my pistol, under great provocation, and in anger. Miss Lewis struck my arm, and my weapon was discharged."

"Do you mean that when you took out your pistol, it was not your intention to fire it?"

"I cannot tell what my intention was. As I said, I acted under excitement. It is impossible to say what may or what may not have happened."

"But did you not threaten Mr. Lewis as you left the lawn?"

"Perhaps! It would have been but natural."

"Where did you go when you left the farm that night?"

"Home, of course."

"But why is it, then, that you were not there when search was made for you the next day?"

"I was disheartened, and disgusted at the turn of events; and in sheer desperation I arose early and went off gunning."

"Did you return?"

"After a day's shooting, I went on to Epping, where I have a house."

"That place was searched a few days later, and no trace of you was to be found."

"I only stayed there one day, and then went to Worcester."

"Why did you do that?"

"Because I knew of the plot which Mr. Lewis was forming against me."

"How could you know that, since you left Lee before any steps had been inaugurated?"

"A friend warned me by letter."

"Who was this obliging friend, and how did he know where a letter would reach you?"

"Before I left I told him where I meant to go. It is immaterial who he is."

"I presume this was Mr. Everly, Was it not?" Marvel remained silent and Mr. Tupper did not press the point, but continued:

"Where were you on the night upon which Mr. Lewis was murdered?"

"I was at the farm."

The lawyer was pleased at this straightforward reply.

"What were you doing there?"

"Is it essential to go into that?"

"It is very essential."

"Well, then, I went there to meet Miss Lewis, having asked her for an interview."

"Did you see her? If so, where?"

"She met me across the river."

"How long did this interview last?"

"Of course I cannot be accurate, but I should say about an hour. The subject which we discussed was one of vital importance to me, and I was not anxious to bring the meeting to a close, before exhausting all the arguments at my command."

Mr. Barnes reflected a moment, and calculated that if Miss Lewis left the summer-house at nine o'clock, granting her fifteen minutes to cross the river, and as many more in returning, this statement of Marvel's, that she talked with him an hour, would just fit the one which she had made, to the effect that she reached the house at half-past ten. This, therefore, satisfied him that he had the matter of time correct.

"Now then, Mr. Marvel," said the lawyer, "please tell us what you did after Miss Lewis left you?"

"I started to walk to the Epping road, but before I reached it I retraced my steps."

"Exactly! You crossed the river, did you not?"

"Yes, how did you know?"

"Never mind! Tell us how you crossed?"

"I meant to wade the stream, and looked for a shallow place, but I stepped into a hole, and was obliged to swim."

"Very good. Now tell us why you were so anxious to cross the river so late at night?"

"It is a delicate matter, but as this seems to be of importance, I will be frank, and tell you the whole story. My first object in visiting the farm, was to persuade Miss Lewis to marry me, without her uncle's consent, since he had refused to grant it. At the meeting between us, she would not do more than promise to send me a definite reply the next day by letter. After she had left me, I could not help thinking that she meant to refuse, and was only delaying the ill-tidings, especially as she insisted that I should go on to Portsmouth, to wait for her letter. I thought of some arguments which I had not used, and returned, hoping to find her still up, and so make one more attempt to win her. That, sir, is the full truth."

"Did you see her when you reached the house?"

"No, sir."

"Did you enter the house?"

"I did. I went into the dining-room, and as far as the door of Miss Lewis's room, but as there was no light in her apartment, I concluded that she had retired, and I left the house as I had entered it."

"Whilst in the house did you see Mr. Lewis?"

"Before I answer that may I ask you a question?"

"Proceed."

"When you ask me if I saw Mr. Lewis, are you not trying to get me to make some admission which might connect me with this murder?"

Mr. Tupper was a little confused at this direct question, and hesitated a moment before he replied:

"Mr. Lewis has been murdered, and there are suspicious circumstances which seem to implicate you. I am only giving you an opportunity to vindicate yourself."

"You are very kind," said Marvel, with a smile, "but it seems to me that it is the other way, and that you are simply hunting for the criminal. Now, if I admit that I saw Mr. Lewis that night, whether I killed him or not, I might be acknowledging myself to be the last person who saw him alive, and that might be construed into an evidence of guilt. I believe I have the privilege of refusing to criminate myself, and I will not reply to the question."

"You are virtually admitting what you seem to wish to deny, since if you had not met him, there would be no reason for your hesitating to proclaim that fact."

"You are wrong. If I say that I did not see him, that will be giving you a positive point. If I did not meet him, it would be proof presumptive that I did not fire the fatal shot. This might be helping to incriminate some other person, which I am equally unwilling to do."

"It is your duty to tell everything that may lead to the discovery of the criminal."

"It is your business, not mine, to trace the crime to its perpetrator."

Mr. Barnes could not but admire the man's cool logic, under the trying circumstances of his position, and it flashed across his mind that Marvel and Virginia were a well-matched pair. It piqued him, somewhat, to notice the quiet smile of satisfaction on Virginia's face, as she sat in her seat, never once raising her eyes from the floor, throughout the examination of her lover. She seemed to have completely recovered her self-control. It was a question in the detective's mind, whether Marvel was shielding himself, or someone else. The examination proceeded.

"Did you return to Epping that night?"

"Yes, sir."

"How did you get there at that late hour?"

"I walked. It is but five miles."

"Five miles, over a country road, through the snow, and at night, is no short walk, especially if one's clothing be wet."

"Mine were dry, however."

"Did you not say that you swam across the river?"

"Yes, but after leaving the farm I went to my own home, and changed for a dry suit."

"Then you walked to Epping?"

"Yes, sir."

"Why did you go to Epping?"

"I expected a letter to reach me there at that time."

This corroborated the story told by young Harrison. At this point Burrows passed to Mr. Tupper a piece of paper, on which he suggested a question. During the latter part of the examination, he had been thinking of the story told by the station-agent, and as Marvel claimed that he had been in Worcester, it seemed like a criminating admission, since the train which Mr. Skene said had brought a stranger had come from that city. Mr. Tupper next asked:

"Mr. Marvel, will you tell us how you were dressed on the night of your visit to the farm?"

"I wore a disguise that I bought in Worcester."

Mr. Tupper had not quite understood the object of the question, but the reply at once arrested his attention, and he pursued the subject.

"Why were you disguised?"

"To avoid being recognized. I did not care to be arrested, and, as you know, the authorities were seeking for me on the charge trumped up by Mr. Lewis. "

"Describe the dress which you wore?"

"I had on a suit of my own clothing, but over it I wore a long, dark-colored ulster which completely concealed my other dress."

"Did you attempt to change the appearance of your face in anyway?"

"I wore a false beard."

This answer gratified Burrows. Mr. Tupper went on.

"What did you do with this disguise when you changed your things?"

"As they were all very wet, and, further, because I did not wish to leave behind me any evidence of my visit to the house, I made a bundle of the whole lot, and, as I crossed over the bridge, I threw it in the river."

"Do you mean the bridge between Riverside and Wadley's Falls?"

"Yes, sir; I crossed the river again, as that is the shortest way from my house to the Epping road."

Mr. Tupper now sought information on another point.

"Mr. Marvel, did you ever see a medallion locket owned by Miss Lewis, which contains her portrait?"

Marvel colored considerably at this question, and seemed confused. After a moment, however, he stammered out:

"Y-e-s, sir; I have seen it."

"When was the last time that you saw it?"

Marvel seemed more than ever troubled, and even Virginia changed her position, and, raising her eyes from the floor, seemed all anxiety. Marvel remained silent so long, that Mr. Tupper at length repeated his question. Marvel hesitatingly asked:

"Why do you wish to know?"

"Come, come, Mr. Marvel, that is not to the point. Answer my question. Is it not a simple one?"

"Well, then," desperately, "if I must, I must. I confess that I did what many men have done. I stole the medallion, and—"

Virginia uttered a cry and started up as though about to speak, but the Squire quickly said:

"Sit down, Miss Lewis! You must not interfere now!" and she obeyed with a groan. Mr. Tupper turned to the witness who was evidently amazed at this little episode, and resumed:

"You had your name engraved on the medallion, did you not?"

"I had my initials put on."

"Precisely. Now let us return to the question. When did you last see this locket?"

"I cannot say exactly. I have it about me at all times."

"Have you it now?"

Virginia made another movement as though to interrupt, but the Squire again stopped her. Marvel promptly replied:

"Why, certainly."

"Please let me see it?"

Marvel at once put his hand in an inner pocket of his vest, but after a moment's search, he drew it out again with a cry of surprise, and exclaimed:

"I have lost it!" There was a silence for a moment, and Marvel rapidly searched his other pockets, but in vain. At last it seemed that an idea occurred to him suddenly, and he said:

"I am a fool, and have been very careless. I remember now that when I changed my clothes at home, after leaving the farm, I did not think of the locket. So it must be, at this moment, at the bottom of the river."

"Ah! Then you admit that you had it with you that night?"

"Did I not tell you that I have always had it with me, since it has been in my possession?"

"Would you recognize it again if you could see it?"

"Certainly."

"Is this it?" He handed Marvel the locket given to him by Virginia. Marvel took it, and after looking at it replied:

"Yes, this is the same. Where could you have found it?"

"Can you not surmise?"

"No!"

"Well, then, I will tell you. It was found in the closed fist of the murdered man!'

"Great God! It is impossible!"

"It is true! At least it is true, if we can believe Miss Lewis, for it was she who found it."

"Miss Lewis found it? This is terrible!"

The silence which ensued was most profound. Every one could plainly see the importance of this latest development, and how, by accidental circumstances, the net was being drawn around the witness. Mr. Barnes himself was considering how strange it was, that this young girl, who had not hesitated to destroy evidence which might implicate someone, presumably her lover, should, by the merest chance, have been the very one to produce the most criminating proof against him. The thoughts of all were suddenly disturbed by the voice of Virginia herself, who stood up defiantly, and with the mark of strong resolve stamped upon her features. She spoke in measured words, and her voice seemed dead to all sense of feeling; indeed, it sounded like only an echo of her natural tones.

"Stop!" said she, "this has gone far enough!"

"What do you mean?" asked the Squire, quickly, foreseeing that some startling development was at hand.

"I mean that you are wrongfully weaving a web around an innocent man!"

"Ah! Then you know who is guilty?"

"I do! I killed my uncle myself!"

This statement naturally caused the wildest excitement. Only two men present seemed not to be surprised; these were Marvel himself, and Mr. Barnes. The former dropped into a seat and buried his face in his hands, giving vent to a passionate outburst of grief. The latter remained almost as unmoved as Virginia herself, who stood like a marble image. A slight smile of satisfaction, however, seemed to play about his features. Burrows, who kept his eye intently on the face of his superior, whilst immensely astonished himself, was convinced of the fact that Mr. Barnes had only heard what he had all along expected. As soon as the commotion caused by Miss Lewis's statement had subsided somewhat, Mr. Tupper resumed:

"Miss Lewis," said he, "you have just made a most astounding confession. But you may not know, that you are not the first who has done so today. This being the case, however, we cannot but accept your words cautiously."

"Do you mean that you doubt my veracity?"

"How can I be sure that you are telling the truth, when you accuse yourself of murder?" Virginia bit her lip and was silent.

"Come," continued the lawyer, "take the stand again, and repeat under oath what you have just declared."

"What use to be sworn?" replied the girl, scornfully. "You would not believe me any more!"

"Do you refuse to swear?"

"Oh, no, since you make a point of it!" She stepped upon the platform again.

"She will stop at nothing to save her lover," muttered Mr. Barnes, under his breath. Mr. Tupper asked:

"Do you still persist in your statement that you killed your uncle?"

"I do."

"How did it occur?"

"When I returned from my meeting with Mr. Marvel, I attracted the notice of my uncle, who, coming from his room, knocked on my door, and called me into the parlor. I went in and he asked me where I had been. I told him, he became violent, and we quarrelled. My pistol was on the mantle where I had left it, and in a moment of rage I grasped it and fired."

"How was your uncle attired?"

"As he was found, of course."

"Did he die instantly?"

"I do not know. I left the room at once."

"How many times did you fire?"

"Once."

"In making this statement you desire to be believed?"

"I do."

"Then show me the piece of paper, on which your uncle wrote the name of his murderer, and which I am sure you have about you."

If Mr. Tupper expected her to refuse, he was doomed to disappointment. Without a moment's hesitation, she drew it out and handed it to him. He read it and seemed puzzled. Then turning to Virginia he said:

"This paper reads, 'If I am dead in the morning my murderer is Walter Marvel!' How does that agree with your confession?"

"You forget that there are two wounds. My uncle wrote that after receiving the first!"

Mr. Tupper had not expected this reply, and the possibility of its being true disconcerted him.

"How do you know this?" he asked.

"During the quarrel which I had with my uncle, he told me of the wound he had received from the lawn, and charged my lover with the crime. It was at this moment that, overcome with anger, I shot him."

"When did you find the paper?"

"In the morning. I think I have said enough, and will retire!" She stepped from the stand and resumed her seat on one of the benches.

"There is no more evidence to be brought before you gentlemen," said the district attorney, addressing the jury, "and no more witnesses. Therefore, the next step is for you to consider what your verdict shall be. However, I should like to detain you a moment, that I may point out one or two things which I think should not be overlooked in rendering your decision. First, there is the matter of the locket. If Miss Lewis tells the truth, how did that trinket come to be in the hand of the dead man, when Mr. Marvel admits that it was in his possession on that night? It is plain that Miss Lewis was ignorant of this latter fact, for otherwise she would have suppressed that, as she evidently at first meant to do with the paper. This brings out another point. It must be remembered that her first, and her second stories, are widely different, and that the second was not offered until she saw how compromising the medallion had proven to her lover, Mr. Marvel. One more point. Her pistol has but one empty chamber in it. She claims that it was on the mantel. Mr. Lewis was seen to fire some weapon from the window. If it was not this one, what has become of the one which he did use?"

The Squire addressed the jury in a few well-chosen words, especially warning them to think well over their verdict, and bidding them to be most careful in charging the commission of so foul a deed to anyone, without thoroughly weighing all the evidence that had been brought before them, much of which indeed, he declared, was of a most conflicting nature. Finally, he sent them into an adjoining apartment for deliberation. In about an hour's time, word was brought in, that a conclusion had been reached, and the jury having returned, the foreman announced the following verdict:

"We find that the deceased, John Lewis, came to his death from a gunshot wound, at the hands of his niece, Virginia Lewis, the latter having openly confessed the commission of the crime!"

CHAPTER XII
JOHN LEWIS SUPPLIES A CLUE

Although the verdict had been anticipated by the majority of those who had been present throughout the examination, all were nevertheless horrified, even though they admitted its justice, in consideration of the evidence. There were some, of course, who stoutly maintained that Virginia was innocent, but they were chiefly her most intimate friends. These proclaimed themselves to be in a position to judge better than those who did not know her so well. Unhesitatingly they asserted, that her whole life and character made it utterly preposterous to harbor a suspicion of a crime of so heinous a nature. Said one: "Does an innocent girl become a hardened criminal in a moment?" But others gravely shook their older heads, and readily recalled instances where equally respectable individuals had been proven guilty of murder. After all, horrible as it is to take life, yet, viewed from a certain standpoint, murder is less dishonorable than theft. One who would scorn even to tell a lie, might yet in anger, or under great provocation, unhesitatingly send another to his last account. So respectability is scarcely a defence against a charge of murder.

The town of Lee is in Strafford County, and the county-seat is Dover; here the Grand Jury meets, and here the trial would take place if there should be one. Squire Olney, at the termination of the inquest, therefore declared that Virginia must be taken to Dover on the following day, together with the record of the evidence, which would, of course, be presented to the Grand Jury. It was decided that she should pass the night at the residence of the Squire, who would personally drive over with her, early in the morning. The Squire, in all his lifetime, had never been placed in a position so painful to himself, and so trying to all his pride in the morality of his town. It was bad enough to have a murder, but that the guilty party should be a woman, and she the most respected and admired female in the town, was simply terrible.

As soon as Mr. Barnes learned of the disposition to be made of the prisoner, for such she was to be considered now, he determined to seek rest at the earliest possible moment. Wishing to go on to Riverside and share the room which had been provided for Burrows, he sought for that young man, but could find him nowhere. He was somewhat annoyed at this, as he wished to talk with him on some of the points brought out in the examination. Finally, concluding that Burrows must have gone to the farm, as it was already after dark, he decided to go there also, and so started immediately. He had walked but a few rods, when he overtook John Lewis, and recognizing him, said:

"Ah! Mr. Lewis, are you going to the farm?"

"I am, and supposing that you would put up there for the night, I have waited to join you as you passed. I could not see you at the moment when the inquest ended, for you were speaking to the Squire."

"Yes! I wished to know what would be done with Miss Lewis. She will stay at the Squire's house to-night, and be taken to Dover in the morning."

The two men walked along, for some little distance, without speaking, until at length Lewis broke the silence; and, when he did so, Mr. Barnes noticed that he spoke very earnestly, as though the subject concerned him nearly. At first it seemed to the detective that this interest was more than was natural; but then he recalled to mind the fact that the girl was a relative, and, as such, would of course attract his sympathy.

"Mr. Barnes," began Lewis, "what do you think of the result of the inquiry?"

As I have already stated, Mr. Barnes was most careful in forming definite opinions, and he was still more so in giving expression to them, he felt a double need of caution at this time, and determined rather to discover what his companion thought, than to commit himself by any direct reply to this leading question.

"Well," he responded, "what other verdict could you look for under the circumstances?"

"I suppose none! Nevertheless, a stigma has been placed on that girl which she does not deserve. At least," he continued, quickly, "that is my opinion."

"You mean that you think Miss Lewis is innocent?"

"I do, decidedly."

"Will you tell me your reasons?" This was exactly what Mr. Barnes most desired; that someone should defend this girl to him. Therefore, if in the subsequent conversation he seemed to be accusing her, it was no evidence that he himself thought her guilty, but only that such a course was the one best calculated to draw out the strongest arguments in her favor, which might occur to Lewis. Mr. Barnes was wise enough not to underestimate the ability of any man. Very often in his experience most valuable hints had been given to him, by persons from whom he had least expected assistance.

"I will try," said Lewis, in reply to Mr. Barnes. "Of course, I was present at the entire inquiry. I was not needed on the witness-stand, as all that I could have testified to would have been the discovery of the body, and that was not deemed of sufficient importance by the Squire. As the deceased was my own father, it is but natural that I should take a great interest in seeing the crime avenged. I therefore listened most attentively to all that was brought out in the examination of the several witnesses. And it is just this that makes me feel so sure that Miss Lewis is actuated more by a desire to shield someone else, than by any other motive."

"Ah! But whom is she shielding? You must remember that she is doing a very dangerous thing when she accuses herself."

"Miss Lewis is a much cleverer woman than you may believe her to be, and she knows, well enough, that she is in no real danger. She has confessed! What of that? When she is made to appear in court she will retract this confession. Then how will you convict her? What evidence is there against her besides her own words? She will tell you that she was excited, that she did not realize what she was saying. What will you be able to do? She is a woman, and the sympathy of the jury will be in her favor. American juries are proverbially lenient towards her sex. She will be acquitted, but where will your real criminal be? In some foreign land."

Mr. Barnes listened with considerable interest to all this, for it was precisely what had been passing in his own mind. He very well knew that a confession of so grave a crime as murder would not by any means assure a conviction, and he had by no means underrated the girl's ability as a bold plotter. Still, he would not dismiss from his mind the possibility that, after all, she might be guilty. The story which she had told was a most plausible one. Moreover, its very simplicity seemed to prevent a suspicion that it had been manufactured. Besides, it fitted so well all the most complicated points in the case. Then, how did she know that there were two wounds? Neither the doctor, nor Burrows, would have told her, and as she was the last witness to enter the room, she could not have heard the previous testimony.

Addressing his companion again, he said: "All that is very true, but suppose that Miss Lewis does not retract?"

"But I tell you she will! Why should she allow herself to suffer the penalty—and such a penalty— when she is innocent? As soon as the real criminal has had time to get away safely, she will tell a very different tale. You will see!"

"Why are you so sure that she is acting a part?"

"Why did she not tell the truth at once, if it was her intention to do so?"

"Ah! Who can be sure of the workings of a human mind, and of the motives which actuate any given course?"

"In this case it seems to me quite simple. When she first testified, she thought that the murderer was safe."

"Whom do they suspect, then?"

"Can you be in doubt? Walter Marvel, of course. Whom else, but her lover, would she risk her life to save?"

"But the dead man was her uncle, her adopted father! Did she not love him enough to refuse to leave him for this very lover? Then why should she not wish to avenge his death?"

"Granted that she loved him, he is dead, while her lover is alive. She will care more for the living than the dead. The uncle cannot be restored; therefore the lover must not be sacrificed. Do you know what she will do? She will exert every effort to save him, and then she will still refuse to marry him. She is a strange woman!"

"How do you know her character so well?" said the detective, sharply. Lewis started slightly, but replied quickly:

"I do not know! I am simply telling you my opinions, formed on the little that I have seen of her."

Mr. Barnes was satisfied with this answer, at least he did not let it appear if he was not, and resuming the thread of their discourse he asked:

"Have you any special reason for thinking that Marvel is guilty?"

"If not guilty, how did his locket come to be in the possession of my father? It is very evident that, even if Miss Lewis tells the truth, she has not accounted for that mystery. This is a point that Mr. Tupper mentioned."

"I mean to investigate that matter, of course, but I have seen stranger things than that explained away."

"Well, then, let me call your attention to another point. Do you remember the story that the Squire told us, of the row at the birthday *fete?*"

"Certainly."

"Very good! If you do, you will recollect that the Squire said that my father kept Marvel's pistol. Now what has become of that weapon?"

Mr. Barnes saw at once the value of this, and it had certainly not occurred to him. He was thankful for this conversation.

"We have not looked for it," he replied.

"You may not have done so, but I have searched everywhere, and it is not to be found."

"Perhaps the Squire may have it."

"I have asked him, and he assures me that my father would not part with the evidence of the assault which had been made on him. More than that, the Squire told me that he kept it locked in a drawer in the parlor."

"How then could Marvel have obtained it?"

"My idea is this. I think that, after his interview with Miss Lewis across the river, Marvel, as he admits, came to the farm. I think he sought an interview with my father, that they quarrelled, and that my father took up the pistol, whereupon Marvel got it away from him and shot him."

Mr. Barnes shook his head. "There is no sign of a struggle. Besides, if that is the truth, how could your father have written the name of Walter Marvel on the slip of paper?"

Lewis thought a minute and then replied:

"I have it! When my father heard the barking of the dog outside, he took Marvel's pistol, and fired at the man whom he saw there. At the same moment a bullet struck him. This was either from Lucas's pistol, or else was the shot fired by Miss Marvel from the summer-house, as she declared. Then, when Marvel came, the weapon may have been on the table right at hand, for, as father was wounded, he would scarcely have thought of locking up the weapon again. As for the writing, that may be as Miss Lewis guessed. My father thought Marvel had fired the first shot, and so wrote a line to that effect, not realizing to what extent he had been wounded."

"But what about the empty shell in Miss Lewis's weapon?"

"Perhaps her first statement was correct, and she had previously fired it; or again, my father may have fired it at Marvel in self-defence."

A silence followed, and Mr. Barnes did not speak, for several minutes, during which time he was thinking deeply. At last however he said:

"You are right; it is of importance to find this missing pistol, but where can we look for it? That is the question!"

"I think I can guess that too," said the other, eagerly—a little too eagerly, thought Mr. Barnes,— although he reflected that, when a novice is working out a mystery of a great crime he is usually impetuous. Lewis continued: "Marvel himself described his movements, on leaving the farm. First he went home, then making a bundle of his wet clothes he threw them into the river, and lastly he went to his old house in Epping. Now either he threw the pistol in the river, or else, remembering that it has his name on it, as young Harrison testified, he was shrewd enough to take it with him, and hide it in the Epping place."

"Your reasoning is very good, and it may be as well for me to go to Epping, in the morning."

"Do so, and whilst you are gone I will have the river dragged, in the hope of recovering the clothing!"

Mr. Barnes stopped, looked at Lewis a moment, then slowly and distinctly he said:

"Mr. Lewis, I would prefer that you go with me to Epping."

"Oh!" said Lewis, quickly, "I should like that, but I thought you detectives preferred to work alone."

"We do, as a rule, but I will make an exception in this case," returned Mr. Barnes, dryly.

By this time they had reached Riverside, and both at once retired to rest.

Mr. Barnes awoke early, and called Lewis, who was still abed when he entered his room, and together they went to Squire Olney's house, where Mr. Barnes explained that something had turned up which would prevent his accompanying him to Dover. With Lewis, he then hastened to the depot where he was just in time to catch the train which passed at 6.30, and getting aboard they reached Epping a few minutes before seven o'clock.

After a little time spent in inquiries, Mr. Barnes learned the locality of the house of which he was in search, and at once repaired thither. Arrived at the place, which was about a mile beyond the more densely built portion of the town, he found it to be as described, in a terribly dilapidated condition, and, recessed considerably from the road, it was almost hidden amidst an overgrowth of trees and shrubbery. Without any hesitation, the two men entered the place, but scarcely had they crossed the threshold of the door, when Mr. Barnes uttered an exclamation of astonishment, for there in front of him stood Tom Burrows, examining a pistol which he held in his hand.

CHAPTER XIII
THE STATION AGENT'S CLUE

Tom Burrows had naturally taken no active part in the coroner's inquest. He was but an assistant to Mr. Barnes, and consequently bound to remain quiet, lest, by intruding, he should interfere with the older detective's plans. For whilst the district attorney ostensibly conducted the examination of the witnesses, Burrows very well understood that he was but following the suggestions of Mr. Barnes.

When Marvel was testifying, however, he could not resist the desire to have him interrogated as to whether he had worn a disguise, and so had sent up his written suggestion. When Mr. Tupper brought out the admission that a disguise, practically similar to the one described by the station agent, had been used by Marvel, Burrows decided that there was no doubt as to the identity of his man. He more than ever determined to follow up this clue alone.

To do this he knew that he must be cautious. He was too well acquainted with the sagacity of Mr. Barnes, not to realize the fact that he must have aroused suspicion by his action in sending his question to the district attorney. He consequently decided to avoid Mr. Barnes at the conclusion of the inquest, and so escape a catechising. In this, the sensational close of the proceedings assisted him, so that it was not difficult to slip away unobserved. Thus, when Mr. Barnes looked for him, he was already on his way to Lee Depot, bent upon taking the same train which had carried the mysterious stranger away from Lee on the night of the murder. Reaching the station he found Mr. Skene, and, without preamble, he approached his subject.

"Do you remember, Mr. Skene," said he, "that you gave me a hint as to the identity of the man who killed Mr. Lewis?"

"Do I remember?" ejaculated Mr. Skene in an angry tone. "Do I remember? Well, darn me ef you an't the cheekiest critter I've seen meanderin' down that road!"

"Why, what is the matter?" asked Burrows, taken aback.

"Matter? Matter enough! Look a' here, you gol-darned eejiot! Why an't you done nothin'? Why didn't you call me on the stan'? Why didn't you stop 'em?" Burrows endeavored to answer, but Mr. Skene waved his hand as a sign to him to be silent, and continued, more excited: "Didn't you git the straight tip from me in this here bisnis? Didn't I tell you who killed Lewis? Didn't I tell you I seen him with my own eyes? Didn't I tell you I seen him twice? Didn't I tell you what train he come on, an' what train he went away on? How much more do you want, you blunderin' lune? Mus' I leave my station an' ketch the man myself? I reckon that's what ye're waitin' on. You want me to ketch him, an' put him in your han's all tied, so he couldn't hurt you, hay?" Mr. Skene stopped to breathe. It is doubtful whether he would have ceased talking except from this necessity. Burrows saw his chance, and tried to speak before the irate old man could resume. But he was not allowed to say much.

"It is all right, Mr. Skene," he began. "There is time enough!"

"Time enough?" interrupted Mr. Skene. "Why, darn your hide, an' the hull thing ended? An't you been an' 'lowed them lunatics to tack the crime onto the fines' woman in this State? An't Virgie bro't in guilty of killin' her uncle?"

"Certainly not," said Burrows, hoping at length to have an opportunity to speak; but again he was interrupted.

"D' you mean to tell me they an't bro't her in guilty? An't Jef Harrison jest druv by an' tole me the verdic'?"

"But, Mr. Skene, that is only the verdict of the coroner's jury. This is not a regular trial."

"Don't you s'pose I know that? I an't a goldarned fool, ef I an't never been to Borston. But what's the diff'rence, I 'd like to know? She's disgraced, an' the hull county'll be talkin' 'bout her. You can't hender folks from talkin', kin you? Well then!" This last ejaculation presumably meant that an unassailable argument had been launched, and he could afford to let his antagonist speak.

"Of course you believe her innocent?" ventured Burrows, and in a moment Mr. Skene was as excited as ever.

"B'leve she's innocent? Do I b'leve it? Say, look a' here! Ef all them white angels that went up an' down Jacob's ladder, as they tell on in the Bible, wuz to let down a rope-ladder right here on this spot, an' as they come' down, they wuz to kneel before me an' swear they seen her do it, it wouldn't budge me a mite. I 'd b'leve they wuz mistaken in the party. Man, I don't b'leve Virgie's innocent! I jest know it, plain an' simple!" This old man's trust in Virginia was impressive. Faith, such as this, might weigh with a jury against a multiplicity of facts.

"But how can you know it? You may think so, but how can you know that she is innocent?"

"How do I know it?" Mr. Skene said this with a sneer, and paused a moment. "How do I know it? How do I know you're a lune? I don't know how, but I know it!" With this sally he turned on his heel and walked towards the baggage-room. Burrows thought he knew how to bring him back.

"Mr. Skene, you misunderstand me. I believe Miss Lewis is innocent also. Won't you help me to prove it?"

The old man turned instantly and came back. He looked sharply at Burrows a moment and said:

"Say, don't come none of your Borston tricks on me! They won't work, an' ef I ketch you lyin' I'll maul you, so help me!"

"There will be no need. I will explain. I am not the only detective working on this case. It was not my fault that Miss Lewis was accused by the verdict." Burrows here adroitly left it to be inferred that it was the fault of Mr. Barnes. It was not a nice thing to do, but he was anxious to divert this man's anger from himself, that he might use him to further his ambition. In this he succeeded too, for the station-agent listened to him patiently, for the first time since the beginning of the interview. Burrows continued, following up the good impression. "I asked you to keep your information secret, because I wished to follow it up personally. This is the first chance that I have had to do so, and I have come to you for assistance. If you give it to me, I think there is no doubt that I can apprehend your man. In that case, of course Miss Lewis will be released. May I count upon you?"

"Kin you count on me? Say, mebbe I wuz hasty! I an't over-patient, I'll 'low, but I wuz riled when I hearn 'bout that verdic'. But no man an't quicker 'n me to 'low he's wrong, so there's my han'." Burrows shook the proffered hand gladly, delighted to have conciliated the old man. "Now then," continued Mr. Skene, "tell me what I kin do, an' I'll do it quicker 'n a streak."

"Listen! You told me that this man did not buy a ticket from you when he left. Therefore, he must have obtained one from the conductor on the train. That will be enough to have impressed the circumstance on his mind. If not, the ticket itself can be found, and that will tell us where he left the train. What I want you to do is, to introduce me to the conductor when the train comes in, and arrange it so that he will not hesitate to tell me all that he may know as we go along, for I mean to take that train to-night."

"That'll be simple enough, for Berry, the conductor, is a nice feller. He'll do all he kin to help you."

"Very good. What time did you say that train leaves?"

"Ten thirty-nine."

Prompt to the minute, the train which he was so anxiously awaiting came along, and was stopped by the agent's flag. Mr.

Skene found the conductor and introduced Burrows to him, at the same time giving a hint of what was wanted. As soon as they had started, the two dropped into conversation, for there had been no other passengers to take up, and therefore there were no tickets to be collected.

"Mr. Berry," said Burrows, "to make no mystery about what I want, I will say at once that I am a detective, and am looking for a particular man. One, answering his description, boarded this train last Sunday night. I desire you to tell me where he was going."

"I should like nothing better than to oblige you, Mr. Burrows, but, really, we see so many passengers that it is not an easy matter to know all about where they get on or off, especially after the lapse of several days."

"Of course not, but consider for a moment! It cannot be a common thing to get a passenger at this hour, at so small a place as Lee."

"No, you are right about that. Nevertheless, I get them all along my route, and there are many stops as unimportant as this one."

"I see I must assist your memory. This man did not buy a ticket from the agent at the station, and consequently he must have done so on the train. Can you not recall that circumstance?"

"Y-e-s—yes—it seems to me that I do. Ah! I have it! The man you want had a full beard and wore a long overcoat—he also had a large satchel— and I remember that he would not let me send it to the baggage-room—but where did he want a ticket for? That I don't get, somehow."

"Haven't you the ticket which you sold him?" asked Burrows, anxiously.

"No, we turn our tickets in at the end of each trip. Of course they would have it at the main office. But stop a minute, perhaps I have the stub." Burrows watched him as patiently as possible, whilst he looked through his book, turning to the right date and glancing over the stubs of the tickets which he had sold on the train. This occupied a few minutes only, at the end of which the conductor continued:

"I am sorry, but it is not here. You see, I use that book when I sell a ticket for any distance, and as there is no stub for anything

from Lee, it must be that your man only made a short ride. The
farmers along the line often do that, and we let them simply pay
the agent where they stop off, the agent giving us the ticket."

"Can you tell then where this man got off?"

"I cannot be sure about it. He must have left the train either at
Epping, the next stop, or one station beyond that, for we seldom
let a man ride farther, in the way that I have described. But stop
here a minute, and I will ask my brakeman if he knows."

The conductor was gone but a few moments, and returned
with disappointment on his face.

"No, he knows nothing; doesn't remember the man at all.
But, see here, the thing is simple enough! All we must do is to
ask the agent at Epping, and if not there, it must have been at
the next."

Epping, a much larger town than Lee, is but five miles from
that place, and therefore it was not long before they reached the
station. Immediately, Burrows and the conductor leaped from
the train, and went up to the station-agent, who was delivering
the mail-bags. It took but a moment to explain what was wanted,
and at once the agent replied:

"Oh, yes, I remember the man well enough. He paid me for
his ticket. I hope there's nothing wrong?"

"This gentleman will tell you," replied the conductor in a
hurry, because he could not keep his train waiting; then turning
to Burrows he continued: "Mr. Burrows, let me introduce you to
Mr. Jennings, he will give you the information which you want.
Good-night, I wish you luck!" A moment later he and his train
were lost to view around a curve, though a deep rumbling noise
remained on the air for many minutes. Burrows turned to the
man beside him and said:

"I am glad to meet you, Mr. Jennings, and I hope that you
may be able to lend me some assistance in the matter which I am
investigating."

"I am at your service, sir. If you'll tell me what I can do for
you, I'll be only too happy," replied the agent, politely.

"I am a detective, and am after a man. I don't say the one who
came here on Sunday is he, but I think so, from the mysterious
way in which he acted at Lee. If you can tell me anything about
him, you will earn my gratitude."

"Well, I don't know as I can help you much. I remember the fellow, partly 'cause he stopped off from such a late train, and partly 'cause he had no ticket, and so had to buy one when he reached here; but I am afraid there an't much more I can tell you."

"Didn't he ask you any questions? Where he could find a place to sleep, at so late an hour, or anything of that kind?"

"Not a word. He just took his satchel, and marched off, as if he knew all about the place he meant to stop at."

"You say he took his satchel with him?"

"Stop a minute; that gives me an idea. You want to find where he put up, an't that the point?"

"That is precisely what I am after."

"Very good! As I said, he asked no questions, but marched off. That's what he did do, but your question about the satchel reminds me. It seemed so large, that his going off on foot, with it in his hand, attracted some attention, and as one of the neighbors noticed that he started off in his own direction, he jumped into his wagon, and as he drove off he said to me, "I guess I'll give the stranger a lift, with his bag!"

"Do you know whether the man accepted his offer or not?"

"Oh, yes, he had not turned the corner there, when Weston caught up with him, and I saw him climb into the wagon."

"Who is this Weston? Where can I find him?"

"I should say he's the very man you want, for more reasons than one. Not only he can tell you where he dropped his company Sunday night, but as he keeps the hotel here, he can put you up for the night."

With a few necessary directions as to how to find the hotel kept by this man Weston, Burrows started towards that place. The hotel in question would scarcely be granted so high-sounding a name in a city, but as it was the largest hostelry in the place, perhaps it was well enough so to designate it. The young detective reached it without any difficulty, and as easily found the proprietor. After engaging a room for the night, he at once approached the main object of his visit.

"Mr. Weston," said he, "I have been informed that you picked up a stranger at the depot last Sunday night, and gave him a lift in your wagon?"

"Yes, that's true enough."

"I would be much obliged to you if you will tell me where you put him down."

"Well, look here, what might be your reasons for askin' about him? I an't a man to git another into trouble, an' excuse me, but you're a stranger to me."

"Well, was not the other man a stranger also?"

"Yes, but for all that I won't do nothin' to git him into any scrape." He looked in a decidedly suspicious manner at the detective. Burrows considered for a moment, and from the manner of his host he almost thought that, despite his assertion that the man was unknown to him, he had recognized him. He also decided that it would not be wise to reveal his real object in hunting up this man. He determined upon a bold stroke.

"Mr. Weston," said he, "I am glad that the secret of my friend is in such safe hands. I thank you for your discretion. Can we finish this conversation where we will not be overheard?"

Weston seemed puzzled, but led the way into a small room at the back of the building.

"Now then," resumed Burrows, "I must see my friend at once, and since you seem to be his friend also, I shall count on your assistance."

"You shall have it, but first you must prove you're his friend."

Burrows now felt certain that he was right in his conjecture that the hotel proprietor had recognized his companion.

The next question was, whether he himself had guessed the man's identity. He continued:

"I suppose you know that our friend has been hiding from the authorities for some time?"

Weston nodded.

"I am a friend of his, and a lawyer, and he wrote to me asking that I should come on here and look after his interests. I started at once, but when I reached the place where he asked me to meet him, he had left there. I have followed him to this town, but, as I am a stranger, I have no idea where he would be likely to stop. I heard at the depot that you had taken him up, and so came straight to you."

"If our friend wanted to see you, how is it he didn't leave his address for you?"

Borrows was compelled to think quickly here, but he was equal to the emergency.

"That is what puzzled me at first, but then it occurred to me that he could not do so, without risking some detective's finding it out also."

"Well, look here, I must be sure you're talkin' straight, so jest tell me the name of the man? We might be talkin' about different parties, after all." This was a trying moment to Borrows. He had hoped, by prolonging the conversation, to surprise Weston into an accidental mention of the name. Now that the question was put, he was compelled to give the name which he suspected to be the right one.

"I am endeavoring to meet my friend Walter Marvel."

Borrows could almost hear his heart beat as he watched the face of his host, but Weston gave no sign, and remained silent for a few minutes.

"Well, I guess it's all right. Mr. Marvel was here Sunday night."

Borrows felt a shiver pass over him, he was so relieved at this reply. Restraining himself as much as possible, in his endeavor not to seem too elated, he continued:

"You say he was here? Did he stop over night in your house?"

"No, he only came in for a minute, then he went on to his own place."

Borrows at once thought of the evidence given by young Harrison, which this statement corroborated.

"You mean the place where he goes to put up, when he is out shooting, do you not?"

This acquaintance with Marvel's habits evidently disarmed Weston of any lingering doubts as to the intentions of the detective, for he replied in a much more friendly tone:

"Yes, that's where he went. Whether he's still there or not I can't say, for I haven't seen him since that night."

"I suppose you can direct me how to find it in the morning?"

"Oh, yes, but if you want to ketch him at home, you 'd better start early. I guess he's off with his gun most of the day."

"I shall act on your advice. I suppose that you have known Marvel a long time, since you are so friendly?"

"Why, no, not exactly. You see it an't any special friendship I have for Marvel, that made me so careful. In fact I don't know much about him at all. I haven't seen him more 'n once or twice altogether."

"But I thought you were his friend?"

"I'm any man's friend when he's down. I heard all about the trouble he had with Lewis, and as I didn't see as how he'd done any different to what I would myself, I wouldn't be the one to help to ketch him."

"But if you don't know Marvel, how can you be sure that he was the man whom you picked up Sunday night?" Burrows was beginning to fear some mistake. However, he was reassured by the positive reply of his host.

"Oh, there an't any chance of a mistake. I suspected who 'twas, by the way he was all muffled up, and because he went off luggin' a big bag without sayin' a word to anyone at the station. So I just called him by name, and he owned up, but he begged me not to tell anyone of his bein' in town. And I haven't!"

"I believe you, Mr. Weston, and I thank you for your discretion. Now if you will show me to my room, I'll thank you, and ask you to call me about six o'clock."

Burrows was well pleased with himself, and with the progress which he had made so far, in the investigation of his clue. He thought that he had managed Weston with considerable adroitness. All that he had hoped when he had started was to find some clue to prove Marvel's identity with the late visitor at Riverside. He had succeeded beyond his hopes, for here was a witness, however unwilling, who could be made to testify that in the stranger, and despite his disguise, he had been able to recognize Marvel himself. Moreover, he now felt satisfied that Marvel had lied, when he said that he had thrown his disguise into the river, and he even hoped to find some trace of it at the old house.

Promptly at six, Burrows was called, and in a very little time he was ready to start. Weston gave him full directions as to how to find Marvel's house.

After walking about a mile beyond the more populous portion of the town, Burrows reached his destination, which he readily recognized from Weston's description. The house itself could barely be seen from the road. It was in the midst of a number of large trees, and besides, as no care had been given to the place in years, it was surrounded by dense shrubbery and covered with vines. Thus everything about it being green, it would scarcely have attracted the attention of a casual observer. Burrows thought it a very good retreat for a man anxious to avoid the scrutiny of his fellows, and entered, more than ever satisfied that some important developments awaited his examination of the interior.

Pushing open the door, which moved noiselessly on its hinges, despite the dilapidation everywhere apparent, he found himself in a small but well-lighted room. In this, which had been originally a kitchen, there was some slight evidence of civilized habitation. The stove bore no signs of rust, and the ashes of a recent fire attested the fact that the owner used it, perhaps for cooking, as a kettle, partly filled, still rested in one of the holes. Burrows observed this at a glance, but the dust apparent in all other parts of the room satisfied him that, except for making a cup of coffee, or other light cooking, the apartment had been abandoned. He thought that he must look further for the room in which he hoped to find some evidence.

He passed through a door and found himself in the dining-room, as a table and cupboards proved. A casual peep into the latter, showed a small store of canned meats and fruits, biscuits, butter, sugar, and the like. The next apartment was the sitting room, but the dust and dirt everywhere bespoke an absence of all care on the part of the occupant. Ascending one flight, he explored two rooms in a similar condition of neglect, before he reached one in which there were any signs of habitation. This was plainly, if not rudely furnished, and contained nothing but what was absolutely necessary in a sleeping-room. A cot-bed; a metal wash-bowl, and a pitcher on a painted wooden stand; a looking-glass without a frame, tacked to the wall; an old dressing case with the top, which originally held a glass, entirely missing; a few chairs, and the inventory is complete. It was evident that the house was used, as has been stated, only as an occasional sleeping place. The few odds and ends had been gathered from the general wreck, and put in this one room, in the endeavor to make it at least habitable. Any further trouble or expense had been considered unnecessary. There was a commodious closet, which had probably decided the selection of the room, for it was filled with a miscellaneous collection of articles, arranged with evident care and neatness, comprising outfits for gunning, fishing, etc.

Burrows glanced about for the clues for which he was searching. The first point to determine was, had the man hidden his disguise in this place? To learn this, he did not go searching blindly about the place, but adopted methods which he had seen used by Mr. Barnes, on similar occasions. Although he was jealous of Mr. Barnes, he admired his ability, and did not hesitate to imitate him. He dropped into a chair and glanced around, looking about him keenly, whilst he endeavored to discover what he wished, by reasoning it out, rather than by chance. Mr. Barnes would say: "Undoubtedly chance is a great factor in all investigations, but the man who uses his brains will have more of these 'lucky accidents,' than he who waits for things to 'turn up.'" Burrows felt the truth of this, and acted accordingly. At this moment he wished to know what had been done with the disguise, and reasoned as follows:

"Marvel crossed the river, therefore, the things were wet. He says he changed them at his house, and threw the bundle into the river. Did he make the change, and, if so, did he throw the things into the river? He had a satchel, and it is probable that it contained the clothes. If so, he made the change, but did not throw them in the river. According to Weston, he took the satchel with him when he started for this house. As this is his sleeping-room, he probably brought it in here, whatever he may have done later. Although cleaner than the rest of the house, there is still a considerable quantity of dust about this room; yet, it is not likely that I can find out, from such a source, where he laid down his satchel. However, if he took out the wet clothes, and laid them down, the water would have converted the dust into mud, and would have left a distinct mark on the floor. There is nothing of the kind about, so he did not put them on the floor. What did he do with them? What would I do under similar circumstances? Burn them, perhaps. But they were saturated with water. Still it is always dangerous to conceal such evidence, for someone generally finds the best-hidden articles, when a crime is connected with them. Therefore, I should have burned them at all cost of time or trouble. I should have burned the satchel with them, building a large log fire and putting it with its contents on top of the logs. In this way, by the time the fire had destroyed the satchel, the clothes would be dry enough to burn. Then I should have raked out and thrown away the ashes, a point which would not strike a criminal as quickly as a detective. At least it seems that it seldom does. I think, I may as well examine the fireplace."

Reaching this point in his reasoning, he went to the chimney and found some ashes. He carefully brushed the pile on to a piece of newspaper, which he took from his overcoat pocket. This done, he laid the whole on the floor near the window, and then, with a piece of stick, gradually moved the soft ashes from the centre to the side. As he did this, he was careful to examine every particle, searching for anything that may have escaped combustion. It was not long before his patience was rewarded, for, first a few iron buttons, and then several other pieces of iron, or metal of some kind, were separated from the *debris*. The buttons, of course, proved that something more than an ordinary fire had been made on the hearth, and it was but fair to suppose that clothing had been burned. The other things, however, puzzled him a while, for though not entirely destroyed, he still found it hard to tell exactly what they were. After some thought he concluded that the majority of the metal had originally belonged to the frame-work of the satchel. One piece still remained to be accounted for. This was a bit of wire. Burrows was almost on the point of throwing this away, as unimportant, when it suddenly occurred to him that it must be all that was left of the false whiskers. There was nothing more that he could make out of the ashes; still he carefully wrapped all up and placed the package in a small satchel, which he had brought with him. Burrows smiled as he thought to himself, "Marvel lied, when he said the locket was still in his pocket. There is no trace of it here, so it is evident that the one found was the same which he had with him that night."

Burrows was now anxious to find the pistol. He recollected that the Squire had told of the pistol which Marvel had left at the house, and as he knew that it had not been found, he deemed it probable that it was the weapon used in the murder. This was not so readily reasoned out as the other matter, for, as a pistol could not be burned, it must be hidden; and as there was no way of guessing the hiding-place, there was but one course open to him, namely, to hunt. This he did, as thoroughly as Mr. Barnes had taught him to do, and, when he went down-stairs again, he felt almost sure that the weapon had not been concealed above. He was just as thorough in going over the rooms on the lower floor, and finally reached the kitchen, without having found it. He had not looked long in this place, however, before he noticed that the tiles in front of the stove had been disturbed. One of the stones had been so poorly replaced, that Burrows muttered to himself, "He must have wanted this to be found." Removing it, he disclosed a hole below, in which was a pistol. He took this out, and another object attracted his attention. This proved to be a small piece of silver-plated metal, and a closer scrutiny revealed the fact that a name was engraved thereon. This name was, "John Lewis."

"Better and better," thought the detective. "How nicely the precautions of a criminal, as usual, serve to convict him. This is a plate which he wrenched from the satchel, and the name proves that he got that at the farm. I am not surprised any longer that he did not disturb any of his own people that night, for he did not go home at all. He obtained a change at the house of his victim. He is a cool hand, to kill a man, and then wear his clothing away from the scene of his crime."

Burrows now turned his attention to the pistol, and at once noticed that there were three empty chambers. He concluded, from this, that Marvel must have fired both shots found in the body. Still looking at the weapon, he noticed that a name was engraved on the stock. He approached the window for more light, and read, "Walter Marvel." At this moment the door was opened, and Mr. Barnes and Lewis stood on the threshold.

CHAPTER XIV
WHEN DETECTIVES QUARREL

When Burrows saw Mr. Barnes in the doorway, for a moment he was confused, but almost immediately he concluded that it was too late for the older detective to take any of the glory away from him. Summoning up his courage, he said:

"Good morning, Mr. Barnes! You are just in time to hear the news. I have discovered the real murderer."

Mr. Barnes looked at him keenly, as he asked:

"Who is it?"

"The man whom I suspected from the start, Walter Marvel!" replied Burrows, with a tinge of exultation in his voice.

"And pray how do you prove this?" asked Mr. Barnes, quietly. Burrows was nettled at the tone of his superior, and answered with considerable asperity:

"Oh, there is proof enough. I am sure of what I say, or I should not make the assertion."

"I hope you are not making any blunder, Burrows? Remember, it is a serious thing for a detective to make a charge of murder against anyone, unless he can assure a conviction at the trial."

"I know that, but I tell you there is no mistake here. I have tracked my man to and from the scene of the crime, and can give you incontestible proof of what I say."

"Go on, I am listening." Mr. Barnes sat down on a chair near him. Burrows forthwith entered into a minute and detailed account of the facts, from which he had reached the conclusion which he had just so positively asserted. During the narration Mr. Barnes made absolutely no comment, and when Burrows reached the end of his story, he was impatient to know what would be said. He already saw that he would not receive the praise which he considered was due to his efforts. Mr. Barnes pondered over the situation for a few moments, and then said:

"Do you realize what you have done, Mr. Burrows?" Burrows did not like to have Mr. Barnes call him "Mr." Burrows, for he knew at once now, that Mr. Barnes was angry, and, determined as he had been to pursue this examination alone, he had by no means counted on a quarrel. Therefore, in a troubled tone, he answered:

"Do I realize what I have done? No harm, I hope?"

"You have been the means of fixing a terrible imputation on the character of a girl, who is the pride of this county."

"How so?"

"It was distinctly your duty to report to me the conversation which you had with the station-agent. I am in charge of this inquiry, and, by your stupidity and vanity, you have caused irreparable harm."

"I don't see that!" Burrows was getting angry now. He did not relish being thus chided before Lewis. But Mr. Barnes did not appear to notice his rising temper.

"I suppose not. Like all young men, you do a wrong act, and then, instead of having the manhood to acknowledge the error, and in some way endeavor to atone therefore, you persist in defending the course pursued. But you shall not make any more mistakes in this case. From this moment you may consider that you have no further connection with it."

"What do you mean?"

"I mean that you will go back to Boston, and remain there."

"And let you take all the credit for my work, I suppose? Mr. Barnes, you are presumptuous."

"I am in charge of this case, and I order you to have no more to do with it."

"What if I refuse?"

"I will dispatch a message to the agency, and request your recall."

"Do so, if you wish! Perhaps I shall send a message also, that will place a different aspect on what you ask them to do. I have discovered the true criminal, and I doubt if I shall be recalled for so doing."

Mr. Barnes stopped a moment to reflect. He did not wish to force Burrows into any hasty action, and preferred, if possible, still to control him. So abandoning for a moment his tone of command, he asked:

"Since you have assumed charge of the affair, will you mind telling me what you wish to do next?"

"I believe that the evidence is all to be given to the Grand Jury to-day. I should go to Dover at once, and relate to them the facts which I have just told you."

"In other words, not satisfied with the trouble which you have already given to Miss Lewis, you will now go and obtain the indictment of her lover, notwithstanding the fact that he is innocent!"

"Innocent?"

"Of course he is innocent! You have proved it by your work. Only, by your delay, you have lost all traces of the real criminal."

"But how can you say that he is innocent, when I have proved that he came here straight from the farm; that he was recognized—"

"By a man who does not know him."

"But here, in his own house, are signs of his guilt."

"Burrows, if this were not so serious a case, I would let you have your way, and then, at the trial, show you what an idiot you are. But as I wish, if possible, to avoid any more mistakes, I will show you how easy it is for me to overturn your castles in the air. According to your latest theory, you make Marvel commit murder and leave the town on a train which started from Lee at 10.39 P.M. Now Miss Lewis left him across the river, went directly to her room, and reached there at 10.30 P.M. Therefore it is plain that Marvel has an easily proven *alibi*."

Burrows flushed at this, but he was not willing to give up his theory without one more struggle.

"The only way in which he could prove that, would be by the testimony of his accomplice, and—"

"Stop! For shame, Mr. Burrows! Would you, resort to so base a thing as slander simply to have the gratification of finding a criminal? To make your chain complete, would you implicate a girl, against whom you have not a particle of evidence?"

"She has confessed her share in the crime."

"She is a noble woman, and is trying to shield her lover from the mistakes of such detectives as you are proving yourself to be."

"You ought to go on the stage," sneered Burrows; "you would make quite a heroic actor, Mr. Barnes."

"Come," said Mr. Barnes, sternly, "no impertinence! Respect my age and experience, if you do not respect me. And now, since I cannot turn you from your folly, which in this case will possibly be a crime, I must resort to compulsion, and again, as your superior, I order you to abandon your project."

"And I refuse!" returned Burrows, hotly.

"Very well! I will give you one more chance. Whatever little ability as a detective you may have, you have imbibed most of your best methods from association with me. Let me tell you that if you do not obey me in this instance, you must never expect any assistance or advice from me again. Moreover, I swear to find the guilty man and to right the wrong which you will have done to two innocent people. Act as you have said you will, and you will live to rue the day when you quarrelled with Jack Barnes."

Burrows regretted the turn of events, but he felt too sure of his position to give it up. He thought Mr. Barnes was actuated to some extent by jealousy, and that he would find it difficult to accomplish all that he threatened. He had no pity for Marvel, for he believed him to be the guilty man, and so he determined to go at once to Dover with his new evidence. In reply to Mr. Barnes he said:

"You have made the quarrel, not I! I am doing my duty."

"What will you do, Mr. Lewis?" asked the elder detective.

"I shall go on to Dover with Mr. Burrows, and see the thing through. I don't say that I think he is right, for, as you say, I should be obliged to accept the theory that Miss Lewis is guilty also, and whilst I thought Marvel the murderer, as I told you before I started here, I must say that I would rather think him innocent, than believe that my cousin had a hand in the affair. Still, she may have been mistaken about the time. However, I must wait for older heads than mine to solve this problem."

"I am glad that you are not as easily convinced by this array of evidence, as our young friend thinks the jury will be. As I suppose you want the truth, I promise you that I will use all my best skill to unravel this mystery."

"Do so, Mr. Barnes, and I will give you a thousand dollars. I have saved some money, and although that is a large sum, I would give it cheerfully."

"Thank you for your generous offer, but I am going to work now, as a duty. The innocent must not, and shall not, suffer if I can prevent it. Besides, my professional pride is aroused in this, now."

The three men then turned their steps towards the town, and walked along in silence. All of the party had much with which to occupy their thoughts, and besides, the recent scene had caused rather a restraint, at least between two of them. Just before they reached the hotel, however, Mr. Barnes asked Burrows:

"How many shots were fired from that pistol?"

"There are three empty shells in it."

"That is to say, it has been used twice since the shot which Marvel fired at the birthday party?"

"Evidently."

Mr. Barnes said no more, and, in a few minutes later, they all were at the hotel, whence they went to the depot. Burrows and Lewis started by train for Dover, and Mr. Barnes for Boston. Reaching that city, he went directly to the agency, and reported all that had occurred. He was closeted with the chief for over an hour, but was unable to convince that personage that Burrows was on a wrong scent. On the contrary, he seemed to think that the young man had shown considerable ability in ferreting out the truth of the matter.

"Well," said Mr. Barnes, "you must choose between me and him. If you refuse to recall him from the case, you must accept my resignation from the agency."

"I should be sorry to lose our best man," responded the chief, "but, really, your request seems a little unreasonable to me. Burrows has only done what we must consider a service, and it would be manifestly unjust to let him suffer for it."

"Then you refuse to call him home?"

"Well, I don't see—"

"There are no half-way measures which you can adopt. It must be either Burrows or Barnes. Come, decide at once! I have no time to waste!"

"Well, then, since you will have it, you force me to accept your resignation, though I regret it very much."

"Sentiment is unnecessary," said Mr. Barnes, dryly, "good morning!" Before the chief could say a word, he was gone, and his superior more than half doubted the wisdom of the course which he had pursued. But that is only man's nature. We often decide quickly, only to regret as soon as the decision is irrevocable.

Leaving the agency, Mr. Barnes proceeded to a telegraph-office, and sent a dispatch to the clerk of the court at Dover, asking for news as to the result of the examination before the Grand Jury. This done, he went to his home and dined, after which he waited impatiently for a telegram from Dover, because he had decided to do nothing until he should hear from the court officer. The afternoon passed, and the evening, till at length he concluded that he would not hear till the following day, and therefore retired to rest. Early in the morning he received the dispatch which read:

"Marvel indicted for murder."

This was only what he had expected, but he could not repress an exclamation of disgust, at what he still thought was the consequence of criminal interference on the part of Burrows. What should he do next?

That was the point to settle, but whilst he ate his breakfast and pondered over this point, a servant announced that a lady wished to see him. He at once repaired to his parlor, whither she had been shown, and was astounded to see Virginia Lewis.

"You are no doubt surprised that I am here?"

"I confess that I am!"

"I have been set at liberty, and Mr. Marvel has been indicted by the Grand Jury."

"I have just received a telegram to that effect."

"What will you do next? I went to the agency in search of you, and learned that you have severed your connection with the case. Will you tell me why you did so?"

"Because they refuse to recall Mr. Burrows."

"Then you do not think that the evidence which he discovered proves the guilt of Mr. Marvel?"

"Miss Lewis, I must tell you that I did not credit the story which you told, implicating yourself, and if I believe in your innocence, I must also believe in Mr. Marvel's."

"Why so?"

"Burrows is no doubt right in claiming that the murderer is the man who made the trip to Epping that night, but I think he is wrong in his identification of this man."

"I thought he had that all thoroughly explained?"

"Miss Lewis, I imagine, from your coming here, that you wish my aid."

"I have come to you because I fancied that you believe Mr. Marvel innocent. I wish you to try to prove it."

"Precisely! Meanwhile you yourself suspect that he is guilty, do you not?"

"I do not say so!"

"It is so, nevertheless. But we shall not get along in this way. You must not fence with me any more. We are on the same side now, and though Burrows has not had as much experience as I have, it will take all my skill to destroy the case which he has made out against your lover." Mr. Barnes used this word purposely to arouse her to action.

"I trust you, Mr. Barnes, and place our affair in your hands. Ask me what you please, and I will reply."

"Very good! In the first place tell me, am I not right in saying that you have believed that Mr. Marvel is guilty?"

"Yes! You are right."

"Very good! That proves your innocence. Now I will demonstrate his, to your satisfaction at least." He explained the discrepancy, as to time, in the theory of the other detective.

"But then," said Virginia, "the real murderer must have placed the pistol where it was found, so as to throw suspicion on Mr. Marvel?"

"Exactly! You are quick to see things, quicker than our adversary, Mr. Burrows. Before we go into that, however, tell me why you consider Marvel guilty? You must have more reason for that opinion than is known to me."

"I have. After we separated across the river, as you shrewdly discovered, he returned to the farm. He admitted to you that he had entered the house, but he did not tell you that he had left a note for me. I found this in the morning and, as I see now, I misconstrued it. That was the secret motive of all my actions thereafter."

"Have you the letter now?"

"Yes, here it is." Taking it from her pocket, she handed it to Mr. Barnes. It read as follows:

"When we parted to-night you spoke as though you could not give me the answer that I wish. Perhaps when this reaches you, you may see things differently. By morning what now seems an obstacle in your judgment may be removed and you may feel free to decide your own and my fate yourself. Should you decide against me, write to me as agreed, and I will leave you and this country forever.

"WALTER."

Mr. Barnes read this carefully, and then said: "I see your mistake. In reading it you placed a comma after the word 'judgment,' whereas he meant it to be after the word 'obstacle.' However, this paper alone will prove the *alibi* so necessary to Mr. Marvel, and so you may rest easy, although I shall not until I have found the man who manufactured all this evidence against Mr. Marvel. There is another point which I wish cleared up. How did you know there were two wounds in the body, and so be able to arrange your story to meet the requirements of the case so well?"

"When Alice fainted, and was brought out of the room, Harry Lucas came with her, and, whilst the doctor was attending to her, I questioned Lucas."

"Of course! Of course! I was a fool to let him leave the room, but then, a man cannot think of everything. You are a clever woman, Miss Lewis, and it will be a pleasure for me to serve you. Now one thing more. Tell me why you did not destroy that paper upon which your uncle had written Mr. Marvel's name, accusing him of the crime? That was a dangerous bit of evidence to keep, if you wished to shield him."

"Yes, I know, but it is just because it seemed so conclusive, that I did keep it. I thought that I should be able to prevent its existence from being discovered, but in that I was sadly mistaken. I kept it for this reason. I was willing to shield Mr. Marvel at any sacrifice, because—because I love him. But I should never have received him again, so long as I knew him to be, or thought that he was, a criminal. Suppose that he had gone away, and then should return after a year or two, never having been publicly accused? Don't you see how terrible my position would be? To be obliged to accuse him of a crime, when I had no proof?"

"Exactly. You were willing to suppress the evidence to save him; but you preserved it to save yourself. Very proper perhaps, but, you see, very risky, considering your primary purpose. Of course that paper will tell against him now. Then, there is the matter of the locket. That certainly looks very bad. How do you account for that?"

"Why—why—don't you see? That was my last hope destroyed. When I heard that Walter—Mr. Marvel—had taken the locket, and remembered that I had found it tight in my dead uncle's hand, the whole thing seemed too terribly certain. But now "

"Ah! You have a theory?"

"Mr. Barnes, you men never quite understand us women. We love a man, and after that we cling to him forever. We hope against reason, and manufacture reasons upon which to build hope. So, ever since the inquest, I have striven to find an explanation of this locket affair. There is one possibility that has occurred to me. Mr. Marvel certainly entered the house after I had retired, and probably whilst my uncle was yet alive. May he not have dropped the locket, and may not my uncle, disturbed by some noise, have searched the house, and accidentally have found the locket?"

"That is very well argued, Miss Lewis, but I fear that it will not prove to be true. Unless Mr. Lewis was killed immediately after, he would scarcely have retained the locket in his hand. Still, it is a possibility. It would do at a pinch, in trying to confuse a jury: But, unless I be greatly mistaken, nothing of that sort will be necessary. I hope to discover the whole solution of this singularly complex affair."

"Where will you begin?"

"Where Burrows did, only I will go the other way. He followed the man away from the scene of the murder, and allowed himself to get on a false scent. I will trace him to the place from which he came, and there discover his identity. Meanwhile, you must go home again. When is the funeral?"

"It is to be this afternoon."

"Then I go back with you. But first, there is something that I can find out even here in Boston. If you will wait for me, my housekeeper will get you some breakfast, whilst I do my errand."

Miss Lewis agreed, and Mr. Barnes went out. He proceeded to the main office of the Boston Maine Railroad and asked for the superintendent. Being shown into the presence of that official, he at once explained the object of his visit.

"I am tracing a man," said he, "and know that he reached Lee, New Hampshire, on the train which is due there about nine o'clock. Can you find the ticket which he gave to the conductor on that train, last Sunday night?"

"Very easily, provided he was the only passenger for that place."

Calling an attendant, he gave him orders to find the ticket, and a few minutes later Mr. Barnes held it in his hand. It read:

"WORCESTER TO LEE."

Mr. Barnes was troubled, for he remembered that Marvel had testified that he had been in Worcester, hiding from the authorities. He examined the ticket closely, and noted that it was rough on one edge, as though a portion had been torn off. He handed it to the superintendent, and asked:

"Can you tell me where this ticket was bought? I see that one or more coupons have been torn off. Therefore, the passenger must have started from some point the other side of Worcester."

The superintendent looked at the ticket, and replied:

"This was originally sold in New York, and is the form used by the Norwich line of steamers. But your man may have bought this half of the ticket from a scalper in Worcester."

Mr. Barnes thanked the superintendent, and left the office.

CHAPTER XV
MR. BARNES ON HIS METTLE

Mr. Barnes and Virginia returned to Riverside farm, reaching there just as the people were assembling for the funeral services. The Squire greeted Virginia cordially, and looked interrogatively at Mr. Barnes, evidently a little confused at seeing them together. Virginia hastened to explain.

"Squire, I hope you will be glad to hear that Mr. Barnes is now working in my interests? He does not believe that Walter is guilty."

"Is that true?" said the Squire, quickly interested. "I am glad to hear it, for though Burrows seems to have made out a complete chain of evidence, if you, Mr. Barnes, with your experience, are unconvinced, there must be a weak spot in it. Tell me, how is it?"

"Mr. Burrows is mistaken," said Mr. Barnes. "His evidence is all good, and most important. His deductions, however, are incorrect. As you say, there is a flaw. I pointed it out to him, but he is obstinate and refuses to see it. He cannot convict Marvel without proving that Miss Lewis here was an accomplice after the fact, if not before."

"God forbid that he should do that."

"I was afraid that he would have brought out this point before the Grand Jury, and that Miss Lewis, as a consequence, would have been still in prison. That he has not done so, shows that he secretly fears that he could not sustain the charge."

"Well, but do you think you can clear Marvel? If so, who did kill Lewis?"

"Your last query is a hard one to answer, but I must do so if I am to prove Marvel's innocence. All I can say now is, that I hope to accomplish that. Now, I wish to see the body again. Will you come with me?"

The Squire and the detective moved towards the parlor, where was the casket containing the remains. Virginia went to her own room. The two men stood beside the coffin, a moment, in silence. Mr. Barnes gazed intently at the charred face, bandaged in silk handkerchiefs to conceal the disfigurement, and the Squire wondered of what he was thinking. In truth, Mr. Barnes scarcely knew himself. He had a dimly defined idea within his mind, and was awaiting its development. Presently, his eyes wandered down to where the crossed arms of the corpse lay upon the breast, and he noted the diamond ring.

"Squire," said he, "I think a mistake will be made if we do not interfere."

"What do you mean?"

"There is a ring on the finger of the corpse. It should not be buried."

"Why not?"

"Because the man was murdered, and anything connected with the body may become an article of value, as evidence of some kind."

"How can a ring amount to anything?"

"I don't say it will, but it may. We detectives, as you know, are cautious, and I should be indebted if you will remove it."

"Oh! certainly, if you specially wish it." The Squire removed the ring with some difficulty.

"I wish, Squire, that you would keep that yourself. Should anything occur which will make it useful to me, I shall know where to get it."

"Yes, I will keep it, and it shall not leave my possession unless I let you know first."

"I thank you, but may I look at it now, for a moment?"

"Certainly!" The Squire handed it to him. Mr. Barnes examined it closely, and noticing an inscription on the inside of the band, went to the light to decipher it. It proved to be "W. to M." The detective started, and muttered: "The same initials as were on the locket!" Then returning the ring to the Squire, he asked:

"Have you that locket? Though that is a foolish question, as I suppose you gave it to the authorities at Dover, with the other things in evidence."

"Yes. They were given up yesterday."

"I wonder," thought the detective, "if I have made a mistake. I may wish to see that locket once more, and I must question Miss Lewis."

At this moment, the minister arrived, and the ceremonies commenced. John Lewis came in with him, and then went to call Virginia, but she declined to leave her room. At this there was little surprise, for what girl would care to show herself before so many people, after such an experience? The service was brief, the main point in the discourse being to impress upon the minds of those present the transitoriness of human life, and the extreme uncertainty as to how long a man might live, or how soon be called away from all that he holds dear on earth; and, therefore, the policy and wisdom of so arranging earthly affairs that one might be ready to answer the call at any time. Whilst the worthy man spoke nothing but truth, it is doubtful if any of his hearers even so much as made their wills the next day, so far off do most men feel from death.

The body was interred in a private cemetery belonging to the estate, situated at one end of the farm, near a growth of timberland. After the funeral, the people dispersed.

Mr. Barnes approached Will Everly, as he was about to leave, and said:

"Do you remember me, Mr. Everly?"

"Certainly; you are Mr. Barnes. Miss Lewis tells me that you are now devoted to the interests of Mr. Marvel. Is that true?"

"It is, and now I wish to intrust to you an errand that may serve him. Will you undertake it?"

"Just give me a chance."

"Have you a fast horse?"

"I have, and can get a faster if there be any need."

"What I wish done is very simple, but it must be done without delay, for I wish to have word to-night, as I shall be obliged to leave here to-morrow."

"I can go where you wish at once."

"Go then to Dover and hunt up the clerk of the court. His name is Ainsley—"

"I know him very well, and where to find him."

"All the better. See him, and tell him that you wish to look at the locket which has played so conspicuous a part in this case. If he has not the custody of it, he will be able to take you to the one who has. See the locket to-night, if possible. Look on the outside and find out what the inscription is. Whether it is 'W. M.' or 'W.

to M.' The word 'to,' if on the trinket will save your friend's life. Lose no time."

Everly needed no second bidding, but was off on a run at once. Mr. Barnes seemed satisfied, and turned into the house. Here he found Lucas, and spoke to him.

"This is a sad business, Mr. Lucas."

"Indeed it is. I would gladly take the place of the prisoner for the sake of his sister, if not of himself."

"Miss Marvel has passed through a trying ordeal. How is she now?"

"She is very ill. Of course she was prostrated at the inquest because of the part which she took in it herself; so much so, that we did not dare to tell her of the charges against Miss Lewis. But through the stupidity of a servant she heard to-day of the fact that her brother is now the accused, and she has been delirious ever since. I have waited after the others to tell Miss Lewis this, but now I am anxious about Miss Marvel and will leave you. I hope that you may be successful in your defence of Walter. I cannot believe that he is really guilty."

"It shall not be for want of honest endeavor, if I fail." Mr. Barnes bowed courteously as Lucas retired.

A moment later Miss Lewis appeared.

"I am glad you are here, Mr. Barnes," said she, "for I want to get to work at once."

"Very well. Let me ask you a few questions. What was your mother's name?"

"Matilda; I don't know her married name. Everyone knows that 'Lewis' is only the name given to me by my adopted father. That was his name, and, as I am his sister's child, of course she must have changed hers when she married; but to what, my uncle never would tell me. So I have been Virginia Lewis, in spite of myself."

"But perhaps you know your father's first name, if not his last?"

"No. Whenever I asked any questions, my uncle would say, 'You never had a father.'"

"Well, your mother's name was Matilda, that is, the first name has 'M.' for the initial. And I feel satisfied that your father's initial was 'W.'"

"Is it a matter of any importance?"

"It may be. The ring that your uncle wore bore the inscription 'W. to M.' I have sent Everly to Dover to find out if the same is on that medallion. I may have overlooked the word 'to 'when I had it in my hand, and, if it is there, it will indicate that there were two of those lockets."

"And that would help to prove that Walter is innocent, would it not?"

"It would help, for it would show that the one which you found in the dead man's hand was not the one which Mr. Marvel had."

"God grant it! Otherwise I should never forgive myself for furnishing that evidence against him. But what about the clothes which he says he threw into the river? The Squire told me that he and my cousin, Mr. Lewis, have had the stream dragged, but did not find anything."

"I mean to have a try at that myself. Now I have another point, which I wish to investigate, and if you will excuse me I will be off."

"You will return and take supper with me, will you not? The proprieties will not be invaded, for Sarah is here with me, and will stay as long as I wish her. Therefore, you can have a room here if you desire."

"Thank you very much. Don't lose heart, Miss Lewis; if it be in the power of man, I will clear your lover from this charge."

Virginia showed gratitude in her face, and the detective went away. From the farm he went to the house of Dr. Snow, and was fortunate enough to find him at home, though he had but just returned from a visit to Miss Marvel, whom he reported as slightly improved. Mr. Barnes proceeded to ask a few questions of the old physician, about the people most nearly connected with the crime and its consequences. Finally he said:

"There is a question that I would like to ask, doctor. Would a man's fingers swell, or would they shrink, after death?"

"That would depend upon the circumstances of the case. If the death was from dropsy, or from some poisons, they would swell, but ordinarily of course they would shrink. Again, the time has something to do with it, for in all cases the tissues must waste eventually."

"Since there is some doubt about it, I must give you a specific case. Take the body of Mr. Lewis, for example. Would you expect any shrinking of his fingers?"

"I think I should, though they may not have done so to any considerable extent in the few days which have elapsed."

"They would not have swollen?"

"No, I am positive that they would not."

"Thank you, doctor, you have settled an important point for me. When the trial comes on, please remember this interview, in case you should be questioned about it on the witness-stand."

"I will testify, of course, though as yet I cannot see what it is that you are trying to prove."

"Pardon me if I say no more at this time. I must think only of the interests which I am serving, and I deem it wisest to work quietly, as yet. Will you oblige me by not mentioning this to anyone?"

"I will be discreet, since you seem to think it is important."

Leaving the doctor's house, Mr. Barnes went to the bridge from which Marvel claimed that he had thrown the bundle of clothing. Looking over the edge, into the water, he concluded that on whichever side it had been thrown, the bundle must have been carried by the current towards the dam; otherwise it would have been found on the banks, which were shelving on the south side of the bridge.

Next, he left the bridge and went to the side of the stream north of the dam, and from that point studied the apparent conditions. "Well," thought he, "if Marvel had sought for a place to lose a thing he could not have chosen better." This conclusion was most probable, for he saw a large number of enormous boulders of jagged rock projecting from the water, which is shallow as it passes over the stones, and these rough projections made innumerable eddies and smaller currents. A bundle of clothing might easily be caught and held among these rocks, and held there against all time, or at least long enough to be of no practical value to Walter Marvel.

The detective saw that he had almost a hopeless task to make this river yield up its secret, if indeed it held one. However, he was not a man easily daunted by obstacles, and he determined to make an attempt that night. He chose the night for his experiment, deeming it wisest to make the conditions, as nearly as possible, similar to those under which the accused had acted. He thought that the currents among these rocks might be different at night, as then the mills would not be working. He closely examined the dam, and conceived a new idea. The dam was made of wood, and as its construction must be clear to you in order that you may understand the course pursued by Mr. Barnes, it becomes necessary to describe it.

The bridge is about a hundred feet south of the point where the water goes over the dam. Standing on this bridge, one notices a smooth body of water flowing towards the place where it rushed over the dam, 'but he forms no idea of the power of the current from this point of view. On the line where the stream dashes downward, he sees some boards projecting above the surface, from each side of the river, towards the centre, for a distance equal to one quarter of the width of the stream. Between these points, where the dam rises above the level, the water rushes over the dam, which is two feet lower along the centre than at the sides. Going below the dam, that is to the north of it, one easily sees how it is constructed. Immense triangles of timber are laid along the rocks, resting on the short sides. Thus their hypothenuses face the south, and on them are nailed the boards which form the dam. Therefore, as the water rushes over, there is a space under the dam where it is comparatively dry. At least, no great amount of water finds its way there, as only what leaks through, drips down.

It was whilst looking at this space, that the new idea occurred to the detective. In order to turn the mill-wheels, sluices are built, which conduct the water in the desired direction. When these are open, it is evident that a strong current sets in the direction of the mill. This is so powerful and there is such a suction downward, that objects on the surface would be drawn below and carried into the mill, were it not that the sluice-gates are furnished with gratings, to keep out such jetsam. Studying this point, it became evident to the detective that if the sluices were open on Sunday night, the bundle of clothing must be looked for at these gratings.

He therefore went to the mill, and asked for the man who had the care of the sluices. From him he learned that they had been closed on the night of the murder, and then persuaded him to have them closed this evening also, so that the conditions might be the same.

Leaving the vicinity of the mill, he went back to Riverside, and enjoyed his supper with Miss Lewis. After the meal, he said:

"Where is Mr. Lewis? Is he not staying here?"

"He accepted an invitation to visit the Squire tonight."

"All the better; the fewer people who know what I do to-night, the more pleased I shall be. Now then, I want a suit of your uncle's clothing; old ones will do."

"I will get what you want." Virginia left the room, returning a few minutes later, with some clothing. The detective placed the articles in a pail of water, allowing them to become thoroughly wet before he removed them. Next he rolled them into a compact bundle, which he tied securely.

"I am now ready for my experiment. My idea is to go to the bridge and throw that bundle over, as Marvel claims that he did, and then see what becomes of it. I am sorry that I cannot ask him at just what point he did this, but I must do the best I can, without this knowledge. The probability is, that he tossed the bundle over as soon as he got on the bridge, and with his right hand. Therefore he would have thrown it over on the side nearest the dam. At any rate, that is what I shall do."

"I see what your idea is, and am anxious to have the experiment tried. Shall we go at once?"

"No. I cannot tell what difference the hour may make on the currents, and, so many days after, they may be totally different. However, I shall go at the same hour as he did. At least it will insure our not being observed. Besides, I wish if possible to see Everly, and I think he will return before eleven o'clock."

"You will wait till that hour?"

"Yes. You left Marvel at the river and reached your room at 10.30. He came here after that, then went to his own house, and back to the bridge, where he must have arrived at or about 11.30."

The evening passed slowly, most of the time being consumed by these two in a discussion of the subject which absorbed their minds, until, at about a quarter to eleven, a horse's hoofs sounded without, and a moment later they were joined by Will Everly.

"Well," said the detective, "what news?"

"I found Ainsley, and through him, was enabled to see the locket."

"Very good! What is the inscription?"

"Simply 'W. M.' the word 'to 'does not appear, and the letters are so close together, there is no chance that it ever was there. It occurred to me that it may have been, and have become worn out, but that is impossible."

As this hope was dispelled, Virginia seemed much disappointed.

"What do you think now, Mr. Barnes?" said she. "This is discouraging, is it not?"

"Do you know if your mother had more than one name?"

"I cannot be certain, but I never heard of any other except 'Matilda.'"

"Still, she may have had another, and it may have been 'Winona' or some other with 'W.' for the initial. We must look that up. If the initials are hers, it will answer our purpose as well. Now we will start on the other errand. Mr. Everly, you may come with us if you wish. We are going to try to recover the clothes which Marvel says he threw over the bridge."

"I should like to go with you, but I doubt if you will succeed. Young Mr. Lewis inaugurated a regular search, and besides I went myself and looked thoroughly, more than once since the inquest. I think I should have made up a bundle for them to find, only I could not supply the locket which he said is in the pocket."

"No! No! We must not resort to manufacturing any evidence. If Marvel is guilty, he must suffer, but if he is innocent he must be saved. Let us work only for the truth." So saying he took up the bundle of wet clothing and started. Virginia and Everly followed in silence, neither of them relishing the last speech of the detective, however just they knew it to be. The trio soon reached their destination, and Mr. Barnes stopped at a point near the rail.

"Here," said he, "if my calculations are correct, is the place from which I think Marvel must have thrown his bundle. I will now explain to you what I expect will happen. I have soaked my bundle, because his was wet. If dry, the clothes would float nearer to the surface of the water, and would soon be hurried over the dam, as the current here is very rapid. But being wet, and therefore more weighty, this bundle will float below the surface, if at all." His companions listened with much interest. He continued: "I will now commence my experiment. Fortunately the moon is bright and we can see easily. First, I will take a piece of wood." He looked about, and soon found a large heavy piece of timber near the saw-mill. Approaching the rail he said: "Now I will throw this over, and you will see that it will be carried, first, against the boarding which projects above the level, and then be swept towards the centre, and over." He let it drop and the result was exactly as he had predicted. "That much was easily foreseen. But my next may not be so accurate, for it is but a surmise on my part. My idea is this. That wood went over readily. But with a bundle of clothing it may be different. If it is first taken against the projecting portion, and then drawn towards the centre, it will go over more slowly than if carried directly. Now, if the weight is sufficient to hold it some distance below the surface, and there are any ragged edges to the wood-work of the dam, the cloth would most likely catch on them. In that case it would not fall into the stream below, but would remain suspended awhile, finally dropping into the space under the dam. Mr. Everly, you will go around to the other side, so that in case it does go over, you can see where the currents take it."

Everly at once obeyed, and, receiving the signal that he was in his position, Mr. Barnes dropped his bundle. Virginia scarcely breathed, so great was her anxiety as to the outcome of the trial. As in the first experiment, the bundle, which could just be seen as it floated below the surface, drifted straight to the projecting ridge; thence slowly it went towards the centre, where it remained stationary for a moment. This moment seemed an age to the girl. She almost thought that her lover's fate depended on that bundle of clothing. At last it moved again, and slid over, partly disappearing, but, as had been predicted, it seemed to catch and remain hanging. Virginia was about to utter an exclamation of joy, when to her dismay it was forced from its slender hold, and carried down into the rapids below. Virginia uttered a groan as she thought the experiment had failed.

"Come, come," said Mr. Barnes, reassuringly, "what did you expect? Surely not that my bundle would drop on top of the other? That would have been miraculous. You noticed that, as I predicted, it caught on the edge? Perhaps the other dropped below, even though mine did not. I may have tied my parcel tighter than the other, and so have left less chance for the cloth to be caught. Come below, and we will search under the dam. Let us see what Everly will report."

Virginia accompanied him, but when they reached the spot where Everly had last been seen by them, he was nowhere in sight. His coat and hat, however, were on the bank, and from this the detective concluded, that the young man, in his zeal, had entered the stream in pursuit of the bundle, and Mr. Barnes decided to await his return before proceeding further with his plan. As the minutes passed, however, first Virginia, and then Mr. Barnes himself became alarmed at Everly's prolonged absence, and he was about to make some search, when a loud shout arrested their attention. It came from the direction of the dam, and Mr. Barnes realized at once that Everly, instead of following the bundle which had just been thrown over, had gone under the dam in search of the original one. A few moments later he was seen emerging from among the timbers which supported the dam, presenting a very wretched and bedraggled appearance. He held a large bundle in his hands, and exclaimed as he came towards them:

"God bless you, Mr. Barnes, you were right! As soon as I saw your bundle catch, I could not wait, but taking off my coat, I went under the dam and searched for what we were after. What is more, I found it not ten feet the other side of where yours would have fallen had it dropped."

"You have done well, and if this is really the bundle that Marvel threw over, you have repaid your debt to him, and saved his life."

Virginia and Everly were anxious to open the bundle at once, but the detective would not permit it until they should reach home.

"We might lose the locket here in the road," said he, "and, besides, Mr. Everly is all wet." So they were guided by him, and returned to the farm, where the detective insisted on a change of garments for Everly, before he would examine the bundle. When it was opened, Virginia claimed that she recognized the clothes as those worn by Marvel on the night of the murder. Mr. Barnes next searched the pockets of the vest, which Marvel had designated as the garment wherein he had placed the medallion, and withdrawing his hand, laid before the delighted gaze of the others a locket, the exact counterpart of the one found in the hand of the corpse.

CHAPTER XVI
MR. BARNES ON THE SCENT

As soon as it was settled, beyond all doubt, that the clothes and locket found under the dam, were the ones on which the fate of Walter Marvel depended, Mr. Barnes was all activity again.

"Now," said he, speaking rapidly, "there is not a moment to lose. We have saved the innocent, but we must yet find the guilty, and he has a week the start of us. How soon can I get away from this town?"

"A train passes Lee depot at one o'clock. You have three quarters of an hour in which to catch it. My horse and wagon are at your disposal, of course."

"Thank you, Mr. Everly; you must drive me to the station. Before I go, I will give you some instructions; though, on the whole, all I wish is, that you two will not tell anyone of what we have found, until you hear from me again."

"But whilst you are gone, must Walter remain in prison?" asked Virginia.

"Yes! It will not hurt him. Neither of you must go to him, for if you do, you might betray what I wish kept secret. Do you promise?"

"But may I not tell Alice that her brother is safe? She is desperately ill, and I fear that she may lose her reason if she does not soon hear that there is no danger threatening Walter."

Mr. Barnes considered a moment and then said:

"If you find it necessary, you may tell her that your uncle, Mr. Lewis, is not dead."

"Not dead!" exclaimed his two auditors in a breath.

"Yes, tell her that he is not dead. That will certainly relieve her mind."

"But how can I explain that, when she knows to the contrary?"

"You must exercise your ingenuity. Tell her that there has been a mistake as to the identity of the corpse, or anything that occurs to your mind, only do not tell her about the finding of this bundle. I do not wish Mr. Burrows to know what I have done, for fear that he may make trouble for me, and perhaps defeat the ends of justice. Now I must be off. Use your judgment, and, above all things, whatever you do tell your sick friend, keep it from getting out. Good-bye! Trust me!"

Mr. Barnes was fortunate in finding trains to meet him as he pursued his way to New York, by a circuitous route. The one which he boarded at Lee, took him as far as Worcester, and thence he went on to Albany, knowing that, from that point, he could easily reach New York. As it was, he arrived in that city before noon on the following day. Leaving the train, he hurriedly proceeded up-town to Washington Heights. Consulting his memorandum book, he turned a few pages, then paused at one which contained the following address:

"John Lewis, Esq.
Care T. Jamison,
Washington Heights, N. Y.

This he had obtained from Burrows, to whom, it will be remembered, had been shown three letters by John Lewis, who claimed that they had been written to him by his father whilst he was at school. Mr. Barnes made inquiries, and very readily found that Mr. Jamison kept a large boarding-school for boys, and that he had done so for the last thirty years. Receiving the correct address, he at once proceeded to the school-house, and was soon in the presence of a pleasant old man.

"Good morning, Mr. Jamison," began Mr. Barnes, "I am looking for a man who has recently inherited some property, but he cannot be found. He is supposed to be dead, and probably is. The case therefore stands thus: If he had a son, that son would inherit, but if not, the property goes elsewhere. I have heard that he did have a son, who was for some time at your school, and so I have ventured to trouble you, hoping that you might be able to assist me."

"I am at your service, and if you will give me the name, I will look over my books and see what I can find."

"The name is John Lewis, and it is about fourteen or fifteen years since the lad was supposed to be here. Moreover, it may help you to remember him, if I tell you that it is further supposed, that he ran away from school and went to sea."

"I am afraid you have been misinformed," said the school-master, shaking his venerable head. "Nothing of that kind ever occurred here. I do not recall such a name of a pupil, but I knew a man by that name once, and have good reason to remember him."

"Will you tell me about it?"

"Certainly! Now let me see! It must have been about the very time that you mention, though I could give you the exact date. A gentleman called here and wished to see the school; he said that he had a son whom he wished to place in a military institution such as this. His name was Lewis. After I had explained our methods to him, he went away, promising to call again. This he did, and, on his second visit, he told me that his son had refused to go to a military academy, and that he had placed him elsewhere. However, he seemed very much interested in the school, and made several suggestions as to improvements. When I explained to him that there were no funds for any such purpose, he generously offered to pay any bills that might be incurred. I protested at first, but he persisted. He even came here himself to superintend the alterations."

"You say that he lived here a short time?"

"Yes, about a month."

"Can you tell me whether his mail was received here?"

"Oh, yes! He was a stranger in the city, and had no other address whilst he was here. So of course his letters came to the academy."

"Whilst he was with you, did his son ever come to visit him?"

"No, I never saw the boy, but he constantly spoke of his son, and if he is the party for whom you are looking, I have no doubt that he has, or had, a son. That seems to be the fact which you wished to substantiate, I believe?"

"Yes, that is all that I wish, except that I would like to find the son. However, as you cannot aid me there, I bid you good morning, and I thank you for your courtesy."

Leaving the academy, Mr. Barnes walked as far as the nearest station of the elevated railroad, and went down-town to Grand Street; thence he walked to the office of the Norwich line of steamers. Addressing the clerk he said:

"Do you keep a passenger list?"

"Well, hardly that, in the strict sense of the term. But we keep the names of all who take state-rooms."

"Can you let me see that list for last Saturday night's steamer?"

The list was handed to him, and he carefully ran his finger over the column until it rested on the name, "Walter Marvel."

He copied the number of the state-room assigned, and left the dock with a smile of satisfaction. "I think I may have some dinner now," said he to himself, and he entered a restaurant where he partook of a substantial meal, after which he went to Police Head-quarters, asked for the Inspector, and was at once shown into the private office of that official.

"Good morning, Inspector," said Mr. Barnes, "I would like to ask whether there has been a report of anyone missing in this city during this week?"

"Why, yes, there has!" The Inspector eyed him keenly. "Mr. Barnes, what do you know?"

"I am working on the Lewis murder case, Inspector. Up in Lee, New Hampshire, you know."

The Inspector nodded, and Mr. Barnes continued:

"I have left the Pilkingtons, because they permitted another man to interfere with me. If my theory be correct, I must trace a man from this city to Lee."

"If you have left the Pilkingtons," said the Inspector, "I will help you. A woman reported here yesterday that her husband has been missing since last Saturday, and that she feared foul play. I put a man on the case, and he has traced him as far as a Sound steamer, so he is probably down your way."

"Is any name given?"

"Yes, but as you must be in a hurry, take the papers with you. I intrust the whole matter to your judgment."

Mr. Barnes thanked the Inspector for this mark of confidence, and then left the building. Half an hour later, he was at a fashionable up-town hotel, and had sent his card up to the woman named. In a few minutes more he was in her presence.

"I see by your card that you are a detective," began the woman, "and I suppose that you have brought me news of my husband?"

"I have found out that he left the city last Saturday night. Did you know of his intention to do so?"

"I did not, but it does not surprise me that he has done so. Where has he gone?"

"I came to see if you can help me on that point. All I know is that he went away on a Sound steamer. Have you any idea of any object which would call him East?"

"Yes, but I may be wrong, and would prefer not to commit myself. I might be betraying what he wishes kept private."

"Will you answer a few other questions?"

"I will answer all that I think I should."

"First, then, tell me how long your husband has been in New York."

"We arrived about two weeks before he disappeared."

"You say 'arrived.' Am I to understand that you came from abroad?"

"Yes. We have been in Europe for many years."

"Had your husband any special reason for returning to America?"

"Yes. But I cannot explain that to you, further than to say that it is a purpose which for many years he has wished to accomplish."

"Why then did he delay the matter so long?"

"I must not tell you that." She colored deeply.

"I do not desire to appear too inquisitive, madam, but if you wish me to accomplish anything, you must give me more information. Tell me this. Do you suppose that it is in pursuance of this purpose that your husband has gone out of the city?"

"I fear so."

"You fear so! Is there any danger then that he risks?"

The woman bit her lip at this slip, and said: "There might be. I do not know."

"Has he gone in search of an enemy?"

"I cannot say!" She seemed decidedly uneasy at the questions of the detective. The latter paused a moment considering, and then asked:

"Do you know the name of this man who is your husband's enemy?"

"I did not say that it is a man, or that my husband has an enemy."

"You did not, but that is evidently the case. Now, do you happen ever to have heard of John Lewis?"

The woman started up in dismay, and excitedly exclaimed:

"What do you know of that man?"

"Then you admit that you know him?"

"I know who he is, but what is it that you know, and why do you mention his name?"

"I know, madam, that your husband left this city for the East on Saturday night last, and that on the following night John Lewis was murdered!"

"My God! This is terrible!" cried the woman, as she sank into a chair, and covered her face with her hands. Mr. Barnes waited a moment for her to recover from her surprise, and then said:

"I will tell you more. An innocent man has been arrested for the crime, and is in prison."

"How does all this interest me? Of course it shocked me to hear so suddenly that one whom I knew, has been murdered, but further than that, what is it to me?"

"That is what I am trying to find out. Was Mr. Lewis a friend of yours?"

"A friend? Far from it, "she answered almost fiercely.

"Ah! Then it is not his death that troubles you?"

"Who says that I am troubled?"

"I do, and I think it is because you know, or think that your husband went to that town expressly to kill Lewis!"

"He did nothing of the kind," she answered, quickly, losing her self-possession in her excitement. "My husband only wanted to recover his child, whom that man had stolen from him!"

"At last we have it!" said Mr. Barnes, with satisfaction. "Your husband then is the father of the girl. In that case you must be her mother, and therefore Lewis's sister?"

"His sister? Her mother? You are mad!"

"Explain it then!" Mr. Barnes was puzzled.

"I will explain nothing! You have got more out of me now than I should have told."

"Then I will hunt for your husband, for he must be the man who killed Mr. Lewis. Let me tell you that I have tracked him backwards, from the scene of the crime, to this city. Another detective followed his trail from the murder, but he did not succeed in apprehending him."

"Then, thank God, he is safe!"

"You are wrong. The other detective failed, but I will not."

"You dare to tell me this, and want my help?"

"We must think of the innocent!"

"What do I care for the innocent? I do not know them."

"Let me tell you who they are. There is the girl, the daughter of your husband!"

"Ah! Is she accused?"

"She is thought to be an accessory."

"Good, I am glad! And the other, who is that? You spoke of a man."

"The other is thought to be the murderer. It is Walter Marvel!"

"What, young Walter? This is worse than I could have imagined! Well, so be it! I care nothing for him either."

"Madam, have you no heart? Would you see the innocent suffer for the guilty?"

"The innocent? How do I know who is innocent? You say these people are accused. The authorities must know what they are doing; there must be evidence against them, and most likely they are guilty. Why should I do anything, and what can I do, anyway?"

"All I ask of you is, to give me the information that I wish."

"What information?"

"Tell me the exact relations which exist between your husband and John Lewis?"

"I will tell you nothing."

"You are determined?"

"I am! Do your worst!"

"Very well, madam! Perhaps I may yet find a way to make you suffer for your stubbornness."

"How dare you threaten me? I'll have you turned out of this hotel!"

"Stop a minute! You forgot that I am a detective. If you ring, I will arrest you."

"Arrest me? And pray what charge will you make? I am not easily frightened."

"I will charge you with complicity in the murder of John Lewis!"

"That is farcical. I have been in New York only."

"You are an accessory before the fact. You knew that your husband went out of the city with a murderous intent. Therefore I think that in this state, under our penal code, you could be indicted as a principal."

"Curse you, you are a demon!"

Mr. Barnes considered a moment, and then said:

"I have half a mind to arrest you anyway!"

"Do so if you wish! But I will tell you nothing, though I should be kept in prison forever."

"I haven't time to wait in the city, or I would try the experiment. As it is, I must be sure that I can get you when I want you." So saying, Mr. Barnes stepped up to the electric call, and pressed the button. A moment later, a bell-boy knocked at the door. Mr. Barnes opened it and said:

"Call a district messenger, and bring me some writing materials!"

"What do you mean to do? asked the woman.

"You shall see."

In a short time the bell-boy returned, and with him, the messenger. Mr. Barnes took a piece of paper, and wrote as follows:

"Send me your best shadow. Important.

"BARNES."

Placing this in an envelope, he sealed it, and addressed it to the Inspector whom he had seen at Police Head-quarters. Handing it to the messenger he said:

"Deliver that as quickly as possible. Here is an extra quarter for yourself."

He then sat down, and commenced to read a newspaper. The woman said nothing for a time, but at the end of half an hour, during which the imperturbable detective had not raised his eyes from his paper, she jumped up, walked to the window, and stood looking out. Mr. Barnes may not have seen her move, so little notice did he seem to take. After a few minutes at the window, she went in the direction of the door, but apparently with no special object in view. Suddenly, with the agility of a cat, she made a dart for the knob, and grasped it. Still the detective made no sign. She turned the knob, and gave the door a pull, but it did not open as she had expected, and after a few futile attempts, she turned on Mr. Barnes like a fury:

"How dare you lock my door?"

"Is it locked?"

"Of course it is, and you locked it!"

"You are mistaken!"

"How is it fastened, then?"

"You said it is locked, did you not? I have not examined it."

"How did it get locked?"

"Since you are so anxious to know, I will be more amiable than you, and tell you. I asked the bellboy to turn the key on the outside."

"Why did you do that?"

"I did not wish to lose your pleasant company, until the arrival of my friend, for whom I have sent. Ah! There's his knock." Going to the door he said: "Turn the key and come in."

The lock shot back and a man entered. Addressing Mr. Barnes, he said:

"I am No. 56."

"A shadow?"

"A shadow."

"What is the meaning of this impertinence?" said the woman, in a rage. But neither of the men appeared to notice her. Mr. Barnes continued:

"Look at this woman well. I will expect you to know where she is when I ask you for her, do you understand?"

"I do."

"Good-morning." No. 56 left the apartment.

"Now perhaps you will explain what this means?"

"I was about to do so. Understand that if you make any attempt to leave the city, that man will prevent it. You may change boarding-places, as often as you please, but remain in the city! That is all! Good-morning." Before she could say a word he had gone.

Mr. Barnes went directly to the Grand Central railroad depot, and started for Lee, where he arrived early on the following morning. Reaching the farm, he found Virginia in the parlor. She advanced to meet him with a cordial greeting.

"I am so relieved to see you back again. What news have you?"

"I have discovered the murderer."

"You have? Who is he? Tell me at once!"

"It is the man who has passed as your cousin!"

"My uncle's son?"

"No, not your uncle's son, though that is what he called himself. I must find him at once! Where is he?"

"He has gone."

"Gone! Gone where? I will follow him to the end of the earth. He shall not escape me. Where has he gone?"

"We do not know. I told you, when I last saw you, that he would pass the night at the Squire's, but it seems that he must have retired to his room, after the funeral, for he was here at breakfast."

"Well? Go on! Go on!" The detective was impatient.

"After breakfast, he again went to his room. We saw nothing more of him until dinner-time. Then I went in to call him, but he was not there. He has not been seen since."

"Perhaps he went to the Squire's?"

"I went over to see Alice this morning, and learned that no one had seen him since the funeral."

"Too late! Too late, after all my trouble!" moaned the detective. He leaned his head on his hands and seemed almost about to weep. Virginia did not know what to say to him, so thinking it best to leave him to himself, she noiselessly left the room. Mr. Barnes remained in one position for fully ten minutes, but suddenly he jumped up, and seemed all animation again.

"Miss Lewis! Miss Lewis!" he cried, in great excitement. At the sound of his voice Virginia came hurrying in, and was astonished at the change in his demeanor.

"Miss Lewis," said he, speaking rapidly, "you say that he went to his room and has not been seen since?

"Yes, he must have come out—"

"Never mind that! Tell me, is it the same room which he occupied when he slept here on the night after the murder?"

"Yes! Thinking that he was my uncle's son, I gave him my uncle's room."

"Your uncle's room? Of course! It is as clear as day. During that first night, Burrows heard mysterious noises. He came down into this man's room, and found it empty. Burrows sat by his door all night, to ask him where he had been, and, although he did not pass him, nevertheless in the morning the man was in the room. Do you understand?"

"Not clearly!"

"It is very simple! There is a secret apartment in this house, and the murderer is at this moment concealed in it."

"A secret room! It is impossible!"

"Anything else is impossible, you mean.. This is not the day of miracles, and a man cannot disappear, in this way, in broad daylight."

"But how will you find it, if it exists?"

"It will be easy enough to find it, if we know that it is in existence. In the first place, there must be a way to enter it from that room in which your uncle slept. Come, we will go there first."

Together they went to the room, and Mr. Barnes looked about for some sign that would guide him aright. After reasoning for a moment, as Burrows had done at the Epping house, he said:

"I have it. I will go straight to it. Burrows heard this man in the secret apartment, and Burrows was upstairs, so I am sure that the place of which we are in search is above. Now what is its exact location? It must be accessible to this room, and yet the room which Burrows occupied is as large as this. Now observe that the closet, in the corner, projects out into the hall. In your room there is a similar closet. On this floor, in the hall, between these two projections for the closets, is the little passage leading from the main hall into the dining-room. I have noticed that upstairs, there are no closets, and of course no such passage-way. Therefore, the space occupied by them below indicates where the secret room is to be found on the next floor."

"But how shall we get in?"

"I think it will be difficult for you to do so, for I expect that the entrance is through the ceiling of the closet in this room. I will now look."

Mr. Barnes opened the closet door, and then started back, as he saw the great mastiff lying on the floor within. The dog arose and went up to Virginia, whining pitifully. Then he went back into the closet, raised himself upon his hind legs, rested his fore-paws against the wall of the closet, and with head upturned, howled in a horribly suggestive manner.

"Do you see," said Mr. Barnes, "the brute knows that there is something wrong up there." Virginia coaxed the dog away from the closet, and the detective stood on a chair and examined the ceiling. In a moment he announced:

"I have it. Here is the trap-door." A minute later he had drawn himself up through the aperture and disappeared. Very soon, however, he returned; and, as he dropped to the floor, he said:

"He is up there—dead! Suicide, I suspect. You must go at once for the Squire. Pardon my not doing so, but I have a reason for wishing to remain with the body until it be turned over to the coroner."

Virginia gladly hurried away upon an errand which she knew promised the speedy release of her lover.

CHAPTER XVII
THE CONFESSION

As soon as Virginia had departed, Mr. Barnes re-entered the secret chamber, passing, as before, through the ceiling of the closet.

His first endeavor was to learn how this man had taken his life. This was not difficult. A small charcoal furnace, and the strong odor of gas permeating the place for some time after he had opened the skylight, which was the only means of ventilation and light, plainly suggested suicide. This point being settled, he examined the other things lying about. These were necessarily few, as the place was very small. The only articles of furniture, were a table and a chair, unless account be taken of a small closet nailed against the wall, in which was a stock of provisions. He also found a suit of clothes. Mr. Barnes pondered over this for a few minutes, and then the idea occurred to him, that it was to bring these, the garments which Lewis had worn on the night of the crime, and for which, it will be remembered, Burrows had searched in vain, that the man had entered the secret room on the night when Burrows was disturbed by his movements. It will also be recalled to mind that the younger detective had a theory which would, in a measure, be substantiated if these were found to be perforated by a bullet, as that would tend to show that the deceased had been shot, that he had then undressed and retired to his bed, to be afterwards awakened and killed by a second shot. Mr. Barnes examined these articles with interest. If there were any bullet-hole it would not fit his own theory of the case. 'It was therefore with much satisfaction that he soon determined that there was none. Next he turned over the papers with which the table was littered, and soon an ejaculation of surprise and pleasure attested the fact that he had made an important discovery. He held in his hand a bundle of manuscript bearing the ominous heading:

"*My Confession,*" followed by the words: "*for Mr. Barnes, should he find this first.*"

With impatience and curiosity Mr. Barnes sat on the one chair, and read the following, occasionally emitting a grunt of satisfaction as point after point in the mystery was explained, and all fitted in with his own theory of the crime. The confession is here given verbatim;

"After years of preparation I find that my plans have miscarried. However, I am a Fatalist, and therefore bow to the inevitable. I have been bitterly wronged, but in some degree I have had a revenge. Now I am forced by the immutable laws of circumstance to choose between my own miserable life, and that of her whom I love most dearly, and I do not hesitate to sacrifice myself that she may live and be happy, even though it be in the arms of a man whom I should like to grind beneath my heel. Yet what has he done to me? Nothing! He is one of the same family as the villain who wrecked and destroyed the life of my dearly beloved sister. Beyond that there is nothing. Strange, that mother and daughter should both love the same name! It is the finger of Fate, and yet there are many who scoff at the idea of predestination. But as I wish to be understood by the one who may find this paper, and that one I am confident will be Mr. Barnes, I must be more explicit. Therefore it will be as well to give a detailed account of the sequence of strange events in my life.

"At the outset, let me say that my name is John Lewis. But, as that is also the name under which I have passed since the tragedy of Sunday night, I will add that I am the man who is supposed to be dead. The corpse is that of Walter Marvel, the uncle of the young man at present accused of my murder. I will now go back to my youth, and relate the events in the order of their occurrence.

"I was born in Richmond, Virginia, and my family was aristocratic. Of course, when the Civil War began, our sympathies were all with the Secessionists. My father entered the Confederate service, and soon, by his gallantry, won distinction, being advanced several times on the field, until at length he had reached the position of colonel. It was during his absence with his regiment, that, in the latter part of '63 some prisoners of war were brought into Richmond. Some of these were wounded and sent to the hospitals. It is a curious fact that however eager men may be, in battle, to destroy each other, after the fight is over they appear to be just as anxious to save the lives of those who may yet have a lingering spark within their veins.

"My sister, together with many other noble women, gave her entire time to the nursing of the wounded, and so spent all her days among the soldiers in the hospitals. Thus, when these prisoners of war were brought in, and the sufferers placed in the kind care of these women, my sister met and nursed many of them. Among the number was Walter Marvel, an officer in the Union army. At once she was attracted to him. How, or why, let those explain who disbelieve in Fate, for he was neither handsome, nor pleasant, either in countenance or manners. Besides, he was the avowed enemy of all that we held to be our sacred right, and for which our young men were pouring out their life's blood on many fields. She was one of the fairest daughters of the South, and it was not surprising that Marvel soon found himself fascinated by her charms. After a time, he recovered sufficiently to be removed from the hospital, and, in the natural order of events, would have been taken to prison, but for the interest which my sister evinced in him. Naturally she possessed much influence with the officers, and she represented to them that, though well enough to leave the hospital, he was still so weak, that if confined in a cell he would probably not survive. Thus she succeeded in having him paroled. So there was opportunity for them to meet and exchange loving vows, although they conducted matters so adroitly that I, who was present all the time in the home, never suspected the true state of affairs.

"At last came the end of the war, and, stricken at heart by the outcome thereof, my father returned home. Moreover, he had been severely wounded, and his wound not having received proper attention, had never thoroughly healed. Great care was necessary to insure it's not giving more trouble. Meanwhile, it subsequently transpired, that during the latter part of '64, Marvel had lured my sister into a secret marriage, a pitfall into which so many innocent and inexperienced women fall, forgetting that their parents have their interests at heart, and therefore are entitled, at least, to advise about so important a step. She would have confessed to my father 911 his arrival, were it not for his weakened physical condition, and the danger which any great excitement might entail.

"So time passed until, at length, it became imperative that she should make the disclosure. She was just about to confide her story to my father, when unfortunately he discovered it himself. He questioned her, and was at first relieved to hear that at least she was a married woman, but when he learned that her husband was a detested 'Yankee,' his rage was simply terrific. He stormed and raged until his strength was exhausted, and he fell to the floor in a swoon. My sister screamed for help, and the servants rushed in and picked up their master. They bore him up to his own chamber and laid him on his bed, but an ominous train of blood marked their progress from the room below, and when, in response to a hasty summons, the doctor arrived, he found that the wound had opened and was bleeding dangerously. Other surgeons were summoned, and after great difficulty the flow was stopped; but the loss of blood in his already weakened condition left him scarcely any strength. Besides, his mental trouble, occasioned by the news which he had that day heard, made his condition critical indeed.

"When the doctors had made him as comfortable as they could, and there was a moment to spare to other considerations, I thought of my sister and sought for her, but one of the servants informed me that she had left the house. I suspected at once that she had gone to her husband, and knowing where he resided, I hurried thither. I rushed into the house, and was horrified to find the apparently lifeless body of my sister stretched on the parlor floor. Assistance was summoned, and as soon as it was safe to do so, she was removed to our own home. It was not until months after, that I learned the events which led up to this last catastrophe. It seems that she had, as I had supposed, sought for the villain who should have been ready and anxious to care for her. When he heard that her father had refused to acknowledge the marriage, he coolly told her that, in that case, it would be best to part. That he 'would not separate a girl from her father,' and other things equally as heartless. Then he left her.

"It was not surprising that my sister's little girl should have been prematurely hurried into the world by these exciting scenes.

Afterwards the mother improved slowly, but surely, day by day. With my father it was different. For months, he lay between life and death. When my sister had sufficiently recovered her own health, she divided her time between her baby and her father, and her experience as a nurse now became invaluable. At last there came a change, and one morning my father awoke, apparently better.

"Matilda, my sister, was at the moment having her breakfast, and was out of the room, I taking her place for the time. Father spoke to me, asking me to relate all that had occurred. I tried to answer evasively, but he immediately showed signs of excitement, insisting on a reply to his inquiries. Under the circumstances I deemed it best to tell him the truth. He listened without comment, until I told how her husband had deserted her, at which he gritted his teeth as he muttered 'the villain.' When I told him of the little stranger in the house his expression softened, and he asked me to send my sister to him. As I left the room to obey he said:

"'Tell her to bring little Virginia with her.'

"I must say here that as yet no name had been chosen for the baby; but Virginia is our native State, and as father called the little one by that name, Matilda would never call her by any other name, in the years that came after.

"The interview between my father and Matilda was touching in the extreme. She avowed her contrition for the deception which she had practised, while he asked forgiveness for his harshness.

"'To think,' said he, 'that I should have endangered the life of this dear little blessing!' and stretching out his arms, he took her child and kissed it, whereupon my sister dropped upon her knees, buried her face in the bed-clothing, and wept like a child. My father soothed her, and deeming it best I slipped from the room, leaving them alone.

"After that these three were inseparable and seemed as happy as could be; so much so, indeed, that we were all lulled into the belief that my father was getting well. All except my father himself. He said nothing, but, when the end approached, declared that he had expected it all along. When it was clearly evident that he would soon die, he called me to him one day, and taking me by the hand, he said: "'John, my son, you have always been a good boy, and I wish you a long and prosperous life. Yet I desire to do something that may seem unjust to you. I hope you may be able to see it as I do. I should die happier!'

"'Do not speak of dying, father,' I cried in a choked voice. 'What is it you wish? I will accede to it cheerfully.'

"'That is my brave boy,' said he, with a smile, and then he paused a while. As last he continued: 'John, I wish to make a change in my will. As it stands, my property would be divided equally between you and Matilda. I wish to alter it so that each of you will have one third. The balance must be invested so that the little one will have something when she is of age. I will arrange so that in case of her death her share must go to her mother, and in the event of the mother's death that portion must be similarly invested for the little one. I wish you to be the executor. Will you do this for me, my boy?' I nodded acquiescence, and he went on:

"'This is just, John! You will soon be a man, and can care for yourself. Matilda is a woman. By a mistake, she has wrecked her chance of winning a worthy protector, and so I must arrange that she and her child shall not come to want.' I assured him that he was only acting as I should wish, and he seemed to be more content. The lawyers were summoned, and all was arranged as he directed. A few days later, whilst he was clasped in his daughter's arms, his spirit passed away.

"I will not prolong my tale in order to give a complete narrative of all that passed, but will simply confine myself to those events most closely connected with this recent tragedy.

"The months rolled by, and never was a word said about the man who had caused all our trouble. Matilda seemed to lavish her whole wealth of love upon her little girl, and as Virgie grew, I cherished the hope that the wound in her mother's heart was healing. How little does a man understand what a woman means when she says that she gives him her heart. Despite all the outward appearances, I was yet to find that Matilda still thought of, and longed for, her husband.

"One morning, when Virgie was about five years old, I was sitting at my breakfast, and Matilda, who had already eaten, was amusing herself with the morning's paper, when a sudden exclamation from her attracted my attention. I anxiously asked what it was, and she handed me the paper, pointing to the following paragraph:

"'We are gratified to see that the Government is recognizing the services rendered by our soldiers in the late war. Especially is it pleasant for us to record, that Lieutenant Walter Marvel has been appointed to a diplomatic mission abroad. This gentleman, by his heroism on the field, has demonstrated the sterling qualities of which he is made, and doubtless will fill his new position with honor to himself and to his country. He will leave for Paris this week. It may not be amiss to mention the rumor, that the gallant officer will take a bride with him.'

"I was much troubled at this, and scarcely knew what to say, for I could not guess how it would affect my sister. However, she spoke first.

"'John, my brother, will you take me to him?' To say that I was amazed at this request would but mildly express it.

"'Take you to him?' said I, 'after all that has happened?'

"'He is Virgie's father, John! You forget that!'

"'Evidently he does also.'

"'He does not even know that he has a child. John, I have thought of this constantly, and it is not right that I should keep him in ignorance, as I have done all these years.'

"'Why, Mattie, what are you saying? What claim can he have on you, after the cowardly manner in which he abandoned you?'

"'Hush! You must not think and speak thus of my husband. If I have suffered, do you not think he has also? He did not abandon me. He saw what was my plain duty, and had the courage to show it to me. I, in my selfishness, would have left my father for him, but he knew that it was my duty to remain at home, and therefore he went. That is the simple truth.' I was almost speechless, so great was my surprise at her defence of him, but I made one more effort.

"'But has he not forgotten you, is he not about to marry again?'

"'Stop, John! You do not know what you are saying. Do you think that I believe for a moment what a newspaper says, when I know my husband as I do? I should have little faith, indeed! John, I must see him before he goes away! If you will not accompany me, I must go alone!'

"I was amazed, but what could I do? She was determined, and I could not allow her to go alone. So she easily induced me to promise to go with her. Preparations were rapidly arranged for the journey to New York, but all of our plans, at the last minute, were upset by the sudden illness of the little girl. Believing, as I do, in Fate, I looked upon this as a sign that we should abandon the idea of seeking out the father. I could not, however, make my sister see it so, and though the steamer had sailed long before Virgie was well enough to travel, she insisted on joining her husband, even though it entailed the necessity of crossing the ocean. She anticipated a happy reunion with her husband, and a future life of happiness and love. As I saw her looking brighter and brighter, day by day, even in the anticipation, much as I detested the man I could not find it in my heart to thwart her. She was so sure of the. joyous welcome with which she would be received, that she had the child's portrait painted, and placed in a locket. In fact she had two made, one for herself, and one which she intended to send to her husband, on her arrival in Paris. This last was the counterpart of the other, save that she had his name, or rather his initials, engraved on the gold case.

"To shorten my narrative as much as possible, that I may surely finish it before I am discovered here in my retreat, I will at once come to our arrival in Paris. It was with little difficulty that I learned of Marvel's whereabouts, for his official duties made him a man of some note. My sister wrote a most affectionate letter, telling him all that had passed since he had left her, and of the birth of the child; with it she inclosed the locket and portrait. This was forwarded, and she waited impatiently for him to hasten to her side. But the days passed and no word came. She made every excuse for him, urging that his new duties must detain him, and making other similar pleas in his behalf. Meanwhile, I instinctively knew that he was but a heartless villain, and I never expected him to behave towards his wife as a man should. At length, even Matilda commenced to' doubt, until the thought entered her brain that perhaps her letter had never reached him. Then she determined to seek him in person. I endeavored to dissuade her from this project, but it was impossible to detain her, and so I went with her to his hotel. We asked to see him, and were shown into a private parlor connected with his suite. There we were allowed to wait but a few moments, and then were joined by a tall, handsome woman, who inquired why we had called. We said we wished to see Marvel in person, to which she replied:

"'He is engaged at present, but I am his wife.'

"'What!" exclaimed my sister, 'His wife? Woman, you are mad! I am his wife!'

The other did not so much as start, but coolly replied:

"'Oh! I see! You must be that little rebel that he met down in Richmond. I have heard all about that affair. He told it to me before we were married.' (Here Mr. Barnes uttered a particularly loud grunt of satisfaction.) 'So you have come to claim him, now that he is somebody of consequence! Quite romantic, I declare! But it won't do, you know. He never will acknowledge you!'

"'You forget yourself, madam!' said I. 'By your own words you have admitted my sister's claim as this man's wife, and therefore must see that you are not his wife at all!'

"'Oh! Indeed? How pleasant of you to come and tell me! But I tell you it will not do! He will not be bound by such a marriage as your sister tricked him into, when he was a prisoner.'

"I thought it best to take my sister away, but she would not stir.

"'I will not go,' said she, 'until I have seen him!'

"'Oh! Very well, if you insist! Though it is useless, I assure you.' The woman turned and left the room. A moment later Marvel entered.

"'Well, madam,' he began, addressing my sister, 'what can I do for you?'

"'Walter—'

"'Excuse me, but you may spare yourself. I have heard from my wife the object of your call, and, besides, I received your letter and so am aware of all the circumstances. I regret the whole affair, I assure you, and since there is a child, which you say is mine, why of course anything that I can do in a pecuniary way to relieve your wants I would be most willing—'

"'You villain!' I began, and was about to grasp him by the throat to strangle him, when my sister caught me by the arm, and with more calmness than I could have expected, she said:

"'No, not that way! He must suffer as I shall. I must be avenged, but death is too tame for my wishes!' With these words she hastened from the room. Hardly knowing what to do, I followed. We entered the carriage which awaited us, and were borne to our hotel, Matilda keeping silent during the trip. As soon, however, as we were in our parlor, she said:

"'John, go at once for a lawyer!' I immediately divined her intention and went out, only too glad that, at last, this fiend was to have his deserts.

"It will suffice here to state that we readily had Marvel arrested and tried. For, however lax the Parisians may be in morals, bigamy is a crime there, as elsewhere, and with but little trouble we secured his conviction. His appointment to his foreign mission had hastened his going abroad, but the newspaper had made a mistake in saying that he would take a wife with him. He had been engaged to marry this woman, but she and her parents had been spending some months in Paris, and their wedding had taken place there, only a short time prior to our arrival. Thus the crime had been committed on French soil, and was punishable there. My sister maintained her strength, and appeared at the trial to testify against Marvel, a circumstance which greatly assisted in securing his conviction; but immediately after, she became quite ill, and died before I returned to America. Thus ends the sad history of my sister and her wrongs. Now, about myself.

"At the trial, when Marvel was sentenced to the full penalty of the law, he started up, and uttered the most horrible invectives against my sister. Then turning to me, he said:

"'As for you, you infernal rebel, you are the one who have hounded me down, and I warn you that when I get out of this trouble, wherever you may hide away, I will find you, and I will kill you, so help me God!' It was terrible to hear him, and as he spoke, I knew that if ever he should have the chance, he would execute his threat.

"It was the certainty of this which instigated me in my subsequent course. I concluded that when we should meet, one of us must die; and I felt that common justice made it but right that he should be the one. Not satisfied with hastening the death of my father and my sister, he must also threaten my life! So I made my plans. If he should come with murderous intent, I would be ready, and if he did not, no harm could accrue.

"I foresaw that some shrewd detective would discover that this man had crossed the ocean to commit a crime, and I determined to let it appear that he had succeeded. I would kill him, dress him in my clothing, and let it seem that I was the murdered man. But as I must further be able to account for my own presence, I plotted to reappear as my own son. To this end, I visited an academy on Washington Heights, and spoke of placing my son there, though I afterwards informed the schoolmaster that I had sent him elsewhere. However, I interested myself in his institution, and offered to make some needed repairs. Then I spent some time at the school, and whilst there, I wrote to parties out of town, enclosing self-addressed envelopes for their replies. These were, in due time, returned to me properly post-marked, and it was an easy matter for me to write fictitious letters, as though to my son, and place them in these covers. These, when the time should come, would be proof enough of my identity, and as I knew that years would pass before I could use them, I concluded that no one would doubt that they were genuine.

"Next, I allowed my beard to grow to its full length, that being the style in which Marvel always wore his. I knew that his would be shaved as long as he remained in prison, but I thought that he would allow his beard to grow again as soon as he should regain his liberty, as it hid a scar from a wound that would otherwise greatly disfigure him. Then I dyed my whiskers, eyebrows, and hair black, in imitation of his, my own being quite red. I had no relatives, and absolutely no friends nor acquaintances in the North, and I determined not to revisit Richmond. Consequently I had all my Southern property converted into cash and forwarded to me. I then looked about for a suitable place to live, and selected Lee.

"I did nothing more in furtherance of my plans, except to speak to all of my new friends of the son who had left me and had run away. I was quite young at this time, but nineteen in fact, although I was fully matured, and looked much older.

"The years rolled by, and nothing occurred to disturb the serenity of our home in this little New England town, except that the Marvel family came here to reside. This I considered another fatality, and for that reason I did not move away.

"At last came the birthday which would make it necessary for me to explain more to Virgie than I had ever yet done. After dinner, I was listening to Squire Olney, but at the same time I was moodily thinking over the past, with its terrible memories, when young Marvel asked to speak to me. I was then startled to hear him, another Walter Marvel, declare that he had won the heart of my little girl. Was it surprising that I should act as I did, and deny his suit? Or, that in my anger I should blurt out a part of the truth? The events which followed are too well known to need iteration here. So I will come at once to the night of the murder.

"I was sitting in the parlor, pondering bitterly over my position. 1 had begun to realize the fact that if I should pursue the course which I had begun, and should prosecute Marvel, it must be at the cost to myself of Virgie's love. I was debating as to the most sensible course to adopt when, suddenly, I heard a pistol-shot, and a bullet broke through the pane. I jumped up, hurried to the window, and distinctly saw a man grappling with my dog. The snow had ceased to fall, and there was light from the moon, which was visible through the clouds as they broke away. I thought this was young Marvel, and that he had deliberately fired through my window, in pursuance of the threat made on the day of the party. I had seen Virgie pass through the parlor and leave her pistol on the mantel, so, quickly possessing myself of it, I fired at the retreating figure. At the same moment, a second shot was fired, this time at me, for it struck me on the head, though it inflicted but a slight wound.

"I learned at the inquest that these shots were fired respectively by Lucas and Miss Marvel; the first accidentally and the second deliberately, though at the time I did not see whence the latter came, and supposed that it was from the man's weapon.

"A very few minutes after this, I heard the knocker at my front door. Thinking that it might be young Marvel still desirous of injuring me, I concluded to go prepared, and took a weapon in my hand. I did not again take Virgie's, for I had time to think before acting, and as I was possibly about to take a life, it occurred to me, that it would not do to use Virgie's pistol, because it has her name on it. At the same moment it flashed across my mind, that young Marvel's also bore his name, and that it was in my possession. I took it from the drawer where I kept it, and went to the front door, where the man outside was again knocking. I opened it and a bearded man entered. When I saw that it was not young Marvel, I led the way back to the parlor. Reaching there, I faced the man and inquired his name.

"'Walter Marvel!' he replied. 'And your day of reckoning has arrived.' For a moment I was dazed, and I did not think of, or remember, that there were two who bore this name.

"'That is impossible!' I exclaimed. 'I do not recognize you.'

"'You will in a moment,' he answered, and put his hand to his hip-pocket. Immediately I understood! This was the elder Marvel, and the time had come for him to take my life, or for me to take his.

"I was certain that he was at that moment getting out a weapon, though as it proved later it must have been that as evidence of his identity, he meant to show me the locket which my sister had sent to him. I think that he wished to know where his daughter was, before going to extremities. Be that as it may, I thought that he was about to raise his hand against my life, and so, having a pistol already in my hand, I shot him, and he died almost without a struggle.

"I at once proceeded to carry out my long prepared plan. I stripped the body, cutting the garments away, with the exception of the long coat which, with much difficulty, I succeeded in removing without destroying, as I decided to wear it away from the house. There was not a moment's delay, for I had long been ready for this emergency, and so acted promptly. I got one of my own shirts, making sure that it was marked with my name, and slipping this on him, made it appear that I had been aroused after going to sleep. Next I arranged the shirt so that it touched the wound and allowed some of the blood to soak through. This served as a mark, and I fired at it, in order that there should be a bullet-hole through the garment, and near enough to the other, for both shots to have entered the same spot. I suppose that my hand trembled somewhat, and that is why, as the doctor testified, this was but a slight wound, and the bullet passed out again. It can be found in the floor, of course, if it be deemed necessary to substantiate my statement in that way.

"Next, to make the identification complete, I placed upon the finger of the corpse the large diamond ring which I had always worn, and which is well known. This was again fatality, for this is a ring which he gave to my sister when he engaged her affections. It was with some difficulty that I got the ring on, for his finger was much larger than mine." (Again Mr. Barnes uttered an ejaculation, and thought to himself: "Exactly, and it was so small a thing as that which led me finally to suspect the truth. If the finger could not swell after death, as the doctor claims to be the fact, then the ring should not have been so tight.") "I then built up a roaring fire and held the head of the dead man in it long enough to scorch and disfigure him beyond recognition. I then laid him down near the hearth so that it would appear that he had dropped there, and had been burned afterwards. Next I hurriedly wrote the slips of paper found by Virgie and the detectives, through which I meant to point to young Marvel as the murderer, forgetting that science would prove that death had been instantaneous, and therefore that the victim had not had time to make such an accusation.

"When I first bought this house, foreseeing the necessity for this crime, I caused this secret room to be constructed, to do which, it was only necessary to close up the closets which originally opened into the adjoining rooms. Here I had everything that I would need in this emergency, and therefore came to this room and quickly shaved off my beard. Then I washed out my hair and eyebrows, using a liquid which I kept specially for this. Thus they were restored to their natural red color, and would easily prevent my identification. Any resemblance in face or voice, I hoped would be accepted as a natural inheritance of a son from his father. I left my own clothing in my sleeping-room to give color to the theory that I had retired. The dead man's effects I packed in a satchel, except his overcoat, which I slipped on over the sailor's suit which I had adopted. I easily caught the train, which passes Lee depot at 10.39, and thus it will be seen that the crime occurred whilst Virgie and young Marvel were together across the river. I left the train at Epping. Here Fate favored me, for a hotel man gave me a lift in his wagon, and claimed that he recognized me as young Marvel. So I admitted that he had guessed my name. Leaving him, I went to the old house belonging to Marvel, and here I burned the articles that I had in the satchel, among which there must have been some wire, which Burrows afterwards, to strengthen his theory, erroneously claimed was a part of a set of false whiskers. Next I hid the pistol, and the piece of plate which had my name engraved on it, and which I broke from the satchel. In re-arranging the stones, I did so in such a clumsy way, that anyone would discover what was hidden beneath.

"It was now but half-past eleven, and thinking there was sufficient time before me, I threw myself on the bed and tried to sleep. I had not been there, more than two or three hours, however, when I heard someone enter the house. I started up, and sprung to the window. The boughs of a huge elm were quite near, and I easily stepped into the tree. Here I remained, hidden by the dense foliage, for, despite the danger, I could not resist the curiosity to know who it was that was in the house. In a very few moments a light appeared, and I clearly saw that it was young Walter Marvel himself. Everything seemed to favor my plot. Waiting until his light was extinguished again, and until I could slip out of the tree without attracting his attention, I stole silently away. I walked to New Market Junction, where I boarded the early morning train for New Market, for, though I could easily have continued on to that place on foot, I wished to give color to the story which I intended to tell, of having come from Portsmouth, by being seen to leave the proper train. During this short ride, the conductor pointed out to me two men, and told me that they were detectives. It was these same two whom I afterwards recognized at the saloon, when the Squire informed me that he was taking detectives to my house. I was startled, not unnaturally, to learn that experienced men would be on the scene of the crime so early, and in my agitation I almost betrayed myself, as I know, because Burrows questioned me afterwards.

"Another unexpected event, was when my dog recognized me at the house, and plainly showed his friendship. Strange as it may seem, this possibility, obvious as it should have been, had not even occurred to me. A man who commits a crime always overlooks something. I was so taken by surprise, that I scarcely knew what to do, for the animal is so savage, that it would of course look strange to the Squire to see him fawn upon a stranger. However, I made a lame attempt at explanation, but poor as it was, it served to lull suspicion.

"That night, as Fate would have it, I was assigned to my own room, and, thinking over the whole affair, it suddenly occurred to me that a *post-mortem* would reveal the fact that one wound had caused instantaneous death, and for all that I could tell at that time, the other might be of the same character. However, I saw at a glance that the only way to explain the presence of the paper which I had written, would be by supposing one wound to have been made by either of the shots which had been fired from the lawn. In that event, the position of the wound on the body would lead the detectives to search for the corresponding hole through my clothing. I therefore determined to secrete these garments in this apartment, and to let their disappearance be a part of the mystery.

"Everything went as I had planned, except that the paper fell into the hands of Virgie, and led her to believe in young Marvel's guilt. Thus, in her efforts to save him, she herself became entangled in the affair, and even accused herself of the crime. To prevent the consequences of this I led Mr. Barnes to where he would find the evidence which I had manufactured against young Marvel. I wished to remain behind, to search for the bundle which he claimed to have thrown into the river, and I would have destroyed it if I had found it. But the shrewd detective would not allow me to leave him. When we reached Epping, we found Burrows ahead of us. He had ferreted out all that I wished to be discovered. I congratulated myself that all would yet be well, when Mr. Barnes at once demonstrated the fact that Marvel could prove an *alibi,* or else that Virgie must be considered an accomplice.

"Thus I have no recourse but to die. The truth must be known, that the innocent may not suffer. It is hard that what I have so long and earnestly guarded, should at last be revealed. I have been a victim of circumstances, rather than a criminal, and it seems unjust. I suppose I should not have raised my hand against my fellow-man, and though it was, as I thought, in self-defence, still it is true that I had long premeditated the killing; and so I bow my head to the stroke of Fate. The one pang that I suffer is, that after all these years, my niece must learn what a villain her father was, and that her uncle is a murderer and a suicide.

"I am confident that Mr. Barnes suspects the truth, and that his skill will place him in a position to unravel the mystery. Should he be the one, as I think likely, to discover my dead body, and this writing, it is the last prayer of a doomed man that if his fertile brain can invent a tale, whereby Virgie could be kept in ignorance of my sin, he will exert himself to that end. If not, I humbly pray that Virgie will pardon me for the misery which I have caused her; that she may enjoy long years of happiness, and that, in time, she may come to think of me as one who loved her dearly, and who now cheerfully sacrifices his life to insure her safety. And now, God's will be done, and may He have mercy on my soul!"

"Amen!" exclaimed Mr. Barnes.

CHAPTER XVIII
DETECTIVE BARNES SURPRISES DETECTIVE BURROWS

"A noble man destroyed by a cruel chain of circumstances," thought Mr. Barnes, as he concluded the perusal of the tale. He then leaned his elbow on the table, and, with his mouth partly open, beat a tattoo upon his teeth with his finger ends, a habit of his when lost in thought, and intent upon some knotty problem. He sat thus for more than a quarter of an hour, and then muttered:

"I have it. That man's secret shall be preserved!"

Carefully placing the document in his pocket, he then gathered up all the writing materials that lay on the table, his idea being to prevent anyone from entertaining the suspicion that the dead man had left any tell-tale writing behind him. Satisfied that this was accomplished, he descended to the room below, and awaited the arrival of the Squire, who, in due time, came with Virginia, accompanied also by Burrows and Dr. Snow.

"Ah! Mr. Barnes," said the Squire, "Virgie tells me that you have solved the mystery of this murder?"

"Yes, sir! Chance has favored me, and I am glad that I have succeeded in saving the accused, without the necessity of a trial."

"Are you sure you can do that?" asked Burrows.

"Oh, yes! I could demand Marvel's discharge, even though I had not discovered the real murderer; for I have the disguise which he threw into the river, and in the pocket of the vest I found the locket which he said would be there."

Burrows was astounded, but was unwilling to give up his pet theory without a struggle.

"How do you account for the initials of the accused being on the locket found in the dead man's hands?"

"They also appear on the one which I found in the vest and which I have here. You may examine it, and you will observe that it is the *facsimile* of the other. Thus it is plain that there were originally two, and I presume that, by a coincidence, these are the initials also of Miss Lewis's mother. She is not certain, as she only knows one of the names, 'Matilda.' The other must have begun with 'W.' "

Mr. Barnes knew better than this, but he had decided to suppress the truth, and therefore he accounted for this point as best he could. He then related the means by which he had recovered the bundle, and Burrows, at the conclusion of his tale, exclaimed:

"Well, Mr. Barnes, you have entirely overturned my theory, and the only satisfaction left to me is, that the innocent will not be made to suffer through me."

"Mr. Barnes," said the Squire, "you have not told us yet who the murderer is, and how you discovered him."

"It is very simple. By an unaccountable prejudice, I suspected that this man was not what he claimed to be. You recall his story of having been at school in New York? I repaired thither, and learned that no such boy had ever been there. Mr. Lewis, it seems, made a present to the academy years ago, and this man must have found some of the letters which Mr. Lewis received whilst stopping there, and, using the envelopes to get the dates right, forged the inclosed letters which he showed to you."

"Then you came back here, I suppose, to arrest him?"

"Exactly, and I find him dead. That would seem to prove that he feared discovery, and took his life, to evade arrest. However, that is not sufficient for me. I must find out the exact object of this crime and will do so. I promise you, that if you will delay the inquest till Tuesday, so as to give me a chance to follow up a clue which I have, I will endeavor to clear up the whole matter."

The Squire willingly acquiesced. Mr. Barnes hastened to New York as speedily as possible, and learned from the spy, that the woman had made no effort to change her place of residence, perhaps realizing the uselessness of so doing after what had taken place in her apartment. He went at once, to the hotel, and, sending his name up, was shown into her presence. As soon as he entered she began:

"I do not know why I have allowed you to come up to see me!"

"I do!" replied Mr. Barnes, tersely.

"Then tell me."

"Curiosity."

"You are clever. Now, satisfy my curiosity."

"I came here to tell you all that I have discovered!"

"Well?"

"I was engaged to find your husband!"

"Yes! Go on!"

"I have found him!"

"Where?"

"Where I told you that I would! He left this city with a murderous intent, and I looked for him in the vicinity of the crime!"

"He has not killed anyone! I will not believe it!"

"No, his guilty plans reacted on himself!"

"What do you mean?"

"He is dead!"

"Merciful God!"

"Yes, the Almighty has been merciful to him, if we consider the wrong that he had done, and still meditated. His victims have suffered far more than he. Now, Madam, let us come to business at once. You must go with me!"

"Go with you? Where?"

"To New Hampshire! Listen! Your husband, as you call him, went up there to commit a crime which he had threatened many years ago, namely, to kill this man Lewis. He reached the house and met Lewis, but the latter had long awaited his coming, and was prepared for his arrival. Before your husband could carry out his design, a bullet ended his career."

"This is terrible! Why did he go? I warned him that the man would not allow himself to be harmed!"

"Ah! Then, as I supposed, you knew his intentions before he went. However, as he did not succeed, you cannot be held on that charge. To continue. Lewis, as I have said, killed Marvel. He then succeeded in making every one believe that it was his own body which was found, whilst he passed off for his son, just returned from sea. This might have been a successful ruse, had not a strange chain of circumstances implicated his niece in the affair, and, despairing of proving her innocence in any other way, he committed suicide, leaving a full confession."

"I don't see what I have to do with all this."

"You will, in a moment. If the truth is exposed, the knowledge must come to this girl of who and what her father was, besides the fact that her uncle killed him. This I have determined shall not be. Justice makes no such demand, and I choose to give this girl a future, unclouded by such a past."

"How will you hide the truth?"

"I must invent a tale which will fit the circumstances, and you must substantiate the story."

"I will do nothing of the kind!"

"Oh! Yes, you shall! You will have no choice in the matter!"

"I tell you I will not! Who is this girl? The daughter of the woman who crossed the sea to take my husband away from me!"

"You and that man, by your heartless treatment of that woman, hastened, I may say caused, her death."

"What do I care for that? If you think I will help you to spare the delicate feelings of this girl, you do not know me!"

"It is just because I imagine that I do know you that I am so confident that you will aid me!"

"What do you mean?"

"You must choose between obeying me, and absolute poverty."

"How so?"

"I will explain. Marvel married this girl's mother, and she is his child. His wife was alive when you married him, and, according to your confession to her, when she met you in Paris, you knew of this first marriage, but chose to ignore it. If you had been united in this State, I could easily have you imprisoned for that bigamous marriage, but fortunately for you, you were married abroad. However, I will not let you slip through my fingers for all that. I think you did what you attributed to the real wife. You were anxious to share Marvel's position and his fortune, and therefore I believe you will do anything for money. So I intend to manage you through your cupidity. If you persist in your obstinacy, I will reveal all that I have learned, and will see that steps are taken to gain possession of Marvel's property for his rightful heir, his daughter. Moreover, you shall be made to give up whatever moneys you now have of his, as they become a part of his estate. This will be simple, for, as you can easily be shown, by the records of the Parisian court, to be the bigamous wife only, of course you would be entitled to no share in his property."

"How is it that you are so well informed?"

"It is my profession to be well informed. I have no time to spare. Choose!"

"You are a devil!" Then, after a few minutes' hesitation, "What is it that you wish me to do?"

"So! You decide that my way is best, do you? You are wise! Well, then, you will return with me, and on the way I will explain what I require of you. Obey me and no harm shall come to you."

* * *

The inquest over the dead body, which had been found in the secret room, attracted even more interest, and a greater crowd than had the first. All looked eagerly forward to the explanation promised by Mr. Barnes, and loud were the praises which he received on every side. At length, the moment arrived, and the woman whom the detective had brought with him against her will, was made to take the stand. Prompted by Mr. Barnes, Mr. Tupper conducted the examination of this witness:

"Will you give your name, if you please, madam?"

"Mrs. Horace Paul."

"You have seen the body of the deceased?"

"I have!"

"Do you recognize it?"

"I do! It is the body of my husband!" This caused a sensation.

"Can you give any reason why he should have wished to harm Mr. Lewis?"

"He knew Mr. Lewis long ago, and did some work for him. My husband was an architect and a practical carpenter. Mr. Lewis engaged him, when he first came to this town, to build a secret apartment in his house. Mr. Lewis was very anxious that no one should know of this hiding-place, and that is why he brought a man from a distant city to do this work. His anxiety to keep his secret, coupled with the fact that he paid my husband an immense sum of money, and stipulated that he should never return to Lee, made my husband suspect that it must have been as a storehouse for money that he wished to use it. He spoke so often of this, that, fearing he might be tempted to investigate it, at length I persuaded him to go with me to Europe. Lately, however, he insisted on returning, as we had used up most of our means. I did not believe, after so many years, that he would again think of this 'hidden treasure,' as he was wont to call it. But now I see it must have been that which brought him here."

After this testimony, she was allowed to retire, and Mr. Barnes took the stand to make a statement.

"Before we give this case to the jury, I should like to say, that I think this man remained after the crime was committed, with the intention of searching for the treasure. Mr. Burrows will testify that he heard him in the secret chamber during the first night after the murder. I think he assumed the personality of the dead man's son, as the best means of enjoying the fortune which he expected to obtain, as well as to avoid suspicion most effectually. Failing to find any treasure, or to inherit under the will, it was still his only means of safety, to remain. Fear, or remorse, at last impelled suicide, a not unusual thing with criminals of an intellectual order."

The verdict of the jury placed the responsibility for the murder on the dead man, and indeed, though they little understood the true facts of the case, that was where it justly belonged.

There still remained one or two points about which Mr. Barnes felt a curiosity, and at the first opportunity, after Marvel's release, he questioned him.

"Mr. Marvel," said he, "how is it that you thought that Mr. Lewis was dead, as we supposed him to be, when I spoke to you, on the vessel, at Portsmouth?"

"I guessed it. I had received a letter from Miss Lewis, in which she used the words 'after the events of last night.' I did not quite understand this at first, though I placed no special importance on them, until you told me that a murder had been committed. It flashed over my mind in a moment, that it was to this that Virgie had alluded, and I feared that she and her uncle had quarrelled on her return to the house after leaving me, and that in a fit of passion she had killed him. That is why I refused to go back with you. I did not wish to be a witness against her. Afterward it dawned upon me that I myself must have been suspected, or you would never have come after me. Then I was anxious to return."

"That explains the point in question, but there is one other matter. Why was it that Mr. Everly sent you a letter that night, and that you went to Epping, instead of going to Portsmouth?"

"I formed the idea of going to Portsmouth, after I reached the farm that night. Previously I had sent word to Everly, asking him to get some money for me, and explaining how he could forward it, without betraying my whereabouts. If he had brought it himself, his presence in Epping might have excited suspicion, as he was well known to be my friend. I knew that we could trust the matter to Harrison, and I suggested him as the bearer of the letter and money. To receive these, I was compelled to go to Epping."

Some months later Mr. Barnes received cards to the nuptials of Virginia Lewis and Walter Marvel, and was pleased to attend the ceremony. The bride and groom went abroad on their honeymoon. A few days after their departure, Squire Olney sent to the detective a certified check for five thousand dollars, with the information that it must be accepted from the newly married couple, as Virginia happily expressed it, "In part payment for our happiness, which we enjoy through you." They had delayed making this presentation until they should be out of the country, lest Mr. Barnes might endeavor to return the gift. Appreciating the intentions which prompted its bestowal, Mr. Barnes accepted the money. He is now his own master, being chief of a private bureau which he has established in New York. I may as well mention also, that Burrows manfully apologized to Mr. Barnes for his actions in this case, and was once more received into the good graces of the more experienced detective.

FURTHER READING

NOVELS

Billman, Carol. *The Secret of the Stratemeyer Syndicate: Nancy Drew, the Hardy Boys, and the Million Dollar Fiction Factory.* New York: Ungar, 1986.

Braddon, M. E. *Lady Audley's Secret.* New York: Dover Publications, 1974.

Doyle, Arthur Conan. *The Complete Sherlock Holmes.* New York: Barnes & Noble, 2009.

Doyle, Arthur Conan. *Memories and Adventures.* Boston: Little, Brown, 1924.

Greene, Douglas G. *Classic Mystery Stories.* Mineola, NY: Dover Publications, 1999.

Nishio, Ishin, Tsugumi Ōba, and Takeshi Obata. *Death Note: Another Note, the Los Angeles BB Murder Cases.* Trans. Andrew Cunningham. San Francisco, CA: VIZ Media, 2008.

Ottolengui, Rodrigues. *An Artist in Crime.* New York: G.P. Putnam's Sons, 1892.

Ottolengui, Rodrigues. *Before the Fact.* Ed. Douglas Greene. Eugenia, Ont.: Battered Silicon Dispatch Box, 2012.

Ottolengui, Rodrigues. *Final Proof; Or, the Value of Evidence.* New York: G.P. Putnam's Sons, 1898.

Poe, Edgar A. "The Black Cat." *The Complete Tales and Poems of Edgar Allan Poe.* Ed. Dawn B. Sova. New York: Barnes & Noble, 2006. 531-38. Print.

SCHOLARLY ARTICLES

Bean, Ethelle S. "Technology and Detective Fiction." *Clues: A Journal of Detection* 24.1 (2005): 27-34.

Harpham, John S. "Detective Fiction and the Aesthetic of Crime." *Raritan* 34.1 (2014): 121-41.

Leddy, Chuck. "Loot vs. Literature: Genre and Literary Fiction." *The Writer* 121.1 (2008): 8-9.

Mason, Emma. "Dogs, Detectives and the Famous Sherlock Holmes." *International Journal of Cultural Studies* 11.3 (2008): 289-300.

Priestman, Martin. "The Detective Whodunnit from Poe to World War I." *Crime Fiction: From Poe to the Present.* Plymouth: Northcote House, 1998. 5-18. Rpt. in *Short Story Criticism.* Ed. Janet Witalec. Vol. 59. Detroit: Gale, 2003.

Routledge, Chris. "Detective Fiction." *St. James Encyclopedia of Popular Culture* (2000): 693-95.

Snyder, Laura J. "Sherlock Holmes: Scientific Detective." *Endeavour* 28.3 (2004): 104104-108.

Taylor, Wendell Hertig. "Rodrigues Ottolengui (1861-1937): A Forgotten American Mystery Writer." *Armchair Detective: A Quarterly Journal Devoted to the Appreciation of Mystery, Detective, and Suspense Fiction* 9 (1976): 181-.

Weiss, Harry B. "Rodrigues Ottolengui, 1861-1937." *Journal of the New York Entomological Society* 59.2 (1951): 93-98.

Xu, Wenru. "Edgar Allan Poe and His Detective Fictions." *Studies in Literature and Language* 7.2 (2013): 59-62.

www.ingramcontent.com/pod-product-compliance
Lightning Source LLC
Chambersburg PA
CBHW021118260626
47169CB00005B/1333